THE MASSACRE OF MANKIND

ALSO BY STEPHEN BAXTER FROM GOLLANCZ:

NON-FICTION
Deep Future
The Science of Avatar

FICTION
Mammoth
Longtusk
Icebones
Behemoth

Reality Dust
Evolution

Flood
Ark

Proxima
Ultima
Obelisk

Xeelee: An Omnibus
Xeelee: Endurance

NORTHLAND
Stone Spring
Bronze Summer
Iron Winter

THE WEB
Gulliverzone
Webcrash

DESTINY'S CHILDREN
Coalescent
Exultant
Transcendent
Resplendent

A TIME ODYSSEY
(with Arthur C. Clarke)
Time's Eye
Sunstorm
Firstborn

TIME'S TAPESTRY
Emperor
Conqueror
Navigator
Weaver

The Medusa Chronicles
(with Alastair Reynolds)

THE MASSACRE OF MANKIND

A SEQUEL TO

The War of the Worlds

BY

H.G. WELLS

STEPHEN BAXTER

GOLLANCZ
LONDON

First published in Great Britain in 2017 by Gollancz
an imprint of The Orion Publishing Group Ltd
Carmelite House, 50 Victoria Embankment
London EC4Y 0DZ

An Hachette UK Company

1 3 5 7 9 10 8 6 4 2

A CIP catalogue record for this book is
available from the British Library.

ISBN (Hardback) 978 1 473 20509 3
ISBN (Export Trade Paperback) 978 1 473 20510 9

Typeset at The Spartan Press Ltd,
Lymington, Hants

Printed and bound by CPI Group (UK) Ltd,
Croydon CR0 4YY

www.stephen-baxter.com
www.orionbooks.co.uk
www.gollancz.co.uk

To
H. G. WELLS
This Extending of His Idea
and
The H. G. Wells Society

'If astronomy teaches anything, it teaches that man is but a detail in the evolution of the universe, and that resemblant though diverse details are inevitably to be expected in the host of orbs around him. He learns that, though he will probably never find his double anywhere, he is destined to find any number of cousins scattered through space.'

Percival Lowell, *Mars*, 1985

'It seemed to me that humanity was on the verge of a deep apprehension of its place in the cosmos. The intellectual world was alive with speculation and hope. Then the Martians came again.'

Walter Jenkins, *Narratives of the Martian Wars*, 1913 & 1928

BOOK I
The Return of the Martians

1

A Call to Arms

To those of us who survived it, the First Martian War of the early twentieth century was a cataclysm. And yet, to minds far greater than our own and older even than the Martians, minds who regard our world from the cold outer reaches of space, that conflict must have seemed a trivial affair indeed, and unworthy.

The further a world is from the sun, the older it must be, and cooler. Thus the earth is older than hot, fecund Venus; and Mars, austere and chill, is in turn older than our temperate globe. The outer worlds, Saturn, Uranus and Neptune, are ancient indeed and locked in the stasis of time and ice. But Jupiter – king of planets, more massive than the rest combined, older than Mars as Mars is older than our world, and warmed by its own inner fire – is, must be, host to the gravest intellects of all. We know now that these Jovian minds have long watched us – watched humanity, the Martians, even innocent Venus. What can they have thought of our War? The fragile sparks crossing the night, the flares of fire on the green skin of our planet, the splash of ink-black smoke – the swarming and helpless populations ... The Jovians looked on all this as a silent god might regard his flawed creations, perhaps, their reflections unimaginable, their disapproval profound.

And yet, claims Walter Jenkins, that great chronicler of the First War, this cosmic scrutiny provides the context within which we, who once believed we were lords of creation, must live out our petty lives. Walter was right. This mighty context was to shape everything about the Second War, and indeed the most important moment of my own life.

On the other hand, I myself, like most people, stay sane by generally not thinking about it.

3

And speaking of grave scrutiny, as I commence this memoir of my own, I cannot help but acknowledge the long shadow cast by that tombstone of a volume which everyone knows as the *Narrative*, the history of the First War penned by Walter, my esteemed brother-in-law – if he can still be termed such after I divorced Frank, his brother – a work that, as Walter's therapist Freud might say, has burned a particular perception of the First Martian War into the public subconscious with the intensity of a Heat-Ray. Let me warn the reader from the off that if it's the grandeur of the cosmos that you want, all told in the lofty prose of a man who was once *paid* to scribble such stuff, then it's another correspondent you should seek out. On the other hand if it's an honest, factual account of my own experience you're after – a woman who survived the First Martian War and had her life pulled to pieces in the Second – then I humbly submit this, history as I saw it.

Although I admit it is an irony that my experience of the second conflict should begin, long before a Martian again set foot on this earth, with a complicated series of telephone calls from Walter himself, emanating from a hospital in Vienna. I, who was patiently building a fresh life for myself in the New World, wanted nothing to do with it. But I have always had a sense of duty. I answered the summons.

A dotty-house, to Jupiter! From the beginning it was a tangled tale indeed.

2

A Meeting of Veterans

My first inkling of the impending storm came in fact in New York, specifically at the Woolworth Building, where Major Eric Eden (retired) asked to meet me, in order, he said, to relay a message from Walter Jenkins.

My young colleague Harry Kane insisted on accompanying me. Harry was of that breed of brash American journalists who are always suspicious of all things European – he would have been even before the Schlieffen War, I think. I suppose Harry came as a kind of moral support, but with a professional curiosity too about a Martian War that to him had been only a distant spectacle of his youth.

So we made our way. It was a brisk mid-March day in the year 1920. Manhattan had suffered what everybody hoped would prove to be the last snowstorm of the year, although the main hazard on that particular morning turned out to be the slush piles alongside every sidewalk, ever ready to soak an unwary ankle. I remember that morning: the swarming, cheerfully ill-tempered traffic, the electric advertising hoardings that glowed in the greyness of the day – the sheer innocent vigour of a young nation – in those last hours and minutes before I was dragged back into the affairs of gloomy, wounded old England.

At last Harry and I pushed through the doors into the Woolworth. The air in the lobby, heated and scented, hit me like a slap in the face. In those days the Americans liked to be *very* warm indoors. I pulled open my coat and loosened my headscarf, and we walked across a floor of polished Greek marble that was speckled with melted snow and grit from the street. The lobby was busy. Harry, with his usual air of amused detachment – an attractive trait in a man a few years younger than me, even if it

5

doesn't sound it – said to me over the noise, 'I take it your Major Eden doesn't know the city so well.'

'You can say that without ever meeting him?'

'Sure I can. Where else would you set up a meeting but here? In London an American would meet you at St Paul's – that's the one with the hole in the dome, right? And a British in New York – well, here we are, in the tallest building in the world!' He pointed. 'And there *he* is, by the way.'

The man he indicated stood alone. He was slim, not tall, and wore a morning suit that looked expensive enough but dowdy compared to the peacock fashions around him. If this was Eden he looked younger than his thirty-eight years – six years older than me.

'And that must be Eden because—'

'He's the only one looking at the artwork.'

Indeed, the man was staring up at the ceiling, which (had I ever noticed this before?) was coated with mosaics that looked Roman, perhaps Byzantine. That was the Americans for you: in this new monument to a triumphant Mammon, they felt the need to reach back to their detached European past.

Harry strode across the floor, muttering, 'And could he look more the Englishman abroad? If this is the best he can do to blend into the background, no wonder the Martians caught him.'

That made me snort with laughter as I followed. 'Hush. You're terrible. The man's a hero.' Eric Eden was, after all, the only living human being who had actually been inside a functioning Martian cylinder – he was captured in the first couple of days in '07, as the military, in their ignorance, probed at the first landing pit at Woking. Having been kept alive, perhaps as a specimen for later examination, Eric had fought his way out of a space cylinder with nothing much more than his bare hands, and had ultimately made it back to his unit with invaluable information on Martian technology.

Hero or not, Eric looked rather nervous as we bore down on him. 'Mrs Jenkins, I take it—'

'I prefer Miss Elphinstone, actually, since my divorce.'

'My apologies. I imagine you recognised me from the posters in the bookshop windows.'

Harry grinned. 'Something like that.'

'It has been a well-announced tour. Just Bert Cook and myself for now, but we should be joining up with old Schiaparelli in Boston – discoverer of the canals, you know – in his eighties but going strong...'

6

I introduced Harry quickly. 'We both work for the *Post*.'

'I've not read your book, sir,' Harry admitted. 'It's kind of out of my sphere. I spend my time fighting Tammany Hall as opposed to men from Mars.'

Eric looked baffled, and I felt moved to interpret. 'Tammany Hall's the big Democrat political machine in the city. Americans do everything on a heroic scale, including corruption. And they were *not* men in that cylinder, Harry.'

'However,' Harry went on, unabashed, 'I've been known to dabble in the book trade myself. Sensational potboilers, that's *my* line, not having a heroic past to peddle.'

'Be glad of that,' Eric said, softly enough. A line which seemed to me the embodiment of British understatement! 'Miss Elphinstone, Walter Jenkins did warn me of your likely – ah, reluctance to become entangled in his affairs once more. Nevertheless Mr Jenkins did press on me the importance of his message, for you, the rest of his family. He seems to have fallen out of touch with you all. Indeed that's why he had to make such a circuitous attempt to contact you, through myself.'

'Really?' Harry grinned. 'Isn't this all kind of flaky?' He twirled a finger beside his temple. 'So the man needs to talk to his ex-wife, and the only way he can do it is by contacting somebody he barely knows, with respect, sir, on the other side of the world, in the hope that he can talk to his *brother's* ex-wife—'

'That's Walter for you,' I said, feeling oddly motivated to defend the man. 'He never was very good at *coping*.'

Eric said grimly, 'And that was presumably even before he spent weeks being chased by Martians across the countryside.'

Harry, young, confident, was not unsympathetic, but I could see he did not understand. 'I don't see what favours Jenkins has done you either, Major Eden. I saw the interview you gave to the *Post*, where you attacked him for claiming to have seen more of the Martians than any other eyewitness, when they were at loose in England. As you said, *you* certainly saw stuff he never did.'

Eric held up his hand politely. 'Actually I didn't say that, not quite. Your reporter rather gingered it in the telling – well, you have to sell newspapers, I suppose. But I rather feel that we veterans should, ah, stick together. And besides, if you take a longer view, Jenkins did me a favour. One cannot deny that *his* memoir is the one that has most shaped public perception of the War ever since its publication. And he does mention me, you know.'

'He does?'

'Oh, yes. Book I, Chapter 8. Although he does describe me mistakenly as "reported to be missing". Only briefly!'

I snorted. 'The man's in the dictionary under "Unreliable Narrator".'

'But he never related my own adventures, as he did Bert Cook's, say, and so I got the chance to tell it myself – and my publishers to label it as an "untold story".'

Harry laughed. 'So it's all business in the end? Now *that* I do sympathise with. So what's the plan, Major Eden? We gonna stand around gawping at frescoes all day?'

'Mosaics, actually. Sorry. Miss Elphinstone, Mr Jenkins wishes to make a telephone call. To you, I mean.'

Harry whistled. 'From Vienna? Transatlantic? That will cost a pretty penny. I know we're all excited by the new submarine cable and all, but still...'

Eric smiled. 'As I understand it Mr Jenkins is not short of pennies, thanks to the success of his book. Not to mention the rights he has sold for the movie versions.' He glanced at his watch. 'Anyhow, Jenkins will make the call to our hotel suite – I mean, mine and Bert's. If you wouldn't mind accompanying me there—'

'Which hotel?'

Eric looked faintly embarrassed. 'The Plaza.'

Harry laughed out loud.

'I myself would have been content with more modest accommodation, but Bert Cook—'

I said, 'No need to apologise. But—' I looked Eric in the eyes, and I recognised something of myself in there – something I could never share with Harry, good-hearted though he was. The look of the war veteran. '*Why* would he call? Could it be they are coming back? And *why now*? The timing's all wrong, isn't it?'

Eric only shrugged, but he knew what I meant.

I was never an astronomer, but since the Martian War we had all picked up a little about the dance of the planets. Mars and the earth chase each other around the sun like racing cars at Brooklands. The earth, on the inside track, moves faster, and periodically overtakes Mars. And it is at these moments of overtaking, called oppositions (because at such instances sun and Mars are at opposite poles as seen in the earth's sky), that Mars and the earth come closest to each other. But Mars's orbit is elliptical, and so is the earth's to a lesser degree – that is, they are not perfect circles. And so this closest approach varies in distance from encounter to encounter, from some sixty million miles or more to less than forty million – the closest is called a *perihelic* opposition. Again there is a cycle, with the minimal perihelic approaches coming by once every fifteen years or so: in 1894, and then in 1909, and again in 1924...

I recited from memory, 'The next perihelic opposition is still four years away. The 1907 assault came *two* years before the last perihelic. Surely they won't come, if they come at all, for another couple of years, then. But if they *were* to break the pattern and come this year, they may be already on their way. This year the opposition date is April 21—'

'And as every paper trumpeted,' Harry put in, 'including our own, that would work back to a launch date of February 27: a couple of weeks ago.'

More grim, memorised logic. In 1907 the opposition's date of closest approach of the worlds had been on July 6. The landings had begun precisely three weeks and a day before that, and the firings of the great guns on Mars had begun four weeks and four days before *that*.

But we all knew that even if the astronomers had seen any-thing untoward on Mars, none of us would have heard about it. Since the Martian War the astronomers' work had been hidden under a blanket of secrecy by the governments. Supposedly this was to stop the panics during the oppositions of 1909 and 1911 and 1914, witless alarms that had caused damage to business confidence and so forth, without a single Martian peeping out of his cylinder – but it had led, in Britain at least, to the possession of an unlicensed astronomical telescope being a criminal offence. I could see the logic, but in my eyes such secrecy only induced more fear and uncertainty.

So, even now the cylinders might be suspended in space – on their way! Why else would Walter summon us all so? But Walter was Walter, never a man to get to the point; I knew that I faced a time of uncertainty before this sudden tension was resolved.

'Well, let's take the call,' I said, as bravely as I could. I linked Eric's arm; Harry took my other arm; and so we walked, as three, out of the lobby. 'I think I can stand an hour or two of luxury in the Plaza.'

'And I,' Harry said, 'look forward to meeting this Cook guy. Quite a character, if half of what he says is true!'

3

An Artilleryman in New York

We took a cab to the hotel, which is on 58th and 5th. The main entrance, if you don't know it, faces Grand Army Plaza, which used to commemorate feats of the Union Army in the Civil War. Since '22 this has been supplemented by memorials to a different conflict. But it was a grand sight to see, in those times.

Eric's suite contained the pampered luxury I expected, with overstuffed furniture and a magnificent view of the Plaza outside. A bottle of champagne stood on a low glass table, uncorked. The air was filled with the tinny tones of a ragtime band, emanating from a wireless set – not the compact government-issue People's Receivers you would have found in every British home in those days, and known universally as Marvin's Megaphones, but a big chunk of American hardware in a walnut cabinet.

And in this setting Albert Cook, in a housecoat, lounged on a sofa, idly glancing through a colour supplement. In my own first experiences with American hotels I had been all but over-whelmed by such luxuries as a private bathroom, a telephone in the room, and cereals for breakfast. But Cook evidently took to it all like a duck to water.

Cook was a little older than Eric, aged perhaps forty; he had neatly cut black hair peppered with grey, and a livid scar on his lower face (though I later heard gossip that he would touch this up for effect). And while there was no sign of Eric's work save a single, rather battered reading copy of his book on a side cabinet, the room was dominated by a poster on a stand: a photograph of Cook in ragged uniform and wielding a kind of club, emblazoned:

MEMOIRS OF AN ARTILLERYMAN

Eric briskly introduced us. Cook did not stand. He grunted at Harry, and eyed me up and down, evidently disappointed to see a woman decently covered up in a trouser suit. For myself, I hope the look I gave him was withering. Since the First War my choice had been to reject any clothing in which I could not comfortably cycle, and I did not go for the prettied-up fashionable versions either but the sturdy suits worn by the munitionettes and others, and Cook could like it or not.

He turned back to his magazine. 'So a half-hour until this blessed telephone call, Eric?'

Eric lifted the champagne bottle from its bucket; it was no more than a third full. He glanced apologetically at me. 'If you'd like me to order some more—'

Harry and I both demurred.

'Please, sit down, let me take your coats . . .'

'And don't let me embarrass you,' Cook said lazily. 'I'll get out of the way when the Prof calls from his foreign nut-hatch. *I've* nothing to say to *him*. I've had nothing to say to him since Putney, when he drank my booze, beat me at chess, and ran out afore the work was begun.'

Harry laughed. 'We've all read the book, man. What work? You'd barely started whatever grand scheme of tunnelling and sabotage you dreamed of—'

'That's as how he tells it. Pompous over-educated toff. I should've sued him.'

'Just as you'll be suing Charlie Chaplin, I suppose.'

Cook scowled, for this was a well-known sore point for him. Chaplin had built much of his cinematic fame on the success of one character, the 'Little Sojer', a comical, good-hearted gunner in ill-fitting uniform, who forever dreamed of being a general while his guns exploded in clouds of sooty smoke. You would have to be a lot thicker-skinned than Albert Cook not to have seen the source of *that*. But Cook had, after all, been no more than a driver.

Seeking to cover over Harry's lack of tact, I interposed quickly, 'I'm not sure any of us came out of Walter's book very well. I've never quite lived down the way he introduced *me* to the world.' The words Walter had used, as he described how his brother had helped my sister-in-law and myself fight off robbers during our own flight from the Martians, were burned into my very soul. '"For the second time that day this girl proved her quality." Girl!

11

And so on. I could have been drummed out of the suffragettes, before they were banned.'

Bert Cook was not listening, a trait I was to learn was typical of the man. 'Should've sued him, no matter what the lawyers said.'

Eric shook his head. 'Don't be a fool. He made you a hero! Inadvertently, granted. I've seen you talking in public – you know how folk respond to the detail – how, when the mob fled from the Martians, you alone ran *towards* them, calculating that was where the food would be . . .'

I remembered the passage, of course. '"Like a sparrow goes for man."'

'That's me.' Bert looked at me now, as if seeking to impress. 'Though I ain't no sparrow. I thought it through, see. As then, so now. And today, out the blue, he wants a nice chit-chat with you, does he? And what is it he wants to discuss? How he feels about getting a daily enema from Sigmund Freud, because he's had the wind up him since 1907?' He looked more intent. 'Or is it about Mars? Another opposition coming up, everybody knows that. What is it – does he know something? He's in a position to find out, I suppose.'

I faced Cook. 'You despise him for his learning and erudition, and his weakness as you see it, yet you want the information he possesses?'

'If it is the Martians having another go, haven't I, of all people, the right to know? Of all people? Eh?' He got to his feet, a little unsteadily, grasped the champagne bottle by the neck and lumbered to a door. 'Show time is – what is it, Eden?'

'Six o'clock. A bookstore on Broadway which—'

Cook belched loudly, and winked at me, lasciviously. 'And then we'll see what's what after the show – eh? Plenty of healthy young American women drawn to a proven survivor like me – survival of the fittest, eh? "Like a sparrow goes for man." Hah!'

I think we were all relieved when he closed the door behind him.

There followed an awkward interval, as we waited for Walter's call. We allowed Eric to order coffee for us, which came with a heap of sugary cakes on a tray.

'So, Miss Elphinstone – Julie.'

'Yes, Major, that's my name.'

'Short for Julia? Juliet?'

Harry snorted.

'Short for nothing. I was christened Julie. I was born in '88, and in that year Strindberg had his "Miss Julie" in the theatres, and my mother was taken by it.'

He nodded. 'Then you were nineteen in '07, when the Martians came.'

I shrugged. 'I was an adult.'

'I was but twenty-five myself. Rather over-promoted, to tell the truth. Many of my men were older than I. In the Army they follow their sergeants, not their officers. Just as well! But there have been much younger recruits in the Schlieffen War, you know, called up by the Russians and indeed the Germans as the fighting has dragged on.'

I wondered how he could know that. There had always been rumours of British 'advisors' at the side of the Germans in the great killing fields in the east, exploring new tactics and weapons – some, it was darkly hinted, based on captured Martian technology.

Eric went on, 'We did well to stay out of that – a quick knock-out defeat for the French.' He actually mimed a one-two punch combination. 'I was a fair boxer at school. Never kept it up, of course...'

Harry burst out laughing, then apologised quickly.

At last, to our mutual relief, the telephone rang.

Harry and I let Eric speak to the chain of operators, from the hotel's own switchboard through to the new transoceanic exchanges, and finally the handlers in Vienna with their 'strong German accents but beautiful articulation', according to Eric. At last he passed the handset to me.

I was surprised to hear, not Walter, but another English voice, strong, cultivated. 'Mrs Jenkins?'

'Actually I prefer Miss Elphinstone.'

'Ah... Yes, I see the detail from the note in your brother-in-law's file. My apologies, then. A heroically long connection to make such an error from the off!'

'To whom am I speaking? Where is Walter?'

'I apologise again. My name is Charles Samuel Myers. I am one of the specialists who have been treating Mr Jenkins for his neurasthenia for the last several years.'

I frowned. 'Neurasthenia?'

Eric Eden pulled a face. 'The privates who faced the Martians – they called it heat-stroke. Or the hots, Bert says. Or, the sweats...'

Once again Harry twirled a finger by his temple. 'Julie, you're talking to a bump-feeler!'

4

An Unreliable Narrator

Heat-stroke. The hots. The sweats. Ghastly soldiers' slang for a ghast-lier condition.

Later I would learn that my brother-in-law had encountered such terms when he had been referred for his first consultation with Dr Myers at a military hospital at a house called Craiglockhart, near Edinburgh. This was in the autumn of 1916, already nine years after the War.

In a dusty office that might once have been a smoking room, Myers had had a series of books with him, like exhibits, Walter had thought: all of them memoirs of the Martian War, including Walter's own, and the first of Bert Cook's self-glorifying page-turners. But the desk was heaped too with records from another conflict, mostly in German: despatches from the eastern front of the still-current Schlieffen War.

'*Heat-stroke,*' Myers said. 'A word coined after our own Martian War. But the condition had in fact been tentatively identified before; British Army surgeons reported the after-effects of shell-fire on the men during the Second Boer War, and even before that it was noted during the War Between the States. And of course since '14 the Germans in the east, and their Russian foes, have been coming up with their own labels. *Gun-dread. Cannon fear. Shell-shock.* Rough translations. I myself have been the first to report the phenomenon in a peer-reviewed publication, the *Lancet.*'

'Good for you,' said Walter, uneasy. At that time he was fifty years old, and by his own admission had not felt strong, robust, since the War. Indeed, he still suffered from burn scars, especially to his hands. Now he was already feeling trapped, he would tell me later. 'I don't see what this has to do with me.'

'But I've told you,' Myers said patiently. 'I believe that the Germans' gun-dread is a similar phenomenon, psychologically, to Cook's sweats. And what it has to do with you, sir, is the contents of your memoir.'

Walter bridled. 'I have suffered much criticism for my "unreliability", as Parrinder has called it. I meant the book as an honest account of my own experience of the War, and my reflections since, for I believe I was in a unique—'

'Yes, yes,' Myers said, cutting him off, 'but what's actually unique about it, man, is that unlike some accounts of the War that you read – Churchill's stiff-upper-lip boys'-story heroics, or else the self-aggrandising of the likes of Albert Cook – what *you* have delivered is a desperately honest account of your own psychological affliction. Can you not see? An affliction *from which to some extent you already suffered*, even before the experiences of the War. Even after the fighting you have clearly had problems: the fracturing of your relationship with your wife—'

'I admit that my experience of the War troubled me. No one of intelligence or sensitivity could fail to bear such scars, surely. But – some psychological disjoint *before*? I cannot accept that, Doctor.'

'But it's all here, man. In your own words. Book I, Chapter 7. "Perhaps I am a man of exceptional moods." Yes! Exceptional indeed. You describe a sense of detachment from the world, even from yourself, as if you are an outside observer... You spent your life before the War dreaming of utopias, did you not? The perfectibility of a world looked at as if from outside, and of a mankind to which, even then, you felt only a peripheral attachment.

'But when the Martians came – look at your own account of your response to the War, from the beginning. You say you fled from that first Martian pit, at Horsell Common, in panic, only to snap back to equilibrium in a trice.' He clicked fingers and thumb. 'In a trice! You showed a peculiar mix of curiosity and dread; you were consumed by fear, and yet could not keep away from the spectacle, the mystery – the newness. At one point you describe yourself actually *circling* a Martian site, at a constant distance – how did you put it, a "big curve"? Ha! A circle, a locus imposed by two forces, perfectly matched, warring in you: curiosity versus dread. As for your detachment from humanity, you could be ruthless, could you not? To save your wife you took the dogcart of, of—'

'A local publican.'

15

'Yes! Leaving the man, who knew less than you about the situation at that point, to die. You saw his corpse, did you not? And later you *killed* directly, did you not? The clergyman you called a curate – did you ever trouble to learn his name, his position? He was called Nathaniel—'

'There is no value in my knowing it! And I believe that, in the course of a dark night of the soul, even at the height of the War, I came to terms over that – action.'

'Came to terms with whom? God? Yourself? The curate? Even that "dark night" line is a quote from a mediaeval mystic. The truth is you called on God, whose existence you once spent a whole book demolishing!'

Walter said, increasingly uneasy, 'And yet I was brought up within the great rotting carcass of that antique religion. I was even forced to accept confirmation to take up my first post, a teaching position. And when faced with the unimaginable, that which lies beyond familiar categories, perhaps the mind reaches for the trappings of familiar myth—'

'Was murder unimaginable to you, afore you did it? I suppose you'd say the Martians drove you to it?'

'Drove me to it, yes, that's it. For it was not premeditated.'

'Was it not? Are you *sure*? You are a man of detachment of mind, remember. And a man of detachment of consciousness altogether, at times.'

'What do you mean?'

'I refer to the later passages of your own book. You describe the great existential shock of the Martians and their weaponry, imposed on the English countryside: "a sense of dethronement", I think was your term. Very well. But at the end of the War – when, as you admit, you were *not* the first to discover the Martians' extinguishing through the plagues – you had a three-day blank, man! Classic fugue. And later – you wrote this book in '13, six years after the War was done – you describe visions, memories still intruding even then. You saw living people as ghosts of the past – "phantasms in a dead city". And so on and so forth.' He looked at Walter with more sympathy. 'Your relationship with your wife broke down, Jenkins. Why do you suppose that is?'

This cut Walter to the core. 'But I spent much of the War seeking her out.'

'That's what you *say*.' He tapped the memoir. 'That's what you *say* in here. But – look what you *did*! You went to Weybridge and

16

London, never to Leatherhead where your wife was sheltering: north to the Martians, not south to your family. That's what you *did*.'

'But the Martians – there were obstacles. The third cylinder fell at Pyrford, between Woking and Leatherhead, and I—'

'Oh, come, man, that shouldn't have necessitated a detour via central London! And are you aware that you don't refer to your wife by name in this book, not once?'

'Nor do I name myself. Nor, for that matter, my brother. Or Cook the artilleryman. It was a literary affectation which—'

'A literary affectation? You name the Astronomer Royal, man. You name the Lord Chief Justice! And you don't name your own wife? How do you imagine she would feel about that? And didn't your hair turn grey? In a matter of days, during the War.'

'But – but . . .'

'There could hardly be more striking a sign of physical as well as mental affliction.' Myers sat back. 'I put it to you, sir – and I have already penned a paper for the *Lancet* on the case – that you are suffering a form of neurasthenia: the sweats, heat-stroke, gun-dread. Symptoms of this include tics, mutism, paralysis, nightmares, tremors, sensitivity to noise, fugue, hallucinations. Do these sound familiar? The difference with *you*, compared to the common soldier of the eastern front, is your articulacy, your intelligence, your self-awareness – even your greater age. Which makes you, together with your account, a fascinating reference point. Sir, our own government, in particular the military authorities—'

'Ha! What's the distinction, under our blessed Prime Minister Marvin?'

'—have encouraged me to refer you for treatment. At this hospital, and others in Germany where gun-dread is being studied. Are you willing to partake in my study? The treatment should be beneficial for you, and may lead to a greater good: the more effective handling of traumatised soldiers of all nationalities.'

'Do I have a choice?'

'But that,' Walter told me, his voice a whisper punctuated by pops and crackles from the long, tenuous wires that connected us, 'was the one question he would not answer. Could not, I suppose, for Myers thought himself an ethical man. Of course I had no choice.'

I rolled my eyes at Harry, who was listening in with Eric Eden, their heads together over the room's second handset. It was hard to know what to say. Despite Myers's attempt to prepare us, the call, when we were finally put through to Walter himself, had been disorienting.

I essayed, 'Walter, I wouldn't take that guff about Carolyne too seriously. Why, I broke up with Frank, remember, and he didn't even write a book!'

'Ah, but I think my brother has too much of *me* in him for his own good. A sense of purpose that takes him away from his humanity sometimes, even from his nearest family...'

'And the treatment? How was that?'

In 1916, in the midst of their European war of conquest, the Germans were necessarily the pioneers in the treatment of this ailment, the 'gun-dread' as they called it. But their attitude was shaped by their own culture. To be brought down by fear was dishonourable, shameful. And therefore their treatment programme, called the 'Kauffmann regime', was a question of psychological pressure and – unbelievable to me – the inflicting of pain.

'I was referred to a doctor called Yealland, British but a follower of Kauffmann, who used a technique he called faradisation. The use of electricity to combat symptoms directly. If you were mute, for example, your tongue and larynx would be prodded with a charge, and the room locked to keep you in, and you were strapped down in a chair, until you *did* speak.'

'Dear God. And does it work?'

'Yes! There's a recovery rate they call "miraculous". What they don't report is a rather high rate of relapse.'

'And in your case—'

'Yealland tried to "treat" the unwelcome memories. You will recall I was badly burned in the course of the War, especially about the hands. And sometimes, when I have nightmares of imprisonment or flight, or when I see the ghosts of the past in the London streets of today, my old wounds ache, as if in sympathy. By provoking pain deliberately in that injured skin, Yealland sought to break the link between the memories and the physical pain, as he saw it, thereby lessening the impact of the former on me.'

'And the outcome—'

He said only, 'After a couple of sessions I chose to terminate the treatment.'

Eric said with feeling, 'Good for you, old man.'

'I wouldn't recommend it over a spa cure,' Walter said dryly.

After that Walter had been taken back by Myers and a colleague called William Rivers, who, sceptical of 'faradisation' and similar techniques, had become followers of Freud and his school.

'Now I am in the rather more pleasant environs of Vienna, and instead of volts it is verbiage, from Freud and his followers. We talk and talk, you see, as the doctors try to discover how a trauma deep in a wounded mind connects to the surface behaviour. I can see there is something in it – but I am sceptical of Freud's claim, as are the British doctors in fact, that every human impulse is at root sexual in nature. For you have the Martians as your counter-example! The Martians, as we know, are entirely without sex – we have physical proof that to reproduce they bud asexually – and so what use Freudian analysis to a Martian? And yet they are conscious beings, they evidently have motivation...'

I rolled my eyes at my companions; I thought we needed to get to the point. 'Never mind about the Martians just now, Walter. I'm sorry to hear of your troubles. I do sympathise. You probably know I left Britain after the '11 election, when Marvin and his strutting bully-boys came to power – soldiers in khaki marching behind King George's coronation coach... I would not wish to be in their hands, as you have been... But you have called for a reason.'

'I have become desperate to get in touch. Not just with you, but with Frank, Carolyne... I could think of no other way but through you, Julie. I could not trace you in New York, so I asked Major Eden to bring a personal message. I hope you will see the sense of it. You have always been—'

'A girl of "quality", as you said in your memoir?'

'Sorry about that! Look – my suggestion is that you go back to England. There is still time. Take a steamer – I have the resources to pay. Gather the family, and I will make another call. Perhaps near Woking – the house I shared with Carolyne is long sold, but—'

'What is it, Walter? Tell me *something*.'

So began for me an extraordinary journey, one which took me from the lobby of the world's tallest building in New York to the foot of a Martian fighting-machine in London – and beyond!

But for now he would say only: 'I have grave news from the sky.'

5

My Return to England

When I looked for a steamer, I found the *Lusitania* happened to be readying for a passage. With Walter's funds behind me, why not travel in style? It didn't take long to arrange tickets for myself, and for Eric Eden and Albert Cook, both of whom, after hearing Walter's dark hints, decided to cut short their American tour (with apologies to Professor Schiaparelli). Their whole lives had been shaped by the Martian War; of course they would come.

Not that I was keen to make the journey at the time. And my brave hero Harry Kane was even less so. 'England ain't a place to be an American these days,' he told me. 'They say that when you open your mouth and let out a Yankee drawl, you're as likely as not to be hauled over by some cop. And meanwhile they got German troopers on guard outside Buckingham Palace. Now where's the sense in that?'

'That's politics for you.'

He grunted. '*I* blame the Martians. You know, I think for a lot of us on this side of the pond your Martian War was a kind of a big splash at the time, and there were false alarms and panics and such here – but when it was all over, well, it was like some remote natural disaster, a volcano blowing its top in Yorkshire or someplace.'

'Do you even know where Yorkshire is?'

'You were crowded off the front page next time there was a jumper off the Brooklyn Bridge. And it didn't stop the Kaiser marching his tin soldiers all over the map of Europe, did it? But for you Brits – sometimes it feels like you never got over it.'

I had to nod. 'Surprisingly perceptive. So you're not going to let my brother-in-law buy you a week on a cruise ship?'

'Some other time, sweet cheeks.'

We said a perfunctory farewell – but as it turned out it would be a very long time indeed before I saw Harry Kane again.

Two days after Walter's call it was time to go. It didn't take long for me to pack. I have travelled light since that dreadful early morn in June of '07, when I was staying with my brother George and his wife Alice in their house at Stanmore, and he, a surgeon, came home from a call-out to Pinner full of news of the Martian advance. He bundled us onto the chaise, promising to meet us at Edgware station after he had roused the neighbours. It was quite an adventure for us, and recorded at second hand passably accurately by Walter in his *Narrative* – for we ran into *his* brother, my future husband Frank, and as a result were brought under the scrutiny of the wider world. But it is typical of Walter's carelessness with human detail that he did not trouble to complete that part of his narrative with a report of the loss of George Elphinstone, my brother, whom we never saw again.

I joined Cook and Eric at the wharf. The RMS *Lusitania* was a floating hotel, with electric elevators, and a telephone in every cabin. The 'Greyhound of the Sea' would fair whip us across the ocean; we should land in less than six days. Of course at that time there was no faster way to do it. The great Zeppelins no longer flew the transatlantic routes, and it was only a year since Alcock and Brown had fluttered across the Atlantic, the first to do so in a fuel-laden variant of the war aeroplanes that had evolved so quickly on the eastern front of the Schlieffen War.

I was irked at the beginning of the show for we had to stay an extra day in dock while the harbour managers arranged the formation of a convoy, twenty or so vessels including ourselves as the largest passenger ship, a number of merchantmen, and a brace of US Navy destroyers equipped with sounding gear and depth charges to see off any threat from the 'U-boats'. Since the early weeks of the Schlieffen War in 1914, no American ship had been so much as scratched by a German torpedo, and it says a lot for the tensions between the nations at that time that such precautions were nonetheless deemed necessary. But there was some convenience for us: the convoy would make for Southampton rather than the *Lusitania*'s usual port of Liverpool, and would deliver us closer to London.

During the crossing I spent much of my time in the on-board library, while Eric habituated the gymnasium and Cook the First Class Lounge, with its stained-glass windows and marble pillars and delicate, fluttering women. There was much black humour among the passengers. We were lucky, it was said, that our convoy didn't include the White Star's *Titanic*, thought by many to be a cursed ship since she was almost wrecked by an iceberg on her maiden voyage – saved only by hull armour of high-quality Martian-grade aluminium.

As soon as we landed at Southampton, squads of the Border Control Police in their black uniforms came on board, accompanied by a handful of regular soldiers in khaki. We three British citizens, with our papers in order and checked while still on board the *Lusitania*, were allowed off briskly, while – just as Harry would have expected – Americans and other foreigners were kept back for closer scrutiny. Once off the ship, the bulky luggage of my two gentleman fellow-travellers was sent on ahead to our hotel in London.

Then, outside the passenger terminal, we three were met by Philip Parris. Philip was Walter Jenkins's cousin. Then in his fifties, he was a bulky, jowly individual, his grey-black hair plastered to his scalp by pomade, habitually dressed in a heavy suit that generally featured sombre black tie and waistcoat adorned with thick watch-chain. He looked every inch the man of business, the man of substance – and the competent kind to whom a man like Walter Jenkins would entrust the welfare of three transatlantic waifs such as ourselves, just as he had once entrusted his wife's safety during the chaos of the Martian War, while *he* followed the Martians around the English countryside as a fly follows a horse. I remember in his memoir Walter dismissing Philip as a brave enough man but not one to rise quickly to danger. Ha! Sooner at my side a man like Parris than one like Jenkins.

Philip led us briskly to the car park, and told us his plan. He would take us to London for the convenience of the hotels, then drive us back out to Woking later, for Walter's family meeting in a couple of days' time. 'I trust you had no troubles with the busy-bodies of the Border Control.'

Eric Eden shook his head. 'Just doing their jobs, I suppose. But when they came crowding aboard – I haven't seen so many uniforms in one place since I left Inkerman Barracks.'

Philip snorted. 'Wait until you see London. I blame Marvin – much too pally with the Kaiser, if you ask me.'

We came to his car, which was one of the new Bentleys; its chassis, mostly of aluminium, gleamed in the watery March sunlight.

22

Cook, whistling, ran a finger along the smooth lines of the bonnet. 'What a beauty.'

Philip grinned back. 'She is, isn't she? English aluminium, or rather *Martian*, and Ottoman petroleum in the tank, and the best leather from the cut-price French markets. And not entirely an indulgence. Aluminium's my game these days, and I need to advertise the wares. I'm going to swing east and pick up the Portsmouth Road to London. Keep your papers handy. We'll pass through the Surrey Corridor, I thought you'd like to see that, but they can be a bit twitchy at the security gates...'

The Surrey Corridor? Security gates? I had been away a long time, but I remembered when you hadn't needed papers or passports even to cross international borders in Europe, let alone to move around England.

He bundled us into the car, whose interior smelled of polished leather.

Near Portsmouth, at Cook's request, Philip turned off the main road and halted at an elevation from which we had a view of the city and the harbour beyond. Portsmouth has always been the main port of the Royal Navy, and that day we could see the English Channel crowded with ships, like grey ghosts in the March mist. Black smoke streaked from their funnels in the breeze.

Cook and Eric, military men both, were fascinated by the sight. 'Something is afoot,' murmured Cook. 'Lot of traffic down there.'

Philip said, 'Wish I'd brought my bird-watching glasses... Are either of you Army men ship-spotters? Not all those vessels out there are ours. Some are German – and some indeed are French, impounded after the Schlieffen War.' He glanced back, almost conspiratorially. 'There are tensions with the Americans. The rumour going round my club – well, it's this. That the Kaiser, straddling the whole of Europe, is feeling restless again. Just as they launched the European war in the west to knock out France quickly and have a free hand to hit Russia before she mobilised, now the German planners are thinking of taking on America before *she* becomes too big to handle. America, you know, has a decent navy but a very small standing army, and problems with her neighbour Mexico. *If* the Germans can get their fleet across the Atlantic, and *if* the Mexicans can be encouraged to cross the border...'

'Madness,' murmured Eric. 'Too many damn war rumours. Keeps everyone on edge.'

'And under control,' I put in.

Cook said, 'But you've got to hand it to the Kaiser. He's winning his war on one continent, through being bold. Maybe he can do it again. Why not?'

I had watched all this martial drama from afar. In a sense it had all followed on from the Martian War. The British Navy, the best in the world, had turned out to be all but useless against the forces that fell on us from the sky. Frank and I ourselves, in our flight to the sea, had seen the Channel Fleet standing across the Thames estuary while the Martians rampaged: 'vigilant and yet powerless', as Walter put it. So, after the War, there had been a drastic rebalancing, with funding for the home army boosted, and the Navy cut, amid much hand-wringing about the loss of tradition and so forth, and bitter inter-service rivalry. Part of the strategy had been, by 1912, our agreeing a rather shabby non-aggression pact with the Kaiser to avoid any naval arms race.

All this had led, in the end, to the betrayal of our allies in 1914.

Philip rubbed his jaw. 'Whatever you think of the national interest and so forth a lot of us were rather ashamed that we stood by as the Germans inflicted a mechanised war on Belgium and France, especially when we had been subject to just such an attack from Mars. No wonder the Americans were disgusted.'

Cook grinned cynically. 'We was too blessed busy dishing the Irish at the time. But as for the Germans versus the Yanks, maybe the Martians will come again and put a stop to the whole thing before it starts.'

And there you had the paradox of Albert Cook. He was not a conventionally intelligent man, and was certainly poorly educated, but he did have a kind of cunning grasp of strategy, of the big picture. For, of course, in that last playful prediction he turned out to be right.

Philip started the car. 'Let's press on. There's a decent pub at Petersfield where we can stop for lunch . . .'

6

The Surrey Corridor

It was early in the afternoon when I discovered what Philip had meant by the Surrey Corridor.

We were passing through Guildford. Just beyond the High Street and before the junction for the London Road, we came to a barrier, like a level-crossing gate. Philip slowed as we joined the small queue of traffic before the gate, which was raised and lowered to allow each vehicle through.

When it was our turn, a police officer came to Philip's window. He wore a regulation uniform as far as I could see, but he had a revolver in a holster at his waist, and no collar number. Philip had warned us to have our papers prepared. Our documents were taken into a small cabin at the side of the road, and inspected at length. I quickly grew impatient with the wait, though Eric and Cook, with more experience of such processes than I, sat it out stoically.

Then came a new adventure. One by one, we three were led from the car and into the cabin. Eric and Cook were released quickly, with Cook returning to the car smiling. 'Bobby in there has a copy of my book. Had me sign it. Ha!'

Which was fine for them. But when my go came, I was detained. The officer in charge was a short, bristling man with a long, mournful moustache of a style I thought of as Germanic – I was to see plenty more examples in London. 'I'm very sorry, miss, but I have to hold you here for now.'

I simply yelled, 'Philip!'

Philip Parris was a man of substance even in General Marvin's Britain. Once he was at my side, I asked again why I was being detained.

The moustached officer glanced at his notes. 'Miss, in 1908

you became a member of a proscribed organisation, the Women's Social and Political Union—'

Philip barked laughter. 'So that's it! You're a suffragette!'

'I was,' I said. Then amended to: 'I *am*. What, is that a crime now?'

'Actually it is, Julie. We'll sort this out.'

With his knowledge of the bureaucracy of the modern British state, and sheer force of character, Philip was able quickly to establish that there was no record of me having participated in such acts as bombings or assaults – neither the assassination of Prime Minister Campbell-Bannerman at the unveiling of the Tomb of the Vanished Warrior, that great memorial to Heat-Ray victims, in '08, nor even the sporadic protests that had intensified after Marvin's quasi-legal election triumph in '11, after which the movement had been banned. In the end, after much telephone negotiation, Philip got me out of choky in return for assurances that I would present myself at a police station in London, and that Philip himself would be a guarantor of my good behaviour.

Though grateful to Philip I was humiliated to have to rely on the help of a *man,* given the circumstances.

Thus my introduction to the new Britain. We drove on.

Beyond Guildford, the Bentley passed smoothly along an almost empty road. And we came into that landscape where Martians had once walked.

The maps that have been drawn up of the battle zone since the end of the First Martian War are familiar enough. It begins south-west of Woking, at Horsell Common, where the first cylinder landed at midnight on Friday June 14, in the year 1907. Then you have that sequence of pits, forming irregular triangles, laid down by cylinder impacts over nine more summer nights, reaching up through Surrey to central London and beyond. (Of course there was more to that pattern of impact scars than I understood at the time, as I will relate.) That loose band of destruction and poison had since become known as the Corridor. By now the natural countryside had recovered, at least as far as the naked eye could see, with green grass in the abandoned fields evident even in the grey light of March.

But we saw the ruins of central Woking itself, still unreconstructed, left as a kind of monument to the fallen. It had become a sad joke that Woking, which had once been notorious as the site of the first crematorium in Britain, had now become nothing but a necropolis itself.

We drove on, through an empty countryside.

Philip said, 'Even after the clean-up all this was left undeveloped. Aside from the physical destruction, the Martians' use of the Black Smoke, and their vegetable infestations, the red weed, left traces thought to be toxic in the long term. So the land's unfit for use.'

'That's the cover, right enough,' said Albert Cook slyly.

The closest the road came to one of the Martians' landing sites was at Pyrford, where we saw a substantial building of corrugated iron and concrete, with barbed wire and watchtowers all around, and armed troops patrolling, and a Union Jack flying jauntily. To reach the site we would have had to pass through another gate, still more massive than the one at Guildford.

I complained, 'I can see nothing of the Martian pit from here.'

'That's not surprising,' Philip said. 'It's the same all over. The pits have become too valuable an asset to be open to Sunday trippers and lemonade-sellers.'

'More than that,' Cook said. 'There's science stuff goes on in there. Like a labor'try. Scientists and inventors and military men, fiddling with Martian gear – trying to make it work for man, see.'

Philip snorted. 'And what would you know of all that?'

The former artilleryman tapped his nose. 'I have my sources. And my readers, even in the ranks of the military, men who agree with me on some points of strategy, they tell me stuff. We haven't had much trouble figuring some of *how* it works. The Heat-Ray, f'r example – and that bighead Jenkins got *this* detail wrong – generates a beam of a special light they call infra-red, that rattles back and forth between two little mirrors, getting stronger and stronger, until, *bang*, out it shoots. *Coherent* – that's the word. The big parabolic mirror on the outside of the cannon is only for sighting, so I understand it, to gen'rate the guide-light that's barely visible to us. And the Ray itself – fifteen hundred degrees it is, nearly hot enough to melt iron. Bet you never knew *that*.

'And the flying-machine, they got *that* working even before the Martians' corpses were cool. But what they *can't* figure is what powers all these gadgets. They all have these little boxes inside of 'em, energy packs... They don't burn coal or oil, and they're not electric batteries.'

'He's right about that,' Philip said. 'There are a couple of German physicists called Einstein and, um—'

'Schwarzschild,' Eric murmured.

'That's it. They have a theory that the power packs are something to do with the energy that's evidently trapped, so *they* say, inside every atom. If only you could liberate it – well, perhaps that's what the Martians have managed. If so it's beyond our understanding, for now.'

'I'll say,' said Cook with some glee. 'But they'd make mighty fine bombs. Maybe you heard of the explosions they had at Ealing and Kensington and Manchester, tinkering with those fellows. Boom! Bash! And half a square mile – flattened.'

Walter himself had witnessed this power. In his *Narrative* you will read how he saw the Heat-Ray camera of a fallen Martian at Shepperton flash river water to steam, and cause a great scalding wave to advance down the river – he still bears the scars of the scalding he received that day. 'Think how long a kettle takes to boil!' he once said to me. 'And imagine, then, the torrent of energy which that generator must have poured into the tremendous mass of the river water . . .'

Philip said now, 'But even so we're working some miracles.' He slowed the car. 'Take a look.'

Glancing around, I saw that we were in the vicinity of Esher. To either side of the road stood lines of wire fencing, tall, topped with barbed wire, with here and there a manned watchtower. Buildings were dimly visible behind these barriers, and people were coming and going, like spectres in the grey afternoon light, watched over by the soldiers or police on the towers. I saw one small girl pressed up against the fence itself, peering out as we passed, her fingers meshed in the wire.

We slowed beside a factory complex. Troops were patrolling the wire here, and Philip made sure a kind of badge was visible behind his windscreen as we paused. We all gazed out.

And, at the centre of a small compound of huts and pits and heaps of clay, I saw a Martian machine.

I recognised it at once, from the reconstructions in the museums of New York – I never saw such a machine myself in '07. It was a handling-machine, a crab-like vehicle that sat on five stiff, stationary legs, and with articulated tentacles working before it. It had no rider. Compared to the dioramas in the museums, which included model Martians riding the things like pilots, it looked as if it had had its brain scooped out.

28

Beside the handling-machine was a crude-looking apparatus, an upright cylinder above which a kind of receptacle tipped back and forth. With graceful if unearthly swipes of its tentacular limbs, the machine fed soil into the cylinder through the tipping device at the top. A white powder filtered out of the base of the cylinder, to flow down a channel to a boxy receiver, from which puffs of green smoke rose into the air – Martian green, an eerie shade that brought back vivid memories to me, if not the others. And even as we watched, another tentacle snaked out of the handling-machine to withdraw a silvery ingot from the receiving device: aluminium.

But this eerie industry was only the centrepiece. Around the central drama of the clay and the ingots and the green smoke, lines of people supported the operation. Shuffling they were, in bland prison-like uniforms and soft shoes, men, women and children. They brought soil to the handling-machine, and took ingots away, and performed other such menial tasks, all under the supervision of armed guards.

Philip, Cook and Eric did not mention the people. They enthused about the gadgetry, what they saw of it as the car crawled past.

'Aluminium, of course,' Philip said expansively. 'That superb material, strong and lightweight as no other metal . . . *We* only began manufacturing on an industrial scale, with the Hall process, a dozen years before the Martians came. And we needed a plant with the power of a Niagara Falls, and an input of aluminium-rich bauxite, to achieve such results. But the metal is abundant in the earth's crust. The Martians could produce aluminium from ordinary English clay!

'I was keen that you should see this, Julie. You are family, after all. *This* is how I have made my, our fortune . . . And I've Walter to thank for it. I tell you now that this humble gadget, the Martian aluminium-smelter, will do more to transform the fortunes of this country than any fighting-machine.'

I considered what I had seen. 'But these fences – the guns – the people working here. Who are they? Criminals?'

'Not necessarily. You know there are a lot of French refugees in England now. Belgians too. Some of them cause trouble: attacks on German business interests, and so forth. And we do have our own home-grown saboteurs—'

'Saboteurs? What, even the children? And all of them tucked

conveniently out of sight in this "Corridor", where they can be put to work? Is this a concentration camp, Philip?'

He had the grace to look embarrassed. He said only, 'This isn't South Africa.'

Bert Cook laughed. 'I bet Keir Hardie and Ramsay MacDonald are in that camp somewhere, fighting for the top bunk like true socialists!'

Philip drove us smoothly away.

A little further north we passed the burned-out ruins of Wimbledon, to our right. A hangar-like building stood bold not far from Wimbledon itself, surrounded by levees and embankments. This was the site of another of the '07 cylinders, the sixth to fall.

Here the road had been raised onto a kind of viaduct, for the land was flooded extensively – as I was to learn, a result of the choking of the Thames by the Martians' red weed; thirteen years after the vanquishing of the Martians, this damage had yet to be corrected. And here I saw gangs of labourers, knee-high in the shallower water, working on drainage ditches or what looked like paddy fields. They were watched over by armed police. The low sun glittered on the water.

Albert Cook said quietly, '*I* was hereabouts, on Putney Hill. Defying the Martians. Apparently the house I was in has got a plaque on the side now, saying so.'

After that we spoke little until we approached London itself.

7

In London

Philip brought the Bentley to an extensive car park outside Waterloo Station. The station itself had been rebuilt as a sprawling pile
fronted by an edifice of concrete and marble – it reminded me of
nothing so much as the Brandenburg Gate.

We were to stay two nights in London; we made arrangements
to meet the day after next, for our excursion back to Surrey to
meet Frank and Carolyne. Eric and Cook left for the hotel Philip
had arranged for us at the Elephant and Castle – and to which
our luggage, save for my rucksack, had been directed. Philip, he
reminded me, now had to bring me to the London police headquarters, relocated to the Barbican, to prove I was no anarchist.

And so, with some time before my appointment, Philip and I
decided to walk.

As we left the car park I found myself staring up at a tremendous poster of General Brian Marvin himself, arms folded, his gaze
fixed sternly on mine:

**IN SOUTH AFRICA I FOUGHT THE BOERS:
NATIONAL HUMILIATION!
AT WEYBRIDGE I FOUGHT THE MARTIANS:
ENGLAND PROSTRATE!
NEVER AGAIN!
VOLUNTEER NOW!**

Philip joined me. 'Doesn't get any better-looking with age, does
he?'

'I'm surprised nobody's given him a better moustache.'

Philip laughed. 'Oh, nobody would dare...'

I looked at him, and mused on the oddities of humanity – of

Philip Parris in particular. He was self-evidently a good man, competent, and a support to his friends. He had enough intelligence and detachment to see the corruption of the regime under which he now lived – even its absurdity. And yet he had not turned a hair when faced with the aluminium-factory camp in the Corridor. We are all complex, I suppose, and none of us consistent.

We walked through the train station itself, an echoing hall, half of which was fenced off by wooden panels. Within was the usual chaos of porters and passengers and portmanteaus, with wreaths of steam everywhere, and the shriek of whistles. But I was puzzled by the half-complete aspect. 'Why all the rebuilding? I don't remember any Martian War damage here.'

'Ah, this is another of Marvin's dreams. Better communications, that was the promise: more road and rail links, the better to move the guns and men around if the Martians had another go – and he's done that, to some extent. But he does have a weakness for the grandiose design, him and old warhorses like Churchill, and all those tycoons from the railways and the coal mines who are in the government now. Vast naval canals joining Clyde to Forth to Grangemouth: warships sailing down Loch Lomond! If the Martians can engineer their planet, why not the British? That's the logic, you see. Well, that's the plan; so far, there's barely a scratch in the Scottish turf. And then there's the tunnel under the Channel. Again, barely a scratch – but we've got the station! The frontage, anyhow.'

There was a W. H. Smith's near the exit from the station, and I glanced over its stock with professional curiosity. In contrast to the vibrant American press, here on offer were mostly what looked like dreary official government rags. The *Daily Mail* was prominent; the *Mail* had been the first to resume publication after the Martian War, and had never let its readers forget it: 'Even The Martians Could Not Silence Us!' I wondered if there was an underground press.

We crossed Waterloo Bridge, itself heavily repaired after the damage of the War. At this time of day the smoke pall hung as heavy over London as it ever had, and from here, suspended over the eternal river, I could see Westminster, where the palace, wrecked by the Heat-Ray, was gone altogether – even the sandstone stump of the Clock Tower demolished – to be replaced by a looming fortress of concrete and glass.

Philip grunted. 'Behold our rulers. The Mother of Parliaments replaced by a bunker – ugh! And over in the City, around Bank, the seat of global finance similarly secured. London's still London. You still get the swarms of commuters coming in from the suburbs in the morning, and trickling out in the evening, day by day. But they all carry papers and passes, and Black Smoke masks or revolvers depending on which drill is on that day ...'

A deep thrumming seemed to make the fabric of the bridge itself vibrate, and a diffuse shadow crossed the river. Looking up I saw a vast Zeppelin, a whale in the sky. The eagle of Imperial Germany was easily visible on its flank.

Once across the river we walked along the Strand a distance, and cut up through Covent Garden. Bunting hung everywhere, and Union flags fluttered, and there were posters of the King and of the heroes of the new military government – Marvin himself, Churchill, Lloyd George. But the streets were grubby, the paint peeling on the buildings, and there were very many beggars. Their hands, open for change, were like grimy flowers.

And I was struck by how many people I saw in uniform, not just bobbies or soldiers. Every public building seemed to have a soldier or two on guard, and even the staff at the hotels and restaurants sported epaulettes and brass buttons. It was the Berlinification of London, I thought. And considering that, I seemed to hear an unconscionable number of German accents.

At Trafalgar Square I was obscurely pleased to see that Nelson, who even the Martians had not toppled, had not yet been replaced on his column by a grinning Brian Marvin, hero of Weybridge. We walked up Charing Cross Road which, of all the locations in London I had seen so far, seemed the least changed, still a warren of bookshops and barrows laden with tattered volumes. As a girl I had always loved coming to London, not for the clothes or the cafés or the shows, but for the books, always the books. This feeling, of stumbling upon a fragment of the past, was so strong that I briefly found myself overcome. Philip, always more sensitive than he looked, gave me his arm, and we walked on in silence. But as a sign of the times I noticed a new book on sale, prominently displayed: *General Marvin and Why We Must Fight an Unending War*, by Arthur Conan Doyle.

We cut through Oxford Street and Portland Place. On the Marylebone Road we ignored placard-bearers urging us to visit Madame Tussaud's, where a new diorama showed the 'true horrors' of the Martians' feeding habits. Philip said the exhibit was popular.

It was with relief, for me at least, that we reached the green spaces of Regent's Park, although the light was fading fast. But even here much was changed. The expanses of grass had been largely given over to vegetable plots, meant as demonstrations for householders urged to grow food in their own lawns. And where once the children flew kites and rode their bicycles, now they marched in crocodiles or dug at the ground, and even put on what looked like a mock battle.

Later I would learn of the transformation Marvin had inflicted on the education system. The motto of the new movement was an old quotation of Wellington's, on seeing a cricket match at Eton: 'There grows the stuff that won Waterloo.' Well, now Eton and the other schools turned out nothing but officers, while the younger siblings of the scholars were enticed into joining a new movement called the Junior Sappers, organised by Lord Baden-Powell: boys and girls as young as five or six, digging trenches and binding mock wounds. All this was part of a general cleansing of the national moral character, as Marvin's supporters called it. I was dismayed, coming at it with unprejudiced eyes from across the Atlantic. Was this the future of Britain – the child soldier?

We passed the Zoological Gardens – now closed up and empty of animals – and crossed the Albert Road to climb Primrose Hill. The view opened up around us as it always had, the hill itself seeming to rise out of the greenery of Regent's Park, beyond which the great reef of the city was visible, the wounded dome of St Paul's, the new concrete excrescences of Westminster and Whitehall, the ethereal glitter of the Crystal Palace, and the Surrey hills in the distance.

Here we stood before what had been the landing site of the seventh Martian cylinder, and the nucleus of what had become the largest single Martian construction during the War. This was fenced off as had been the pits in Surrey. But of the three inert fighting-machines Walter had glimpsed here on that hot sum-mer's day at the end of the War in 1907, one had been left stand-ing, a tripod stark and disconcerting in profile. A fairground had been set up, a roundabout with cars and horses, a steam organ, coconut shies, balloon races. Thus, around the feet of the ghastly monument, small children played. I looked up at the brazen cowl of the thing, that mechanical component so like a head.

And it was at that moment that I had what Philip described as my 'turn'.

After I recovered – I sat on a bench for a while, with Philip hovering solicitously – we took a taxi to the police centre at the

Barbican, where I was processed with cold efficiency, though it was nine at night before I was released.

I allowed Philip to escort me back to the hotel at the Elephant and Castle, where I retired immediately, taking a cold supper in my room. I slept little, trying not to think of that which had disturbed me, on the Hill.

The next day was free. I felt I needed to see something of the real London, away from Philip's kind but suffocating embrace, away from the military cynicism of the others. I still had old friends in the city, and I hastily called a couple from the hotel and made arrangements.

I left the hotel early, avoiding Philip and the others.

Lunch was at an oyster house in Lambeth. Here I met a school friend who ran a soup kitchen. For all his grand visions, and whatever he might have done for national security, Marvin had delivered an economy that was faltering at best. I was told that though trade unions and the like had long been banned, there was plenty of agitation, in the mines, the railways – even in Woolwich Arsenal, which manufactured a large percentage of the country's munitions supply, all such unrest brutally suppressed. And at the very bottom they were opening up the workhouses once again. My friend had plenty of clients. I was lucky to be here in March in a place like Lambeth, said my friend, for in the summer the bugs came out.

That evening, by way of contrast, I called another old friend, the wife of a banker. We met in a tea shop – I relished the smell of coffee and tea and cigarette smoke, and the rattle of the dominoes – and Hilda loaned me a dress for the evening, and we went to the Savoy on the Strand, which I playfully told Hilda was nearly as grand as the *Lusitania*. We had caviar and crab and mushroom salad, and a bottle of hock. The place was full of the usual menagerie: the bounders and the flappers and the roués and the Varsity youth, their cheeks flushed with the drink. We danced to the Havana Band, and we let ourselves be charmed by handsome German officers.

The Savoy was relatively uncrowded, I thought, but Hilda reminded me it was not yet the season. For now the upper classes were still mostly ensconced in their draughty country houses, but they would swarm in London during the summer – like the bugs in Lambeth, I thought to myself. There wasn't much to enjoy in Marvin's morally uplifted Britain. He hadn't quite had the nerve to prohibit alcohol, but prices had been sharply increased by tax levies. The government had shut down most sports (none of which I followed anyhow), save for cricket which Marvin regarded as 'manly', and football, but only as played by military personnel on leave. But if you had money there were still places in London to spend it. The well-to-do had no problems with the new way of things, Hilda told me, unless it was to complain about the reintroduction of wild boar to the English countryside so the Germans could hunt *Schwein.*

Between dance numbers a kind of dumb waiter was circulated through the room. It had to be pushed around, but fine metallic tentacles curled from it, grasping bottles to pour, even mixing cocktails: Martian technology, of course, and a pretty advanced experiment in its application. A glimpse of the industries of the future, perhaps, but it seemed grotesque to me. The beautiful people clapped and laughed in delight...

We went on, deeper into the wilds of London... To a dance hall in Soho, where a band from America played 'Tiger Rag', and the dancing was as fierce as the music...

None of it seemed real to me, and the more I thrust myself into these foolish adventures the more unreal it felt, a puppet show on the slope of a volcano. I kept thinking of those striking words Walter had used in his *Narrative,* to catch the mood of the last days he and Carolyne had spent in Woking before the cylinders fell: 'It seemed so safe and tranquil.'

And I said nothing to my friends of what had given me my 'turn' on Primrose Hill. In the gloom of that March evening, even as the children of London had played around its tremendous feet, *I thought I saw the Martian turn its head.*

8

A Meeting at Ottershaw

The next morning, even if I was a little tender, I was ready for Philip and Eric and Cook, and our drive to Surrey. It was March 25, a Thursday.

It was a little after lunch when we gathered at last in Ottershaw, some three miles to the north of Woking where Walter and Carolyne Jenkins had once shared a home – and, though this site was only a couple of hours' walk from the location of the first Martian landing, it was just outside the Surrey Corridor perimeter.

Marina Ogilvy, our hostess for the evening, had long been a friend of Carolyne's, though the closest relationship had been their husbands'. Benjamin Ogilvy had been a noted amateur astronomer, with his own small observatory in Ottershaw. In that eerie summer of '07, he and Walter had watched through Benjamin's telescope those reddish sparks on the disc of planet Mars, those gushes of gas, that turned out to have been signs of the firing of a mighty cannon. What a disturbing thrill it must have been for Walter and Benjamin to see it with their own eyes! And the first landing at Horsell Common, so close to his home, must have been a kind of vindication for Benjamin the amateur – that and the response of the Astronomer Royal himself, who had come out to Horsell: the crowning moment of Benjamin's life, perhaps. To be followed pretty rapidly by his death, in the first few hours of humanity's encounter with the Martians.

Despite this grisly outcome, or even because of it perhaps, Marina had kept on the house, and she had maintained her husband's observatory, neither of which had been damaged during the War. She had even let out the observatory to a local amateur-astronomical group, of which a profusion had sprung up, now that the night sky had become an arena of threat for all of us. Later, of course, the telescopic observation of Mars by amateurs had been banned by the Marvin government under their Defence of the Realm Act, DORA, of 1916; now Benjamin's grand old telescope was without mirrors and eyepieces.

Anyhow, Marina had generously offered to host our telephonic meeting with Walter. Hers at least was one telephone number Walter had retained, even if he had lost contact with Carolyne, his ex-wife. Carolyne had quickly sold the house on Maybury Hill after her divorce. I suppose the reason for the breakdown of her marriage is obvious, if you read the *Narrative*. But it seemed somehow fitting to be in a location so close to the start of it all.

So here I was, with Philip. Here were Eric Eden and Bert Cook, who had followed in my wake, so to speak, both of them alarmed or intrigued by the tantalising promise of Walter's news.

And of course my own ex-husband had to be summoned to the gathering too: Walter's brother, Frank Jenkins. Thus the Martians, those interplanetary matchmakers, brought us together once again, for we had first met during the great flight from London. Frank had been a medical student then, and I at nineteen a few years younger with ambitions to become a journalist. And for a while it had worked. Frank completed his studies, and settled down to what had evidently always been his ambition, to become a general practitioner, and we bought a house in Highgate.

Bur Frank had always had something of his brother's sense of destiny about him. Though heavily committed to his practice, he would often let himself be called away on what I described as his 'missionary' work among the destitute in the East End. And in '16, when the DORA was passed, Frank surprised me by being drawn to Marvin's new programmes of military service. He had quickly enlisted in the Territorial Force, a volunteer reserve, which Marvin, with typical cunning showmanship, renamed the 'Fyrd', a nod to deep English roots.

'Oh, for pity's sake!' I had protested. 'I can understand a schoolboy enjoying all the marching about. But you – you're a man of healing.'

'I heal humans,' he said. 'I would *kill* Martians. And at High Barnet, remember, it was your brother's revolver that saved us from the ruffians who wanted your cart, Julie, that and a bit of my boxing from school, not my nascent medical skills, or even your high spirits. There are times when one must fight...'

Well, to be a witness to self-assumed greatness was never

enough for me. And besides – it is hard to record this so bluntly, but it was a difference between us – I had never wanted children. Not after the horrors of the Martian War; whatever you may have read of Walter's mental torment, that was its lingering effect on *my* psyche. Other survivors reacted similarly. Eric Eden, for example, never married. It is just as well the rest of the human race doesn't share that flaw; indeed after the War there was a sharp rise in the number of births in Britain.

Frank understood, I think, but did not share my reluctance. Since we had divorced, Frank had married again; he had a child, and I was happy enough for him. But I wasn't terribly comfortable, here in this relic of our calamitous past, and I dare say nor was he.

So the six of us gathered early that afternoon, replete on Marina's tea and finger sandwiches: myself, Carolyne, Philip Parris, Frank, Eric Eden and Bert Cook. It was a vivid scene, with our faces glowing like moons in the light of a single, shadowed electric bulb – there are only dim lights in an observatory, of course. I remember the smell of oil and furniture polish and clockwork, with the domed roof over us adding a peculiar echo to the soft sounds of our voices. The telescope itself, angular in the shadows, had an eerie Martian-like quality that made me unwilling to turn my back on it. It was rather cold, too. I could feel my own tension rising – a tension that had never gone away since Walter had approached me in New York.

It was something of a shock when the telephone finally rang.

9

A Call from Germany

Bert Cook had some practical skills, and, with odds and ends from the observatory tool box and the remains of a broken Marvin's Megaphone, he had managed to rig up a small loudspeaker so that we could all hear Walter's thin voice, relayed from Germany. Though Walter asked first to speak to Philip, that good man firmly passed the handset to the man's former wife.

'Walter? It's me. Carolyne. I'm here safe and sound – we all are.'

'Carolyne? I . . .'

'What's this all about, Walter? And where are you, for heaven's sake?'

'I am in Berlin – not in Vienna any more, as when I called Julie in New York. For with the coming emergency they let me out of the nut-hatch and ferried me here.'

I asked, speaking loudly for the pick-up, 'What "emergency"? And who are "they"?'

'Julie! I'm grateful you came. "They" are a stellar assemblage here at the Academy of Sciences, drawn from across Germany – indeed across Europe. Drawn to this rather well-equipped bunker under the Academy's tennis court, and I can tell you with some authority that many of our crowned heads are in similar bunkers, dotted around the planet: the Kaiser, the Emperors of China and Japan – no doubt the American President – and our own King George with his family is I believe deep in the turf beneath Balmoral.

'As to who has been gathered here, you might call it a brains trust – with myself roped in on the basis of my *Narrative*, and I feel as if I am the comic relief. The Buster Keaton of Martian studies! You have Einstein and Schwarzschild and Rutherford, experts on one aspect or another of the atom and its energies. Hohmann and Tsiolkovsky, analysing and predicting interplanetary trajectories. They've even got the chap – what's his name? – who once wrote a facetious but provocative essay on the future of humanity, and almost by accident came up with a sort of vision of the Martian form. "The Year Million Man" – it was called something of that sort. You may have heard me speak of him before. No longer young – about my age in fact – an odd, bouncing sort of fellow with a squeaky voice, but full of ideas.

'And you have the astronomical exchange wires buzzing with sightings from Hale in Wisconsin and Lick in California and Nice in France – though that's now under German control – all of it organised and marshalled by Lowell's team at Flagstaff; shame the old man himself isn't alive to see this. Even the Vatican observatory at Castel Gandolfo has pitched in . . .'

Philip took the handset and spoke more sharply. 'Get to the point, Walter. Sightings of what? What are you on about? What is it they are all observing, man?'

Again my own inner tension tightened a notch, and I could see it in the faces of the others.

But Walter named a planet we were none of us expecting: *Jupiter*.

We stared at each other, confused. Jupiter!

Philip snapped, 'Walter, damn you! What about Jupiter?'

'Why, a sigil has been observed on its cloudy face.'

'A sigil?'

'A mark, luminous and sinuous – entirely contained within the feature we call the Great Red Spot, as it happens, but easily visible from the earth. Indeed Dyson in England claims to have seen similar sigils on Jupiter's larger moons, but that is disputed.'

Eric Eden said, 'A sigil? You mean like the marks observed after the War, on Mars and Venus?'

'That's it, yes,' Walter said when this was relayed. 'The conclusive observations were made by Lessing, who told me that—'

'As I recall the Mars and Venus sigils were identical, aside from scale.'

'Of course they were. They were made by the same agency.'

'The Martians?'

'Of course the Martians! Who did not, by the way, have the time to complete the construction of a similar symbol of possession of the earth back in '07, though the work was begun.'

41

'It was? A sigil on the earth? I never heard of that,' said Eric, evidently confused. (As I was – this was a reference to the geometry of the Martians' first fall upon the earth, of which, as I have said, I would learn more.) Eric pressed, 'And the Jovian sigil—'

'Quite different in character, obviously – the Jovians' was a near-perfect circle—'

Frank broke in, 'For God's sake, Walter, can you never get to the point? What has all this to do with us, and your brains in Berlin?'

'Everything,' said Bert Cook. 'For he's giving us the bigger picture. Aren't you, Walter?'

'Bert Cook?' said Walter. 'How odd to hear your voice again.'

'How's your poker play?'

'How's your chess? You're right, though. This is indeed the bigger picture. The context of our petty lives. For, you see, if the nebular hypothesis is to be believed, a kind of migration between the worlds is a *necessity* if life is to survive . . .'

As most people understand today, the nebular hypothesis of Kant, Laplace and Maxwell posits that the further a world is from the sun the *older* it must be, and the older, too, its freight of life and mind. But since the first life emerged it has faced challenges. Our best physics has it that as the sun itself ages it is cooling, year on year. *That* is why the Martians were driven to the earth, as an Ice Age without end crept upon their planet. Some day our own world will suffer the same fate: the oceans will freeze from the coasts, the rains will diminish, the higher forms of life will die out and the lesser shrivel to sleeping spores. Whither mankind? A mature but doomed civilisation *must* reach out to the younger worlds for room to live. It is the logic of cosmology; it must be so.

'Which,' Walter said, 'is why the Martians *must* come again to our younger earth. Oh, they have made a stab at Venus – and that is the ultimate prize in the far future, for ourselves too. Within Venus is only Mercury, younger still but a lifeless cinder. Yes, Venus is the goal.

'*But* –

'But out on the rim sits Jupiter, largest planet of all – fully seven times as old as Mars, even. *And the Jovians are watching us.* Their sigil proves it! It was clearly painted on the Red Spot as a response to the Martian invasions of Earth and Venus. This ancient and enormous planet may be the seat of—'

Frank grabbed the handset. 'Into the inferno with Jupiter,

Hubble and all! You wouldn't have dragged us all together, from across the damn ocean, just to talk about Jupiter. And nor would the King of England be stuck in a hole in the ground. What is it you really have to tell us, brother?'

But – typical of the man! – still Walter hesitated, as if gathering his thoughts.

'We've seen the shots,' Walter said, almost gently. 'The gun shots on Mars.'

And there it was – at last!

This was the way of it with Walter, of course. If you've read his *Narrative* you'll know he wasn't a man to walk in a straight line. In the First War he had set off from the ruins of Woking in search of his wife, at Leatherhead, and ended up on Primrose Hill, at the greatest concentration of Martians in England. And as then, so it was now, with this rambling affair of second-party messages and transatlantic crossings and diversions via Jupiter: in the end here we all were facing the Martians once again.

The tension broke within me, as if I had received a grim but not unexpected diagnosis of illness. I remembered again how I thought I had seen that solitary fighting-machine on Primrose Hill move its head-like cowl, as if in anticipation. It had distressed me – I thought I had been seeing things . . . Perhaps *it* knew, through some machine telepathy of its own . . .

Philip was angry, reasonably enough. 'You have such news, Walter, and you yattered on about Jupiter? *When*? When did the firing start? On February 27? Because if they kept to the same timetable as last time that's when they'd have fired, with an opposition on April 21—'

Cook snarled, 'And if it's so, the governments have kept it quiet after all—'

'No,' Walter said softly. 'Earlier than that. The strategy's evidently different this time, although it's not yet obvious how. The guns started firing earlier – nine days – on February 18.'

Frank was as furious as his cousin by now. 'You're saying now that they started to fire in February! Why, that means the landings must be close – what, days away, no more? And it is only now you warn us, with this farce of messages across the Atlantic?'

'I'm sorry,' Walter said, still more quietly. 'You must understand that the information I have is partial, gathered in shards and scraps – the security is heavy here, and it was difficult for me to get in touch with you at all – then it took time for you to come together. I suppose I might have planned it better. I did my best, Frank, to give you this warning. I did my best.'

Oddly enough, I believed him.

And Cook, an artilleryman himself, picked up on the key detail. 'You said *guns*, Jenkins. The *guns* started firing. Not *gun*.'

'That's it. More than one this time, Bert. More than one gun, on Mars.'

We looked at each other in horror, we veterans of the First War.

Walter continued to speak, his voice frail and faint, dogged. 'We think we saw the casting of the new weapons – just as, in retrospect, we glimpsed the casting of the first at the opposition of 1894, when the workers at Nice and Lick saw an anomalous glaring on the surface. They had one cannon last time. *Now it's ten.* Ten we've seen to fire, anyhow. A belt of them in low latitudes, spread around the planet.

'The smoke released by the firings themselves, a great bruise that has spread across the face of the planet, has made the sequence difficult to observe. Nonetheless we've been able to map it against Schiaparelli's scheme of the canals. Perhaps you know that the canals are tremendous affairs, some thousands of miles long – and they meet, in groups of three or four or five, with geometric precision, at "nodes" as Lowell called them, or "oases". The greatest of these is Solis Lacus, the Lake of the Sun – a sort of nerve centre for the whole planet, I suspect, from which any point can be reached. But there are others, at Trivium Charontis, Ceraunius, the Cyane Fons.'

Philip the industrialist said, 'These junctions of the transport network may be centres of population, of manufacture. And if you're seeking to build an interplanetary cannon—'

Cook nodded. 'You'd do it there. All right. Ten cannon instead of one. Last time it was ten shots—'

'This time there were a hundred, Bert. Ten from each gun. Last time a flotilla; this time a veritable fleet. Or rather two fleets; they seem to be separating, in space, into two groups of fifty or so—'

'Hang on,' I said. 'But what about the oppositions? Why come now, *four years* before the next minimum approach?' There was a complaining whine in my voice, I admit. Like everybody else in those days, I would watch the skies at every opposition with Mars, even the most unfavourable. But I knew that the next most

44

likely date for an attack was years hence. Not now! It's not fair! *That* was how I, quite unreasonably, reacted.

But Walter was reason itself, in his fashion. 'Last time they came in '07, two years before *that* minimum. Perhaps they planned, and abandoned, a follow-up shot for the perihelic optimum at '09, and even thereafter. There's no reason to suppose they haven't expanded their capabilities to exploit less favourable oppositions – why not?'

Eric said, 'Actually I would say that serious military thinking has argued against another invasion. After all, their first shot was a hopeless attempt. The Martians couldn't stand the different atmospheric pressure, they couldn't stand the difference in gravitation, our bacteria finished them off – them *and* their red weed. Hopeless from the start.'

'But that was only a scouting mission,' Walter whispered. 'You have to start somewhere. Columbus in the Americas. And *he* thought he was in Asia! Consider how difficult it is to observe the earth. As seen from Mars, the earth is an inner planet – as Venus is to the earth – that is, closer to the sun. They must have known little of our world, before launching that first cylinder. And yet they knew *something*.

'Remember the timings of the firings of their great cannon? Ten shots in all, each fired at our midnight, Greenwich Mean Time, and each landed at local midnight. Now the Martian day is longer than ours – nearer twenty-four and a half hours – and "midnight" at the cylinders' launch site did not coincide with that in Britain. So their timetable, for symbolic or other reasons, was keyed precisely, not to the time at the launch site—'

'But to the time at the target,' Eden said softly. 'Even the launch timing! I never thought of that.'

'Nobody has, before me. As to the rest, consider how different our earth is to their own world, how much they must have learned, and how quickly! Their seas are shallow and cover only a third of their world; our deep oceans cover twice as much of the earth. And so the oceans have become our highway of choice – on Mars, it must be the land.'

'No wonder they were baffled by our ships, then,' Frank said. 'Off Tillingham, I saw them amazed by the torpedo ram that got amongst 'em. And what of our bacteria and viruses? That was new to them too, evidently.'

'Another lacuna in their knowledge when they came, yes. I speculate they must have eliminated whole microscopic continents of such creatures deep in their past, perhaps while they were in the process of remaking their own bodies. So long ago that they simply forgot such perils – as an educated Roman, say, would have been surprised to be savaged by a wolf at the heart of a city in second-century Italy. But they learned, the hard way, and next time will come prepared.'

Cook leaned forward. 'But there's a question of intelligence, you see. Of signalling and communications. Every soldier knows that. All those Martians who came here are *dead*. How could they have got the message back, then, about gun-boats and germs, back across space to Mars?'

Walter said tensely, 'I explored this issue in my memoir. I observed the Martians in life as closely as anyone – yes, I still maintain it is so, Major Eden! And I still argue that what I saw with my own eyes, of their ability to carry through complex communal tasks *all without a word being spoken*, is evidence of some kind of telepathy. A direct link, mind to mind. Why, isn't it logical? The Martians have stripped away their bodies until they are nothing *but* mind. And if a Martian mind may speak to another across a pit in England—'

Cook rubbed his chin. 'Then why not between worlds?'

Philip, the voice of common sense, guffawed. 'Oh, this is all fanciful.'

'So would the idea of warriors from Mars have been once, cousin,' Walter said regretfully.

Eric objected now, 'But if that's so, why the sigils, the markings on the faces of the worlds?'

Cook said, 'Nothing wrong with that. It's just as a Navy tub will still fly the White Ensign, even though those boys talk to each other with the wireless telegraph these days, instead of with flags like ol' Nelson in his day.'

'Or perhaps,' Eric said with an uncertain grin, 'it's a marker. Telling the men from Jupiter to keep off.'

'Or vice versa,' Walter whispered. 'Which is the point I've been trying to make ...'

As this conversation unfolded, of the mind-reading of the Martians and other exotica, I glanced at Carolyne, Walter's former wife, who had not been addressed since the beginning of the telephone call. She sat rather slumped, her face an expressionless mask – not bitter, somehow accepting.

Cook said, 'Well, at least we'll be prepared this time, if we can get the guns up before they open their shells – and if we can predict where they'll fall.'

'But they may not land in any kind of neat sequence,' Walter said. 'Oh, there will be constraints of graphic geometry.'

It was a remark that baffled me at the time – he was referring to his sigils again – but it turned out to be key to the whole issue, as I will relate in its place.

'But we *know*,' Walter went on, 'that even last time the cylinders did not simply drop from the sky. We know they must have slowed at least, to avoid being smashed against the ground like so many falling meteorites. Most observers saw green flashes as they fell – I did myself. Tsiolkovsky and others speculate this is some kind of motor, a rocket perhaps, which slowed and directed a cylinder's trajectory.'

'That's a nasty thought,' Cook said softly. 'So we can't predict anything from the dates of the launch. They could land anywhere, any time they liked.'

'That's it,' Walter said. 'And though they fired off ten cylinders per night, there's nothing to stop them joining up in space, and coming down together. We can only wait and watch. There's a global network of spotter 'scopes watching the skies, international and highly secret. We might have a few hours' notice, at best.' He sighed. 'But to me their destination is obvious, and I've made my case as forcefully as I can to the authorities. *They must return to England.*'

The six of us absorbed that dread but oddly authoritative warning in a brief silence. I think I had expected it – I had seen the Martian on the Hill! Even so it was a shock.

And Eric said, 'Walter, I'm not challenging your judgement, but I still don't see it all. As I understand the way you've explained it, they came to England last time because London is mankind's largest city, as you could see from Mars. At opposition they have a fine view of the right side of our world, and our cities must glow like fireflies. And if you had assumed, as the Martians seem to, that we must be a unified civilisation, as *they* may be, then you come to the World Capital for a quick decapitation. Fine. But, look, they could land anywhere on the earth. Why England *again*?'

'Because of what I saw at Shepperton. Bert, I thought you saw it too. When Marvin's guns downed a fighting-machine, and the battle was done, *the others came back for it*, and carried it back to the pit at Horsell. You know, it's easy to speak of the Martians as evil and unethical and so forth. We should not judge their ethics on the way they behave towards us, for we are vermin – farm animals at best – to them. No, we must judge them on how they behave to each other. They talk, they co-operate – they come back further injured. And that's why they'll return to England. For their fallen.'

I thought with a shudder of the pickled specimen of a Martian, on display in the entrance hall of the Natural History Museum in Kensington.

At last Philip said, 'So this is why you called us.'

'I am aware I have called some of you, Julie for instance, back from places of relative safety.'

'Never mind that. You did the right thing, Walter,' I said as firmly as I could. I was already thinking ahead, planning. I would call on my sister-in-law, she with whom I had fled the Martians last time . . .

Eric glanced at Cook. 'I think I'll go back to my old regiment, at the Inkerman Barracks. What about you, Bert?'

Cook's eyes narrowed. 'Oh, if the Martians come again I know *just* where I want to be.'

Frank stiffened. 'And I'll get my wife and son to safety, and I thank you for that, Walter. But as to myself – if the Martians do come, I will have my duty as a doctor and a soldier, of the Fyrd at least.'

'Of course you will,' I said coldly.

Walter whispered, 'And – Carolyne?'

She looked up. 'Now you think of me?'

'Always. You know that I – before – that I thought you lost . . .'

'Oh, Walter—'

'Philip?'

Walter's cousin looked up. 'I'm here.'

'I must ask you to care for her, as you did before—'

'Oh, you fool, Walter.' Carolyne snatched the telephone hand-set, and yelled into it, 'You bloody fool!' And she slammed it down into its cradle.

Marina Ogilvy took her hands.

Philip shook his head. 'You're right, he is a fool. And so *indirect*. Always was. But I wonder if all of this – never mind the babble about Jupiter – was all, really, about saving you, Carolyne.'

I said cautiously, 'He does love you. He always did.'

'I know,' said Carolyne bleakly. 'I read about it in his book.'

10

To Stanmore and London

We all stayed over in Ottershaw that night.

Marina took one more call from Walter, in the small hours, and then she woke the rest of us. He had been able to confirm the likely date of the landings. It would be at midnight, Greenwich Mean Time, the morning of Monday March 29. The logic of firing and landing, the separation of those dates, was at least similar to the sequence of 1907. Still there had been no public announcement.

Monday, then. Our meeting at Ottershaw had been on the Thursday. We had little time. On the Friday morning, after a breakfast and hurried farewells, we scattered to our various destinations.

That morning, as a first stop, I intended to get to Stanmore, to my sister-in-law's home. Since the death in '07 of her husband, my brother George, on whom she had always depended, Alice, never strong, had become distracted, vague, reliant on friends and relatives on whom she would inflict silly, selfish talk that was ever laced with phrases like, 'If only dear George were here ...' For better or worse, part of my motivation for my flight to America had been to get away from her cloying dependency; Alice was only five years older than me, but it was like having to care for a somewhat dotty aunt. Yet I had returned a few times to help Alice through various genuine crises – illnesses and such. And, I admit, there had been times when she had supported me in turn.

Frank approved my plan readily enough, for he had seen Alice crumble in many a crisis, beginning with the greatest of all, when we had met during our flight from London during the First War. But when it came to caring for Alice it was a question of, 'Sooner you than me.'

49

Frank himself still lived at our old house in Highgate, north of London, the base of his practice and now home to his second wife and their son; he had bought me out. Now Frank intended to drive back to Highgate, and he offered me a lift to Stanmore – not much of a diversion for him. I agreed, though we haggled until I forced him to accept half the petrol cost. It was a playful fight but with an edge; that's as good an outcome as you can expect from the most amicable divorce, I suspect.

So we said our goodbyes to Ottershaw and our friends. Frank's cousin Philip was heading back to his own family, who had settled on the south coast after the destruction of their home at Leatherhead during the First War. Bert Cook and Eric Eden asked only for a lift to the station for a train to London, from where they would find a way to their respective regiments. Though neither of them was any longer serving, they were confident they would be taken back in the course of the new emergency. And London, Cook said, would soon be like a 'great clearing house' for troops and equipment, to be deployed wherever the Martians finally decided to come down.

As for Marina Ogilvy, she decided to stay put in Ottershaw, only a few miles from the Horsell Common pit where the first of the invaders of '07 had fallen to the earth, on the basis that 'lightning doesn't strike twice'. She was right about that, as I would confirm when I saw her again.

So we drove, Frank and I, heading north.

We decided to avoid the direct route which would have taken us through the militarised Corridor with all its complications, and made a wide detour. We went west as far as Bagshot, and crossed the river at Windsor. I remember our drive through towns and villages, the people going about their regular business: very ordinary scenes, even if there were rather more Union Jacks and military uniforms in evidence than in the old days. Windsor, with the royal castle at its core, bristled with security.

We took a hasty lunch at an inn outside Slough. We sat near a gaggle of young mothers, and working men who spoke of the coming FA Cup quarter-final between rival teams of marines and sappers, and a few solitary drinkers flicking through copies of the *Daily Mail*. The day was bright, bathed in the light of a clear and pleasant sky – it had been a late spring, and Frank said there hadn't been much warm sunshine in the year up to that point, so we were lucky.

'Lucky!'

Frank forced a smile. 'How eerie it is, to be one of just a hand-ful in England to know the truth.'

I put my hand on his. 'We made it through before. So it will be again.'

He nodded. Then, awkwardly, he withdrew his hand.

Before we left the inn Frank made another call to his home, having spoken to his wife from Ottershaw early that morning with a cryptic warning. This time his maidservant answered, saying that his wife and child had already left, driving in the family's second car. 'Making for our beach cottage in Cornwall,' Frank reported to me. 'Which we took in the first place as a bolt-hole in case – well, in case of a day like this. And near enough to Falmouth if we needed to get out of the country in a boat, like last time.'

I said firmly, 'You should go to them.'

He shook his head. 'I have my duty. I'll go home – having dropped you off – and shut the place up. The maid has a sister in Wales; I'll bundle her onto a train before the flight from the cap-ital gets underway – as we both know it will, don't we, as soon as Marvin makes his announcement? Then I'll head for Bloomsbury, tonight.' He meant, I knew, the apartment off Gower Street he had once rented as a medical student, and had later, nostalgically, bought outright to serve as a pied-á-terre when he needed to stay in the city – it was only an attic room. 'From there I can walk to the barracks at Albany Street.'

'Nothing I can say would persuade you to be more sensible, will it?'

He grinned. 'You're a journalist. When you've sorted out your sister-in-law, do you expect me to believe *you'll* find some hidey-hole while the greatest story of the century breaks around your head?'

'We're both idiots. Or neither.'

'I'll drink to that,' he said, raising his pint mug.

He dropped me at Stanmore without incident.

I had a key to the house. I found my sister-in-law was already away, according to the neighbours – 'taking the waters' in Buxton with a like-minded old lady – and so, I hoped, safely far from the action to come, if as everyone expected it would be concentrated in London. She was, however, planning to be home 'in only a few days'. Well, there wasn't much I could do for her now.

51

I stayed in the Stanmore house that Friday night. I dithered over my next step. I could make for London, the cockpit of the last War. Or I could flee – maybe I could even still get back to America.

And while I still hesitated, the next day, at about lunch time, the nation finally heard – by newspaper specials, by posters and proclamations, by loudhailer vans, and from Marvin himself, speaking into our homes though his Marconi-wireless Megaphones – the news that a new 'flight' of Martian projectiles had been observed, and was now confirmed as heading for central England. The country was immediately put on an emergency footing: a mobilisation order was declared for all regular forces, reserves and the Fyrd, and so on. The pronouncement was topped off by a bit of booming Elgar. Even for the privileged few like myself who had advance warning of the new invasion, this coldly stated confirmation came as a dreadful shock.

My own necessary course of action now seemed clear. I was a journalist; I must go to the action: to London. Hurriedly I packed my rucksack, and hoped I was not too late to be able to get a train.

Before I left Frank gave me a quick call. I remember his words very well, for although I later learned what became of him from his own account and a detailed diary he managed to keep, this was the last I was to hear of him for more than two years.

'My God,' he said. 'My brother was right!'

11

In London

Frank, so he would tell me later, stayed in his apartment on Gower Street much of that Saturday. His only visitor was the postman, who brought, as Frank had expected, his call-up papers and joining instructions for the next day, the Sunday.

Frank had prepared as best he could in the morning before the pronouncement, and so before the rush. He had done a little shopping for pocket-filling essentials any soldier would require, even a medical specialist such as himself: packets of biscuits and dried fruit and a water flask, spare socks, bandages and blister ointments for his feet, and suchlike. He had never smoked, believing the habit, against most advice, to be deleterious to the health, but he would later wish he had bought cigarettes even so, for they served as currency among soldiers. With the banks still open he withdrew a healthy amount of cash. And he bought a commonplace book, a thick block, and pens and ink and pencils. It was this pad, casually bought for a few pennies, that would become his chronicle for the next years, filled with the smallest handwriting he could manage.

When he went out again after the pronouncement he was surprised to find rationing already imposed.

In the late afternoon of the Saturday he took a walk – there wasn't a free taxi-cab or omnibus anywhere – across a city organising for war. At the great rail termini, at Charing Cross and Waterloo, barbed-wire barricades had already been set up, the entrances manned by soldiers and police. It seemed that only a handful of civilians were being allowed onto the trains today, and there were angry exchanges and tearful scenes. But behind the wire Frank saw soldiers massing, great crowds of them in the process of being moved from one part of the country to another.

And at Victoria, Frank glimpsed a train bearing huge guns being manoeuvred towards the station. As it always was, London was the hub of it all, a great switching-centre for the country, just as Albert Cook had predicted.

There were soldiers everywhere, in fact.

The parks of London had been given over as temporary military camps, vehicle depots, and grazing for their horses. In the streets he came across columns of troops marching in cheerful mood, being greeted by catcalls from the urchins and blown kisses from strolling girls. Once Frank saw a detachment of the Royal Naval Volunteer Reserve, marching off to their own oceanic battlefield. And on the steps of St Paul's, under a dome still bearing a Heat-Ray scar, a senior officer, he thought a colonel, harangued the crowd, picking out men in civilian clothes: 'Will *you* join up? Will *you*?'

Frank sensed no real fear, no apprehension, not that Saturday. Rather there was a sense of excitement, if anything. In a way, he says, it was as if everybody had been waiting for this moment since '07. Frank thought all this could be regarded as a triumph by Marvin and his government. However cynically motivated – for the years of militaristic harangues from the government had surely had much to do with control of the populace – and however misguided and brief this sense of exhilaration would prove to be, better to be optimistic at such a moment; better to be purposeful, rather than afraid.

And Frank would write in his diary, one of the first entries, of how he had marvelled that the post offices were open – on a Saturday! 'It *must* be a national emergency,' he noted.

Towards evening he laid out his uniform. He didn't brag about it – even I didn't know much about it – but Frank the doctor, though a mere Fyrd volunteer, held an honorary rank of Captain in the Royal Army Medical Corps. He would tell me he was proud of wearing the polished badge, the Rod of Asclepius, on his dark blue beret.

He says he slept well. This was despite the din outside: regardless of official restrictions, some informal, unplanned evacuations had begun, and there was too the noise of a few wild celebrations across the city on this last night of peace.

I have no reason to doubt him, though I slept badly, in the sylvan calm of Stanmore.

12

The Mobilisation

Frank was woken at six by a clamour of church bells, as were we all across the country that Sunday morning. In London there followed whistles and shouts, and the squawks of loudhailers from trawling vans.

Frank had laid out his breakfast the night before, expecting an early start. He did not turn on his own Megaphone, though he suspected he was breaking some minor ordinance by not doing so. He washed, shaved, donned his uniform and boots and great-coat and blue beret, shoved his toilet kit into his backpack – he holstered his service revolver – and he turned off the gas and electric, pocketed his papers, and left his flat.

Outside, Gower Street was transformed.

Police and military seemed to be everywhere. New posters on walls and lampposts and placards on patrolling vans declared the imposition of emergency regulations: martial law, a curfew, rationing, various restrictions on movement. And a boy was selling papers just outside Frank's building, yet another *Daily Mail* special – on a Sunday – with an image of Churchill, Marvin's minister of war, rolling up his sleeves:

THEY DARE TO COME AGAIN
WE HAVE PREPARED
WE HAVE A PLAN
THEY SHALL NOT PREVAIL
LET'S GET ON WITH IT!

Frank did not trouble to buy a copy. Nor did he pay much attention to the exhortations of a government that was probably already in flight; Churchill might be an honourable exception, as he had been in the First War.

Though there were pedestrians everywhere, there were very few civilian vehicles on the roads. The reason became obvious when Frank reached his own car, which had a military requisition notice pasted to its windscreen, along with a reclaim docket. Frank just laughed and pocketed the reclaim slip. He would manage to keep this docket safe, in fact, throughout the Second War, but he never saw his car again, nor received a penny in compensation.

However he had plenty of time, and the walk to Albany Street, his muster station, was short. It was quite a contrast to the day of the great panic in which we had both been caught up in the last War, when the Martians had advanced on the capital. He had the general impression that, like himself, people seemed to know where to go, what to do – there was an air of purpose, not the collapse of order. Not yet.

In another echo of his previous experience he walked across to Great Ormond Street, meaning to spend a few minutes in the chapel of the Foundling Hospital there – it was after all a Sunday. In the grounds the Boys' Band played martial tunes. Frank knew that many of the boys who passed through this place went on to the armed forces, swapping one institutional life for another, and he wondered how many old boys might be preparing to face the Martians that morning. Inside the grand two-storey chapel Frank found a service in progress; a notice claimed there would be services all day.

From there, with no more prevarication, Frank marched direct to Albany Street.

In this broad residential street of grand terraces, now hastily boarded up, he found himself part of a growing throng. He said it was like joining a crowd for a football match, save that all were in uniform, or else were sweethearts or mothers or children clinging to those in uniform. They were regulars mostly, but some were reserve or Fyrd, as Frank was. Some were kilted – they were men of the Argylls and the London Scottish – and there was a detachment of what he learned were Guards, even a troop of marines in their blue war-kit.

But there was organisation. Military policemen, armed with clipboards and pencils, briskly read each newcomer's call-up notice and directed him to his station – or her, for there were many women in uniform throughout the crowd. A bleak moral victory for the suffragettes!

Thus, gradually, Frank was filtered to a crowd of medical types gathering at the junction of Albany Street and Albert Road, male officers wearing blue caps like his own, and women of the Imperial Military Nursing Service in their nurses' uniforms and capes. They joined a column forming up inside Regent's Park itself; they would be marched across the Park to Baker Street, for transport to 'your position at the anticipated front', as an MP put it. From this Frank deduced that by now the cylinders' fall must have been predicted quite precisely.

One young woman in uniform and topcoat bravely approached Frank. 'You must be Captain Jenkins?'

Frank stood a bit straighter. 'Only a Fyrd volunteer – feel something of a fraud – but, yes, that's me.'

'My name's Verity Bliss. They put me in charge of this lot.' She indicated a group of shy-looking women behind her. Verity looked mid-twenties, with a sturdy, sensible face, and short-cut brown hair. 'And that chap over there,' she pointed to an MP, 'tells me that you're in command of us, at least until we get off the train.' She hesitated. 'Do you know – the train to where, sir?'

He grinned. 'I didn't even know we were taking the train. VADs, are you?' The VADs, for Voluntary Aid Detachment, were unpaid nursing volunteers recruited through the War Office and the Red Cross.

'That's it, sir. We were munitionettes, working at Woolwich. We joined up together.'

'Good for you. But, look – the "sir" doesn't fit comfortably. How about it's "Frank" and "Verity" until we're off the train, eh?'

She grinned back, but said, 'Not in front of the MPs, sir.'

Their column, gathered inside the park rail, was almost lined up now. A senior officer – a Brigadier-General perhaps, Frank was too far away to see his rank, but he looked old enough to have served in the Crimea, let alone the First Martian War – climbed on a box and called out in a ringing voice, 'Well, it's your time, men – and women. I know you're mostly reserve and Fyrd, but you've units of the Guard with you, and you are honoured to fight alongside such men. Now give me a British cheer, and have a good go!'

Well, they all cheered, of course.

And then Frank and Verity, and the other doctors and the nurses and the VADs, all marched with the rest across the park.

*

Now it was Frank's turn to have flags waved at him by school-boys, and kisses blown by a few girls. Frank was thirty-eight. What he had seen of war personally had horrified him, and like most educated British folk he had a healthy cynicism about Marvin and his warmongering, and the militarisation of society. But he had a feeling he would remember this as one of the proudest moments of his life.

At Baker Street station they joined in an elaborate game of queuing up before entrances and turnstiles meant for a comparative trickle of commuting clerks. The station itself was a box of noise – the ringing and clanging of shunting engines, the shriek of whistles, thousands of excited voices echoing like a gull colony – but above it all there was a sense of organisation. In some ways, Frank would say to me, he had always thought the efficiency and order of the railways, including the underground, was one of the finest expressions of our civilisation. During the first Martian attack the railways had kept functioning even after the government itself had effectively collapsed, and here they were now, an essential part of the defence of the nation.

It was mid-afternoon, and Frank was already tired from all the standing around, when at last they were bundled onto a Metropolitan Line commuter special that was standing room only before it finally pulled away.

In Frank's compartment a tommy accompanied bawdy songs with a mouth organ, and at times he heard the skirl of bagpipes coming from a carriage further up the train. The mood remained cheerful enough, though the MPs assigned to each compartment kept a watchful eye.

Soon they were beyond Hampstead and out in the country, passing through Wembley and Harrow. They did not stop at intermediate stations, but the train did slow, and local people came out to clap and wave flags, passing up food and apples and even postcards. Frank saw troopers leaning out of the windows, trying to grab bottles of beer. And, once out of the city, Frank saw columns of troops marching, and howitzers and field guns drawn by motor and by horses. He wondered if the farmers and publicans were having their horses requisitioned: war in those days demanded a great number of horses.

The general flow was away from London, towards the north-west, towards Middlesex and Buckinghamshire, a pattern that did not go unnoticed by the more experienced soldiers on the train, who spoke in a variety of accents, mostly from the rich linguistic pot of London:

'I reck'n someone knows where they're coming down this time.'

'Yeah, some ast – ast – *rologer*.'

'Last time they came dahn in Surrey, din't they? Tryin' sumfin diff'rent this time, looks like,' said an older, scarred man.

'So what? Big guns would've knocked 'em flat las' time, and will this time if'n we get the chance.'

'Won't be like las' time. Coming down somewhere else, in't they? If that's diff'rent, the rest will be. Stands to reason they'll try something new. They lost, din't they? They'll learn.'

'Huh. *We* don't always learn.'

Laughter at that, and ribald comments about the failings of various commanding officers.

But the scarred man did not laugh. 'If'n they're smart, they'll learn. Look at the Germans. They flattened the French in 1870, and they hit 'em even harder in '14, and they won *again*.'

Nobody had a reply to that.

13

Approaching Uxbridge

The train stopped at Ickenham, and they were disembarked. This, Frank knew, was short of the terminus of the line, at Uxbridge.

Frank and Verity, herding their little flock of MOs, nurses and VADs, saw little of the village of Ickenham before they were marched out into the country. They heard mention of units of troops from all over Britain: the 4th Battalion, 5th Fusiliers; the 2nd Battalion, King's Liverpool Regiment; the 1st King's Own Shropshire Light Infantry. There were divisional troops too, specialists with their equipment: artillery batteries, Royal Engineers. There was wireless kit and cables for the field telegraphs, such mundane gear as a field bakery, and more exotic items such as sections of pontoon bridges and the envelopes of spotting balloons, hauled off along the roads by horses or trucks – all generally heading further to the south-west, towards the town.

Verity touched Frank's arm and pointed at troops on motorcycles heading up the roads and across country, off to the west. 'Scouts,' she said.

'Heading where they expect the battle to be joined.'

'I imagine so.' She shivered, and Frank imagined she was thinking that those forward units might be among the first casualties of any action – though somehow that prospect still seemed unreal.

Before very long the marching column broke up, and Frank's group was led to a series of field hospitals, tents erected in the fields. The MP who brought them there briskly summarised orders he read from a sheet. 'Get yourselves set up. You've got a water supply and oil heaters, or should do. Tents over here, beds over *there*, supplies and whatnot over *there*. Bandages and a blood store, and knock-out drops and surgeons' saws...'

Not all the medical staff were terribly experienced, Frank saw, and some of them paled as these words were delivered with gruesome relish. 'That's enough, Corporal, we get the idea.'

'Then get to it.' At the last minute the MP remembered to salute his senior officer, and made to turn away.

'Hold on,' Frank said. 'What about the rest of it?'

'What rest of it?'

'We've been on our feet all day.'

'And *I've* been walking around shouting at people all day, sir, and you don't hear me complaining.'

'We've only eaten once—'

'Field kitchens over there.' He pointed. 'You can work out your own rota for that. Lavatories thataway.'

Frank looked around again; he had the sinking feeling he was missing something obvious, and was on the point of making a fool of himself. 'Yes, but – where do we sleep, Corporal?'

The MP stared at him, and grinned. 'No sleep for any of us tonight, Captain. Balloon goes up at midnight. Or rather, something big and fat and heavy from Mars comes *down* at midnight. Then we've got the nineteen-hour window, and when *that's* done – why, *then* I reckon we'll all be due a good kip.'

Midnight, Frank thought. So they were coming at midnight, just like before – just as Walter had noted. Scanning the young, apprehensive faces that surrounded him – many of them could only have been children last time – he kept his own sudden nervousness to himself. *Nineteen-hour window*, though: what could that mean?

It was late afternoon and the light was already fading. Seeing that he would get no more from the MP, he briskly set Verity, the junior MOs and the rest to organising the field hospitals and their equipment – hoping very much that he gave the impression that he knew what he was talking about – and then went stomping off to find 'somebody in charge', as he would later note in his journal.

He came upon a kind of command post: a lot of senior officers, and map tables and field telephones and wireless units and telegraphs, and a coffee urn. It took some moments before a young officer named Fairfield, a lieutenant-colonel, took pity on him. 'Sorry about this, Doctor – Captain. The trouble is we are running around ourselves to get organised, and you MO types don't fit easily into the command structure.' He was perhaps in his late twenties, a decade or so younger than Frank, with a clipped public school accent and an air of wry amusement. 'Coffee?'

'No, thank you, sir.'

'I know what you're thinking.'

'You do?'

'Good job it's not raining, as we're all stuck out in the field, what? Although it will be raining Martians soon enough.'

'Where, sir? *Where* is the cylinder coming down? I know the telescopic spotters have been tracking them.'

Fairfield raised an eyebrow. 'Not so much "cylinder" as "cylinders", Doctor. But the one that interests us seems to be heading slap bang for the middle of Uxbridge, which is bad luck for that unlovely town. Population's already been evacuated, by the way, so you don't need to worry about them.' He glanced up. 'Closer to the hour we'll have planes up there, even a Zeppelin I'm told, courtesy of the Kaiser. They *might* give us a better fix.' He eyed Frank. 'To be honest I'm not sure how well you've been briefed.'

'Hardly at all. An MP—'

'Well, that's typical. What you do need to know is that a regular arrangement for treating the wounded has already been established. You will have aid posts at the front itself – that is, the site where we have our best guess about where the cylinder will come down – and behind that, within stretcher-bearer distance, you have casualty clearing stations, and behind *that* it's ambulances back to the field hospitals, which is where you come in. You haven't drawn the short straw, you see, Doctor – the forward staff, the MOs and the rest, are already at the front-line stations.'

Frank nodded. 'Thank you. That's clear enough. The MP said a couple of other things. *Nineteen hours*—'

'He has been talkative, hasn't he? I'm told that after the first cylinder fell last time, near Woking—'

'At Horsell Common.'

'It took that long, you see, for the Martians to unscrew the bally thing, and for the Heat-Ray gun and other nasties to start poking out, and for those fighting-machines to climb out and stretch their legs and get to work. So *this* time we should have that window of opportunity, to shell the thing while they're helpless.'

Frank felt suspicious of his confident tone. '*If* all goes as it did last time—'

'Of course I would hope we will finish the thing off in two hours, not nearly twenty. Is there anything else, Doctor?'

'You said "cylinders". There was only one at a time before.'

'Ah. Well, that is something new. The astronomers have been definite about this, if a little late in the day. Can't blame them for that, I suppose.' He faced Frank. 'There are more than fifty of 'em coming in, all across this part of the country.'

Fifty. Frank remembered his brother's talk of the array of cannons spread across Mars, firing night after night, and the fleets of cylinders forming up in space. And now that deadly barrage had crossed interplanetary space and was about to fall *here*. Fifty together! And from what Walter had said there would be another fifty following after...

The lieutenant-colonel clapped his shoulder. 'Anyhow, *we* only have one to worry about.' He glanced at his watch. 'Now look, if there's nothing else urgent...'

'Thank you, sir.'

'Carry on, Captain Jenkins.'

Once the sun had gone down, it felt like a long wait until midnight.

Frank's staff had got the field hospital organised as well as it could be, and he was relieved there had been no significant balls-up with the supplies. But there was only so often he could check and recheck it all.

At about seven, he gratefully accepted Verity's idea of mounting a few exercises, with volunteers playing the roles of incoming wounded. The VADs especially went at this with a will, if inexpertly. Frank knew that there could be gruesome accidents at munitions plants, but he had the impression that most of the VADs had little experience beyond their training.

At nine he encouraged those who felt like it to use the hospital beds to nap. Few could sleep, though several lay down.

At ten he ordered his people to eat, have coffee or water. He caught one of the junior doctors with a hip flask, which he confiscated and locked away in a chest, promising to hand it back after the 'battle', as they were calling it – unless some wounded had a greater need of the rather good brandy it contained.

At eleven he ordered his staff to use the latrines, in a rota. He murmured to Verity, 'But of course I'm expecting rather a few loose bladders before the night is out, come what may.'

As midnight approached, the two of them were tucked in behind a barricade of sandbags, looking towards the lights of an empty Uxbridge. They both had medical bags at their sides, and they wore regulation steel helmets. The sky was clear that Sunday night, with only a light mist obscuring the stars.

They spoke little, as they waited. Verity seemed too nervous to say much of herself. He gathered she was single, and had only just moved out of her parents' home into an apartment near Woolwich with some of the other workers when the call-up came. He tried to distract her with talk of himself. Naturally she had heard of Walter.

'I was only twelve last time,' she said. 'We had been visiting family in the Midlands when the news started coming out of London. My father got us on a boat to Ireland, out of Liverpool. I missed the whole show. But your brother's book – it made it so real. I met him once. There was an illustrated edition. He came to Foyles on the Charing Cross Road to give a talk. I remember he complained about the drawings, though. I got him to sign a copy for me.'

'Of course you did,' Frank said, gritting his teeth.

'Captain, *you* saw one fall, didn't you? A cylinder. Last time.'

'Yes. The sixth, that came down at Wimbledon. That was at midnight too.' He glanced at his watch; five minutes to twelve.

'What did it look like?'

'The cylinder? Like a falling star, sliding across the sky. Green flashes.'

'Green? Then that's what we must look out for, I suppose.' She raised small binoculars and scanned the sky.

For a time neither of them spoke. Frank imagined a great circle drawn around Uxbridge, the quiet, deserted town at the centre, with its electric street lights pointlessly glowing, and a ring of troops like themselves with their guns and field hospitals and binoculars, all waiting, waiting. From somewhere a Cockney voice floated, singing to a carol tune: *Why are we waiting? Why-y are we waiting?* Chuckles of laughter, a soft command to be still.

'Captain, it's gone midnight. My watch has a luminous dial . . . Midnight plus ten seconds. Fifteen now. I don't see any green flashes—'

There was a crack, a detonation high in the air above them. Then a searing light that smashed down from the sky, coming from directly above them. White light – not green at all. Plunging at the dark earth.

'*Down!*' Following sheer instinct, Frank lay flat, and pressed the back of Verity's neck to force down her head.

Then the shock hit them.

14

The Landing of the First Wave

I learned later that the astronomical spotters had got some of it right – at least the number of projectiles, and the rough location of their fall. None had anticipated the manner of that fall.

A total of fifty-two cylinders landed on central England that night. Tsiolkovsky and co-workers later calculated, given comparisons with the 1907 assault, that they must have launched in five flotillas, each of ten or so shots: launched on February 18, and then on the 20th, 22nd, 24th and 26th.

(The cylinders to fall the next night, at that moment still en route to the earth, had been fired off on the interleaving nights, from the 19th through to the 27th...)

As Tsiolkovsky had suggested, the Martians used engines during their interplanetary flight to tweak their trajectories, the lead volleys slowing to allow latecomers to catch up, so that in the end all the cylinders of the first wave fell simultaneously – at least within the limits of accuracy of the timepieces of the military observers who saw them fall – at midnight of Monday, March 29. And the last cylinder to be fired on February 26, unlike its brothers having none to wait for, landed on the earth four weeks and four days after its launch – the precise same timing as with the cylinders launched in '07.

(And meanwhile, as we would soon learn, the second-wave cylinders were still co-ordinating their own fall, out in space...)

That first fifty-two fell together in a great ring of twenty miles diameter, roughly centred on the town of Amersham in Buckinghamshire. The circle of impacts reached out beyond High Wycombe to the south west, Wendover to the north-west, Hemel Hempstead to the north-east – and it brushed quite precisely over Uxbridge to the south-east, where Frank was stationed. The cylinders came down in a chain, each a little more than a mile from its neighbours on either side. There were no green flashes this time, no attempts to slow the craft – if true craft they were, rather than inert missiles fitted with steering engines.

The purpose of that first wave was evidently *not* to deliver Martians and their equipment intact to the earth, as had been the case with the Horsell cylinder, and its siblings of the First War. The sole objective was destruction.

In their analysis of the 1907 event, Denning and others with expertise in the kinematics of meteorites had pointed out that by landing their cylinders relatively softly, the Martians had actually thrown away a kind of advantage of position – the advantage of the sky over the earth. Indeed, Walter's account of his experience of close proximity to a cylinder-fall on houses in Sheen during the First War gives a vivid impression of the damage done even by these relatively gentle landings. Barringer, meanwhile, has studied the Canyon Diablo crater in Arizona, and has suggested that it may have been formed, not by volcanic action or by such events as a steam explosion, as others have suggested, but by the uncontrolled fall from space of an iron-rich meteorite a few tens of yards across – that is, of a similar size to a Martian cylinder. A hole in the earth some half-mile across and two hundred yards deep: there you have a measure of the harm such a fall can inflict. (Incidentally, one speculative writer – the 'Year Million Man' essayist whom Walter met in Berlin – has irresponsibly suggested that the Barringer crater *was* created by such a cylinder, an early Martian visitor of the remote past.)

This was the simple but cruder tactic adopted by the Martians to begin their second assault on the earth: to use the brute kinetic energy of these dummy projectiles to smash any resistance before it had a chance to escape, let alone respond. Thus the event that befell England that March night.

Consider the impact of a single cylinder. In its last seconds of existence the Uxbridge cylinder must have angled in from the west, across the Atlantic Ocean. It punched its way through the earth's atmosphere in a fraction of a second, blasting away the air around it, leaving a tunnel of vacuum where it had passed. And when it hit the ground, it delivered all its energy of motion in an instant of heat. The cylinder itself must have been utterly des-troyed, says Denning. A narrow cone of incandescent rock mist fired back along the cylinder's incoming trajectory, back through the tunnel in the air dug out in those last moments – some more distant observers thought they had seen a vast searchlight beam. Around this central glowing shaft, a much broader spray of pulverised and shattered rock, amounting to hundreds of times the cylinder's own mass, was blown out of the widening crater. Then the shock waves came, a battering wind, a searing heat. Even the ground flexed and groaned, as a crater a mile wide was dug into the flesh of the earth.

In that same moment the event was repeated in that grand ring, all around the target circle: seen from the air (as photographs taken the next day proved) it was a circle of glowing pits, every one still more impressive than the Arizona crater, and all neatly punched into the English ground.

And any military units which had been within a mile of the infall were lost.

Many had believed that England would not be subject to a second Martian attack, but enough had believed it possible, and enough more had feared it, that the authorities had been compelled to prepare. The result had been a reconfiguring of our military and economy, of our international relationships, and a coarsening of the fabric of our society. All this had delivered a much more effective home army, and when the attack had finally come the mobilisation, after years of planning and preparation, had been fast and effective.

But as a result of that promptness of mobilisation a little less than half the new British Army, as measured in numbers of regular troops and front-line materiel, was destroyed in the first minutes of the assault – most of the lost troops leaving no trace. And even those on the periphery of the landfalls, like Frank, endured great trials.

The violence was astonishing, overwhelming. Frank lay flat on his belly, face pressed into the earth, hands over his head. It felt as if the world itself were coming apart, the very bedrock shuddering, his own body hurled and wrenched. Waves of heat washed over the trench above him. And then came a kind of hail – fragments of hot rock, he thought, that stung where they hit him.

The contrast with a moment before was astounding – the orderly processes that had led him to this point smashed and shattered in a moment – as if he had suddenly been born into some new, primordial realm, a helpless mote.

Only when the ground had stopped shaking, the waves of heat

and noise had roared past, and the thin hail of hot rock fragments had ceased to fall, did he dare to look up, over the parapet. But by the light of his torch there was only billowing dust to be seen, as if the world had been erased.

Verity's face was pale in the gloom, blank and bewildered. When she spoke it sounded as if she had had the breath knocked out of her. 'What was *that*? The Heat-Ray?'

'Not that . . . I don't know.' Frank stood up. 'A terrible disaster.' He glanced around. The night had become darker; the lights of Uxbridge were extinguished. By the glow of a few surviving lanterns he saw the camp was in disarray, tents blown over, even a great field gun toppled on its side. And the field hospitals were blown down, the beds and other supplies scattered. 'This will take some clearing up.' His very words seemed foolish as he spoke. How could any human agency cope with this?

There was the sound of a motor-cycle revving. Verity pointed. 'Look.'

A scout, goggles and gas-mask fixed, headlight bright, rode a motor-cycle into the billowing smoke: already heading into the zone of destruction. Soon more prepared to follow, their lights disappearing into a curtain of dark, beyond which, Frank saw, a reddish glow was slowly gathering, where Uxbridge had been.

'That's where we need to be,' Frank said. 'Where the wounded are – if any survive at all. Come on. Pick up your bag.'

'But the hospitals—'

'Plenty of muscle here to put all that back together. What we must do first is to find our patients.'

He led the way beyond the parapet, torch in hand. They both donned their gas-masks, meant for protection against the Black Smoke, but now the goggles and filters served to protect eyes and lungs from the dust of the shattered landscape. Glancing behind him, Frank saw that more of the MOs and VADs were following their lead, carrying torches and lanterns. Sparks in the dark.

The ground they crossed was broken, as if a great wave had passed through it. And, Frank saw as he moved forward, it was littered with wrecked guns and vehicles, and with human remains. A limb here, an open hand there, a detached skull: some of the more complete bodies lay draped over the parapets of trenches. *Disarticulated*: a clinical word that floated to the top of Frank's stunned mind. Not even burned, most of them, just torn apart. His staff peeled away to check these ghastly relics for signs of life.

Verity stood at Frank's side, her gloved hand over her mouth. 'Perhaps this all seems very small, if you're looking at it from Mars.'

They came upon a couple of soldiers walking out of the dust, one dragging the other, who appeared to have a broken leg and was badly burned on the face. Frank and Verity ran to the men, and helped lower the wounded fellow gently to the ground.

'It's nothing,' the man said, his speech distorted by the damage to his face. 'A cushy. Nothing...'

'Don't talk,' Verity said. She briskly examined the wounded man. 'He's bleeding out. He needs a tourniquet on this leg. Cold water for the burns on his face. Get the leg set and splinted...' She looked at Frank, her uncertainty evident despite the masked face. 'If you agree, Doctor.'

'Of course. Go ahead.'

As she worked, Frank stood and looked around once more. The dust was clearing a little now. Still a tremendous heat came from the direction of the cylinder's fall, and that red glow was still brightening – whatever was left of Uxbridge must be burning vigorously, he thought, and the fields and the forests around the town.

From the camp, others were coming out, medical staff but also common soldiers, NCOs, even the officers, meeting the handful of men and women who came limping out of the disaster. One older man, an experienced MO, bent over and vomited helplessly. When he straightened up, wiping his mouth, he said, 'What can we do here? It's a butcher's yard. What can we do? What can we do?'

'Medicine,' Frank said, as determinedly as he could. 'Come, follow me. Fan out.' He pointed. 'I saw movement, there...'

So they found their patients, among the dead. Most of the beds of the field hospital remained empty. But throughout the night Frank and his team went back into the broken landscape, over and over. All this was lit sporadically by torchlight and lanterns: human forms coming together, dimly glimpsed in air laden with soot and smoke.

15

Monday in London

Monday morning has never been my favourite time of the week. Especially if one is tied to the routine of an office and the commute, when a lazy Sunday evening at the end of which one somehow felt as if one is *oneself* again is revealed to have been a deception, and with a hurried breakfast heavy in the stomach, there's nothing for it but to swarm ant-like to the great hives of the office districts. But there can scarcely have been a more dreadful Monday morning to wake to than that of March 29 – in London not since the days of the First Martian War itself, perhaps, or in Paris since 1914 when the Germans came to town. And many of us were already awake, I suspect; it had been a sleepless night for me ever since midnight, and the Martians' first landfall.

I had reached central London from Stanmore, not without difficulty. I stayed in a hotel on the Strand. I had taken the room at an exorbitant cost – everything had been heroically marked up in those final days and hours – but, unexpectedly free of the burden of my sister-in-law and being a journalist, I had determined to be in the thick of things: the story of London in the Second War, whether the Martians got that far or not, would be a tale for the ages. Bluntly put, I expected a retrospective commission from the *Saturday Evening Post* to boost my savings.

Before Sunday was over the telescopic spotters had done their work, and the government and the military authorities had already alerted the people through the papers and the Megaphones and the loudspeaker vans that the Martians were on the way, that this time they were heading for Middlesex and Bucks, well away from the city – that the Army was on the move and ready to deal with them. They were coming back! It was terrifying; it was *thrilling* – thrilling if we really were ready for them, at least, though none of us mere civilians knew how ready we actually were.

So there I was at midnight, fully dressed, waiting for the show. What did I expect, that night? Perhaps to see a falling star or two, as when, under a clear sky on a short June night, Frank had watched the sixth cylinder of the '07 wave fall towards Wimbledon, while my sister-in-law and I dozed – a green flash, falling silent beyond the hills – and then there would be the clatter of distant artillery as our boys got their revenge for the last time.

Not a bit of it. As Churchill would put it later, the dastardly Martians returned to the pitch, but refused to play the game by the rules.

Peering from my sixth-floor window towards the north-west, for I had made sure I got a room with a view on that side, I saw what appeared to be a sudden storm: tremendous flashes of white light like bolts of lightning that reached down to the ground from high in the air, miles high it seemed to me, and not a bit of green about them, all in a kind of eerie silence.

Then, a full minute later, the sound broke, like tremendous claps of thunder falling on the city; I heard the smashing of windows. There was a deep shuddering of the very fabric of the hotel too, and I sensed tremendous energies pulsing through the earth beneath us as through the air. (I was some thirteen miles from the nearest landfall of the Martians' dummy projectiles, as I learned later.) It was over in a moment, though the horizon slowly turned red from distant fires.

In the returning silence, the hotel's fire alarm bell was rung with vigour. I heard footsteps running in the corridors, voices calling for the building to be evacuated – we were to take the stairs, not the elevators. I suspected this was unnecessary, but I was ready to go. I grabbed my rucksack, packed up as ever, and left my room, pocketing the key, to join the swarms for the stairs.

Out on the street there was a surprisingly large amount of traffic, mostly motor-cars but a few horse-drawn chaises, most of it already heading east towards Aldwych, away from the 'storm', and disregarding the traffic lanes despite the efforts of a couple of special constables to impose discipline. People already fleeing, then. I was one of a flood of guests spilling onto the pavement from the hotel, most of them in night-gear and overcoats, for the March night was chill. But people looked bewildered and a little shame-faced, for that tremendous light show, the terrifying noise,

71

the shaking of the ground had already ceased. Aside from that suspicious redness to the sky off to the west, there was nothing to be seen. People speculated aloud about what had happened – had the Martians been shot down even before they landed? There were wild rumours of super-guns carried aboard German Zeppelins, and suchlike.

But one old fellow with a Kitchener moustache held forth: 'I tell you what we *don't* hear, and that's artillery fire. I was in Rye during the Battle of Paris in '14, and even from that distance we could hear the bark of the Germans' howitzers as they advanced to the centre. Middlesex is a lot closer than *that*. Now, whatever that herculean storm was, we don't hear our boys firing in response, do we? So what's going on? Every one of our guns spiked already, eh?'

It is telling of the temper of the cowed Londoners of the day that his wife plucked his sleeve to hush him, and others looked away uneasily, or glanced for special constables and the like who might put a stop to his demoralising words.

Well, with the show apparently over – and the hotel not shaking to pieces or bursting into flames – we guests were encouraged to return inside. A fair fraction seemed over-excited and unwilling to retire to their rooms. In an imaginative move the manager opened up the restaurants and bars; there were drinks to be had, and soon a cold buffet was laid on, with coffee and tea. I heard grumblings from the staff, roused from their own beds: 'Wish them blessed Mar-shins would come in the middle o' my shift and not at the end of it.'

I stayed a while, drinking strong coffee and trying to find out any news. Every room private or public had Marvin Megaphones, of course, but they brought nothing but bland assurances that the enemy had landed just where the astronomers had predicted and that our forces were vigorously engaging them – no specifics, amid lashings of uplifting patriotic music. I tried making a few calls to contacts in Middlesex, but all the lines that way seemed to be down. I even called the *Observer*, for that paper has run a few of my cultural pieces from New York, but the duty editor said the telegraph lines were down too, and there was no news even by wireless.

Eventually I filled my pockets with sandwiches, attracting odd looks from the hotel staff, and retreated to my room. I thought I should stay until the dawn, even try to sleep. I lay in my bed, clothed save for topcoat and shoes; at least I got warm. I heard nothing more from the war front, if such it was – no more thunderous detonations, and no clatter of gunfire.

It all seemed alarming and mysterious and not at all what we had expected. It was as if not a Martian but some tremendous unpredictable god had stamped on the earth.

The sky was lightening, as seen through my open window, when I was woken by the smell of smoke.

That was the end of the night for me. I washed hastily, grabbed my coat and bag – slurped a last mouthful of cold coffee from the cup I had brought with me from the restaurant – and hurried out of my room and once more to the stairs.

In the street, there was a faint light to the east. But the dawn was matched by a lingering red glow in the darker sky to the west. The wind, though gentle, blew from that direction, and that was the breeze that brought the stink of smoke to my nostrils. I imagined the whole of Middlesex was ablaze, and as it turned out I wasn't far wrong.

The street had been transformed since I had come out at midnight. There were roadblocks and temporary gates all along the Strand now, manned by special constables, most of them identifiable only by the arm-bands and tin hats they wore over their civilian clothes. No vehicles moved, and those few parked in the street had been slapped with military requisition notices. Some new set of regulations had been hurriedly brought into play, evidently, a new phase of a well-rehearsed plan.

Yet amid all the restrictions people were up and about. Some had the look of city workers to me, early birds perhaps even now expecting a normal day in the office, while the suburbs burned. But others were evidently on the move, more than last night; they brought children and old folk with them, some in prams or walkers or in bath chairs, and they were laden with goods, with suitcases and packs on their backs. They were all heading east, away from the western glow. These were sights that brought back to my mind once more the ghastly summer days of '07.

But this was different, it seemed, so far. The government had not yet given up. The special constables and fire wardens and others were standing their ground, and even exhorted people to go back to their homes, to do their duty. Individuals could be singled out. 'You, man – that's the arm-band of a fire-watcher. St Martin's, that's where you should be, with your whistle and your bucket of sand, not running like a rabbit.'

73

A few argued back, in that dawn – the absconding fire-watcher, for one. 'Come off the high horse, Ted, you're a doorman at the Rialto, not Winston bloody Churchill. The guv'm'nt have took my motor-car, they've took my dogcart, and if it had occurred to 'em they'd have took my mother-in-law's wheelchair too – no, no, Ma, don't try to get up, you keep it – but they can't yet *reck-wee-zish-un* my two poor feet, and if you've got any sense left you'll join me.'

Even I was picked on for not carrying my gas-mask – in fact I had it but not on show; it was in my rucksack. 'You'll regret not having it to hand when the Black Smoke comes, missus.'

If this was going on in the West End, I imagined the same scene played out across the city and the residential suburbs: the authorities struggling to keep the city functioning with their rules and regulations and an appeal to duty, and no traffic moving on the streets save for military and other official vehicles. And yet as seen from the air, a trickle of dark, struggling dots must already have been filtering through the streets and alleys, laden, on foot, yet making their clumsy way, the people of London swarming and converging and massing, I guessed, on the great trunk roads leading south and east – opposite to the direction from which the Martians, this time, would surely come.

And, even in the Strand, even at this very early hour, in amongst the gathering crowd of evacuating residents I saw folk who had evidently come much further, and were travelling *into* London. Some walked only with difficulty; they had scorched clothes, blackened faces. These were families, with old folk and little ones, all on foot – and all much less heavily burdened than the Londoners who were only now beginning their journeys. There was a first-aid post in the hotel, and VADs came fluttering out to offer assistance to the worse-off of these poor wretches; waiters and bell-boys came out too with cups of water. The journalist in me longed to talk to these refugees, to learn a story or two from individuals, but the special constables, ever vigilant over morale, kept us apart.

Restless, impatient, I gave up on the hotel and struck out myself along the Strand, pressing west against the flow and heading for Trafalgar Square.

Charing Cross Station was closed entirely now, barricaded with barbed wire; the rail lines, like the roads, had been requisitioned for official use. It was still early but a few stores were open; I saw fist-fights in a grocery. And queues formed outside a bank branch with its door barred and firmly closed. I would learn that the Bank of England had already suspended specie payments, and the other banks had no choice but to close. That was the first inkling that the new Martian attack already had global implications; with the closure of London's investment markets, through which in those days flowed much of the world's money, there would be an instant financial crisis.

In the Square itself I stood on the balcony of the National Gallery and looked out, with Nelson, at this great confluence of the city's highways: the roads becoming steadily more packed with pedestrians, and only a handful of vehicles, police and military, pushing through the crowds and the roadblocks. Even here, as the morning light gathered, I sensed a steady drift eastwards, an instinctive flight away from the glowing enigma to the west.

About eight in the morning the newsboys appeared with their first specials of the day, and were mobbed; small fortunes in pennies were handed over in minutes. I did not join the scrums around the boys, but waited a few minutes until I could get my hands on a discarded but mostly intact copy of the *Mail*. Hastily printed, heavy on headlines but short on images, the rag contained what seemed like authentic news to me, and I silently praised the publishers for defying the government's ban on the truth when it mattered most. Indeed, in screaming headlines, there were scraps of news from the front itself.

HUGE DISASTER
IN MIDDLESEX AND BUCKS
'HALF OF ARMY LOST IN MOMENTS'

A few words, a handful of facts – alarmist, you might think, but, as I would confirm later, the essence of the case was there, in a dozen words.

Meanwhile the Chief Commissioner of Police urged us to keep public order. Parliament, the Privy Council and the Cabinet councils were all in session, we were told, and communications with the military commanders in the field were being kept up. The Royal Family was no longer in London; even before the weekend a warship had taken the King to the safety of Delhi. I heard murmurs of satisfaction from fellow readers at this news: 'As long as they're out of it and safe, bless 'em ' To me the King was nothing but a stamp-collecting dullard, but I was often struck in those days by the ardent loyalty to the Saxe-Coburg-Gothas of their most disadvantaged subjects – even those who despised Marvin's government.

Meanwhile major movements of troops and materiel were reported from Aldershot, headquarters of the Army and home of three divisions, and north of the Thames out of Colchester, and special trains were carrying stocks of weapons and shells out of the Woolwich Arsenal. Food stores across the city were already depleted of stock because of panic buying, and the government was diverting the inflow of fresh supplies to special warehouses, to be doled out through the rationing system.

I read the paper twice, then gave it to a man begging to see it in turn.

Aimless, I walked, letting instinct guide me.

I went down to the river and along the Embankment – or at least, along the narrow strip of walkway still permitted to the public – and crossed Westminster Bridge. From there I saw military vessels pushing up-river. Some appeared to be barges laden with troops, and I thought I recognised the low profile of torpedo rams, like the *Thunder Child* which thirteen years before had done so much to preserve my own life. Such a boat, I realised, would be able to pass under the bridges and reach further into the upper stretches than most capital ships. I also saw what appeared to be heavy naval guns, dismounted and being lugged upstream on smaller boats and barges.

From the river I walked down the Bridge Road and then south of Waterloo. In Lambeth's narrow streets, though the government's proclamations bloomed as dense on the walls and lamp-posts as elsewhere, there was comparatively little sign of the alarm that was gripping the West End. When you had little, I supposed, you were even less motivated to abandon it. But on the Cut the food stores were shut up, and I saw one had been looted, its smashed window left gaping like a missing tooth.

Before the homely grandeur of the Old Vic I found a handful of children on the step, barefoot and begging. I gave them pennies, though much good it would do them with the shops shut up. I wondered how quickly Marvin would get his new system of ration distribution up and running: very quickly, I prayed, for in places like this hunger was only a meal-time away. Indeed, during the First War, even as the Martians rampaged in Surrey, the police had struggled to contain food riots in areas like this. There had been long-term consequences; Frank had been among the first of the medical teams to go into the East End after the War, and had never abandoned his mission – and the police, battle-hardened, had never softened in their attitude to the desperate poor. There was a story Walter Jenkins had never told.

Reminded of Frank, I wondered what had become of my estranged husband, somewhere in Middlesex. Indeed, I had already begun to wonder if he was still alive.

16

Into the Cordon

As Frank would later record in his nascent journal, he and his medical staff were told they were to be moved some seven hours after the first Martian landfall – a little after dawn that Monday morning.

But where Frank had expected the surviving units to be pulled back in the direction of London – and the wounded had already been taken that way, in ambulances, or the walking wounded on foot, all evacuated but for the moribund who waited to die in tents in a farmer's field – instead, so Lieutenant-Colonel Fairfield came to tell Frank and Verity in person, a percentage of the surviving force was to be moved west, *inside* the Cordon.

'Which is what we're starting to call the great circular earthwork the Martians have created, all in an instant. Or a "marswork" perhaps,' Fairfield said with a smirk, exercising his sometimes laboured humour.

The three of them stood in hot, murky air; smoke had swirled all night from the burning countryside around them, and some had tried to sleep in their gas-masks. Even now Frank had to blink to keep the grit out of his eyes. Overhead, aeroplanes buzzed like gnats. Frank had had a chance to shower, at least, and to change his bloodied clothes – he hadn't slept – and yet he had an odd sense of unreality, as if the daylight was a sham. He had to concentrate to follow what Fairfield was saying.

Fairfield showed them aerial photos of a ring of craters, fifty-two in all. 'Wounds executed with surgical precision,' Frank said.

'I suppose that's an apt comparison,' Fairfield said. 'But it's difficult to get the scale of the thing. This is a composite photo, you know. The chaps worked through the night to assemble such images, and maps of the new terrain – and that's not to mention the peril to the flyers who took the shots. Each of these craters is all but a mile wide. *This* smudge,' and he pointed to a blur at the very centre of the circle, 'is Amersham, a fair-sized little town. All but lost within the perimeter – see the scale of it? The second wave, though. That's what comes next. All this is just a stage-setting.'

'The second wave.' Frank recalled that Walter had spoken of a hundred cylinders on the way; only fifty or so had landed yet. 'The next will surely be the war craft, like the cylinders of the last invasion. But where *will* these next cylinders come down? Can we say, yet?'

'With some degree of certainty; they're only eighteen or so hours out now. Some will hit the interior of the Cordon. But others, the first to fall, will hit—' Fairfield jabbed at the photograph with a forefinger, following the arc of craters. 'Here, here, here ... In the existing pits of the perimeter, you see. Not every crater will be targeted, as you can see, but a respectable number will get a new visitor.'

Verity seemed baffled. 'Why would they land on terrain they have already churned up?'

'Because they will have smashed up any resistance there first, *before* they begin to unscrew a single cylinder,' Frank said. 'Now they think they can land in peace.'

'That's surely the idea,' Fairfield said. 'But there's still a flaw in their thinking – a loophole. They didn't get us all, and we've time to respond – to bring up more troops and guns from the rear and from the reserve divisions. Surround them even before they land.'

'"Surround them",' Verity repeated. 'Which is why *we're* going inwards.'

'That's it. We're taking a fighting force *inside* the Cordon, you see, through the craters and to the relatively unharmed land within, so that there will be a welcoming party ready on all sides of each cylinder when it comes down. And meanwhile fresh troops will be brought up to plug the gaps we leave from the far side.

'And you'll be coming with us. So I'm afraid it's to be a day of walking for you, walking and digging in – it's not far, but tricky countryside, as you can imagine. The scouts and sappers have gone on ahead.' He eyed Verity. 'I'm not ordering you to do this, miss. You VADs are volunteers. If you wish to be released—'

Verity said boldly, 'When the fun's only just started? Not on your life, Lieutenant-Colonel.'

Fairfield grinned. 'Carry on, then.' He snapped out a smart salute and walked on down the line.

'Brave of you,' murmured Frank.

She snorted. 'You should see the alternative – if I skulk away from here I'll have to go back and face my mother, who says she once met Florence Nightingale. Sooner the Martian horde than *that*. Come on, Doctor Frank, let's get our things packed up.'

Frank had always kept himself reasonably fit. After that confrontation at High Barnet in the First War he had taken up his school-days boxing again, since the skill had proved so useful in a crisis, and later he had responded with relative enthusiasm to the demands of the Fyrd trainers for their recruits to achieve physical readiness. Even so, he would write, he was already exhausted by the time they had got the field hospitals and their ancillary stations emptied out and torn down and stowed away in motor-wagons and horse-drawn carts.

At that, the equipment he and his medical staff handled was a good deal easier than the heavy weaponry, ammunition and other gear that the regulars had to manage. 'I never saw a bunch of men look less fit than a random selection of British privates,' he told me. 'But give them a task and they get it done, grumbling as they go – smoking, swearing, complaining, every one a miniature Hercules.'

He said, though, that at the time he found the demands of the physical work a relief. Better to be engaged in the outside world than in the contents of one's own head.

There was a brief respite for lunch, of cold meat and bread supplied by the field kitchens. And then, in early afternoon, the column formed up to make its way north-west, past the ruins of Uxbridge. Fairfield and other officers walked or rode alongside the marchers and the vehicles, and scouts zipped up and down the line on motor-cycles, fairly bouncing over the broken ground. Frank imagined the scene as viewed from above, like Fairfield's photograph mosaic – perhaps as seen from one of the Martian cylinders that was falling to the earth even at that moment – the great circular scar in the landscape, and all around men and women and their machines and horses, creeping towards the barrier of smashed earth, and crawling gingerly through it.

As Frank understood it, they passed through the Cordon at a

80

point where two of the Martians' craters, side by side, abutted each other. Smoke drifted everywhere. At the periphery of the craters the damage was partial. They came to a house like a shell, with one wall left standing and the interior floors, unsupported, hanging limp; broken water pipes leaked slow floods into the heart of the ruin.

The ground underfoot here was relatively undisturbed, but in places it was littered with tumbled trees, or churned up to expose the chalky bedrock of the country, rock the colour of bone. In the worst of it the sappers had laid tracks of canvas and planking, but that was meant more for the benefit of the vehicles than the walkers, and Frank and his team, each laden with a pack, had to step carefully.

They had bypassed Uxbridge, or the site of it, when, close to a sign for a place called Denham, they came to a flood. The Grand Union Canal, badly disrupted by the Martian assault, was drowning the countryside. The sappers had put together a pontoon bridge over which the vehicles were driven or dragged, but the foot-sloggers had to walk through thickening mud. Frank soon found it wasn't the wetness that troubled him but the way the mud sank under every step and clung as he tried to lift out his feet, draining what little energy he had left. Around him, all the mud-spattered individuals started to look alike, officers and other ranks, volunteers and regular, women and men. Just lumps of clay and mud, struggling on.

Frank and his band of medics came to a group of soldiers, as mud-covered and unrecognisable as the rest. They were working on an overturned cart; a bored-looking horse stood idly by. One of them called out, and Frank was surprised to recognise a German accent. 'Can you help us? . . .'

At a nod from Fairfield, Frank went over with a couple of his junior doctors, and a handful of VADs. They all took a break for a smoke and a sip of water from their flasks, and, standing in the mud, inspected the problem. The cart was undamaged but it had tipped over in a hole hidden by the brown flood, and it had dumped its cargo, a large and impressive-looking machine gun, into the water.

'Even when we get it out,' said the German who had hailed them, 'it will take us all day to clean it – but we must get it done, for we have an appointment with the Martians.' He stuck out his hand to Frank. 'My name is Schwesig. Heiko Schwesig. My rank is Feldwebelleutnant; I am in charge of this weapon and this team – we are on detachment from the imperial army, as is this fine G8 . . .'

Schwesig's unit had been assigned to guard duty at the German consulate in London – in those times it was necessary for an embassy from that power even to a friendly city like London to be heavily armed. When the Martian threat had been announced this unit and others had volunteered to bring their weapon to the fight. 'The Martians are not waging war on Britain after all,' said Schwesig in his precisely accented English, 'but on all mankind. Of course we must be here.'

Verity, with a dubious eye, was sizing up the challenge of the stranded gun. 'A bit of exercise – just what we need today.'

'Need a hand?' This was a brisk female voice.

Frank turned to find himself facing a sturdy woman of perhaps fifty, evidently muscular, her face broad and weathered, greying black hair tied back in a scarf. She wore what looked like fisherman's waders, and a leather coat buttoned around her barrel of a body. Behind her, its engine turning over – unnoticed in the general din of the day – stood a hefty-looking tractor.

Schwesig grinned. 'Madam, you are the least muddy person I have met all afternoon.'

'I should hope so too, or my husband will never forgive my borrowing his leggings. But he's had no time for his precious fishing since he was called up by the reserve, and left me to run the farm for him.' She pointed with a thumb. 'Said farm being a few miles back that way, near a place called Abbotsdale if you know it. And this sort of pickle is the precise reason I thought I should bring Bessie out to meet you fellows.'

'And glad we are of it, too,' Schwesig said, and he shook the farmer's hand. She introduced herself as Mildred Tritton.

With Mildred's expert handling, it was the work of a moment for 'Bessie', the tractor, to free the gun from the mud, get it loaded in its horse-cart, and on the move again. Then Fairfield briskly commandeered the tractor and its willing driver for more pressing assignments.

Verity watched her go with a sigh. 'And there was me hoping for a lift. Never mind. On we go, Captain Frank . . .'

It wasn't far to their final position, as checked by Fairfield on the mud-spattered, hand-marked map he carried. And the medics weren't the first to arrive in this farmer's field; already troops were digging in, setting up trenches and latrine ditches, and building parapets of hastily filled sandbags facing back the way they had come.

They were now far enough behind the Cordon for them to find themselves in what felt like unsullied British countryside, a place of green hills and hollows and hamlets; a heron skated low over open water nearby. Dairy cattle were being shooed from the field to make way for the soldiers, lowing in apparent irritation.

It was still early in the day, comparatively, only mid-afternoon – they had come only a few miles from their old position. And they were all exhausted to some degree, Frank thought. None had slept much, if at all, last night.

But still they were put to work straight away and were willingly enough. Frank observed an awareness of time, a sense of urgency. 'Midnight they're coming,' went the whisper: in the trenches, in the hastily erected field kitchens, among Frank's own staff, the doctors and orderlies, the nurses and VADs. 'Midnight, coming again, the Martians. Got to be ready . . .' They had all seen the sheer blind destructive power so casually wielded by the Martians just the night before. They had all been briefed on what might come next, the Black Smoke and the Heat-Ray. And here they were, the first line of defence for England and all mankind. Frank heard Fairfield and other officers and the bristling NCOs uttering exhortations as they worked their way along the line, but Frank scarcely thought it was necessary. They all *knew*.

At six they were fed, but they kept working.

By now, despite the 'nineteen hours' window of opportunity still anticipated after the landings, a fight was expected, and the medics were set to digging their own protective trenches. The field hospitals were positioned well back from front-line troops and the expected landing site of 'their' cylinder – marked as 'No. 12' on Fairfield's map – but the Heat-Ray was known from the last War to have a useful range of several miles. So, trenches it had to be. They ate as they worked, taking breaks of only a few minutes from the digging and hauling.

By seven thirty the sun was down. Frank and Verity made a final tour of their installation.

'Looks rougher than the first set-up,' Verity said. 'But then everything's been dragged a few miles through the mud – as have we all.'

Frank said, trying to project a confidence he did not truly feel, 'We'll do all we can.'

She laughed. 'Now *that* is a doctor's line! Comforting and meaningless. You've been in the job too long, Captain...'

Night fell, and the clocks worked their way towards midnight.

Fairfield, on his last tour of inspection before the deadline, wasn't terribly sympathetic over the medics' mounting anxiety. 'Had a couple of operations in my time,' he said. 'Bullet in the shoulder, picked it up in the Sudan. When you're waiting for your turn on the slab – *that's* what this is like. Now it's your turn to wait for the surgeon's blade, Doctor!'

Frank used the latrines at ten, and again at eleven when they were getting more crowded. This routine reminded him uncomfortably of the night before, as if he were stuck in some over-scripted play that he must rehearse over and over.

A last cup of coffee, which he took to his position in the trench. He clambered down a short wooden ladder and settled behind a sandbag parapet, wondering if he would ever climb back up again. In fact he found it hard to imagine a time, any reality, beyond the midnight cut-off. In the earth at his feet, gleaming in the light of the oil lamps strung along the trench, he saw a flint nodule, creamy white with a rich black interior.

'Chalk country, Doc,' came a familiar voice. 'Sappers know the landscape. Have to. Nat'ral geologists, you could call 'em.'

Frank turned, startled. 'Bert Cook!'

Cook was wearing a reservist's uniform, as muddied as the rest. Under his steel hat, Frank saw, he had blackened his face with burnt cork. The officers had suggested it, but most of the troops hadn't bothered; Martians brought no snipers. 'Hello, Doc,' Cook said. 'Heard you were here – with this unit. Made my way along the perimeter to find a friendly face.' He glanced at his watch. 'Just in time for the late sitting of the show, eh?'

'I shouldn't be surprised, Bert. I suppose *you* would always come back.'

'"As a sparrow goes for man", as your brother quoted me.' He sounded charged, excited – yet calculating, Frank thought. 'And here I am, right underneath 'em. This is what I've been waiting for, ever since the beggars died off in '07 – waiting for them to come finish the job they started.'

'You say it with such relish, Bert. You are a riddle.'

'I'll give you a riddle. What's green and flashing and flies like a bird in the sky?'

Frank stared at him.

Cook grinned, and pointed upwards.

17

Cylinder No. 12

It took Frank some time, with the help of other survivors, to put together a coherent account of what followed. But then, as it turned out, he would have the time – plenty of it.

It was at the stroke of midnight that Fairfield's Cylinder No. 12 made its entrance, with that vivid flash of green overhead, and then a concussion, a slam on the ground.

Frank, huddled down in his trench, felt it as a shuddering in the earth, and a gust of air that knocked the breath out of his chest. In the trench the duckboards creaked and cracked, some of the loosely constructed parapet of sandbags collapsed, and here and there people whimpered and huddled. It was not as bad as the calamitous infall of twenty-four hours earlier, Frank realised immediately, but *nearer*.

Then, just seconds after the cylinder's fall, Frank heard shouting. 'Advance! Advance!' 'Bring those bloody guns up!' 'A light here, throw a light!'

Frank stood on a firing step and looked ahead, out of his trench. He saw a greenish glow coming from a hole dug new into the churned-up ground, with earth scattered around, and small fires in the nearer distance where there were trees and grass and buildings left to burn. Men and field guns were silhouetted against the eerie green light, and picked out by wavering torchlight, already advancing towards the new pit.

And, from somewhere far behind, Frank heard the cough of artillery: the big guns firing from behind the lines, the giant eighteen- and sixty-pounders. The plan was that those great shells would smash up the cylinders before the ground troops even closed.

Frank's new friend Feldwebelleutnant Schwesig and his gun

crew, mobile, fast, and well-trained like all German troops, were among the first to reach the perimeter of the new pit itself. Later Schwesig told Frank what he saw. There was the cylinder embedded in the earth, standing vertical, a great pillar of steel some thirty yards across – and, no doubt, a hundred yards long, as it had proved when the inert craft had been finally dug out of the ground after the First War. Schwesig and his crew prepared their G8 gun for what seemed to them the remote possibility that anything from within that cylinder should survive the blast of the field artillery already being trained on the target. There was no rush; they had nineteen hours' grace before the Martians could move out in force, so they believed.

But the rules of the game changed again.

There was a crack, a flash of greenish light. Schwesig saw it as a band of light around the top seam of the cylinder, under its flat lid. Then that disc of metal, itself weighing perhaps five thousand tons, was suddenly detached and cast aside like a straw boater, to fly across the pit. No hours of patient unscrewing this time!

Then, in another instant, a tentacular, metallic arm lifted out of the craft, bearing a compact device not unlike a moving-picture camera: a device that Schwesig remembered well from his briefings. It was a Heat-Ray generator. Schwesig hurled himself flat into the dirt. He saw a ghost-pale beam of light pass not feet over his prone body, and thought he felt the air itself blasted to a tremendous temperature.

Around him men who had not been so fast to react flashed into white flame, as the Ray swept like a hose around the perimeter of the pit. All this in mere seconds after the opening of the cylinder.

Nineteen hours! The cylinder had *not* waited inertly for the human attack, not for nineteen hours, not even for nineteen minutes.

Lieutenant-Colonel Fairfield was a little further back, on a slight rise, observing. He could not see the heat beam itself, or indeed the projector being wielded from the suddenly open cylinder, but he saw men, machines, vehicles and horses incinerated in a glare of light, all around the pit. Then he saw more beams, coming presumably from projectors within the cylinder itself, reaching up into the sky, beams barely visible in air that was already filling with smoke. He looked up, wondering – and saw detonations, high in the air, almost like fireworks, he would say later. These were artillery shells, incoming from the remote big guns, on their way to smash the Martian cylinder before it ever opened – that had been the theory. None of the shells reached the ground, never mind its target. A few spotter planes too were caught like moths in an invisible flame, brief flares against the midnight sky.

And then, returning his gaze to the pit, Fairfield saw a great cowl, like a bronze helmet, lifting smoothly on three unfolding legs. It was a fighting-machine – a great tripedal engine of war, returned to the earth after thirteen years, rising out of the smoke of the disintegrated corpses of hundreds of men.

All this and not yet a minute since the cylinder had landed. Fairfield comprehended it in an instant. If we had deduced that the Martians were at their most vulnerable on first landing, so had they themselves, and they had done something about it.

Verity Bliss, in the medics' ditch with Frank, was too far back to see any of the first moments of the conflict in detail, but she quickly got the general picture – so she would tell me later. That great cowl of the first fighting-machine was already advancing, looming out of the pit. Verity grabbed Frank's collar, and hauled him by main force out of the trench. 'We must run! It is the only chance!'

Frank had heard the cries of freshly wounded; in his head he had been frantically preparing to go over the top, to help who he could, he and his staff. But he could see he had no choice but to agree; the whole position would soon be overwhelmed. Out of the trench he came, and he and Verity rounded up the rest of their staff, yelling and pushing: 'A doctor's no use to anyone fried! Run, scatter!'

But even as he ran away from the pit – and thus heading *deeper* into the Martian Cordon – Frank was conscious of others running the other way: gunners scrambling to man their weapons, even individual troopers hurling themselves into trenches and taking pot-shots at the Martian with their rifles.

Glancing back over his shoulder, he saw the Martian advancing remorselessly into this fire, with that peculiar, horribly familiar three-legged motion, a mobile war-machine without wheels. It was a tripod, like a milking stool tipped over and bowling along at a tremendous speed – a traumatic memory of thirteen years before, he told me. But even as it advanced the fighting-machine kept its upper body steady, that great cowled 'head' a superb platform for targeted fire.

'Down, you fools!'

A firm hand in the back forced Frank to the ground, with

Verity sprawled alongside him. Frank twisted to see the soot-smeared face of Bert Cook, grinning, his teeth white in the light of Frank's torch. 'Sorry about the rough handlin', miss.'

Frank protested, 'Bert—'

'Lie still, I say!'

And Cook kept them pressed down even as a second fighting-machine swept *over* them.

Frank, twisting, saw one immense leg, the best part of a hundred feet tall, swing through the air, as the cowl far above twisted as if in search of prey. By the light of fires lit by the Heat-Ray itself, he glimpsed too the metallic net on the thing's 'back', a detail with grisly associations. Though the Heat-Ray stabbed this way and that, it never came close to the three of them. He survived – *they* survived – and the Martian passed.

'Can you see the pattern?' Cook yelled in Frank's ear. 'They're going for equipment, guns and ammo – and men who fight back, they'll get a lick of the Ray too. But if you submit – well, you might get stomped on accidental—'

'They're leaving us alive,' Verity said.

'Course they are. That's why they're not using the Black Smoke, I imagine. And we all know for why, don't we?' He smacked his lips, as if hungry. 'They're harvesting. And you know why? Because we're defeated already. *Already*. Oops – here comes the second machine – down!'

Again he pressed their heads into the dirt, as hundreds of tons of articulated metal waved in the air above them. And then came a third fighting-machine, and a fourth, rising gracefully from the pit.

'This is the life!' yelled Bert Cook, through the din. 'This is the life!'

18

The Flying-Machine Over London

On the Monday night I had slept badly.

Before midnight, when the next batch of Martians were due – so the rumour-mongers had it, and by now they were well informed – I had returned to the West End. I had been out on the Strand, in fact, in the night air. With the restrictions on traffic the city was free of engine noise, and I could clearly hear the voices of people out and about as I was, and the clank of a train leaving Charing Cross, perhaps a troop-carrier. And to the north, I thought by Covent Garden, I heard voices raised in revelry, even the shrill sounds of a ragtime band, and then a thin police whistle. Marvin's regime had not quite sucked all the gaiety out of the city, then; not even the Martians had managed that.

It is an odd thing, looking back, how bright London had been made in the night, in those years between the Martian Wars. It was not quite Times Square, but the West End would ever be ablaze with electric lighting, and even the meaner districts to the east and south of the river shone with electric, and with old-fashioned gas where the supply was kept up. All of it bright enough that the sky above was masked from sight – as if the British who had been threatened from the sky now wanted to shut out the night altogether, to pretend it did not exist.

But in spite of the customary glare that night, at midnight, as Tuesday began, I saw green flashes, off to the north-west: the Martians coming down for the second night in a row, really not so far away from London, and right on top of my ex-husband. I heard a brief barrage, like a flash storm, far beyond the horizon, and thought I saw flickers of white light, like immense explosions. But it was over quickly – within minutes. Could the battle be concluded so soon? I refused to be drawn into the speculation of the anxious strangers around me, who were as ignorant as I was myself. But I stood, and waited, and listened.

After perhaps half an hour of silence from the front, it might have been more, I went back indoors. Again the hotel had kept the bars open, though there were markedly fewer guests than the previous night, and fewer staff too. I took more sandwiches for my pockets, and a glass of hot toddy, and retired to my room. Of course there was no news to be had on the Marvin's Megaphone, nothing but patriotic music, sad or uplifting. I turned it off and tried to nap.

I was out again at dawn.

That Tuesday was a fine, clear day, with a nip in the air although March was nearly done with us, and the sky was deep blue and streaked with low cloud to the west. I had my rucksack on my back, with all my worldly goods, for I did not know what the day might bring. None of us did. But I did not check out of my room at my hotel on the Strand – I had the key in my pocket; perhaps I would yet return. (I never did; I have the key still, before me as I write.)

I walked to the river, the heart of the city. Though I do not count myself a Londoner I suppose it was an instinct to go there at such a moment. The river could be a strange sight in the dawn light, even on days when Martians weren't attacking, for you would see folk picking their way through the exposed mud of the banks, seeking treasures washed down the drains: coins, lighters, pens, cigarette and card cases, even bits of jewellery. These 'mudlarks' were a symptom of the return of extreme poverty under Prime Minister Marvin, a condition Dickens would have recognised.

But that morning the water itself was crowded and noisy from engines, hooters, bells, and raised voices. There were some of the Navy boats I had seen the day before, gun platforms and torpedo rams among them. And I saw too a scattered host of civilian ships, ferries and yachts and quite grand river-boats, all making their cautious way downstream – towards the sea, and away from the fighting. Some of those on the yachts and cruisers stared curiously at the mudlarks, and at me, and at the city's great buildings. I imagined great houses further upstream, at Marlow and Maidenhead and Henley, abandoned for the duration. Some of these well-heeled refugees raised Kodaks.

And then I saw the flying-machine.

I glimpsed it out of the corner of my eye at first, a shift in the light, off to the west. When I looked that way I saw a disc, flat and wide, a smooth profile – very large, and evidently moving very rapidly, for it was greyed with distance, and rose up *beyond* the clouds. It was a Martian machine, of the kind which I had seen once before, in the sky over Essex, from the bobbing deck of the paddle-steamer on which I, Frank and Alice escaped to France during the First War. I strained my eyes, trying to make out any details – any differences of form or operation from that glimpse thirteen years ago. This great flyer moved smoothly and silently, with a grace that made it seem to belong to the realm of the air, like a cloud, like a rainbow, rather than to the dullness of the ground. But then it has long been remarked that all Martian machines have a sense of living grace about them, in contrast to our own clanking, spatchcocked gadgets.

It is a remarkable truth that of all the gadgets humans retrieved after the First Martian War, it was the flying-machine that was the first to be made operational. It flies, in fact, not by dragging its way through the air with propeller blades as our aeroplanes do, but rather by gathering in the air, raising it to a super-hot temperature, and then letting it expand explosively from an array of vents which may be swivelled and turned. As for the heating agent, this seems to be a development of the Heat-Ray technology; the energy generators used by a flying-machine are evidently closely related to those used in that weapon. According to Rayleigh, Lilienthal and others, the Martians' flying-machines are adapted to the conditions of Mars's air, which is much thinner than ours, and of different composition. In thin air one would not use wings to rest on the air to support the craft, as our heavier-than-air aircraft designs have done since the Wright brothers' experiments. Rather, you would shape your craft to push the air out of the way, streamlining the ship like a stingray, a form to which the Martian machines have been compared.

It had taken days in the First War before that flying-machine had been spied. Everyone supposed that the Essex machine must have been constructed from components carried in several cylinders, brought together and assembled. But now I was seeing this new machine only hours after the Middlesex cylinders had landed. In addition there had always seemed an uncertain, experimental aspect to the flying machines as observed during the First War; *this* beast seemed much more confident. I realised with unease that Walter was right, that the Martians must have learned a great deal from their first dealings with humans, and had come back far better prepared, for our thicker air and other terrestrial conditions.

The machine came out of the west, following the line of the river – and thus heading for my position. I remembered that the Essex machine had been scattering the Black Smoke across the land, but there was no evidence of that dark agent this time. The machine passed directly over me; I ducked, but kept looking up. I saw that the hull was brazen, like the cowl of a fighting-machine, and its undersurface was grooved, perhaps for stability in the air, and its sharp rim was oddly feathered at the back.

And I saw now that the flying-machine had escorts: biplanes, two of them, which swooped and darted like flies beneath the belly of the behemoth. I thought they must be a German design – or even Russian – rather than anything British. I wondered what harm even the Red Baron, hero of the Russian front, could do to the Martian machine, if he ever got close enough. Yet it was cheering to me to see that the invaders did not have the skies entirely to themselves.

I watched the Martian and his escort pass on down the Thames, until I lost him in the glare of the rising sun. And then I heard the cries of the newsboys, for the day's first specials were out.

I hurried from the Embankment and back into the city. Though the sun was barely up the city was coming to life once more, and the crowds were out, and I had to battle to get hold of a flimsy *Daily Mirror*, exorbitantly priced at a shilling:

EXPLOSIONS IN MIDDLESEX
MORE MARTIANS LAND
BRIEF BATTLE WAGED
FRESH CATASTROPHE FEARED

And even as the newsboys made fresh fortunes, the government was stirring, the loudhailer vans cruising the blockaded streets, the bill-posters slapping fresh proclamations onto the lampposts:

LONDONER!
SAVE YOUR CITY!
GO TO THE KING'S LINE!

This new directive was set out over a portrait of the King, who looked a bit bewildered in an elaborate military uniform, but a better choice to stir the soul than a picture of Marvin, I knew by now.

I saw that 'all able-bodied men between sixteen and sixty not already engaged in vital war work' were 'encouraged' to grab a pick and a shovel (bring your own; equipment not supplied) and to make their way to the 'King's Line', which was to be a defensive perimeter cutting across the country between the Martians and the city. A map was appended, showing the Martian Cordon where it swept closest to the city to the north-west, near Pinner. Our Line would be a bow-shape five to ten miles back, following the lines of the trunk roads, but advanced a little ahead of those highways, perhaps for ease of communication. Thus the Line would run from Ashford, north-east up through Twickenham and Richmond, then roughly north through Brentford, Ealing and Wembley to Hendon, and then north-west to Edgware – its terminus coming alarmingly close to Stanmore, to where my sister-in-law might have returned, I noted. Tractors and digging machines both civilian and military were already drawing up to the Line, I read, which was being surveyed by the Royal Engineers and marked out by scouts; there would be a complex of trenches, earthworks, pillboxes and redoubts, manned by troops hastily deployed from Aldershot, and with artillery batteries reinforced by Navy guns. Later the British forces would be joined, in a gesture of friendship, by German detachments already being rushed across the Channel from occupied France.

A woman close to me, middle-aged, well-dressed, stern-looking, read the poster through a pince-nez. 'My husband fought the Boers, you know.'

'Did he?'

'Died out there, in fact. *They* resisted like this, with entrenchments and tangled-up barbed wire so you couldn't advance. I suppose we are now against the Martians as the Boers were against the British, rebels against a superior army.'

'The Boers put up a good fight even so.'

'That they did. But this defence line—' She snorted. '"Able-bodied men", indeed.'

I smiled. 'No women, you mean?'

'They'd rather use a German than a British woman.' She glanced at me, taking in my trouser suit, short hair and pack, not with any trace of disapproval. 'And do you think this line of theirs will work?'

'Do you?'

'If the Martians kindly give us a chance to build it.' She flicked the poster with a fingernail, and walked away.

It was a morning of maps. On an inside page of my *Mirror* I found an extensive report on 'The Flight From London' during the Monday. The great trunk routes out of London to the south and east had been packed by civilians, making for Southampton, Portsmouth, Brighton, Hastings, Dover – even for Essex as Frank, Alice and I had once fled. The police and military had set aside lanes along the highways so that the walkers did not impede the flow of personnel and material into the capital. And the Red Cross, with government approval, was hastily setting up reception camps at places like Canterbury, Lewes and Horsham. At least this time there was some order to it – so far, anyhow.

As for myself, my own instinct was still to remain in central London. To be in the thick of it: Julie Elphinstone, War Correspondent! It had a ring to it. But I had my personal duty as well. I thought of Alice, helpless if she had returned to Stanmore – and just beyond the limit of the King's Line, where you might expect the fighting to be worst if the Martians thought as the Germans would have, and tried to turn the British flank. Perhaps I should go to her.

As I stood there undecided, another flock of newsboys came out, another set of specials, with the ink not yet dry on the first. This time there was news brought back from spotter planes who had been bravely flying over the Middlesex salient. The fighting-machines were already on the move, already pushing out of their huge Cordon.

19

The First Hours Within the Cordon

Through the early hours of Tuesday, after the Martians' lightning-fast scattering of the Army's resistance, Frank and Verity and a handful of their staff, and a number of troopers detached from their units, huddled in hastily improvised foxholes and trenches.

And they watched as the fighting-machines stalked across the broken landscape within their Cordon, probing at the wreckage of our military emplacements. The night was dark, but Frank was able to follow their movements from the light of the burning of vehicles and dumps of fuel and ammunition. He would see their legs, long, graceful, articulated, passing before a crimson glare. Once or twice a searchlight was opened up, pinning the Martians in brilliance, but the sources once revealed were incinerated in an instant. Frank heard little gunfire, saw little evidence of any resistance, confused or otherwise.

After a few hours of this, Verity whispered to Frank, 'Anything that moves – anything mechanical – they fire on. Even if it isn't a weapon, a gun. I imagine they'd fire on a field ambulance if we could get to one. But they are sparing the people, unless you're silly enough to take a pot-shot. Just as your friend Bert Cook said – and, don't worry, I do understand why: the Martians have to feed – as will we, in fact, at some point. Where is Cook, by the way?'

'Long gone,' Frank said. 'Looking for Martians. Bert was always going to follow his own agenda, rather than the Army's.'

'I think it's starting to get light.'

'Hmm. I wish it wouldn't.'

Verity glanced around at their charges, the young medics and the VADs, many of whom were huddled up against each other for warmth, as innocent as small children. 'Look at them. I envy them their ability to sleep.'

'They're all exhausted. No sleep on the Sunday night for most of us either, remember.'

'True.' Then, hearing something, she twisted and looked out of the trench.

Frank raised himself carefully, up on his elbows. In the gathering pre-dawn light, he saw yet another fighting-machine picking its way with speed but apparent care through the ruined landscape. And at its feet scuttled something smaller, a fat body on multiple legs like a crab or spider, the whole the size of a small motor-car perhaps.

Verity breathed, 'What's *that*?'

'A handling-machine. It's odd to see one outside a museum . . . If the handling-machines are out they'll be bent on construction as well as destruction.'

'Maybe they're building a fortress.'

'Something like that. A stockade, perhaps, all the way around this zone they have conquered.'

She glanced at him. 'It really is a cordon, then.'

'It seems so.'

'With us on the inside . . .'

'Just as well I'm here, then.'

The woman's clear voice, contrasting to their whispers, coming from behind him, startled Frank. He rolled on his back, scrambling for his revolver, and clumsily slipped down into the trench.

A horse whinnied, as if mocking him.

Frank found himself facing Mildred Tritton, who was seated on a battered old dogcart to which two sturdy horses were harnessed.

'Good morning,' she said cheerfully. 'And as it is just about morning, the light ought to be good enough to tell you I'm not *quite* a look-alike for an invader from Mars.'

Feeling foolish, and though it defied instinct to abandon his cover, Frank got to his feet. 'I apologise,' he said, sheepishly holstering his gun. 'We've had rather a bad night. What can I do for you, Mrs Tritton?'

'Mildred, please. I have a feeling it's more a question of what *I* can do for you just now. This is actually the third trip I've made out to the perimeter this night, or morning – once I discovered, by means of a rather nerve-racking experiment, that the Martians would not fire on a wagon pulled by a horse, not unless it's loaded up with a howitzer I suppose. The Martians go for machinery. They did for old Bessie, you know. My tractor.' Her face worked. 'I find that rather hard to forgive.'

Verity said, 'The poor Martians! They've made a formidable enemy.'

'You said three trips?' Frank asked.

'Yes, collecting up benighted souls like yourselves and taking them home.'

'Home?'

'I mean my own home – my farm is near Abbotsdale, which is a village a few miles thataway,' and she jerked her thumb over her shoulder. 'First trip was out of the goodness of my heart. Second trip I picked up your Lieutenant-Colonel Fairfield. Pleasant chap, and one of the more senior officers to have survived – in this part of the Cordon, at least. And he told me that while the telephone and telegraph are out – the Martians seem to be busily cutting the wires – the field units have wireless telegraph, and that still works, and there's some co-ordination going on among the survivors. Those caught within the Cordon are being withdrawn from the perimeter for now, and brought back to suitable rest stops – suitable meaning away from a Martian pit at least, for the cylinders fell throughout the cordoned-off zone, not just at the edge. I took Fairfield to Abbotsdale, and he requested I come back out for the rest of his unit – I think he was particularly keen to find you, Doctor Jenkins.'

'Frank,' he said heavily. 'And we're more than grateful that you did.'

'Load up, then,' she said briskly. 'I can take a round dozen in the cart. Any of you who feel up to walking, you're welcome to follow. I'll come back for the rest, have no fear. I brought breakfast. I have ham, cheese, bread, and buckets of fresh milk – a couple of your strong lads can unload. Oh, and clean drinking water. Given what the Martian Smoke can do to the soil, you're advised not to drink from streams and broken mains and such just yet.'

'Still not quite dawn,' Frank said. 'But it's as if the sun has come out. Thank you, Mildred.'

But she seemed distracted. She said softly, 'What strikes me, Doctor, is how deuced *young* your people are.'

'Indeed. Well, nobody old is foolish enough to go to war.'

20

An Occupied Countryside

After a hasty breakfast, and with the cart loaded, Mildred snapped her reins, the horses pulled with a patient, heavy plod, and the cart headed across the rough ground of the field. Frank himself rode up with the farmer – somewhat reluctantly, while there were others of his people who had no place to ride at all, but his more experienced subordinates insisted that as commanding officer he should take the lead.

It felt very odd, even dream-like, to be out of cover, even if there were no Martians in sight. As they rode they spoke softly, with Mildred asking Frank about his background. She was interested to find out about his relationship with Walter, and had read his book; Frank later told me he felt the typical younger brother's jealousy at this, even in such circumstances. Across the field, a cluster of cows lowed mournfully. 'I'm sure Jimmy Rodgers won't neglect his milking, Martians or no Martians,' Mildred said sternly.

They hit a particularly deep gully in the field, and the cart jolted violently.

Frank said, winded, 'So you're not troubling to use the roads, Mildred?'

For answer she pointed into the distance ahead, misty with the dawn. Now Frank saw Martians, two fighting-machines walking in the greyness, astonishingly tall – like church steeples come to life in this English countryside, he thought.

'*That's* why,' Mildred said. 'They're everywhere – coming in from the pits at the perimeter and from those in the interior – they're cutting roads and rail lines, as well as the telephone wires – best to keep out of the way of them altogether, don't you think? So we'll stay off the roads, and bypass the villages. But it's up hill and down dale all the way...'

Mildred was proved right about that. Even crossing the fields, the going was steep, all dips and climbs. The landscape had a closed-in feeling to Frank. It was like a vast green mouth, on this cold March day. He supposed a military man would fret about the lack of long eye lines.

Mildred studied him. 'You don't know the Chilterns, do you? Sixty miles of high ground, from the Goring Gap in the south-west where the Thames passes, to the Hitchin Gap in the north-east – as I am sure the military planners in London and Aldershot and wherever are working out as we speak. Chalk country, lots of crowding hills and narrow valleys. It seems evident to me that the Martians have seized this place to serve as a sort of base of operations. A fortified perimeter from which they can strike out elsewhere – at London, presumably. And in the meantime we're all stuck here.'

'We? But who is "we"?'

'That's one of the questions that needs to be discussed. Here's the brief. I'll drop off your troops in Abbotsdale, and I'll take you to the Manor – it's not far.'

'The Manor?'

'Where you will be the guest for the day of the Dowager Lady Bonneville. Emily has your Lieutenant-Colonel Fairfield already, and other senior officers from this part of the Cordon, and she has summoned other significant figures from Abbotsdale and nearby villages – the local bobby, the postmaster, the bank manager, that sort. Jimmy Rodgers, with the largest land-holding hereabouts—'

'There's to be a gathering hosted by the Lady of the Manor?' Frank had to laugh. 'It's all rather medieval, isn't it?'

'Look around you. You're on a horse and cart, crossing a field! There may be interplanetary engines stalking around, but I rather think we *are* somewhat medieval now, don't you? As for Lady Bonneville, I suspect she will have more of a problem with the Germans in your units than with the Martians. Old school, you see. On a more practical note, we have to think about the welfare of your toy soldiers. Hundreds of them, I imagine.'

'Thousands, probably, if they survived.'

'There's an awful lot of you, and a lot of empty bellies. I don't imagine you brought over much in the way of supplies?'

He thought about that. 'There were field kitchens... No, I don't suppose we brought a great deal. A day or two's worth, perhaps.'

She sighed. 'You expected a short campaign in a well-provisioned countryside, not a siege. In the short term we'll have to rely on our stores. But soon enough – these men of yours. Mostly young, yes? Strong, fit, used to discipline.'

'If we can maintain it.'

'Oh, they'll maintain it when I have them ploughing my fields.'

Frank felt bewildered. It was only a few hours since he had been cowering in a scratch trench under attack from an invading force from another world – and now here was this remarkable woman with her talk of ploughing fields. 'You've thought it out, haven't you?'

'We can't use tractors, of course; the Martians evidently won't allow us to use motors. Hard work. And we will have to *clear* the fields, or some of them.'

Frank glanced around with, he would later admit to me, a town-dweller's blank incomprehension of the countryside. 'Don't you feed yourselves already?'

She smiled. 'Not for, oh, thirty or forty years I think. Not since the imports of cheap grain from Europe and America began, and the farmers went out of business. So the land was turned to foresting, or dairy cattle. Well, no more American grain for us for a while. Lucky for us that a lot of folk around here remember the old ways...'

They spoke on of other practicalities. The stranded troops had some medical supplies, but there were injured among the civilian population too, and the stock of the pharmacies was limited; what they had would have to be pooled and rationed. Electricity hadn't yet reached many communities out here anyhow; the Manor had its own generators, but they would require fuel which would be irreplaceable, so the lights will soon be out. Water would always be an issue, but there were old wells in Abbotsdale that could be opened up with some muscle...

As the journey wore on, Frank felt himself weakening. He had after all missed two nights' sleep. He fought not to shiver; he wrapped his arms around his chest. And he became aware of aches and pains that he hadn't noticed before – a pull of one ankle, a wrenched shoulder. The world, the green country around him, seemed bright as it ever had, and yet he had a growing sense of unreality, as if all of this was a sham that might be ripped aside at any moment, to plunge him back into those midnight scenes of smashed bodies and broken minds.

Mildred watched him. 'Are you all right?'

100

'Nothing a stiff whisky won't cure...' He heard these words as if from a distance.

To his horror, he found he was weeping.

Mildred Tritton pulled up the cart. After a soft word from Mildred, Verity scrambled up beside him, and held him. Mildred snapped the reins, and the cart rolled on slowly. After a time, with Verity at his side, the weeping receded, and he fell into a half-doze.

21

At Abbotsdale

They approached the village at last. Frank looked dully on a church no more than fifty years old, a new school, a scrap of common land that had been spared enclosure. This was no suburb, but the social and technological progress of the nineteenth century had wrought great changes on places like this.

The cart slowed at the gate of a handsome manor house, a much older building, set back from the road. Outside, weapons – rifles and revolvers and even flare guns – had been heaped up and covered by a tarpaulin, hidden from Martian eyes, Frank supposed. As the MOs and VADs and nurses clambered out of the cart, the manor gates opened and two scouts emerged, riding bicycles. They rolled off in the direction of Amersham, wobbling as they went, to a chorus of catcalls from the MOs: 'Put your back into it, lads!'

Mildred clucked at the horses, and turned to Frank. 'Well, here we are, for better or worse. Now look, don't be alarmed when I take you into the house, the spaniels are perfectly harmless even if there are rather a lot of them . . .'

Frank joined Fairfield and other officers, gathered together by Lady Bonneville over coffee in a grand but musty dining room. Fairfield detached himself to greet Frank, barely interrupting the earnest talk.

Already the officers and their aide were getting organised. A local map had been spread out over the dining table, and was being marked with the landing sites of the Martians, as they were reported in. Within the Cordon itself Frank saw now the impact pits of the second wave, including a cluster of landings over Amersham, at the very centre of the complex.

As for the immediate situation, a priority was communications. A simple Marvin's Megaphone wireless receiver would pick up the government's broadcasts from the Marconi station near Chelmsford, as long as there was power, and already there had been broadcasts aimed at those trapped inside the Martian Cordon: '*You are not alone.*' Frank was assured that later it would be possible to rig up 'crystal sets' which could detect wireless signals without any external power supply at all. Getting messages out was another issue, however; the small field wireless kits were limited in range, and there had been little success so far. But a lieutenant of the sappers spoke of tunnelling all the way under the Cordon perimeter itself and laying cables.

As the morning wore on, there was some news from outside. On this Tuesday, their first day on the earth, these new Martian invaders had already left their vast encampment. The cylinders having landed at midnight, the fighting-machines had moved out a mere six hours later, in the dawn, and thus establishing a precedent which would be followed later in this War, as I will relate.

The first sightings of this movement had been by units within the Cordon. According to reports from the exterior, once out of their perimeter the Martians had fanned out quickly in groups, evidently heading for specific targets. There were a lot of fighting-machines on the earth now, estimated at more than two hundred if the capacity of the forty-eight crewed cylinders was similar to the fleet of '07; there were dozens of machines in these early attack groups.

And attack they had. They had made straight for bases at Colchester and Aldershot, the very guts of the Army. They had gone too to Salisbury Plain where the military training ground had been used to amass reserve troops; the slaughter had been great. (After the War, Frank was astonished to be shown dramatic pictures run in the *Mirror* of a fighting-machine standing over Stonehenge; of course there were no newspapers in the Cordon.) The big Navy dockyards at Chatham and Portsmouth had been hammered too, though many of the capital ships had been able to put to sea – that was thanks to quick thinking by Churchill, who overrode the Admiralty to get it done. And throughout the country, wherever they roamed, the Martians routinely cut road and rail links and bridges, and telephone and telegraph wires, and blew up electricity stations and gasometers, and even fired coal heaps. There was some resistance, and a couple of fighting-machines had been got by lucky shots from artillery pieces, but that was all; they were too fast, too destructive. This time the Martians had done their homework, Frank realised; they were hamstringing southern England.

And when, on the Wednesday morning, the Martians moved at last on London, of all of us – all of my scattered and broken family – it seems to have been Frank who was aware of it first.

22

How the Martians Moved Out of the Cordon

As the most senior of the medical officers who had survived to make it to Abbotsdale, Frank had been offered a room in the manor house. But Frank is nothing if not a man of conscience, tedious company as that makes him at times. So that night he bedded down on a straw-filled mattress in the Abbotsdale village hall with his junior MOs and the nurses and the VADs, men and women separated for decency by a big old canvas curtain used in the annual pantomime – he told me it was crudely painted to look like a fairy castle, which after the unreality of the last few days struck him as somehow appropriate. For a while he was kept awake by the uneasy joshing of men as exhausted and disturbed as he was. But he snuggled under a blanket and a heap of his clothes, and was soon out like a snuffed candle.

He was woken by a drone of aircraft engines.

He sat bolt upright, in pitch dark broken only by cracks of flickering orange light coming through imperfectly fixed curtains. Around him men were stirring, muttering. With the wariness of the war veteran he had so suddenly become, Frank had kept his trousers and socks and shorts on, and he was glad of it now as he felt around in the dark for his jacket, boots and revolver.

That deep thrumming gathered in intensity, coming from the north and east, he thought. Aircraft, undoubtedly; he recognised the sound of the big screws. At last somebody ripped aside a curtain, exposing a window facing north. The sky was full of drifting orange sparks: Very lights, flare shells, falling slowly. In the hall, all the faces turned that way, shining in the orange light.

'My God,' said one man. 'Somebody's putting on a firework show.'

'That's Amersham way, I think,' said another. 'And – look at that! The big shadow, like a man on stilts! The Martians are moving!'

There was a hand on Frank's shoulder: Verity Bliss. She was fully dressed, with her steel hat fixed over her hair. 'It's all kicking off. Lieutenant-Colonel Fairfield sent me to fetch you.'

He pulled on his boots. 'Come on, then.'

They pushed their way out into smoke-tinged air. In the road, men and women stood around, excited, pointing. The orange glare of flares in the direction of the Martians' central Amersham pits was strong. Frank saw there were villagers among the khaki-clad crowd of troops, boys and girls scared but excited, wide-eyed to be up before the sky was properly light.

And – yes, Frank could see it now – there were the fighting-machines, tall and stately, casting shadows in the flare-light. The Martians formed up and began to stride away, to the east.

Verity said, 'Maybe we should count the machines. One, two, three ... The shadows make it impossible.'

'Don't worry,' came a cultured voice. Lieutenant-Colonel Fairfield joined them, dapper in his peaked cap and topcoat, although Frank noticed outsized carpet slippers on his feet. 'We've got scouts out, and we're trying to get signals to the commanders outside the Cordon.'

Frank pointed to brief explosions of Heat-Ray fire. 'The chaps sending up the Very flares seem to be getting it.'

'Yes. Brave men, volunteers all. But we thought we needed to get a good look at what was going on, whatever it cost us. For it's not just *our* Martians that are on the move. They seem to be converging from around the Cordon – we've had sightings from as far south as Slough, north as far as Hemel Hempstead. Flocks of the things, and converging thataway, towards Uxbridge.' He pointed east. 'I'm afraid there's not much doubt about their target this morning.'

'London,' Verity said breathlessly.

The aircraft noise rose to a deep grumbling roar, and they had to shout to make themselves heard.

Fairfield said, 'And up there's the other reason we're lighting the Martians' pits.'

Frank grinned, suddenly exhilarated. 'To guide in the bombers!'

And there they were, Frank saw, coming in low from the north, illuminated from beneath by the orange gleam of the flares. Frank suspected they had flown out of Northolt, the base of the Royal Flying Corps. They were huge, heavy aircraft, beefy biplanes. These were not RFC craft – the British military had no such planes – these were German bombers, Gothas and Giants, craft crash-developed in the crucible of the Russian front, some of them immense with multiple engines fixed to their wings. It was a sight that could scarce have been dreamed of ten, twenty years before.

Now they began to drop their bombs, big heavy pellets that sailed down through the air. *Slam! Slam!* Even from Abbotsdale the detonations felt heavy, like physical blows, and Frank fancied he saw destruction in those distant Martian pits, fragments of smashed machinery wheeling in the air. He had seen for himself how a decent human weapon, a Navy gun, could down even a fighting-machine.

But the Martians fought back. Frank saw the pale gleam of the Heat-Ray lancing up from the ground, and the fighting-machines turned their armoured heads, even as they marched to the Cordon perimeter. The German bombers were heavy craft and slow to turn; one by one they were caught by the Heat-Ray and erupted into flame, and some exploded spectacularly as their bomb loads detonated in the air.

'Bats, flying into a flamethrower,' Fairfield murmured.

'Yet still they come,' Verity said. 'Still the Germans come! To think, if I hadn't joined the VADs, I could have missed all this!'

Fairfield nodded. 'Well, there'll be plenty of work for you, given the way the Martians are chucking the Heat-Ray around. You'd better get organised, Captain Jenkins. And see if you have any German-speakers to hand, in case we find any air crew.' He glanced east, where the sky was brightening. 'Nothing more we can do for London now.'

23

Our Flight from Stanmore

As the dawn gathered that Wednesday morning, outside their Cordon, the Martians formed up.

In the First War, in striking from Surrey towards central London, they had been observed making a crescent formation, advancing bow first: an arc of armour and firepower whose flanks it would be all but impossible to turn, military analysts had since concluded, and not unlike the Prussians' advance towards Paris in the war of the 1870s.

Now again they formed a crescent as they came out of the Cordon, with its prow pushing along the Western Avenue over the ruins of Uxbridge, its arcs reaching back beyond West Drayton to the south and towards Bushey to the north. And this time there was no mere handful of machines; observers counted at least fifty during the course of the day, perhaps a fifth of the entire force that had been landed in the heart of England in this new armada of cylinders.

Thus they advanced. All across a swath of the western suburbs of London the alarms started to sound, and Army units, men and materiel, scrambled to their positions.

And we, my sister-in-law and I, were in Stanmore, to the west of the great improvised barricade that was the King's Line. I could not see the action yet but I could picture it: to the west of us the Martians, to the east of us the British defence line, and we two between them – caught in a closing trap!

Alice had indeed returned from Buxton, where she would have been safe, for now, but her instinct was to come home. Since my own return on the Tuesday, I had made what preparations I could for our evacuation. I was determined that we would use our bicycles first, so that we could flee as fast as possible – but that laid a constraint on how much we could carry. I had kept my rucksack packed, and with every means of persuasion short of physical force I had induced Alice to compress her essentials into a single suitcase – she would have used more space for family jewellery and photographs of George than for underwear, which tells you all you need to know of her priorities. And she would chatter on about her spa holiday – who had said what to whom. That had taken all evening, until it had been too late to leave on the Tuesday night, and I had watched with envy and a kind of shame as the neighbours had one by one slipped away, a few in motor-cars somehow not requisitioned by the government, the rest on foot.

And all that day, as best I could, I followed the news of the Martians' attacks on their targets around the country: fast, precise, evidently ruthlessly planned.

On the Wednesday, we woke from a restless sleep to the sound of church bells and sirens, and police lorries with loudhailers urging those remaining to hide in cellars or to flee. As I learned that the Martians were moving this day on London, I felt profound regret that I had not succeeded in getting us away earlier – and a deepening fear that whatever we did now would be too late.

Even so I had to shake my sister-in-law out of her bed. 'George would not want us to run like rabbits,' she said, as I argued with her over the necessity of brushing her hair.

'We should go north,' I said, thinking fast. 'If we can get to the Midlands towns there may be trains, to the Lakes, to Scotland even—'

'George and I – this was our home, his library is still here, his surgical tools.'

'George is thirteen years dead! It's up to us now, Alice. We must save ourselves, for George can't.'

'France.'

'What?'

'Not Scotland. France. George had a patient there, a man from Nantes, came to England for treatment. He wrote to me after '07, and said that if the Martians should come again to England we should go back to France – to him.'

'France, again...' Even then it occurred to me that there was no reason to believe the Martians would spare France, any more than they had England, not this time. Where was safe? And even to get to France we would need to reach the south coast.

To cross London! 'Alice, the city's going to be a boiling ant-hill today. We cannot—'

'We must,' she said. 'Or I won't go anywhere.'

And that was the compromise we came to; I could not shift her. We would flee, yes, but only by plunging into the capital on this day of turmoil.

We left the house at last, with the sun rising on a pointlessly clear and fine spring day – the last day of March. The house was near the station, and I remember those big beautiful villas all shut up, their owners long gone, their windows blank rectangles with the curtains closed and the low sunlight glinting. Alice told me that some of the residents had boasted of burying hoards of coin or jewellery, like Saxons before the Vikings.

Thus began our flight. At my insistence we cut north at first, for I knew that the King's Line did not extend far north of Edgware, and at its terminus we might be allowed to pass, and then turn south.

And meanwhile, to the south-west of us, the Martian front was approaching the King's Line.

24

On the King's Line

When the Martians had imposed their Cordon in Middlesex and Buckinghamshire, Eric Eden, formally restored for the duration to his rank of Major, had happened to be outside the perimeter, rather than trapped inside, and he and his fellows had been hastily ordered back.

But now Eric found himself once more on the front line of a Martian war.

This time he was in an entrenchment that had been hastily cut across the line of Western Avenue, close to the junction with Hanger Lane, just north of Ealing – a section of the King's Line. He was standing on a fire step, peering over a parapet of sandbags and looking west, the direction from which the Martians would come. His view was impeded by a heavy gas-mask, and he held his rifle in his hands, tipped with bayonet. With the goggles, and with the roar of the guns already opening up behind the lines, he could see and hear very little.

And yet he was confident, for he knew that at this point, where, since the landings, it had been expected any Martian advance on London must first come, human resistance had been made the strongest.

Winston Churchill himself, Secretary of State for War, had patrolled the lines the day before, even as frantic construction works had proceeded. It was said that he had been the most senior figure in the government to stay in the city, and had done much to organise its defences. Forty-five years old, tall, bold, more soldierly than ministerial, he had stood on the trench parapet, fists on hips, mud on his shoes, and pronounced, 'Break them here, men, break through their thin crust, and we'll break them everywhere. For there aren't so many of them. And if you should go down into the sleep of the just, *take one with you*. Hundreds of them, millions of us: we cannot help but prevail!' That had won him cheers aplenty. He was a man to lead you to triumph or disaster, but at least to *lead*.

And Eric knew that there was cause for optimism beyond Churchill's public words. Because of his own special experiences, Eric was among a privileged few to have been told that a little further behind this line, should it be breached, along with more artillery and machine-gun nests and troops, there was a most secret weapon.

At last the time came for all these hasty plans to be put into operation.

It had still been early morning when the guns started firing.

It began with an artillery barrage launched from deep behind the lines. The heaviest weapons of all were some miles back – some were Navy guns, dismounted and transported on lorries and railway carriages. Their shells flew over the King's Line, over the manned trenches, and pounded the ground ahead, to the west, like tremendous footfalls.

Eric, cautiously poking his head over the parapet of his trench, could see the shells falling, and the sprays of dirt rising from the shattered ground, the fires starting in abandoned properties, and the scraps of forest and parks and common churned up and ablaze. He knew the plan: there would be a 'creeping barrage', as the great guns were tilted up, and the lines of shell-fall worked steadily back over the ground, as if to clear it. The Martians were not immune to shell-fire, as was well known from the First War. The plan was that the bombardment would do most of the work; the great fighting-machines would be smashed and toppled, and then it would be the turn of the troops to rush ahead with automatic weapons and rifles, to pick off individual Martians as they tumbled from their broken craft.

Even as the shells fell, Eric looked around, to left and right. The trench line twisted and turned out of his sight line; it was built in a zigzag scrawl so that the blast of a detonation could not spread far along its length, a lesson the British had picked up from the Boer resistance fighters in South Africa. Everywhere men were lined up, on the firing steps and on the duckboards behind, ready to go over the parapet, and spotters peered through binoculars into the wall of smoke and flame. This was a war machine, he realised, the entire

112

set-up, a unified system of men and machines and earthworks dedicated to a single purpose – planned and set up in mere days.

And now, at last, the cries started up.

'There!' 'And there!' 'Yes, yes, I see – all along the front – here they come!' There was a stir along the line, the men on the fire steps pointing. Eric wiped mud from his goggles and peered hard into the swirling smoke.

He saw them come for himself, the triple narrow legs spinning and flexing, the great feet falling to the ground, and the knot of equipment above – the cowl, the dangling metallic tentacles – with, somewhere within each machine, a living Martian. They seemed to coalesce from the smoke itself, as if emerging from a dream, and they came in great lines, a leading rank with more visible behind. Even at first glance the Martians loomed over the human works, giants in the mist. They made no sound that Eric could detect – there was only the clamour of the guns still firing.

And the fighting-machines were responding to the artillery barrage. Eric saw how, even as the machines walked forward with that peculiar bowling gait, their bronze cowls turned and twisted, and their agile appendages aimed Heat-Ray projectors this way and that, with dazzling speed. And one by one shells that had travelled miles from their guns popped in the air, breaking into harmless shrapnel above their targets.

But the spotting was not perfect; even the Martians were mortal. A big round smashed one Martian square in the 'face'. A great howl went up from the trenches, and Eric saw fists waved. The fighting-machine staggered, its hood now a tangle of twisted metal and crimson – perhaps the splash of Martian blood. The balance was lost, the controlling intelligence gone, and it staggered and fell, knocking against one of its fellows, and the two of them began a stiff-legged tumble to the ground, like great trees falling.

'Two!' cried a young private close to Eric, his face hidden by his mask. 'Two!' He stood up, waving a gloved fist.

'Down, you fool!' Eric grabbed him by the scruff and dragged him below the parapet.

And when the Martian hit the ground there was a detonation as if a fifty-pound shell had landed not many yards away, and Eric, huddling, felt a surge of intense heat. There were screams, now, as men not in shelter were struck by this fiery pulse.

When he dared glance over the parapet again, Eric witnessed one of those remarkable instances of mutual co-operation and aid among the Martians which had struck observers during the

First War. Even while the artillery barrage continued, even while men behind the trenches brought up field guns and howitzers for some close-in turkey-shooting, other Martians broke off their advance. Some leaned over the wounded, making a kind of tent over the fallen ones, even as they continued to shoot the shells out of the sky. They were so close to the line that Eric could hear the rattle of shrapnel harmlessly hitting their hulls. And meanwhile others bent over the fallen, and with extensions of their long metallic tentacles began to drag the wounded machines back from the line of fighting. If precedent was followed, Eric knew, the fallen Martians and their machines would be taken all the way back to their pits inside the Cordon.

But all this was a sideshow, Eric saw. The guns started to fall silent now; the artillery curtain could not be drawn further back without the shells landing on the British lines themselves. Most of the Martian line came on unscathed.

So the barrage had failed. Eric heard the men around him muttering their dismay and fear, and he felt his own tension rise as those great feet steadily approached the trench system. Still the troops held their position, or most of them, with a rattle of automatic fire, even snipers' bullets pinging harmlessly off the legs of the giant machines.

But soon the Martians were free to target the ground positions almost at their feet. The fighting-machines raked their beams the length of the trenches, systematic and calm, as a farmer might sluice out a drainage ditch with a jet of water. Eric had to watch men not many yards away from him caught in the beam and erupting into flame.

Eric himself held his ground, waiting for the lash of the Heat-Ray on his own back – but when at last the whistles blew and the bugle sounded, and the NCOs began to yell 'Fall back! Fall back!', he did not hesitate to follow.

The over-eager young man whom Eric had already saved once jogged alongside him after they had scrambled back out of the trench. 'Next stop Shepherd's Bush,' he said. 'That's where we'll stop 'em.'

Eric, who knew more than most, said through his mask, 'Maybe we will, Tom. Maybe we will.'

And where the Army retreated, so perforce did what was left of the civilian population.

25

How the Retreat Began

That dreadful morning I and my sister-in-law had ridden our bicycles as far as we could, my sister with her suitcase slung over her shoulder with a bit of rope. Then when the roads got too busy we abandoned the cycles and trekked, making south-east, heading steadily for central London.

We passed down the Edgware Road, through Colindale and West Hendon and Cricklewood. We had to fight our way – often literally – through a wash of refugees heading generally east-ward, rather than south as we were. There were some grand folk who even now insisted on carrying valuables, either in carts or wheelbarrows or even on the backs of servants, and some more pathetic types, such as a middle-aged woman I saw struggling to push another lady, much older, jaw sagging, in a bath chair, a mother or an aunt perhaps. I would have stopped to help but Alice hurried me on, and perhaps it's as well she did. And just behind this froth of civilians came defeated military: ambulances and lorries and omnibuses carrying the wounded, and a few units dishevelled but apparently unwounded, some walking in forma-tion but others more or less running, their discipline already gone.

We had some difficulty, then, and lost a good deal of time, before we reached town.

From Paddington we hurried through the densely packed streets south of the Marylebone Road until we reached Marble Arch. Here there seemed some semblance of civil order still, though there was a thickening flood of refugees coming down the Bayswater Road from the west and into Oxford Street. Specials and a couple of regular police were on duty at the Arch, and in Hyde Park the camps that had been set up for the soldiers were open to the newly displaced, and signs promised tea, water, food, rest, medical care.

Alice was unduly impressed. 'Oh! The spirit of London – the great city is not done yet. Can we not stop for a while, Julie? We have walked so far already today. A cup of tea would be a tonic!'

But I heard gunfire coming from the west, and thought I smelled burning. 'We may have little time,' I replied. 'Come, stick to the plan. We must press on.' So I urged her away from the park, and won the day by sheer persistence.

It is just as well that I did, for I think that by that hour – it was mid-morning – the Martians were already at Wormwood Scrubs.

26

The Martians at Wormwood Scrubs

In the last stretch of the retreat down Western Avenue, the order came filtering down to try to slow the Martians' advance before they reached the Scrubs. Eric knew something of what was at stake. He passed on the new orders; he turned and pushed back himself, shouting, arms waving, ordering the men to hold.

But the Martians came again, advancing out of the west from under a lurid, smoke-laden sky, standing over rows of houses, the cowls casually turning to and fro, each lick of heat causing houses and vehicles and people to burst enthusiastically into flame. Now they were so close that Eric seemed to see every detail of the Martians' construction clearly, even the chains of metallic rings that comprised their supple tentacular upper limbs, and he felt again a shudder of horror, an echo of those long hours when he had been trapped in the cylinder on Horsell Common.

And yet he walked towards this army of monsters even so, as did the men around him, firing rifles, hurling grenades. One man commandeered an empty ambulance and drove it into the whirling legs of a fighting-machine; the Martian stumbled but did not fall, and then kicked the ambulance across the road as a boy might kick a can, and moved on. A few seconds' delay of a single machine's advance, bought at the cost of a man's life.

When the Martians at last drove into the tangle of streets just south of the green spaces of the Scrubs itself, a bugle sounded, calling a general retreat. Eric waved to his men. 'Fall back! Fall back!'

But even as the retreat began, glancing to his right Eric saw the walls of the prison – a gaol hastily commandeered by the order of Churchill as the King's Line was established in the last hours and days – and he saw great doors opening. A group of lorries towing flat-bed trailers burst from the gates. On the back of each truck were devices covered in tarpaulins, and men and women in protective suits. Careless of the troops who scrambled to get out of the way, these vehicles lined up, taking positions that roughly blocked the road before the Martian advance. As soon as the lorries were stopped, their drivers dived out of their cabins and ran back to the protection of the prison. The tarpaulins were whisked away – and Eric saw the men around him goggle.

For, arrayed on the back of each truck, were Heat-Ray cameras. Old now, battered, some visibly patched, these weapons had been retrieved from the wreckage of the earlier Martian expedition and put into store. At great risk, and considerable loss of life – as Eric, drafted in as a relative expert on Martian technology, had witnessed for himself – human engineers had discovered how to operate them.

Now brave souls standing on the trailers swivelled the generators on the big mounts to which they had been attached. They looked like searchlights, Eric thought. And one by one they were turned towards the advancing Martians.

At the last moment Eric threw himself over a low wall and out of the way.

The Martians slowed. It seemed to Eric that the lead machines, or their occupants, looked down at the humans, their crude vehicles, and the purloined Heat-Ray cameras, as if curious.

And then –

Nothing! Eric could see the operators frantically working the controls rigged up to the Heat-Ray projectors, controls that no longer did their bidding.

After that brief hesitation, the Martians resumed their advance in complete safety.

In a flash Eric thought he saw why this ploy – Churchill's secret weapon – had not worked, and it occurred to him that he should have anticipated it before. But if he had warned his superiors, would he have been believed?

For all Walter Jenkins's boasting, he, Eric, was probably the man who had seen the Martians closer than anybody else, for he had spent long days cooped up in the Horsell cylinder. And he had seen the Martians work together, and with their technologies. Like Jenkins he had come to believe that the Martians communicated through a semblance of telepathy, though in his view this was more likely to have been achieved through some subtle technology with equivalent function. We know that the Martians have achieved a union of the biological and the mechanical, externally at least: their great machines are like suits they don for specific purposes. If that's so outside their bodies, why not within too?

And if a Martian mind can talk direct to another Martian mind, why not to a Martian machine?

The Heat-Ray generators would not fire, it seemed, not if there was a Martian in their sights. It was an obvious precaution.

'Undone by a safety catch!' Eric muttered to himself, behind his wall.

But the day was not yet lost, he thought. For in his visits to the laboratories where the Heat-Ray engines had been studied, he had seen other ways in which the generators could be destructive. There was still time; the Martians had not yet reached the line of the lorries with their projectors.

Gathering his courage, Eric dumped his rifle and scrambled over the wall. As the position broke down people were already fleeing before the feet of the advancing Martians. But Eric did not flee. He ran straight for the nearest abandoned trailer, and scrambled aboard.

The Heat-Ray generators were heavy, and it took him precious seconds to turn them – but at last he had one generator barrel pointing into the mouth of another, both of them turned away from the Martians. The human-built control box was simple – and, he saw with relief, it had a timer mechanism. He says he would have stood his ground and followed through his plan even without that stroke of luck, and I believe him, but he much preferred to inflict some damage and keep his own life in the process. With the Martians closing on his position, he set the timer for thirty seconds.

Then he scrambled off the trailer and, ducking, running, rolling, made for the cover of another wall, low but stout.

He saw what came next.

Ignoring Eric, if they saw him at all, the Martians made for the two Heat-Ray generators he had pushed together. As always in such cases, the Martians were more interested in retrieving their own technology than in the antics of humanity. Two machines leaned over the assemblage, as Eric watched, and he counted down the second hand on his wristwatch: 'Four – three – two – one—'

His thinking had been simple. A camera would not fire on

119

a Martian, but, perhaps, *it would fire on another camera*. So Eric hoped.

And so it proved. When one of the two Heat-Rays was triggered, it fired at point-blank range into the carcass of the other, injecting lethal energies, sublimating the hull, liquefying the many mysterious parts of the camera, perhaps shattering the arrays of crystals and mirrors within – and, at last, destroying the casing of the mysterious power generator, that featureless sphere no larger than a cricket ball which, experts like Einstein and Soddy had argued, must somehow harness the energies of the atom.

Nuclear energies suddenly released, in a London street. Even amid the ongoing battles, the detonation was heard all over London. Two fighting-machines were smashed, broken to smithereens which wheeled through the air. Three others were damaged, two enough to disable them.

Much of what occurred during the early days of the Second War was to remain classified as secret; it was many years before I learned from Eric himself (in an airship sailing over the Arctic wastes, as I shall relate in its proper place) what he had done that day. It was the act of a *franc-tireur*, people would say, yet in that act Eric Eden inflicted more damage on the Martians than they suffered in any other single incident that day. He himself was badly burned, but survived.

But he did not stop the Martian advance.

Once the wreckage of their fallen had been cleared away and sent back to the Middlesex pits, the remaining fighting-machines, still more than forty of them, resumed their march into London. Now, with the King's Line breached and the Army's last attempt at a surprise attack foiled, there was nothing and nobody to stand in their way.

27

A Flight Across Central London

My sister-in-law and I had continued to flee.

From Marble Arch we pushed our way down Oxford Street and Regent Street to Piccadilly Circus and the Strand, and then to the Embankment, myself urging my sister-in-law along – or sometimes vice versa, for it had already been a long day of flight and terror for both of us. Of detail I can remember little. By then the streets seemed full of people rushing hither and thither, but all heading away from the Martian advance. It was like a tide receding across a stony shore, perhaps, the detail chaotic and unpredictable, the general drift evident. And there were so *many* people – for even if London had already been drained of millions in those few days, millions more remained. The river too was crowded with shipping, boats and yachts and even barges heading steadily downstream, although a few Navy boats struggled in the other direction.

And meanwhile the Martians were coming. The western sky, livid red since before dawn, was stained by smoke and flame, a sullen glow that seemed to be advancing closer. Already, looking that way, you could glimpse a Martian here or there, that terrible machine walking above the houses and offices and shops, like a man wading across a coral reef.

As for ourselves, we still had our basic purpose in mind: to head south and east, to get to the coast – to flee to the continent, as we had the last time the Martians came. But how were we to cross the river? The bridges were crammed with people, and I thought we would have to fight our way through.

But my sister-in-law came into her own. Suddenly she took the lead, hurrying me along the river, heading east past Temple and Blackfriars, on past the medieval heap of the Tower – which still bore the scars of Heat-Ray licks from the '07 War – and then through the wharves and warehouses of Wapping.

And there she brought me, bemused, to the mouth of the road tunnel to Rotherhithe.

We found our way blockaded by burly men, dockyard workers, who had piled up scrap in the road entrance, and thrown barriers across the spiral stairs meant for pedestrians. One man, arms folded, stepped in front of us. 'Tunnel's closed.'

'Is it?' Alice asked, breathing hard, sweating, somewhat dishevelled, weighed down by her suitcase, but determined.

'Ain't choo 'eard? Martians in town.'

'But our intention is merely to pass through. If you would stand aside—'

'Local folk on'y. No toffs.'

I closed my eyes, wondering if it would be class war that killed me.

But Alice was unperturbed. 'Is Fred Sampson here?'

''Oo?'

'I'm sure you know him. The local union organiser. Fred and his wife Poppy, and their children—'

''Oo wants him?'

'If you would kindly tell him that Mrs Elphinstone is here – Alice Elphinstone – he might remember me as "the Fabian lady" . . .'

When the message was transmitted, to my astonishment, Fred Sampson did indeed remember his 'Fabian lady'.

For some years, I now learned, and since the deprivation under Marvin had begun to bite, Alice and others of her Fabian Women's Group had been coming to Limehouse, Wapping and other dockyard areas to alleviate the plight of the working poor. Alice herself, with her medical connections through her deceased husband, had brought aid to Fred's own smallest child, an asthmatic whose lungs did not prosper well in the riverside district's damp, smoke-laden air.

As we waited at the barrier I frankly stared at Alice, as if at a stranger. 'The "Fabian lady"? I thought they were banned.'

'Not banned. Frowned upon, compromised – yes. I joined anyhow. One thing led to another, and here we are.' She looked at me coldly. 'I know you think I'm weak and foolish. That is how your brother-in-law portrayed me in his *Narrative* – a cruel sketch. And with George gone, after the war – and I admit I took it badly – that is how people perceived me.'

'That is the way you behave!'

'Are human beings only *one thing*? Yes, I was terrified that day of flight, scared out of my wits, but that isn't *me*. And I don't care to explain myself to the likes of you – despite your bullying, Julie, for that's what it is, even if I've had cause to come to appreciate your help in the years since. Let's leave it at that, shall we?'

So there you had it, an astounding personal revelation on that most astounding of days. I sometimes wonder if there was anybody Walter mentioned in his wretched *Narrative* who had *not* come away mortally offended.

Anyhow we were ushered, as polite as you please, into a road tunnel that had become, in the hours and days since the Martian landings, a shelter – a veritable town under the city, with food, latrines, a water supply – even electric lights working off a small generator. We had meant to go on, but discretion proved the better part of valour. Exhausted, bedraggled, there we stayed, safe and snug, at least for a time.

It was only later that I learned how the Martians completed the work of that terrible day.

28

The Fall of London

The Martian vanguard, before which Eric Eden's unit retreated, had proceeded along Western Avenue, on through White City and Bayswater until they came to Regent's Park, and then had crossed the park, to Primrose Hill.

As everybody knows, it was on the Hill that the Martians of 1907 had begun the building of their largest single excavation, a vast pit that had crawled with their handling-machines and excavators, before the plagues killed them all. And here too had been left a single, inert fighting-machine as a symbol of that defeat – inert, or so we believed. I had thought I saw the thing twitch, in those last days before the Martians returned to earth – *and now witnesses saw it move again*, turning its cowled head, defanged as it had been by the loss of its Heat-Ray camera, and trying to lift legs that had been set in a concrete plinth. Truly it can be said that Martian machinery has the quality of life, even loyalty to its masters.

And now, on the last day of March 1920, about twenty fighting-machines stood tall on Primrose Hill, from where they were visible from afar across the city – and of course, since the Heat-Ray was a line-of-sight weapon with a range of miles, anywhere the Martians could be seen was vulnerable to the fire. Meanwhile the rest of the machines, another twenty or so, fanned out in twos and threes towards specific targets.

Targets, yes: that was to be the game for the rest of that day, and into the night. With human resistance already vanquished, the machines turned on the greatest city in the world. And this time the damage was not random and haphazard, as it had seemed to be when that first war-party had ventured from Surrey into the city in '07. Now they had intelligence from that first expedition;

now they had the recent scouting of their flying-machine. This time the destruction was deliberate and purposeful.

Beams aimed by the raiding parties stalking across the city, or delivered direct from Primrose Hill, destroyed our transport links, beginning with the great rail termini: Euston, King's Cross, Charing Cross, London Bridge, Waterloo, Victoria, Paddington, all of them. Our war-making abilities were smashed, too; Chatham and Woolwich Arsenal were already wrecked from the fighting-machines' strikes of the day before, and now the explosives factory at Silvertown was targeted, going up with a glow like a sunrise – it created a bang that was heard in France. Many of our great buildings and show centres were cut down, including Olympia and White City and even the Crystal Palace.

The symbols of our power too were wrecked: the headquarters of the British military at Horse Guards, Whitehall, our seat of government in the ugly new block at Westminster, which did not withstand the Heat-Ray any better than its elegant predecessor had. At the Bank too, the heart of the world's financial system was cut up. How much of the purpose of these buildings was understood by the Martians on the day has since been a matter of debate – what would a Martian know of stocks and shares? For myself I believe that save for sites with obvious functions like the Woolwich munitions factory, the Martians judged the significance of a site on the grandeur of the buildings, and the density of human activity they had seen around them; they did not need to understand a specific purpose to assess a target's importance to us.

It went on all day.

With much of London already ablaze, the targets became less prominent: the gasometers were blasted, the cathedrals broken – St Paul's demolished at last – the Albert Hall stove in, and it was as if the Martians used the spires of the Wren churches for target practice. Even Bart's hospital was smashed, it turned out. And there was casual massacre: the refugee boats on the river washed with fire, the crowds on the bridges incinerated, before the bridges themselves were cut, one by one.

The Martians did not have it all their own way. Gun emplace-ments still operated across the city – some of them, I learned later, having been set up years earlier in anticipation of a possible air war with Germany. And, I would learn, capital ships had come up the river as far as Greenwich – any further and there would be a fear of grounding – and had fired their own huge guns into the carcass of the city, seeking Martians. One or two shots hit home; the machines on the Hill were particularly vulnerable, and one fell. But each aggressor was eventually silenced by the Heat-Ray. And besides, it seems that more harm was being done to the city itself, and no doubt its inhabitants, by the almost random landing of the shells; it must have taken a stern heart to order Navy guns to fire into the centre of London.

Rather more damage was wrought, in the event, by aircraft. Towards evening, from out of the darkening sky – and as imagined in a thousand lurid coming-war fictions – German Zeppelins approached London, not in enmity but in solidarity. Flying from occupied airfields in France, this stately flotilla was led by Heinrich Mathy in his L.31, the 'Super Zeppelin' – Mathy, the German hero of daring raids on Paris during the worst of the fighting there. The Zeppelins came in high, and got their bombs away, and did some damage; a couple more fighting-machines on the Hill were toppled like nine-pins, and one got a three-hundred-pounder in the cowl which knocked him out of the game. Also there were British craft in the air: RFC Be.2cs flying out of their bases at Hounslow and Romford, buzzing like hornets around the great carcasses of the Zepps.

But it was not long before the Martians responded. With their swivelling hoods, their manipulator arms directing the Heat-Ray cannons, they were able to mount an anti-aircraft response much more effective than any human force could have managed: they shot down the planes as easily as they had swatted artillery shells from the sky. One beam caught Mathy's own ship as she tried to turn. The airship flashed to flame, and to the horror of those Londoners watching the show, it took the craft three or four minutes to drift to the ground, a grisly lantern. One could only think, I was told, of Mathy and his crew, roasting slowly in the sky.

I can record one more bit of heroism. Battling through the invisible lanes of the Heat-Rays, while its fellows burned and fell all around, one of our planes, a feeble Be.2c biplane, *kept on going*, making for that nest of monsters on Primrose Hill. It hurtled at one cowled beast as if to ram that bronze carapace, and it fired off a round of incendiary bullets before the Heat-Ray, inevitably, smashed it and its pilot to atoms. But those bullets got through, one evidently penetrated some break in that cowl, and the head of that machine blossomed in flame. This was seen all over London. I learned later, and record here, that the pilot was Lieutenant William Leefe Robinson of the RFC, twenty-five years old.

That, at any rate, was the end of resistance from the air – and indeed of any organised resistance at all. But the slaughter and destruction continued for hours more.

After the War I returned to the Strand, and saw the detailed destruction inflicted there by the passage of a single fighting-machine. The Martian had inflicted a sequence of blasts, the first at Exeter Street, just off the Strand, which caused damage to the Gaiety Theatre; the next close to the Strand Theatre at Catherine Street; the third and fourth in Aldwych; and then the Martian veered north, striking at the area between Aldwych and New Inn, and then the Royal Courts of Justice and Carey Street. Lincoln's Inn Chapel, four centuries old, was demolished. If you visit the site today you can still see the traces of that Martian's few minutes of passage, decades later. All that from a single pass by a single machine. Imagine such damage repeated and magnified across the city! But even so you cannot imagine the night itself, the screaming and fleeing people, the gas mains flaring, broken water mains gushing, the chaos and the noise and the light.

The people . . .

When I write or speak of those times, I am never more like Walter Jenkins in the telling. Walter, who saw a mob, not a group of terrified individuals; Walter, who clung to the *idea* of people above the actuality. In that way perhaps you could say that even his wife had to compete with a kind of ideal of herself for room in Walter's imagination. Walter was nothing if not humane; but I think he had trouble perceiving the human. But there are times when I sympathise; when writing of wholesale and purposeful destruction it is easier to list grand buildings lost, than to look at human suffering square in the face.

What of the people of London, that day and night, as the monuments of their city exploded around them? In fact, for all its faults, Marvin's government had striven to learn the lessons of the First War, and had implemented its plans competently enough. So when evacuation became inevitable there were planned escape strategies, and even refuges for the evacuees; in the poorer districts there were shelters and hiding places, in basements, the underground stations, even the sewers. Londoners fled or hid more or less according to the plan, and though the loss of life and the casualty numbers were great, the human disaster was not overwhelming. Most Londoners would survive that night, to face an uncertain future.

But I did not know this at the time; in my own shelter I could only huddle and wait.

In one extraordinary final touch, I would learn, a fighting-machine came to the museum district of South Kensington. At the Natural History Museum, the roof was cut open by a careful slice of the Heat-Ray, and the pickled specimen of a Martian in the entrance hall, that grisly souvenir of the First War, was retrieved and carried away to the Middlesex pits. A long-standing duty had been fulfilled.

And as the night fell, the Martians on the Hill began to call.

'Ulla! Ulla!'

It was heard across London – we even heard it in our tunnel. And if some self-proclaimed expert tells you that Martians are disembodied creatures of brain without emotion, let him listen to the recordings that were made of those cries, of victory, of vengeance, of exultation.

'Ulla! Ulla!'

We heard it in our tunnel, deep beneath the sheltering Thames, Alice and I, huddling with the families of the dockyard workers, and we prayed for it to end.

'Ulla! Ulla!'

BOOK II
England Under the Martians

1

I Receive a Call in Paris

I was summoned to Berlin, to visit my estranged brother-in-law Walter Jenkins.

It was the beginning of May 1922 – with the Martian boot having been planted firmly on the neck of England for over two years, and with all of educated mankind, I suspect, looking fearfully at the skies, where Mars was swimming towards its next opposition in June.

Summoned? Is that the correct word? *Persuaded to go*, perhaps, by Major Eric Eden. But it had begun with Walter himself, who had written to me from Berlin, asking for help in a scheme he had come up with to 'deal with the Martian canker in England'. All Walter's mail was routinely scrutinised by his doctors and the military people in Germany and England, and so this came to Eric's attention. And he, perhaps surprisingly, saw some merit in Walter's plan – whatever it was being kept a secret from me for now.

It was my *duty* to see Walter! So even Alice told me, she who had hardly been out of our apartment in Bagnolet since we had arrived in Paris.

If the reader has stuck with my account thus far, then you will know I am not one to take kindly to pressure from overbearing men, with which my world has always been too well stocked. I took my time over whether to accept the commission – indeed I slept on it, through a still, unnaturally warm Parisian spring night. Yet I was still undecided when I woke to my morning view of the ruin of the Eiffel Tower, smashed by German shells eight years before.

In the end I went back to Walter's letter, and I concentrated on his own words, directed to me personally. 'Please come ... Just as two years ago, of all my extended "family" it is only you, Julie, whom I feel comfortable in contacting at this time. Of course my choice is somewhat limited since my brother, your former husband, is lost behind the Martian Cordon...' Which put me in my place!

Still, I had the resources to respond, and was without burdens. My sister-in-law Alice had slotted easily enough into the gloomy culture of a defeated Paris, and had even found worthwhile work aiding the poor of that occupied city; short of a cross-Channel invasion by the Martians she could last without me for a while. As for my own work, I was making a respectable if precarious living as a correspondent for the New York papers, with the help of much mediation from Harry Kane. I was no war reporter, but Harry said that my accounts of aspects of life in an occupied city, on everything from clumsy German policing to the Parisians' desperate attempts at fashion and art, held a certain audience in Manhattan and Queens and New Jersey in grim fascination. But it was an eminently interruptible career, and, who knew? Perhaps I could get good material out of this fresh adventure.

You will have guessed, by the by, that I saw little chance of my actually being involved in any successful scheme to beat the beastly Martians.

I determined to respond to Walter's request. Not long after breakfast I was packing my rucksack, and hunting for my Baedeker, and telephoning the railway companies for a ticket to Berlin. And I called a number Eric had given me, of an agent in Berlin who, I was assured, would arrange hotel accommodation for me.

When my taxi-cab called Alice was barely awake, her hair tousled, her dressing gown tied tight. But we said our farewells cordially enough – she approved of my trip – before the cab drove smoothly away.

Of course if I had known then the truth of my mission – or rather the great *Lie*, as I came to think of it – I would probably have stayed in bed.

2

A Meeting in Berlin

The brand-new German-built rail connection from Paris to Berlin, from the capital of a conquered nation to that of the conqueror, was direct but not terribly fast. So it was not until early the next morning that I completed my journey of six hundred miles or so, and debarked at the grand new Alfred von Schlieffen station in the west of Berlin, named, provocatively, after the mastermind of the recent European war.

I took another taxi-cab to my hotel. The cab was as scrupulously clean as the roads we travelled. And whereas my driver in Paris had been a slovenly fellow in a soft hat and disreputable jacket, who had been rather too attentive as I had climbed in and out of his vehicle, my driver in Berlin was a woman, young, smart, with efficient hair under a peaked cap. Her conversation was a comment on the weather and a query as to whether this was my first visit to Berlin, all delivered in clipped, rather monotonic English. I half-expected her to swivel round and offer me a game of chess, like the mechanical Turk of legend.

At my hotel, another uniformed figure was eager to greet me as soon as I set foot on the pavement, and almost wrested my rucksack out of my hands. I quickly learned that the British consul, who had arranged this domicile for me, had not spared the pennies: my hotel was the Adlon, which has the prestigious address of No. 1, Unter den Linden.

Restless after my travelling and having slept well enough on the train, I quickly took possession of my room, showered and changed, and went straight back out into the Berlin morning. I knew that Walter was waiting to see me, but I could not resist the briefest of tours.

So I strolled along the Unter den Linden, joined the crowds in the Potsdamerplatz, walked up the Leipzigerstrasse, and allowed myself the briefest of ventures into the Wertheim, a vast department store into which, it seemed to me, you could have crammed most of Oxford Street, if that broadway had been cut up and stacked on two or three levels. It was a Friday, a working day, but the crowds, affluent, noisy, and spending freely, swarmed with a kind of springtime gaiety, I thought. And there were uniforms to be seen everywhere, from the foremen and lift attendants in the Wertheim to the military costumes of many nations – including the sombre khaki tunic and flat cap of the modern British officer, a sensible ensemble and shade that stood out amid the more gaudy colours and spiked helmets of the continentals.

And among the soldier types, even here in the rich, modern, electrified heart of Berlin, I saw wounded – mostly men but not exclusively – in smart uniforms but with bandaged faces or arms, some in bath chairs, some with limbs plucked away. They made a brave sight, as such veterans always do. The war the Germans had started in 1914 continued still, despite the presence of Martians on the earth only a few hundred miles away, and had become a great grinding of flesh in the east, as the Germans pushed ever deeper into the tottering Russian empire. Or so it was said; little news was released to the public. The missing eyes and limbs of these Berlin veterans were, however, like mute reports from that remote battlefield.

It was not yet lunch time when I dragged myself away from these spectacles and summoned another cab, which would take me to my meeting with Walter.

Driving east, we soon left behind the city's historic core, or what passes in Berlin for such, and crossed into a more modern realm, of sprawling suburbs studded by immense factories. I glimpsed railways and rectilinear canals; it was almost Martian – no wonder Walter had been drawn here!

The address Walter had given me turned out not to be an apartment, as I had expected, but a street corner opposite a factory, a tremendous structure buttressed by brick pillars and fronted by glass, all under a curving roof; the building dwarfed the handful of trees that adorned the pavement before it, and the people who came and went through its doors.

And its scale overwhelmed the man who sat on a bench on the far side of the road, wrapped in an over-large overcoat, sketching busily. This was Walter, of course.

Having paid off the cabbie, I approached him tentatively. As I sat beside him he leaned towards me, but that was as much as I got in terms of signs of recognition or affection. He continued his impulsive sketching in bold black charcoal, but I could not make out the subject.

At length he closed the book and turned to me.

He was fifty-six years old now. In some ways he had not changed: still the unkempt mass of hair, once red from his Welsh ancestry, so his brother, my husband, had told me, but grey as steel since his experience of the First Martian War; and that peculiarly large skull, the broad brow from beneath which blue eyes peered. He wore white gloves to protect his scarred hands. His face, under a heavy layer of some medicinal cream, was immobile of expression. His eyes were odd as he looked at me, with a strange brightness, an alertness – the eyes of a hunted animal.

'Julie. It was good of you to come all this way.' His voice had been left gravelly from the inhalation of smoke.

I cautiously touched one damaged hand. 'I'm glad to see you too, Walter. But I don't yet know—'

He said, bluntly, 'I need you to go to England, you see. To fulfil my scheme. I mean, into the Cordon, the Martian zone.'

My breath caught in my throat. That was Walter for you, either a fog of prevarication or as direct as a knife in the gut.

'They all know about it, of course. Eric. All the way up to Churchill, I'm told. Seem to think it a good idea, somewhat to my surprise.' He studied me. 'Does all this come as a shock?'

'I – don't know. Perhaps I anticipated this on some level: a warning from the subconscious, as your friend Freud would probably say. Given all the trouble they went to – the Ministry of War isn't going to put me up on the Unter den Linden for nothing, is it?'

He laughed. 'I don't suppose so. But we do have some choice over our actions. Such as my choice to meet you here.'

'In the open air, before a factory? Just as well it isn't raining,' I said tartly.

He looked at me. 'I never thought of that. The Martians, you know, did not anticipate the rain before they came in '07, as they drew up their plans in their arid utopia in the sky. If you've never seen rain fall, perhaps it is hard to imagine it – and if they'd been unlucky with the weather in '07 a few showers might have laid their Black Smoke before it harmed a soul! Ah – I sometimes think I am half-Martian myself.'

135

'Nonsense,' I said firmly. 'You've been spending too much time alone. Or with the bump-feelers of Vienna, which is nearly as bad.'

He tried to smile. 'As to the palace of industry over there – it is a turbine factory, belonging to Allgemeine Elektrizitäts-Gesellschaft.'

'AEG. I know of them; their shares are popular in New York, especially since the European war kicked off.'

'A magnificent sight, though, isn't it? This whole area, the north-east suburbs, the Fabrikstadt, the factory-city. And to me this is the jewel in the crown. *Modernist*, they call it. Whatever that might mean.'

I got up and walked back and forth to get a better view of the monstrosity. 'It's big enough to be a Zeppelin hangar. But modern? It reminds me of Rome. Some of the great secular buildings: the market-places, even the huge bath-houses.'

He nodded. 'A shrewd comparison. Secular, not religious, not a cathedral as our forefathers built; *this* is the spirit of our age. Certainly it is *new*. As is all of Berlin. Only fifty years ago, a couple of generations, this was nothing but the capital of Prussia; now we are in the capital of *Mitteleuropa*. And speaking of capitals, how is Paris?'

I shrugged. 'Unhappy. There is muttering of strikes, of a new generation of charismatic leaders to drive out the Germans and restore national pride – Communists, perhaps.'

Walter nodded. 'I am sometimes surprised that the modern Germans who built *that* –' the AEG factory '– do not rise up and knock over the pompous princeling and his lascivious, sly son, who presume to govern them as if this were still medieval Prussia.

'But do the Martians see *any* of us as civilised? Oh, they recognise our mechanical prowess, and its danger to them; even in the First War they hit powder stores and the like. But they may see our machines, our cities as the product of a kind of blind reflex; we might ourselves decide to stamp out an ant colony despite its apparent sophistication.

'And they may not see this as a *war* at all. Why, they may not know the meaning of the word. From our new mountaintop eyries the astronomers have scrutinised the Martians as never before, even though the stargazers work under blankets of secrecy. We can see it for ourselves: a planet ordered on a global scale, its scarce resources managed by a unified civilisation, with

136

the geometry of the canal system its finest single expression. Wallace points out that a water shortage need not be a drive for global unity so much as a source of division – he uses the British example in India, where the control of water led to the cementing of social inequality, with the water in the hands of an elite. Perhaps – but I would argue that any such conflict, any war, *must* lie in the deep past of Mars – the geological past!

'My idea now is that the first wave, in '07, were not soldiers at all. They were explorers – even farmers, perhaps. They came to deal with what they had seen as a wild world, a world of insensate animals – and they were armed with nothing more lethal than a farmer's tools. Some have remarked that the Martians have not innovated since the '07 War, as we have – with our aeroplanes, for instance. But of course the Martians would not advance their technology; their society is a million years old, and such devices as the Heat-Ray must have been perfected long ago. Adapt it for terrestrial use, yes, as they have the flying-machine ... But their strategy – surely we should have expected *that* to evolve. And so it has, all unforeseen by the strutting peacocks who rule us. The nonsense of the nineteen hours! How many lives did that bit of complacent foolishness cost?' He glanced into the bright daylight sky. 'And now the planets are swimming into alignment again. Another chance for them to cross that dark gulf.'

'Mm. So what's your big idea, Walter? What am I to do in England?'

'Simple enough. *Speak to the Martians*. We must negotiate, you see. It's the only way.'

That startled me. 'How? And why would they listen?'

'How? With symbols, of course.'

And he hurried on before I could interrogate him over that detail!

'As to why – well, there's at least a *chance* they'll be predisposed to listen. Why do you imagine this party of Martians are here in the first place? The damage they have caused to England, horrific though it may seem to us, is ... incidental. It was intended only to secure their position. And after two years of occupation, they have learned of the ways of our earth – of us. Surely that is why they have come. Why, you only have to see their flying-machine pass by, a great eye over city and field—'

'They are scouts,' I said, seeing it.

'That's it. Gathering information to inform the greater invasions to come. So, you see, this lot at least, sent here to observe

137

us, perhaps even trained to do so, may be predisposed to *listen* to our communications – or at least, to credit us with the capability of communicating.'

He opened his sketchbook now, and began to scribble once more as he spoke. It was a kind of reflex, I thought, as if he had forgotten I was still with him. I had imagined that he was sketching the AEG factory, but rather he was covering page after page with abstract symbols: circles, beautifully drawn, crowded in with wilder, spiral-like patterns.

I guessed, 'So your idea is to parley? But what of the very first night they landed on Horsell Common back in '07 – you were there, Walter – the Astronomer Royal with his white flag—'

'Yes, with poor Ogilvy, and their reward was a dose of the Heat-Ray. But that's not to say it's not worth trying again. Oh, I admit it, to attempt interplanetary communication appeals to the utopian in me. I've been following this chap Wendigee who advocates sending wireless signals to Mars, to parley for peace direct. Churchill supports my scheme, you know – he was given copies of my opened letters. But *he* has always been a man who can see wider possibilities. At the very least we can play for time, he thinks. Thus might a wily Inca have drawn the conquistadors into long negotiations, until the time came to slit a few throats, steal horses and guns and ships, and carry the war back to the monarchs of Spain.'

I rubbed my face. 'Given the way it turned out for the Incas, it might have been worth a try. But why me, Walter? What have I got to do with it?'

'There is a logic. Look – work backwards. We need to open some kind of a dialogue with the Martians; let's take that as a given. Now – according to Eric and others – there's only one man, one human being, deep inside the Cordon, who is at present coming into peaceful contact with the Martians – or at least non-lethal.'

I frowned. 'I'm surprised there's even one. Who?'

'Cook. Albert Cook.'

'Your artilleryman! Why, he's a –' I waved a hand '– a music-hall turn.'

'Never in his own head,' Walter said solemnly. 'And to be fair to him, according to the intelligence, he *has* been able to establish some kind of rapport with the Martian occupiers. Remarkable! As to how he maintains these contacts, and to what purpose, Eric Eden isn't telling me, *if* he knows. Now, Cook won't listen to the military, for they wouldn't listen to him, so *he* believes, when after the war he expounded his theories on how we should prepare for a future rematch. No, it has to be another, a lone, self-motivated survivor as he was. *You*, you see, "Miss Elphin-stone", were one of the few characters I named in my account, the account that made Cook famous, or notorious.'

'And *that's* to be the reason he will speak to me? It sounds a little flimsy. And besides, why not you yourself, Walter?'

'Well, he might be suspicious of me. He does feel I mocked him, traduced him and his theories. Never my intention. And besides—' He raised a scarred hand; it shook.

'Very well. And if, through Cook, I do get close to the Mar-tians—'

He held up his scrawls. 'Show them these.'

This seemed faintly insane, on first hearing. I essayed, cau-tiously, 'These abstract designs—'

'Not abstract. You don't recognise them? More images I find it hard to get out of my mind. Here, the circle – an eternal, perfect figure, and the one we know the Jovians use as their own sigil, lifted in their mighty clouds, plastered over the faces of their moons. The Jovians! – of course they would use the circle, with its lucid perfection, its infinite number of axes of symmetry...'

I had little interest in the Jovians. I pointed to another sketch. 'But this other,' I said. 'I remember now.' It was like a spiral, spread across the page, drawn with the right hand with clockwise loops – like a clock spring pulled out of shape. 'This is the sigil the Martians made, on the surface of their own world, and on Venus—'

'Not *on* Venus,' he said pedantically, 'but in the clouds of Venus, somehow – for the cloud-tops of that young planet are all that we can see of it. But this is not the Venusian sigil; *it is my attempt to capture the mark the Martians had begun to make in Surrey.*'

'What mark? In '07, you mean? You spoke of this before, but I remember no such device.'

'We weren't looking at the time,' he said with that twisted smile. 'What with all the running and the screaming. The design became clearer after it was over, and the battlegrounds could be more carefully mapped. I have a chart here...'

Tucked in the pages of his book, he had folded an ordnance survey map showing London, Surrey, Middlesex, Kent – the region across which the Martians had rampaged. 'Can you see? With these orange flags I show where the Martians came down, starting with Woking down in the south-west, and working up through what is now the Surrey Corridor past Kingston and Wimbledon, and across London to Primrose Hill, and then to Hounslow and Hampton Court and Merrow...' He took his graphite and made a faint swirling line, an open spiral connecting these points. 'Can you see it? We always marvelled at the closeness of the landing sites of the cylinders, after a journey of forty *million* miles. Now, I claim, the accuracy was rather better than that. The landing pits of the cylinders are the anchor points of—'

'A sigil! Like the one on Venus.'

'That's it. I believe if they had had the time they would have finished the figure – how? With earthworks, or canals, or lanes of the red weed perhaps. And then, with the earth wholly conquered, they would have created an even greater form, sprawled across the Sahara perhaps, or the Antarctic ice. A symbol of their victory, visible across interplanetary space!'

I sat back. 'Ah! And this is the "graphic geometry" of the war that you mentioned when you spoke to us in Ottershaw, is it not?'

'Indeed. And when you think on it, that is the one thing that unites us, this interplanetary symbolism: ourselves and the Martians – perhaps the inhabitants of Venus – even the Jovians! Never forget the Jovians, Julie, never forget; before them we are like children squabbling at the feet of a fully armed soldier...'

But, my head full of the Martians, still I was not thinking about the Jovians just then, not listening to what he was trying to tell me (I should have been! I should have been!).

We turned to business. He had prepared a packet of drawings for me, he said – symbols, the interplanetary sigils and certain other geometric forms. He had even brought a light leather satchel for me to carry the drawings! All I had to do was to set these before the Martians, and... Well, it got a little vague after that.

It was hard to refuse him, so fragile was he. And besides, I rather grudgingly thought the plan was worth a shot. (I had yet, of course, to develop any suspicion about the true motives of Eric and those to whom he reported. That disillusionment came later.)

But the effort of discussing all this seemed to exhaust him.

'I do miss it all, you know.'

The non-sequitur caught me off guard. 'You miss what, Walter?'

'My old life, *before*. Sometimes I look out my old work, you

140

know. All foolish conjecturing, of course, but like the residual scent of a dead flower it brings back a mood, a time... My life then, the writers and thinkers with whom I corresponded and clubbed, the editors – the magazines! The *Pall Mall Gazette*, the *National Observer*, the *Saturday Review*. All gone now, and even the archives burned or flooded, I imagine... We never got back the press we had in the old days, did we? All those papers and journals, lustily competing – the governments blame shortages of paper and the like, but the habit of secrecy is a more compelling reason for the silence of the press. I am not a strong man, I know. I remember, I remember – ah, Carolyne! Have you seen her? I do miss her...'

He went on in this manner for some time, in broken sentences now, as if talking to himself, and forgetting I was there. He grasped his charcoal in one withered hand, and drew his sigils and circles over and over, striving for a perfection his damaged body could never deliver. I sat with him, but our conversation was effectively over.

3

A Journey to the Coast

After returning to my hotel I telephoned Eric Eden – who, I had been informed, was in Paris, on some errand of his own. I told him I would undertake his commission. He had been waiting for my response. The arrangements began immediately.

As per Eric's instructions – he was polite but specific and left me in no doubt that I must obey to the letter – I made my own way, the next day, from Berlin to Bremen. I stayed one night in a small hotel, a short walk from the rail station; there, another phone call warned me to be ready for an early start the following day, for the inception of Operation Get Julie Across the Channel.

Early indeed. I was woken before three in the morning by a smart rap on the door. A young officer in khaki and flat cap stood there smiling at me.

'Miss Elphinstone?'

'Guilty as charged.'

He told me I'd be given a lift aboard a long-planned naval convoy, weather conditions and whatnot being favourable – and it was time to go. Despite the hour I was all but dressed, and seeing him standing there in his spruce, carefully ironed uniform, I was glad of it.

'You'd better come in while I finish up.' I collected my boots and overcoat, and the last few items to stuff into the rucksack. I checked one more time that the leather-bound packet of papers Walter had given me was safely tucked away; from now on until I encountered the Martians themselves this packet would never leave my person.

The officer stood just inside the door, hands clasped before his belt-buckle, eyes averted from the particulars of a female's hotel room. 'My name's Ben Gray, by the way – Second Lieutenant for my sins.' Clipped Harrovian tones, not unlike Eric's. Slim, dark, his well-groomed face blandly handsome behind a rather weedy moustache, he might have been twenty-five. 'My regiment—'

'Save the biography; it's all the same to me, Lieutenant.' But it seemed unfair to dislike him, like taking against a puppy.

I was done in a minute. I caught a glimpse of myself in the room's long mirror. I kept my hair cut short, and it was service-able after a finger-brush. With a last glance around, I led him out, closed the door and locked it behind me.

'Leave the key in the lock,' Gray said. 'The manager will take care of that.'

'And the bill—'

'Paid for.' He guided me towards the lift.

'How efficient. Look, Lieutenant Gray, I'm quite capable of putting myself on a train. Indeed on a boat.'

He laughed. 'Major Eden predicted you'd say that, almost to the letter, Miss Elphinstone. "Orders is orders" – that's what he told me to reply.'

'Know him well, do you?'

'Tolerably, given he's my senior officer, and a fair bit older. When I was stationed at Inkerman he gave us briefings on his experience in the First War. He's a clubbable sort of chap when off duty – well, you know that, miss.'

'Old Harrovians together?'

He grinned, sheepish. 'As you put it, miss – guilty as charged.'

We reached ground level, crossed a deserted lobby, went out into the crisp air of a morning already growing lighter, and turned for the rail station.

'And as to why you've been assigned me as an escort for the day, miss – Major Eden is crossing too, but from Brest – which is—'

'The French military port, I know.'

'A warship for him, a fishing tub for us. The fact is that crossing the Channel isn't the pleasurable jaunt it might once have been, not with Martians on the prowl.'

Martians on the prowl? I was not privy to military intelligence, but I didn't like the sound of that. I was, however, committed.

We came to Bremen's main station, and I was surprised to see a crowd there, gathering in the subdued half-silence that seems appropriate in the small hours, and most of them, in this German station, evidently British or French.

There was plenty of khaki, and the blue of Navy uniforms

– mostly men, some women. But there were civilians too, men out of uniform, women, children sleepy-eyed and dismayed. My journalist's eye caught details: a man hugging a little girl to his chest, both weeping; a girl of perhaps sixteen fixing a flower to the cap-badge of a sailor no older than she was; a boy of eleven or twelve standing to attention before a father who was evidently giving him orders of the 'be a man for your mother' sort. The predominant language seemed to be English, but there was plenty of German, even French spoken too, some attempted by tongues strong with the accents of the Mersey and the Thames and the Tyne. The two years since the Martians landed had been plenty of time for fraternisation, it seemed. It was not a large station and the crowd's murmur, subdued as it was, seemed to fill up the space beneath the vaulting roof.

'My sister and I have been rather tucked away in Paris. I had no idea so many troops were stationed on the Continent.'

Gray was glancing around, evidently looking for a muster point. 'It's more or less a continuous process, miss. People and assets crossing back and forth. We have bases in northern Germany, and across the Low Countries and France, the provinces facing the North Sea and the Channel. Southern England is a war zone after all, and our allies are generously allowing us sites for stores, training camps, hospitals, even weapons development. Anyhow I think I see our train.' He dug papers out of his tunic pocket. 'If you'll follow me . . .'

So my journey resumed, with a short rail trip from Bremen to Germany's North Sea shore – short, but scarcely pleasant, in a compartment so cramped it was standing room only, windows slammed shut to keep the engine smoke out, and before the sun was high it was a pit, the air stinking of sweat and thick with tobacco smoke. Well, if Second Lieutenant Ben Gray could withstand it, a man from a much gentler background than me, so could I, I told myself. After all, I had seen worse in the First War.

I did wonder how Eric Eden, a landlubber himself, was faring.

4

Aboard the *Invincible*

As it happens, as he would tell me with some relish later, Eric was having the time of his life, at that point in the morning anyhow.

Having completed a mission involving our ambiguous German allies – a mission of which I would also learn later – he, along with a number of other senior Army officers, was hitching a ride aboard the HMS *Invincible*, which as Gray told me had sailed from Brest; in fact she had put to sea the day before. She and her sister ships would sail north through the Channel, there to join more capital ships coming down from Scapa Flow, to shield our convoy from Martian attention as we dashed across the North Sea to England.

Invincible was a battlecruiser, in the jargon. Such ships were heavily armed but bore lighter armour than the great dreadnoughts, the idea being to sacrifice resilience for mobility and speed. Indeed, at sixteen years old *Invincible* was the lead ship of her class, and probably the oldest and slowest of her kind – not a cheery prospect for Eric to reflect on.

But Eric, as was his wont, had not restricted himself to the officers' cabins, as many of his peers would have. The night before sailing he had toured the mess halls giving the crew impromptu lectures on his brief but unforgettable encounter with the Martians on Horsell Common, of the kind he had given many times during his book tours, in his amusing, self-deprecating style: how, while those around him had laid down their lives, he had been clumsy enough to have fallen 'arse over tit' into the great cylinder itself... English heroes don't go in for bombast, which is where Bert Cook got it wrong, in my view. The novices aboard *Invincible* showed much interest in the Heat-Ray, its performance and characteristics, as well they might. The more experienced men told them grimly to wait and see.

The *Invincible* put to sea in the dark; Eric, sleeping soundly, missed the departure. He was roused in the small hours by bells ringing and a gruff cry: 'All hands to breakfast!'

The evening before, Eric had been speaking to a group of stokers and other men of the engine room, and his imagination had been caught by the technicalities of their posts. Now he found himself breakfasting with them in the mess, squeezed onto benches by one of the great tables that had been set out. On such ships the various specialisms work, sleep and mess together in dedicated halls, and when the ship is underway a meal-time is a rush, an industrial process in itself, the feeding of hundreds of men of the thousand-strong crew. The meal, of bacon, scrambled eggs, toast, and potatoes boiled to mush, was surprisingly good. Eric had heard that men of the lower classes would sign up for the Navy solely on account of the availability of decent food and board, and now he could believe it.

Eric's friendly stokers had just come off a night shift. The *Invincible* was old enough that she still ran on coal, and the men, dressed in loose vests, were sweating, black with soot and coal dust, and breathing hard. They drank sweet tea from soup bowls, great measures that they gulped down one after another.

When the meal was done, inspired by his companions, Eric cheerfully volunteered for a shift shovelling the coal. 'I'm no expert but how hard can it be?'

The officer he spoke to was dubious, but evidently decided it would be good for morale to have a hero of the First Martian War mucking in with the rest, and he gave the nod. So, half an hour later, down in the bowels, Eric found himself stripped to the waist, handed a shovel, and stationed at a sprawling hillside of black coal before the gaping man-high doors of a furnace.

He was welcomed with the usual inter-service banter: 'Bit o' hard work, for once, sir?'

'We do work in the Army, you know. I'll show you how to use a trenching tool some time . . .'

The labour of shifting a shovel-load of coal and chucking it through the big doors into the flames was heavy, but simple enough – if you only had to do it once. But Eric soon found himself tiring. And he quickly realised there was a rhythm to it, for the trick was not to release too much heat from the furnaces as they were fed. So it was a two-man job at each door; one

146

would shovel and chuck with a rhythm, the other would open the door in time to catch the load, then shut it again to trap the heat. Expert crew could manage a shovelful per second, if the two stokers worked together well.

As he worked Eric's thoughts softened to fancy. He could *feel* the ship was underway, from the thrumming of the deck plates beneath his feet. He knew intellectually, of course, that it was the release of heat energy from the burning coal that powered the big Parsons steam turbines that drove the ship forward. But down in that pit it felt as if it was the labour of the stokers, toiling in synchronised rhythms like parts of the machinery themselves, that pushed that heavy boat through the waters of the Channel.

Stuck down there as he was, however, Eric saw or heard nothing of the wider picture as, in the gathering light of that morning, across hundreds of miles and all along the coasts of Britain and Europe, the great ships of the Channel Fleet and the Grand Fleet put out from their bases at Brest and from Scapa Flow – the British base most out of reach of the Martians – and units of the German High Seas Fleet sailed too, in a grand co-ordinated operation. Safety in numbers: that was the idea behind the convoy, and the swarm of shipping I was to join was one of the largest yet to put to sea.

Not that any of this was to save us from the Martians.

5

At the German Coast

The Frisian coast of north Germany, between the Elbe estuary and the Dutch border, is hardly a coast at all. It is as if the land disintegrates into islands and sand bars and shallows, offering a dubious navigability that changes with the conditions of the tide and the weather. That Sunday morning, somewhere out on the ocean beyond, Eric was already busily shovelling coal. But it was from this coast that I, with hundreds of troops and many other passengers, was to be taken across the North Sea.

We were transferred off the main rail line from Bremen to the line that runs along the coast, which was used to disperse us among the fishing villages and small harbours that line the shore. Travelling companions briefly acquainted said briefer goodbyes. Once I was off the train myself I breathed in air laden with salt and a reek of seaweed, but at least it was fresh after the train.

Then, somewhat bewildered, I was led with Gray and a dozen others to the groyne of a minuscule harbour, where the crew of a small fishing smack made ready to take us. The morning was already bright, the sky empty and clear, the sun lifting over the horizon. I looked up and down the coast; lights twinkled, not yet doused from the night. It was going to be a fine spring day once a thin mist burned off.

And out to sea, out beyond the sand bars that glistened in the lapping water like the backs of sleeping whales, I could see a veritable fleet of small craft. There were lighters, tugs, fishing smacks, steamers and pleasure boats; and further out I could see larger vessels, like grey shapes in the mist: colliers, freighters, ferries, tankers. Flags fluttered, no doubt celebrating many nations, but all too remote for me to make out.

At last our crew, who spoke only a rough, heavily accented

148

German that I found unintelligible, gestured to us to come aboard the smack. Ben Gray tried to offer me a hand aboard; I disdained him, and in the end it was I who helped him. I was, however, the only woman aboard.

The smack stank of its regular cargo of fish even more than had the harbour. The crew wore sweaters, heavy leather coats, and shapeless hats; to a man they had thick beards. Clutching packs and bags and rolled-up blankets, with our overcoats and greatcoats tucked close around us, we passengers sat on equipment boxes, upturned baskets, even on the greasy, damp deck. We fitted in wherever we could; if we got in the way the snarls of the crew told us about it quick enough. One young private found himself sitting on a peculiar piece of wood, large, shaped, stained, and he made to throw it out of the boat. More snarls from the skipper put him right. There was a small cabin, fitted out with a couple of bunks and a tiny galley, I saw, and a couple of fellows crowded in there to leave room on the deck. I heard a crackle of static; the cabin was fitted with radio gear, of a robust military-looking type.

Once we were aboard, we cast off from the harbour and gingerly made our way out through the sand banks, propelled by oars and, after a time, by sail.

'It's going to be like navigating a maze,' I said to Gray.

'Indeed. And a maze whose plan can change with every shift of the tide, every storm. Takes an expert to know it, and not to ground the boat – at least, not to ground without meaning to . . . Don't be offended by the captain having a go at you about that bit of wood, Collins, by the way. *That*, you see, is a sort of detachable keel. The boat is all but flat-bottomed here as we slide over the sand banks; when we get out deeper he'll fix the keel – how, I don't know, perhaps it's driven through a slot in the floor – and then we'll ride steady.'

'Yes, sir. What was it he called me, sir?'

'Best not to know, lad. Best not to know.'

Now I began to see more small boats like our own heading out to meet the impromptu fleet that waited to collect us, craft crowded with passengers squeezed in and silhouetted in the morning light, emerging all along the coast. 'Reminds me of the First War,' I murmured. 'The evacuation from Essex.'

'Yes, we've all been briefed on that,' Gray said. 'At least *this* is planned.'

'How reassuring,' I said. 'And is there a reason why I'm

shivering in a small boat, instead of fast asleep on a passenger liner sailing out of Hamburg?'

He laughed. 'There is a logic, actually. It's a sort of extrapolation from what we're learning in England. The Martians treat humans as a farmer might treat ants. When a nest gets big enough he'll kick it, stamp it, flood it, poison it. But even so an individual ant, scuttling off, might get away with it. Do you see?'

I did, and I remembered Walter's similar parallels of humans with ants and their colonies.

'Well, on land we've learned how to move about the country without alarming the Martians too much. They watch on a big scale, not the small.'

'And so at sea as on land.'

'That's it. A thousand little fishing smacks might come and go without attracting the attention of the Martians, even if one of 'em had Churchill himself on board, whereas if the *Lusitania* sailed from Hamburg with just you on board, Collins—'

The private grinned. 'With a few society beauties. Might be worth it, sir!'

An older man grunted. 'Careful what you wish for, laddie. But speaking of being spotted by the Martians—' He peered up into a morning sky of blue perfection. 'I haven't seen a flying-machine yet. But you couldn't give them a better day if they sent one up. I mean, the North Sea's not known for its glorious sunshine, is it, Lieutenant? Typical!' His accent was northern, I thought, perhaps Liverpudlian. The man had stripes on his uniform arm, and a burn scar on his cheek, not unlike Walter's injuries, though lesser. Now I considered him more closely I was unsure of his age – younger than at first glance, perhaps in his thirties.

Gray said, 'I don't know you, Sergeant.'

'Lane, sir. RE.'

'You've seen action but not agin the Martians, I'm guessing.'

'Russian front, sir.'

I admit I stared at the man after that frank admission, and so did others in the fishing boat. This Sergeant Lane, the blunt scarred reality of him, was like a rumour congealed into fact. So British troops really were, even now, serving alongside the Germans in the depths of the Siberian war.

Lane said now, 'Plenty of spotting out *there*, sir, by Zepps and planes, though the Russkies do their best to shoot 'em down. But a spotter on a Zepp can't see through cloud and mist.'

'And that's where the Martians are different, Lane. They *can*

150

see through cloud layers, through mist, even in the pitch dark. I say "see"; it might not be seeing as we know it with our baby blues. The boffins have no clear idea how this is done, but there are guesses. You shine in the dark, you know, Lane: the body heat you give off is a kind of radiation, like light, invisible to our eyes, but there to be measured. Perhaps the Martians can track that. And a Marconi wireless transmission will pass through mist as if it ain't there. Anyhow, if we do move out in the mist or in the pitch black, we're not discommoding the Martians at all – only ourselves. So we may as well move in bright summer daylight, like this, when – if they can see us – at least we can see *them*.'

Lane grunted. 'Goes against human nature, sir.'

'Yes, Sergeant, it does. But these Martian lads aren't human, are they?'

We inched our way out through the sand banks, and then to open sea, where at last the crew were able to fit their removable keel. After that the bilge swam with water that leaked through the keel's attaching seam, and the men complained of wet feet and backsides, but we rode the water steadily.

The shore receded behind us, flat and all but featureless, turning to a dark line on the horizon. I watched it go with some trepidation; Germany was a foreign land and could never be home, and nor indeed could France, but they were a much more secure resting place than where I was going now.

We were transferred to our larger transports without significant incident. Out in deep water, somewhat to my relief, the passengers from my vessel were taken on board a kind of small river cruiser. She was called the *Lady Vain*. She was expensive-looking, but her smooth white paintwork had been splashed over by Navy grey, and the polished planking of her decks was scarred by the soldiers' boots and littered with their gear. I could have done far worse, given that the fleet included herring-boats and coal-carriers!

Gray and I were admitted to a forward lounge, under the small bridge, fitted with padded seats and benches, and lined with portholes out of which we would get a good panorama of the North Sea as we sailed steadily west. Though crowded with soldiers who sat or lay sleeping on every square inch of floor space, the lounge was relatively comfortable. There was even a steward, who, after we were all boarded, came round with trays of water and fruit juice. He greeted my companion: 'Morning, Mr Gray.'

'I'm afraid it's Lieutenant *pro tem*, Perkins.'

When he'd moved on, I said, 'So, Lieutenant *pro tem*. The steward knows you, does he?'

'Through the chap who owns the boat – has one of those big riverside villas at Marlow, you know the sort, and *he's* a friend of my father. Used to go up for Henley and to play tennis.'

'I'm sure you did.'

He winked at me, and raised a glass of fruit punch (without alcohol). 'We'll see enough discomfort in England. I thought I'd pull one of the few strings within my reach to make our journey a little more pleasant.'

I touched his glass with mine. 'Right now I'm glad you did – and will be more so in ten or twelve hours, I dare say.'

For that was how long our passage was predicted to take: across the North Sea from the east Frisians, passing not far south of Dogger Bank, until we reached the Wash, where we would be transferred to another flotilla of small boats for the final step to the shore. If all went well, I might be in England, without getting my feet wet, before sundown.

But it was about lunch time when we heard the rumours that Martians had been seen.

Soon after that a sound like thunder was heard.

I recognised the consternation on the faces of Gray and others, and understood its cause. For we, part of a great convoy of ships, were still in the open sea, suspended between Germany and the British Isles. And the gunfire was coming not from the west – not from the English coast, where we might have expected to encounter Martians – *it came from the north*, the open ocean. It was disconcerting for me to discover that none of my companions, no matter how experienced and battle-hardened, had any idea what was happening.

6

The Battle of the North Sea

On the *Invincible* Major Eric Eden had been fast asleep. Showered, fed, dressed in a clean uniform, he napped on a heap of blankets on the carpeted floor of an officer's cabin, which, he told me later, even in the middle of an interplanetary war, had leather armchairs and pictures of Nelson on the wall. It was about noon, but he was exhausted after a mere half shift of feeding the maw of the boilers below. He would tell me he had even slept through the bells that summoned the men to the chaplain's services, for the day was a Sunday.

That was when action stations were sounded, with the tinny note of a bugle.

Eric woke immediately. He had never heard the call before, but understood its portent immediately – and would have moved even if the officers around him, Navy and Army alike, had not been quicker still. Eric had no specific station. He considered going down to the coal bunkers once more; perhaps he could lend a hand. But he could not resist trying to discover what was going on. So he pushed his way out to the open deck.

He got to the rail in time to see the White Ensign being hoisted overhead. All around him was apparent chaos as the crew ran to their positions, and the big guns swivelled on their mounts, and black smoke from the funnels streaked across the sky. He spared a thought for the men of the boiler crews, toiling down below.

Looking out to sea he saw that the *Invincible* was one of a neat line of ships playing follow-my-leader bow to stern, the ensigns fluttering and the black coal-smoke pouring from their funnels. Some of them were dreadnoughts, their characteristic profiles shallow in the water, with the two huge chimney stacks and the four vast gun placements fore and aft. To Eric it was a tremendous sight, the scale surprising, inspiring.

And he perceived that this great rank of ships was turning, following a huge arc scrawled across the grey sea. The sun was high in a featureless blue sky. He was suddenly disoriented. The battle group was changing course, but which way? And, more to the point, why?

Then the guns started to bark, from the ships ahead of the *Invincible*. He thought he saw the streak of shells, but as yet he could discern no target.

'This'll be fun,' said a man at the rail next to him. He was a Navy man, a rating, but not of this crew; his cap proclaimed him a man of the *Minotaur*. His accent was northern, perhaps Northumbrian.

Eric, bewildered, asked, 'What do you mean?'

The rating looked at him for the first time. 'You're the Martian chap. Heard you speak.'

'The Martian chap.' Eric laughed softly. 'I suppose you could say that. But I'm as bewildered here as I was in that blessed cylinder.' He glanced at the sun. 'What time is it?'

'Not long after midday.'

Eric tried to remember the schedule. 'Then we're stuck somewhere in the middle of the ocean. We're not expecting to run into Martians until we hit the coast... Are we? And which way are we turning? The sun's too high; I can't even be sure which way's south.'

The rating pointed to his right. 'South's that way, where we came from. We sailed out of Brest – you remember that much—'

'Yes, yes.'

'We made north through the Channel. We were going to rendezvous with units of the Grand Fleet coming down from Scapa Flow, and then escort the passenger fleet in to the English coast.'

'But we're nowhere near the coast. And we're turning – what, east? Not west, towards England.'

'Because the Martians are out there, sir. Out of our sight still – but they're *there*, to the north. I can only tell you the scuttlebutt, mind. A Zepp spotted them, a cluster of fighting-machines, out in the middle of the North Sea. Where they had no right to be. Zepp himself was unlucky to be there, he was on his way home after scouting the big Martian nest in England – or lucky for us he happened to spot them. Zepp managed to get off a message before he was shot down—'

'By the Heat-Ray?'

'That's it.'

'Martians can't swim, damn it. It makes no sense. And they brought no ships. They *can't* be out in the ocean.'

'But even a man who can't swim,' the rating said calmly, 'may stand in the shallows, and wield a sword.'

Then Eric saw it. 'Dogger Bank. Of course.'

The rating nodded grimly. 'Only a hundred feet or so deep at the shallowest, and many miles from land. Not a bad platform from which to fight, eh? If you're in a fighting-machine a hundred feet tall, and we know they can extend those legs of theirs even higher than that...'

The two of them speculated for a while, about how the Martians could know of the existence of the Bank. It was a parallel of my own overheard conversation on the fishing boat. If the Martians could 'see' through mist and fog, and in the dead of night, why not 'see' through a hundred feet or so of water? Perhaps those flying-machines of theirs had mapped the sea beds as efficiently as they must map the dry land. And as to how the fighting-machines could have reached the Bank—

'They have no boats,' Eric mused. 'But, as you say, they could simply *walk* there. Under the water. It must seem quite unnatural to creatures of a world of shallow seas...'

'Makes sense for the Germans to give us a hand, anyhow. Even the Channel's not so deep. If the Martians can just walk over to Europe...'

'But what of today? What are the tactics, do you think?'

The rating, clearly an intelligent man and experienced, if of low rank, seemed pleased to be lecturing an officer. 'I'll tell you what *I* would do, if Admiral Jellicoe asked.' He used a forefinger to sketch an invisible map on the palm of his hand. 'Here's Dogger, and your Martians. Here's the passenger fleet that's going to pass within easy striking range of the Heat-Ray. Well, I'd put a call out to divert the convoy south – while *we*, instead of steaming north-west to England, are sweeping starboard like so, to head east.'

'Ah. Passing between the Martians on the Bank and the passenger fleet.'

'That's it. Give those Martians something to think about. Meanwhile the Grand Fleet coming from the north will divert east also, passing to the north of the Bank.'

Eric frowned. 'All in a line? Instead of steaming straight at the Martians?'

'That's the tactics. You keep your ships together in a group, so they protect each other, and you show your flank so you can bring your guns to bear. Now, we'll have been firing our big guns as soon as the Martians were in range, even if they're over the horizon and too far to spot, for it's always worth the chance of a lucky strike. After all, we've got a longer reach than the Martians; that Heat-Ray of theirs is strictly line of sight, while *we* can lob a shell miles over the horizon.'

'Hmm. But they have the ability to strike our shells out of the sky.'

'That's why you have to overwhelm them; you can't shoot down every hailstone in a storm, can you?'

'That you can't.'

'The Germans have tried their undersea boats against 'em. But the Martians can see through the water clear as air, and pick 'em off like lumbering whales. Anyhow, we have to try. Can't have 'em blockading England.'

Eric could not argue with that sentiment.

Then the *Invincible*'s own guns opened up.

For Eric it was as if he had suddenly been dropped into a battle zone. The ship had four twelve-inch guns and sixteen four-inch; when they all started to blaze the ship shuddered, the noise was deafening, and the cordite added to the black coal-smoke from the engine stacks to wreathe the ship in a choking haze. Yet still Eric clung to his place at the rail, with the rating alongside him. And Eric could see the gunfire erupting from all the ships of the group, strung out in their line to west and east.

Now the rating stood on a rail and yelled, pointing. 'There! I can see the shells come down! We must be close to the Bank!'

Eric, peering, saw plumes of water rising up, columns that he thought might be two hundred feet high or more, rising and feathering in the air.

But now, too, he saw explosions of a different kind, in the water along the flanks of the ships in the line – detonations, spouts. Of course it was the Heat-Ray, all but invisible, but when it hit the ocean it caused the very water to flash to steam, explosively, in great volumes.

'Closer than we thought,' the rating muttered. 'They can *see* us.'

And then the Martians on Dogger Bank found their range.

A beam hit a vessel only a couple ahead of the *Invincible* in the line, licking it almost lovingly. Everything the beam touched flashed to flame or melted or exploded – the ship's hull, the superstructure. Soon the ship was wrapped in smoke and steam, its armoured hull plate cracked and crumpled, its funnels gashed and falling and spewing smoke and steam. As the ship began to list – less than a minute after the first strike – Eric saw men throwing themselves desperately into the water, some only to be boiled alive, their screams terrible, if they entered the cauldron stirred by the Heat-Ray. The deck of the next ship in the line already swarmed with men trying to reach those in the water with ropes and belts, even as the battle continued.

Before the Martians, the human vessels looked horribly primitive, slow and lumbering, the smoke billowing from their stacks a symbol of their wretched crudeness. Yet each of those wallowing tubs carried over a thousand crew. Eric felt naked and exposed. The doomed ship's heavy armour had given it barely any protection. And the *Invincible* was a battlecruiser, Eric remembered, with thickness of armour deliberately sacrificed for speed and manoeuvrability.

Still the shells poured down onto the Martian position. The rating had hold of a pair of binoculars now, and claimed he could see the brazen cowls of the Martians – 'A whole flock of 'em,' he claimed. 'And one down! And another!'

But even as the Martians defended themselves against the incoming hail of shells, those bronze cowls twisted this way and that, and one ship after another in the line was maimed by the Heat-Ray.

Then one ship simply disappeared in a huge detonation, out of which tremendous components came wheeling, cast by the residual spin of smashed turbines. There could be no survivors of such an end, Eric realised.

The rating said grimly, 'That's bad, if the Martians are working it out. Hit the magazine and a ship like this will go up like a Guy Fawkes firework...'

The Heat-Ray touched the *Invincible*.

Looking down, Eric saw thick armour below his position crumpling like paper in an invisible fist – as if by magic, as if from no tangible cause – and fragments, white-hot, dripped into water that boiled. Eric heard screams now, and men tumbled like toys into the water. He braced for the detonation that would kill him – but the ship, shuddering, limped on.

157

'Hit! But still afloat.' The *Minotaur* rating slapped Eric's shoulder. 'You any kind of doctor, sir?'

'A nurse, maybe.'

'Come with me, then.'

Eric found himself hurrying down a gangway to an enclosed chamber that, he quickly learned, was used as a 'distributing station' during battle. Here the wounded were brought as fast as they could be gathered, sorted by a kind of rough triage, and then treated by medical officers in their white coats before being carted off to rest areas deeper in the ship.

Eric helped as best he could, lugging the wounded, carrying supplies, even wrapping bandages tight around a splinted broken arm. The flow of the injured was relentless, bewildering. He would tell me, much later, that the experience had taught him a greater respect for battlefield medics – for Frank, for instance. Even to continue to function in such conditions, to *think* – to make one life-or-death decision after another, over and over – seemed heroic to him.

But it was hellish not to be able to follow the battle. There were no portholes, no way to see what was going on, but Eric could hear the explosions all around, the guns still firing, a rougher roar that was the effect of the Heat-Ray hitting the water, and bangs and shudders all around the ship, which was starting to list, ominously.

Afterwards he found it hard to say how long he served in that station, racked throughout by a sense of imminent doom; it might only have been minutes, or perhaps half an hour. Compared to the muddy chaos of a land battle, he had always thought of naval warfare as a rather remote, abstract affair – not like this.

Then, though the noise of the battle did not cease, he heard cheering from above decks. Eric was between patients, and curiosity burned – more than curiosity, a compulsion to know if he was likely to live or die. With a stab of guilt he broke away, promising himself his absence would be brief, and scrambled up a gangway to the deck.

Up there, still the air was alive with the whistle of shells, and the sea churned with the wreckage of ships. He managed to find his Northumbrian rating. 'There!' The man pointed across a stretch of ocean where still the shells rained. 'There!' he cried, over the continuing roar of the *Invincible*'s own guns.

And Eric saw it, a line of low shadows on the northern horizon, grey in the mist, the smoke stacks high, the guns sparking. Fire, all along the horizon; it was an astonishing sight.

'That's the Grand Fleet out of Scapa! The dreadnoughts! Now those Martians will be sorry, you'll see!'

But then the Heat-Ray found another of the battlecruisers of the *Invincible*'s line. There was a vast explosion, and the ship seemed to burst, and then implode, and she was gone.

From my yacht, we heard thunder in the north, and saw flashes. But we saw no dying ships, or fighting Martians.

I learned that some thirty per cent of our convoy's Navy escort was lost in the action, but only five per cent of the passenger ships. The loss to the Martians was unknown. This kind of loss was typical, but still the passage of people and goods across the oceans continued. As Eric's rating had remarked to him, and as Sergeant Lane had said to me, everyone agreed we could not allow the Martians to blockade Britain.

I myself sailed far south of the battle zone and towards England, without incident.

7

A Landing at the Wash

Once safe from the perils of the high seas our convoy broke up, with the larger cargo vessels making for the great ports of the south and east coasts, while the military vessels made for their own home ports.

As for my party, we came into the Wash at last, where, close to the shore, a fleet of fishing smacks and the like was waiting to greet us, a mirror of the arrangement at the Frisian coast. With Lieutenant Gray, Sergeant Lane and a small mob of other passengers, I and my rucksack were loaded once more into the foul bilge of a fishing vessel, and we had to endure another tortuous journey through the shallow sandbanks that all but choke that tremendous bay. It was evening by now, and how our skipper – a crusty old salt with a beard like Martian snow – navigated us through it all to the lights of the shore I don't know; we heard curses and the ringing of bells coming from the dark as others of our scattered fleet ran aground. But make it we did, and I was relieved to have my feet back on solid ground once more.

We were, I discovered, in the estuary of the Great Ouse and not far from King's Lynn. Motor-cars painted a dull military green were waiting here, and Gray quickly went to commandeer one to transport me onwards. Sergeant Lane had his own unit to find, but he waited with me politely while Gray tried to sort things out.

The car driver, however, insisted on checking over my papers and identification. I quickly discovered that a passport was no longer sufficient documentation to allow a subject of His Majesty even to set foot on English soil, and there was something of a stand-off as Gray debated with the driver. 'Damn it!' he said. 'I never thought of that. We should have got you military papers.'

The driver was a woman, perhaps forty, smartly uniformed, competent, apologetic. She looked me over and grinned. 'Well, you don't look terribly dangerous, ma'am. I'm allowed to transport one prisoner under guard. I'll have to check that rucksack, though. And I'll need another warm body in the back with her – in addition to yourself, Lieutenant.'

Gray sighed. 'Very well. Sergeant Lane?'

'Sir?'

'You're volunteered. Now let's get aboard this jalopy and make for the bright lights of King's Lynn...'

Lane complied with a grin. 'Better than the barracks. First round's on me, miss,' he muttered to me as he clambered into the car.

We spent Sunday night in the town, of which I saw very little.

Gray and Lane, I learned, spent some of the evening at the cinema, where they saw *The Kaiser's Lover*, a Hollywood drama of the early days of the Schlieffen War, with screen stars mugging between footage of the actual events. And from the look of my companions the next morning, they appeared to have stayed up long after the show was over.

As we boarded the train I teased them. 'Gave the film a thorough critique, did we, gentlemen?'

Gray grunted. 'Film – balderdash – I don't remember any bally Americans saving Paris single-handed.' The train lurched into motion and he blanched.

Lane laughed. 'Looks like it's not just wartime memories coming back to you, sir.'

'Oh, hold your peace, Ted, and enjoy your day off.'

'Right you are, sir.'

We headed south-west through Peterborough and Northampton towards Oxford, where we would change. After a long time away I peered out curiously at a partially occupied England. Our route passed well to the north and west of the Martians' Cordon. But you could see camouflage colours roughly splashed over buildings, rail tracks, even telephone lines clumsily concealed – and few vehicles moving anywhere, for the Martians targeted mechanical transport. Though Martian forays outside the Cordon were rare, they did occur, and no part of mainland Britain was entirely immune from attack. Of course a skimpy layer of camouflage would not deter a determined Martian – they could detect the heat of a concealed engine, for instance – but their machines were few, and they could not check everything, so such precautions were worthwhile.

The train made other stops too at places I did not recognise – the detail of southern England had changed. One striking location was a sprawl of what appeared to be hastily thrown-up barrack blocks, hutments of wood or concrete panels or even corrugated iron, which must have been hideously uncomfortable in the summer. These blocks were set out in grid systems. The Union Jacks flying everywhere, and a perimeter of dug-in artillery pieces, made me think of a military camp; on the other hand a handful of children playing in a desultory way in a meadow close to the small rail station reminded me of a holiday village – like Caister Camp in Norfolk, where George, Alice and I had spent a brief holiday in the year before the First War. The rail stop had no name.

'What is this place?'

Gray was half-dozing. 'Mm? What time is it?' He glanced at a pocket timetable. 'Camp A-One-43, I should think, if we're on schedule.'

'Camp? I see children playing.'

Lane said, 'You have been away a while, haven't you, miss? This is a Winstonville – that's what the Cockneys call 'em.'

'Oh. A refugee camp.'

'Rather more than that,' Gray said. 'It's a functioning township, with shops and doctors' surgeries and schools and chapels, all thrown up in the blink of an eye. One of dozens, if not more – they label them by the road-numbering system, you see...'

I was familiar with the general idea. All of this was a consequence of the unending Martian threat to London. There were still millions trapped in the capital, and a significant percentage of our national resource was spent on provisioning the Londoners, trying to enable their escape – and catering for refugees, who came out in vast numbers. Hence such camps as this.

London had always been more than a sink of people, however. It had been at the centre of Britain's economic activity, as a financial centre, a port, even as a manufacturing centre – the Woolwich Arsenal alone, now smashed and burned out, had been our most significant munitions factory. After the Martians struck we needed a national reorganisation, and for better or worse that was what we got. So the other ports of Britain, from Hull to Harwich, Southampton to Liverpool, were now taking cargo that had once unloaded in London, and new transport networks,

162

camouflaged against Martian attack, were being thrown together. New manufactories of all kinds were being set up across the country, with the aid of loans from the Germans and Americans and others; huge areas of the north of England had been torn up and transformed into giant open-cast mines for the ores, readily available, that now yielded aluminium with the Martian process. But there were the usual mutterings of profiteering; even with the Martians for company, the rich got richer and the poor poorer.

The government itself had been shaken up too. Much power had been devolved to regional governors, under Prime Minister Lloyd George who was with the Cabinet in exile in Bamburgh. (General Marvin was long gone, dead in 1921 at the hands of the Martians, after a foolish advance that he, shamed by Churchill's example, had insisted on leading in person.) The royal family was still ensconced in Delhi, and from the beginning I had heard nothing but pleasure from the people that the King, at least, was safe.

'"Winstonvilles", though?'

Gray eyed me. 'I take it you know that Churchill is Governor of London. He thinks big.'

'A bit of a lad,' Lane said, grinning. 'Good old Winston.'

At Oxford we changed trains at a brand-new station, in an industrial belt that now appeared to encircle the historic core of that university city. It was early afternoon, but I thought the outside air was odd, with a kind of electrical tang to it – like sniffing ozone at the seaside – and it had a peculiarly greenish tint that brought back unwelcome memories. I wondered what was being manufactured in these great new factories, with their Mars-tainted technologies.

I was relieved to board the connecting train, which would take us directly south through Southampton to Portsmouth. When we passed through Abingdon, Gray said we were about as close to the Chilterns, and the Martian Cordon, as we would get. All along the train, I saw as it followed a wide bend in the track, faces were pressed to the glass, staring out to the east in awe and trepidation. But of the Martians I saw nothing – not that day.

8

In Portsmouth

In Portsmouth at last, we were met off the train by a despatch rider with revised orders. I was to first report, not to HMNB Portsmouth, the Navy base, as I had expected, but to a military hospital outside the city. Gray accepted this change of circumstance with a kind of cheerful resignation; indeed he seemed pleased to have a grain of fresh evidence of the caprice of command.

As a car was found for me, I made my clumsy goodbyes to Sergeant Lane.

'It's been a pleasure, miss. I'll call my unit and find out if I'm still to make my way to Harwich. Probably another train ride, and paid for out of my own pocket.'

'Criminal,' I said.

'Ain't it, though?'

Gray was eyeing him speculatively. 'Well now, look, Sergeant. You know that my mission is to escort Miss Elphinstone here across London and all the way into the Martian Cordon. And you know about as much about *that* as I do. Why don't you hang around for the evening? I could make a couple of phone calls, get you transferred *pro tem*. Unless there are duties for which you are absolutely essential elsewhere.'

Lane rubbed his chin and glanced north, the direction the Martians lay. 'Hmm. A veteran of the eastern front, venturin' into the Martian pit. Not many men can say that, can they, sir?'

'I wouldn't imagine so.'

'And it is your round.'

'Let's get Miss Elphinstone settled first . . .'

The Queen Alexandra Hospital, a sprawl of red-brick buildings that dated to before the First Martian War, was outside the city, a short tram-ride if you hadn't got a military chauffeur as I had. They were expecting me at reception – and I was surprised to be met there by Marina Ogilvy, wife of the astronomer at Ottershaw. It was an awkward encounter: in fact, in my surprise, I struggled for a moment to recognise her.

A brisk matron took charge, and led me to a private room. Marina came with me. En route I got a glimpse into a ward; I saw men evidently badly burned, cocooned in bandages, or with obvious respiratory problems. This was the kind of injury you came to expect from contact with the Martians, if you survived at all. We were a long way from the front line of the Second Martian War here; this was the first set of casualties I had seen since leaving England two years before, but it would not be the last.

At my room the matron told me I faced a series of injections – 'Your friend can stay with you.'

The area within the Martian Cordon was quarantined, I was told. Though attempts were made to maintain supplies and otherwise support those trapped, there had been reports of such war-zone horrors as cholera and the typhoid, and I was to be inoculated as best as possible.

'And you will be given other vaccines of a more experimental nature,' the nurse told me vaguely. 'It's all quite routine.'

That last was, as it turned out, a fresh encounter with the Lie. But I felt no alarm at the time. One trusts nurses!

After the injections were done I lay on a bed, sleeves rolled up, and while we were alone briefly, I spoke with Marina. 'I do apologise for not recognising you back there.'

She smiled tiredly; she was a woman who had always seemed tired, in my recollection of her. 'Oh, don't be. It was my husband who had the famous face after all.'

'I suppose I understand why they called on you. In the First War your husband was among the first to try to communicate peacefully with the Martians—'

'The first in the war to lose his life, along with Professor Stent and the rest, silly fools all.'

'Perhaps. But their motive was a good one, wasn't it? And now here we are attempting contact again.'

'You're right, of course. I think I'm here to attach a kind of legitimacy to the enterprise. I'm a symbol of my husband. *Silly* fool,' she said again, savagely. 'I heard that Lady Stent, the Astronomer Royal's widow, refused to have anything to do with it. But that may be just rumour. Few people refuse their duty these days.'

The matron returned and briskly told me I was free to go, though I might experience symptoms such as mild nausea for a while and I should 'go easy'. There would be no more long-distance travel that day.

Otherwise I was free to wander. After so many days in company that was mostly male and exclusively military, I could think of nothing better than to escape; it was a pleasant May evening, even if it was a Monday, and I itched to walk. Marina agreed to accompany me. But my night off took some negotiating by telephone with Lieutenant Gray – I still did not have the right papers. We worked out a kind of deal.

Shortly afterwards a taxi-cab pulled up outside the hospital, with a single passenger: Ted Lane. The sergeant's brief, from Gray, was to keep a discreet watch on us for the evening: 'That man will do anything to get out of buying a round,' Lane grumbled. But he was cheerful enough, and I trusted his competence as much as Gray evidently did.

Since the cab was paid for, we used it to take a tour of the city, including the dockyard and the harbour. When I had seen all this before with Philip Parris it had bristled with fighting ships; now the ships routinely anchored far out to sea, out of reach of marauding Martians.

We were dropped in the Commercial Road, and took a stroll, with Lane tailing us at a discreet distance. It was easy to lose him in the crowd, for there was plenty of khaki about, as well as Navy blue. The other predominant colour seemed to be black. Marina told me that black was something of a fashion now. 'As if we're all back in Victoria's day,' she said gloomily.

Aside from the fashions, another striking difference from Paris or Berlin was the lack of motor traffic on the streets: a few omnibuses and ambulances, police cars and military vehicles, only a handful of taxi-cabs and private motor-cars. On the other hand there was a flood of horse-drawn traffic, which brought with it the straw and manure and an earthy reek that had been lost from the streets of Britain since before the First Martian War. It was all down to a shortage of petrol, Marina said – that and a general discouragement from using motorised vehicles, which attracted Martians.

In the city itself we saw little of the defences of Portsmouth. I did spot searchlights and gun emplacements; I learned that there were rings of guns five and ten miles from the city centre, and others placed around the docks area, with anti-aircraft installations and lamps.

166

I saw the mark of Martian activities past: the careless splash of brick and concrete and glass, the brush of the Heat-Ray.

And I saw more subtle signs of war. Portsmouth's busiest shopping street looked barren compared to Berlin's meanest, I thought. Every food store had a queue outside it, a line of patient men and women and a few children, their clothes drab and well-worn, all clutching empty baskets and pink scraps of card that proved to be ration papers. There were servicemen in the lines – you could tell by the shabby greatcoats they wore or by their battered military caps. Some were evidently wounded internally rather than externally, like poor Walter. You came to recognise a kind of nervousness, a shaking, a turning away of the head.

In search of happier sights I looked for bookshops, but there was a shortage of paper, among other essentials, and I found only second-hand stores, or rows of trashy American thrillers. Burroughs's sagas of human heroes biffing the Martians on their home soil seemed to be selling well – alongside, ironically, a new, cheap edition of Walter's *Narrative*. The only newspaper widely available was the *National Bulletin*, a worthless government rag started in Marvin's final days.

We stopped at a small restaurant where I ordered an omelette with mushrooms and fresh-baked bread, accompanied by sweet tea. It was plain but nourishing food. Even so the prices were exorbitantly high, I thought.

Then we went in search of entertainment: not easy to find. Most posters you saw, rather than advertising the films or the shows, were of the uplifting, instructional or hectoring kind:

VOLUNTEER!

or:

A MEATLESS DAY IS A DAY CLOSER TO VICTORY

or:

TAKE ONE WITH YOU!

This last below a stern portrait of Churchill

The theatres were running sentimental shows such as revivals of *Tommy Atkins* and *In Time of War*. The audiences thronging outside the theatre doors looked keen enough, but it all seemed a little desperate to us, and we wandered on, arm in arm.

At about nine o'clock there was a new rush of people, and I gathered that a work shift had ended. Among them were munitions workers from the new factories, all women, their hair and skin discoloured orange and yellow from the toxic materials they habitually handled. These 'canaries' seemed intent on drinking as much as possible as rapidly as possible, and for all the moral strictures of our new England there seemed no shortage of cheap alcohol in the city that night.

Marina was amused to see them. 'Funny how old Marvin always railed against the suffragettes. Now his successors need women to fight their war. Still haven't given us the vote, however. Not that that means much nowadays – no elections since 1911—'

'What about people's rights?'

'Responsibilities trump rights, for the time being. That's the argument.' She shrugged. 'Who am I to argue? The Martians are *here*.'

The canaries deserved their entertainment, but we had had enough. We summoned Lane, our patient shadow, and the three of us took a horse-drawn chaise to our hotel.

Oddly enough I felt satisfied to be back in England, grim and war-struck as it was. Berlin, immersed in its eternal politicking and war-making, and Paris, obsessing over its own humiliations, seemed irrelevant now, a distraction. As Marina had said, the Martians were *here*, in England; here was reality, here was where the history of all mankind pivoted. And here was I, engaged. A rare burst of idealism for me, you might think! And it was not to be rewarded.

I did not sleep well. I felt somewhat nauseous, and the sites of the various injections itched or ached. The vagueness of my mission concerned me, and occupied my waking thoughts.

I need not have wasted the brain power. For when the military car came in the morning to take me, Marina Ogilvy, Ben Gray and Ted Lane to a poky office in HMNB Portsmouth, Eric Eden quickly disabused me of the notion that my mission had anything to do with communication at all.

9

A Secret Assignment

'After all,' Eric Eden said cheerfully as he poured us all some rather terrible coffee, 'what would be the point, if you think about it? Would we have paused if the Tasmanians had insisted on telling us their theories of the universe as we worked them to extinction?'

Gray, Lane, Marina and I sat on uncomfortable upright chairs before a desk, behind which Eric sat at ease. This was a Royal Navy briefing room, if a small one; there were charts of seas and oceans on the walls, as well as the customary portrait of Lord Nelson – and, almost as an afterthought, a map of southern England with the Martian positions around Amersham overlaid in glaring red ink. The desk top was empty save for a clutter of stationery, and my own leather satchel.

Eric's face bore new scars. This was a relic of his heroism at Wormwood Scrubs, I would learn much later.

'We used to debate all this at school,' Gray said now. 'The morality of empire.'

Ted Lane pulled a face. 'Of course you did.' But Gray was of that class so blessedly privileged that he did not even know when he was being ragged.

'To get back to the point,' I said somewhat testily, 'if this isn't about communication – what, then?' I tapped the leather satchel I had placed on the table, the packet of Walter's sigils. 'I've come a long way with this, Eric.'

He steepled his fingers. 'Walter did believe everything he told you. And it really was his idea in the first place, the whole communications angle. We just – embellished it.' Eric actually laughed.

I was growing angry. 'What, then, is the truth?'

'We haven't been idle since 1907, you know. *We* being military intelligence, to which I have become at least partially attached, given the uniqueness of my experience. From the Martians' point of view, it has always seemed to me a strategic error for them to have come, and *failed*. The first shot always had the best chance of success. Now, if they have come back to study us, we've had plenty of time to study them. Everybody knows how we've been able to make industrial use of some of their inventions – the aluminium smelter, for instance. But we've been looking into other aspects.'

My arms prickling from the injections, I was starting to intuit the truth – or rather, the Lie. 'Other aspects like their biology?' I prompted.

He eyed me. 'Quite so. Everybody knows, as Carver first argued, that it was the germs that killed the Martians. I remember the lovely lines in Jenkins's tome very well: "The Martians – *dead*! – slain . . . by the humblest things that God, in his wisdom, has put upon this earth." But precisely *which* of those humblest things? For Jenkins's words about "putrefactive" and "disease", pinched from Carver's papers, are the purest speculation, you know.'

'Ah,' Lane said with a soldier's crafty smile. 'And you clever beggars have been finding out which bacteria, have you? With all respect, sir.'

Eric nodded. 'Not me in person, of course . . . Have you heard of a place called Porton Down, Miss Elphinstone? Hush-hush Army laboratory, out in Wiltshire.'

'I know it,' said Ted Lane. 'Or *of* it. Belonged to my lot, didn't it? The Royal Engineers.'

'That's it. Set up during the Schlieffen War to look at the possibilities of chemical warfare – gassing, you know.'

Lane grunted. 'Stinks shells. Worked in Russia.'

Gray eyed him curiously.

Eric went on, 'When the Martians returned we set Porton on the germs, with a crash programme to determine which precisely was the pathogen that killed the Martians. The whole thing was another bright idea of Churchill's, actually, if arrived at belatedly; the man does have a certain ruthless genius.'

Lane leaned forward. 'How could you test it, though? All them Martians from '07 were dead.'

'Ah, but they left their corpses behind – plenty of tissue to experiment with. Did you know that one Martian was *born* during

170

the '07 invasion? Found partly budded off its parent – dead as the rest, of course. That provided particularly sweet materials for the sample labs, I'm told. And you needn't look at me that way, Miss Elphinstone; I doubt that the Martians are showing much pity for human infants within the Cordon right now.'

As he spoke, I could feel my injection sites itch and crawl, and I realised what had been done to me. '*They found it*, didn't they? The boffins at Porton Down – they found the pathogen that killed the Martians.'

'Indeed they did – with a little help from equally advanced laboratories in Germany, which, if you want to know, was the true purpose of my own recent jaunt to the continent. Don't ask me for the Latin names, that was never my bag. But it's a very old bug, and it's been with us a long time – you find it in every population – must have come with us out of Africa, you see, that's if Darwin and the rest are right about our origin there, the bug having no doubt scythed down our man-ape ancestors before they developed immunity. Well, we can be sure that by now the Martians have fixed themselves to resist *that* one. So we found another. An even nastier cousin, to which the Martians had no exposure last time, but distant enough related that any protection they cooked up after the last lot will do them no good. And it works; we have enough samples of fresh Martian tissue to have proved that.'

'And those "tests" I went through last night—'

'It happily reproduces in the human bloodstream, but does no harm to the carrier.'

'*It's in me.* This archaic killer. You put it in me. And you want me to carry it to the Martians, under this pretence of communication.' There was the Lie, revealed and spoken aloud. I immediately felt foolish not to have suspected it before.

And I saw that my companions, Ted Lane, Lieutenant Gray, even the down-to-earth Marina Ogilvy, shrank away from me.

My mission, in the end, was simple. I was to enter the Cordon, and get as close to the Martians as I could – with or without Cook's help, though the artilleryman seemed the best option.

'We'll only get one shot,' Eric said. 'And so we've got to make it count. Bring them all down at once. Remember, another opposition is approaching. If more cylinders are meant to come our way, we believe our chances agin them will be that much greater if the Martians in England, spotters for the fleet, are knocked out before the reinforcements – or perhaps the main forces – even get here.

'Now, one benefit we've extracted from Martian technology is a blood storage system – for much of the supply on which they subsisted in their interplanetary flights in the cylinders was externally stored, you know. We use the technology ourselves, on the battlefield. We've every reason to believe that they're using a similar system in their big central pit at Amersham. A sort of big larder, full of human blood. And *that's* what you've got to spoil, Julie. Should take most of them down in one fell swoop, and the open sores the infection creates ought to pass it on to the rest. So you see, you need the Martians to trust you, to let you all the way in to the heart of the nest. Which is where Cook is going to provide vital cover.'

'Why didn't you tell me all this? I mean, before squirting your venom into my veins.'

'Because, frankly, it was judged there'd have been a high chance of you turning down the job.'

'Am I to commit mass murder, Major Eden?'

'Are you to save the nation, Miss Elphinstone?'

And it was as if I saw my own epitaph.

10

A Night in Hampshire

As the next stage of my journey to the Cordon in Buckinghamshire, I learned, I was to be taken through London. Though millions remained trapped there, or perhaps because of them, the capital was a great hive which the military infiltrated with relative ease, beneath the attention of the Martians – mostly. I was to join a regular expedition.

That evening I was escorted out of Portsmouth, by Ben Gray and Ted Lane, to stay in a rather fine house in the country – I never learned its name, and did not ask – out in the meadows beyond Eastleigh. The owners had either abandoned the place when the Martians returned to England, or had had their property requisitioned, and now it was used to house officers, while the grounds had been given over to respite accommodation for active troops on leave. In the years since the owners had left, the property had lost a lot of its glamour, as evidenced by the muddy boot prints in the hallways, the khaki greatcoats hanging in the cloakroom, and the lack of staff save for a few injured troops, evidently given light behind-the-line duties. One poor chap who served us dinner had half his face a mask of scars.

For, yes, despite the house's fall from grace, that Tuesday night we went down to dinner, of soup and rather stringy beef, served in the old-fashioned formal way, in a dining room lined with paintings of weak-chinned generations of owners. And there was wine from the cellar and port served in fine glasses, and at the end the cigars came out, a very expensive treat shipped from Cuba. Much of the conversation was light, touching on the scandalous antics of various film stars, perhaps for my benefit as the only civilian present and one of only three women. Gray put in anecdotes about the eccentric behaviour of Churchill in his bunker at Dollis Hill, where – so it was said – the Governor of London would host meetings of his inner cabinet in his pyjamas and dressing gown, with a goblet of brandy at his side and a budgerigar perched on top of his balding head.

Most Army officers were, after all, drawn from the privileged classes, and all this seemed normal to them. To me it was a strange evening, a poignant reminder of an England that was all but lost. And an England, I thought as I watched poor Ted Lane try to decide which bit of cutlery he was supposed to use next, from which most of the English had always been excluded.

I slept restlessly that night in a room that felt stuffy, on a mattress that felt too deep, a bed piled too high with blankets. Perhaps I was simply disturbed, as I had been since my injections in Portsmouth, by the thought of the lethal pathogens I carried in my body – as if my body itself had become a battleground. Or perhaps I had simply become too used to my comfortable but relatively austere life in Paris.

I was woken very early by sounds outside: voices barking commands or raised in laughter, a hiss of water, even a smell of what might have been cooking bacon. I pulled on a dressing gown and went to my open window.

As I have said, the grounds of the house had been given over as a rest and recuperation area for men brought back from the front and they were all men here; women had separate stations. I saw them now, queuing in the low sunlight of an early May morning, at tables for an open-air breakfast of sardine and bacon and potatoes and bread and a mug of tea; they were fed from a 'company cooker', as they called it, like a big kitchen range on wheels. Or they gathered around communal shower centres to wash – I caught cheeky glimpses of pale flesh – and there were wagons laden with disinfectant and delousing powder through which those just back from the front had to be processed.

Some, that morning, had already been called to training. I saw one group busily burrowing into what had once been a croquet lawn, I think, disappearing into tunnels like human moles. Others, in full kit, faced a row of targets dangling from a line, like big leathery sacks. At a snapped command from the NCO they charged en masse at the targets, yelling; they did not fire their rifles but stabbed at the sacks with their bayonets, like men taking on bears. With their big eyes and beak-like mouths and dangling tentacles, the sacks were scarecrow Martians. I learned later that,

174

although it seemed unlikely any soldier would survive to face a Martian outside its protective machines, the very physicality of bayonetting was thought to be good for a soldier's morale. Do it often enough, make yourself muscle-weary with it, and you grow into a kind of blood lust, an unhesitating willingness to kill – and that was a good mental state for a fighting man to reach for. The work was quite precise, I observed. The men were trained to thrust their blades into the Martians' mouths or eyes, and at the junction of the arms with the body, where the anatomists have observed nerve clusters.

As I watched there was a sudden clatter of rattles, a cry of 'Smoke, Black Smoke!' Everyone in hearing range dropped their gear, fixed hooded masks over their heads, and pulled down sleeves and trouser cuffs to leave no flesh exposed. But it was only a drill.

And there was a soft knock on my door: a call to the day's duty, and London.

Before the day was much older we had packed up our bits of luggage and were driven back into town to the rail station, and loaded up on a train full of anxious troopers, novices and veterans alike, being despatched to their postings. So we three, Lane, Gray and I, shared a compartment with a dozen men, who crowded the seats and sat on the floor – one fellow even stretched out on the flimsy-looking luggage rack overhead – and filled the little cabin with their cigarette smoke, as we rattled northwards, to London.

We slowed as we passed another train, coming down from London, and I peered over curiously. The train itself was splashed with paint, black and brown and green – camouflage colours. I saw troops in there, heading for their relief break, grimy and exhausted, many sleeping. Carriages marked with red crosses were like mobile hospitals. And there were carriages crammed with civilians too, evacuees, men, women, and children, many of them as grimy as the troops, blinking in the light – and in the case of the children staring in wonder at the green countryside, which perhaps they had never seen before.

Ted Lane, by the window, amused himself by pulling faces at the little Londoners and trying to make them smile.

Later we had a pause in our journey. The train simply stopped in open country, somewhere near Alton I think. The loco-motive was shut down, and workers in khaki swarmed along

175

the carriages dragging tarpaulins loosely over the roofs, and our view from the window was obscured.

Lane touched my shoulder. 'Martian about – or so some spotter will have called in, and the message sent on to the signalmen.'

'Probably a flying-machine,' Gray said. 'They come out for the odd raid, as if testing our defences. And they cut the rail links if they see them. So you conceal the tracks by splashing them with camouflage-colour paint, though that has to be renewed as it gets rubbed off by passing stock. And the trains too, the roofs of the carriages painted, a bit of tarpaulin to blur the outlines. Wouldn't fool a human spotter, but might a Martian. And we have to be still. A moving train—'

'Why are we whispering? The Martians might see us, but they can't *hear* us.'

He grinned. 'Natural reaction, ain't it? Anyhow you started it.'

Of course he was right.

We were held for hours before at last we moved. In the interval we had none of us spotted a flying-machine.

11

My Return to London

The train journey ended south of London, at Clapham Junction.

Here our train-load was exchanged with more relieved troops, all grimy and damp-looking, their clothes and kit shapeless and well-worn, even mouldy in some cases. The dominant impression was of exhaustion. Nevertheless these hollow-eyed fellows had greetings ready for their replacements.

'Hello! Nice haircut, mate, but the Heat-Ray will give you a trim for nothing.'

'Got a fag to spare?'

'Look at that one, Fred. Ruddy like a raspberry and as full of juice. Them Martians will have a fine time with *you*, you mark my words, suck and suck and slurp!...'

I suppose it has been the way of soldiers to goad each other this way, back to the days when Caesar came with his legions, perhaps to this very spot. But I saw that while this badinage was continuing, nurses and MOs stood with men in a worse condition: walking wounded festooned with bandages, on crutches – there was a line of men who seemed to have lost their sight, all standing with one hand on the shoulder of the fellow in front. All looked exhausted, bewildered, *shocked*, and those who could see were blinking in the light. It was not a promising welcome committee. And still I was far from the Martian centre, the cause of all this.

We filtered through the station, hundreds of us, to the gull-like cries of the NCOs and MPs.

Once we were out of the station we joined a unit of troops, laden with kit, already formed up. And then we set off on foot. We walked out to St John's Hill and turned right, towards the river.

It was my first return to London since I and Alice had fled from the initial advance of the Martians from Uxbridge, more than two years earlier. Falling back on my journalistic experience, I tried to keep my mind open, my reactions fresh. And to begin with, I had oddly positive impressions.

I saw a stretch of blue sky above. I heard little but a lapping of water somewhere nearby – that closeness puzzled me – and the singing of birds, and the quiet voices of the men as they walked along. The air smelled clear if a little stale, like a blocked drain, I thought. Many of the buildings had a peculiarly streaked effect on their grimy surfaces, pale stone showing under the black. The coming of the Martians had extinguished London's smoking chimneys, and the rain had weathered away some of the buildings' grime, centuries thick. I wondered what was going on in the parks – if the trees and birds were flourishing, if wildlife had come in from the country. It was a Wednesday in May; I felt a burst of absurd springtime optimism.

And then – too soon! – we came to the river. But not to its old bank.

Where the water lapped, I saw from the signs, was York Road. To our right was a small park area, sodden and flooded. And before us was the river itself, evidently spread up from its old course and over the feet of the buildings. I looked out across a stretch of grey water, to the silhouettes of buildings on the far shore, their foundations drowned as on our side.

Where the cobbled road surface ducked under the water there was an improvised jetty. Here a series of rowing boats waited for us, with more standing out on the river. The NCOs spoke their orders, and we shuffled down towards the water.

Once in my boat I sat cautiously at the prow, beside Gray, while Lane sorted out men to take the oars, and a rough type in a heavy waterproof leather coat sat at a tiller in the stern and glowered at us.

I murmured to Gray, 'What is this vessel?'

He shrugged. 'Scarcely matters, does it? Might even have been a lifeboat from one of the warships the Martians smashed up in the Pool...' He fell silent, watchful, as the boat inched its way down the flooded street, and over what I supposed to be a drowned embankment. 'Always the trickiest part, over the streets, there's all sorts of hazards – was on a boat once that got spiked by a smashed lamppost, sharp as a bit of broken bone, and that was no fun.'

178

We joined a line of similar boats. The oars lapped, and gulls wheeled overhead, calling, perhaps seeking food. The old route of the Thames was easy to make out as we progressed, for I could see the spans of bridges, every one of them broken as if snipped with scissors: Battersea Bridge, Albert Bridge, Chelsea Bridge. But the far bank was as drowned as the Clapham side, or more so; the river, vast and extensive, seemed to spread far inland to the north and east, over Chelsea and Westminster. The water itself was scummy, dirty, and scattered with debris – bits of wood, the remnants of clothing, dead birds and animals. The heat-twisted hulk of a battleship protruded, rusted and pathetic, above the lapping current. And it smelled foul, even in midstream. It was hard to believe this was the river of empire. Our pilot navigated cautiously, peering to left and right and every so often calling a halt if he suspected we were about to encounter some submerged obstacle.

Gray was watching me, as if interested in my reaction. 'More marvels for your newspaper stories, Miss Elphinstone?'

'Hardly marvels... The flooding. Is that the work of the Martians?'

'Not directly. Indeed I doubt the Martians, from their arid world, know enough about hydrology to have managed this deliberately. No, this is all accident and neglect; nobody is in a position to maintain the drains and the flood gates and the pumping stations. So the Thames is regaining its old banks: flooding lost lagoons at Hammersmith, Westminster, Bermondsey, the Isle of Dogs, Greenwich.' He smiled. 'The old rivers are coming back too, bursting out of the culverts into which we had forced them. I have a friend who swam down the course of the Fleet, for a dare, from St Pancras to Blackfriars. Of course as much damage is being done underground as at the surface.'

I thought that over. 'The Underground tunnels, for instance?'

'An awful lot of people sought shelter from the Martians down there, for an awful long time. Moving them has been a regular duty.'

So much damage had been done here – so much suffering! I felt ashamed of my own self-absorption.

We rowed our way carefully north-east – I think we followed the line of the drowned King's Road, through Chelsea towards Belgravia. To my right the broad, placid river could be glimpsed between the surviving buildings; to my left I thought I glimpsed the great museums of South Kensington rising pale. And ahead, the jagged ruins of General Marvin's new Palace of Westminster protruded from the water like the skeleton of some vast aquatic mammal. Still on the river, we passed Buckingham Palace – its roof was *melted* – and skirted the Victoria Memorial, and our pilot seemed to make his way more confidently over the drowned St James's Park.

At last we came to Trafalgar Square. Along with the boats that had preceded us we berthed on the Gallery steps which rose up out of the water; iron posts had been driven into the stone for the purpose. Once I had climbed out onto the steps, looking away from the water, I had a brief, odd feeling of normality, of routine, despite the khaki-clad men all around me. But a glance down Northumberland Avenue showed the waters of the swollen river glinting in the sun between the buildings, the surface littered with unidentifiable debris.

Gray came up beside me. 'Now we have lunch.'

'A little late for that.'

'You're in the Army now, Miss Elphinstone; you eat when you're fed. And then it's a walk for us and the troop, I'm afraid.'

'Which way?' I knew my destination was to the west and the Cordon, eventually.

But he pointed east, towards the Strand. 'That way, along the new shore. Dry enough, if we cut up a couple of streets. The Strand, you know – a Saxon word for "beach", and that's no accident, for this was once the bank of the ancient river.'

'How far?'

'All the way to Stratford.'

'Stratford? East, then, not west to where the Martians are – I imagine there's a plan.'

'As much as the Army ever has.'

12

From Aldwych to Stratford

So that extraordinary day continued.

We walked, but I am used to that, and was glad of the exercise after days of travel on boat and train. Our troop headed along the Strand – where now, as I have previously remarked, I had the opportunity to inspect the war wreckage of landmarks familiar to me – and then through Aldwych and around the London Wall to Aldgate, and then on up Whitechapel Road to Stepney and Bow. As we progressed the scouts would peel off to the locations of telephone equipment, left by those who had come this way before; they checked the gear and made hasty reports. The engineers suspected that the Martians could detect our wireless transmissions, and could track us that way – but they could not detect our telephone calls, or the wires if hidden underground.

As we walked, though we saw little evidence of fire, we passed tremendous craters, as if great bombs had fallen. These were the scars of Heat-Ray strikes. The Heat-Ray will incinerate a human in a flash, and demolish a building – but such is the density of energy it delivers that the fires it sets, in urban situations anyhow, tend to blow themselves out. So London had been spared the great fire-storm that many had predicted when the Martians brought the Heat-Ray back to the city.

But what the Martian assaults had done, by breaking the skin of modern London, had been to uncover the ancient city beneath. I was fascinated to learn that the Martians' destruction of the Guildhall had revealed the remains of a Roman amphitheatre, a structure long hypothesised but its existence never confirmed. Gray told me that even as the Martians still strutted over London in the present, archaeologists came to study what was exposed of the past. 'Makes you proud, doesn't it? That we still have such a perspective, even in *this*... Do the Martians seek abstract knowledge? If not, then that separates us from them.'

Now I saw that the men around me, on a murmur from their officers, were raising their gas masks to their faces, and Gray quietly advised me to do the same. He pointed to a churchyard, not far off the road. The church itself had been smashed, and the ground around churned up too.

'The graveyards?'

'In some of the older churches there are plague pits. Best to be cautious.'

We walked on.

You might ask where were the Londoners in this, those millions who still remained. *Hiding* – that's the short answer. I was told that the surviving population had learned to stay back from the main thoroughfares, but they still inhabited the great warrens of back streets, especially in the East End rookeries – that was if they hadn't found shelter underground, in the sewers or railway tunnels that were not yet flooded. Thus they avoided the Martians, with their Heat-Ray, and their harvesting. And they did what they could to keep themselves alive, and not just on the rations the emergency government managed to provide: they foraged in the wrecks of stores, where tinned goods and so forth could still be found, and they grew vegetables, even kept chickens and a few pigs, in gardens and allotments and the smaller parks.

The government kept an eye on the population. A system of ration cards was one way of ensuring every man, woman and child was logged in a great register somewhere. The police still functioned, after a fashion, augmented by Special Constables; crime levels were lower than you might have expected – because, it was said, the rations doled out were more nutritious than the diet of many East End Londoners before the Martians came. And people were put to work, on one project or another: on salvage work, or maintaining the surviving sewers, for example, as I was to discover for myself.

Hidden the people were, but, as we walked, occasionally children would peek out from an alley or the doorway of an abandoned shop, with grimy, rat-like faces, and big eyes. The soldiers threw them bits of chocolate, even a few cigarettes. 'For your mum and dad!' The children would grab the treasures and scuttle back into the shadows.

'Poor little mites,' Gray said neutrally. 'After years of this they don't know whether to fear us or the Martians.'

Ted Lane growled, 'I had family living around here – came to London to make their fortunes, if you can believe it – all evacuated now. A summer's day like this isn't so bad, but the winter's a misery. Nobody dares burn a fire, see, for fear of the Martians seeing the smoke. The sooner we put a stop to this business the better.'

'No one will disagree with you there, Sergeant,' said Ben Gray.

We reached Stratford, an area I did not know well. It seemed to me that the stroke of the Heat-Ray must have been heavy here. The streets were mere mounds of rubble in rows, with the names picked out by hand-painted wooden signs, if at all. In some places the damage was such that the very cobbles had been smashed and lifted. But life persisted, as it always does, and green sprouted in the lee of the broken walls. I remember particularly rosebay willowherb standing proud in the wreckage of parlours and kitchens.

And we came to a manhole cover.

The file broke up from its rough marching formation, and the NCOs gave brisk orders to the men to disperse to cover. 'If you've any tanks that need emptying, do it now. Then we'll be going down the rat-hole one at a time, so get ready.'

It was the work of a moment for a couple of men, hastily volunteered, to brush the cover clear of debris, and to get it lifted. Beneath, I saw rusty rungs leading down into the dark.

I faced Lane and Gray, who were both grinning at me. 'Is that—?'

'A sewer,' Gray said. 'A marvel of Victorian engineering.'

Lane sniffed. 'And a couple of winters' rain will have sluiced it nice and clean.'

'There is that.'

I glared at them. 'Why didn't you tell me?'

They glanced uneasily at each other.

'Well,' Gray said hesitantly, 'I suppose we thought – if you'd known—'

'What, I would have had a fit of vapours? Just as Major Eden decided I had to be tricked into my mission. Oh, for God's sake—' I pushed my way to the open manhole mouth, grabbed an electric torch from a startled corporal, and looked down into the pit. 'Tell me where this goes.'

Gray explained, as best he understood it himself. This great drain was part of the Bazalgette system, devised and built in

Victoria's reign to clean up the city. Once London's drains, all along the course of the river, had flowed more or less direct into the Thames by the shortest route. It was when the filth and stench had driven even the Parliamentarians indoors – the water was foul well upstream of Westminster by then – that it had been determined something must be done.

'So,' Gray said, sketching maps in the dirt, 'Bazalgette drove great transverse "intercept" sewers from west to east, running parallel to the river's course and cutting across all the other big north–south conduits. The idea being, you see, that the flow of water should be diverted east, so that the big discharges into the river itself would come much further downstream – further than Westminster anyhow. One of these transverse channels runs from Chiswick eastward. But the big one, the high-level sewer, runs from Hampstead to Hackney to Stratford – to *here*.'

I glanced at the unassuming manhole, and then westward. 'So if you plod upstream, so to speak—'

'You'll get all the way to Hampstead, deep underground and out of sight of any snooping Martian. And from *there* it's only a few miles to Uxbridge and the Cordon. And then – well, you'll see when we get there. It's a circuitous route we've followed, I know, to go east afore heading west again, but it's the safest passage we have.

'Anyhow, that's the good news,' he said wryly. 'The bad news is the day is too far advanced for us to make it all the way to the Trench today.'

'The Trench?'

'You'll see.'

I glanced around at the ruins. 'There's barely an intact roof to cover us. Where will we spend the night?'

And Lane and Gray glanced at each other, and at the manhole at our feet.

Albert Cook would have approved, I thought grimly. Londoners running in their own sewers, just as he foresaw during the First War. And yet, despite my bravado before these overbearing men, I felt a deep dread at descending into the clammy dark – indeed, a dread that had gathered for days as I had worked my way, step by step, closer to the heart of the Martians' dark empire on the earth.

13

Into the Sewer

Just under the manhole there was an equipment cache: sets of leather waders like an angler's, and gauntlets, and protective caps for the head, rather like a pilot's. There was an immediate fear among the men that there wouldn't be enough of the stuff to go round, a fear that proved all too justified, but as the stock was broken out Ted Lane made sure I got a set.

Once we were kitted out it took some time to get us all down that hole, one at a time – there were dozens in the party. It was a vivid experience for me when it was my turn, with Lane below me and Gray coming after. I remember how greasy the rungs of the ladder were, perhaps some measure against rust. As I descended I looked up at the diminishing circle of day, which by that time was already fading, and wondered what kind of landscape I would see when next I emerged into the light.

Then I was in the water, which was thick and muddy.

By the light of electric torches we moved away from the manhole. The tunnel in which I found myself had a profile like an egg-shape, perhaps to give it structural strength. The bricks seemed to sweat, glistening with damp. I could feel shingle on the floor, through the thickness of the waders and my shoes. We were walking against the current, but the water was not quite waist-high, and the current was no more than a gentle push. And I was relieved it was nothing *but* water, as far as I could see, with none of the horrors I had imagined: no waste, no dead rats – or worse, live ones.

Even so it was tiring, and we soon fell silent as we plodded into the dark, one step after another, with only the pools of light cast by the torches of those ahead visible, their distorted shadows making them seem hulking, inhuman forms. We did not speak much, though at first a few noisy fellows whooped to get an echo. And the jokers had a go: 'Just think, lads. One quick rainstorm and we'll all be flushed like turds, all the way to the North Sea!' But they soon shut up.

I could not track the time, with one gloved hand gripping my torch and the other skimming the greasy wall for balance. It was one of those experiences when you simply have to put your head down and endure, for counting the seconds won't make it go by any faster, and you're better off trying to forget where you are, what you are doing – who you are, if you can.

So I got through it, as did we all.

It was a huge relief when the walls opened out around us, and we came to a broader chamber. This was a cylindrical cave, the walls and flat roof more roughly finished than those of the sewer itself, and I surmised that this place was more recently built – constructed, indeed, since the Martians had arrived. The walls had been cut back at an angle so there were places where you could sit and lift your feet out of the water, or even lie down if you were lucky. This peculiar architecture was sustained by pillars of clay that had been left uncut to support the roof above us. Soon we were arrayed on the brick ledges like toys in a shop's store room, with candles under-lighting our faces and the shallow water casting shimmering reflections on the brick roof.

Talking softly, we broke out water and food and blankets from our packs. I was obscurely fascinated by the details of the men's uniform, up so close – the greenish khaki woollen tunic and trousers, puttees, boots with iron toecaps and heels, the peaked cap – and by the contents of the their kit-bags: each man had a toothbrush, soap, towel, spare bootlaces, a mess tin and fork, a razor, even a sewing kit, along with reading matter, mail from home, photographs and locks of their children's hair ... A mouth-organ or two. And probably French letters, tucked discreetly away.

The toilet was just an offshoot of the tunnel, a little way out of sight in either direction – more easily managed by men than women, but I found a way. We were in a sewer, after all.

'A strange place to stay the night,' I said to my companions, as Gray broke a chocolate bar and shared it with us. 'But I have been more uncomfortable.'

'You want to try kipping in a trench in Siberia,' Ted Lane murmured. 'And it's as safe a spot as you'll find anywhere within fifty miles of here.'

186

'I wonder where we'll all be this time tomorrow.'

Gray said, 'I know where we're *supposed* to be, which isn't always the case, and that's good enough for now.' He wriggled down and pulled his cap over his face.

I lay down too and made myself as comfortable as I could. I did not expect to sleep, not in such circumstances – deep in a sewer, under occupied London, with the men snoring all around me. But the echoes off the brick walls and the water and the breaths of my fellows merged into a kind of susurrus, broken by the plinking of water drops somewhere, and I was neither warm nor cold. I drifted gently into slumber.

I woke once to hear someone whimpering, off in the candle-light. It sounded like a child. There was a gruff rumble, a murmured, 'Yes, Sarge,' and then silence.

14

Emergence

The next morning we completed our subterranean journey under London and surfaced, blinking in the dawn light, in the ruins of Hampstead.

There was no time to sight-see. We were hastily bundled aboard a small fleet of motor-omnibuses, waiting in a shell-cratered school yard. The vehicles were nothing but London buses, I saw, their company markings roughly covered over with camouflage paint, the dull green and brown and black that were the colours of England that summer. I was pleasantly surprised to find these vehicles ready and waiting for us on time – a bit of Army planning that had worked out.

I was still more surprised to find Eric Eden waiting for me on one of the buses, somehow spruce in a clean-looking uniform. He grinned. 'Beat you here – don't ask me how! We had to send you by the most secure route, uncomfortable though it may have been; I am a less valuable shipment.' He eyed me. 'I'm glad to see you're healthy and in one piece, given your travels so far, Miss Elphinstone. And I take it you are – I mean, the special package has been no burden?'

He meant, of course, the tainted blood that coursed in my veins. 'Oh, everything is blissful,' I snapped back.

We boarded promptly and the bus rolled away, one of a small convoy on an otherwise empty road – heading west, I saw from the angle of the rising sun, towards the lair of the Martians. The scouts, I learned, had assured the officers that there were no Martian patrols nearby, and it was comparatively safe to dash across this last bit of open ground.

Eric sat with me on a scuffed leather seat, with Gray and Lane sitting behind. The rest of our group slumped down in their seats, broke out water flasks, and started cadging cigarettes from each other.

Ted Lane, an NCO himself, watched this display with amused contempt. 'Look at 'em, all grumbling and groaning. You wouldn't think they'd all just come from eight hours' lovely kip safe in that rat-hole, and a slap-up breakfast on top of that.'

Eric laughed. 'Well, they can grumble all they want when my back's turned, as long as they follow orders. And as long as we've got the right quality. In a set-up like the Trench you need a mix. You want your fighters, but also men who have been miners, navvies, gangers on the railways – that sort, with practical skills. And a well-trained sapper is worth his weight in gold, of course.'

But after only a short journey, the troopers grew restless, pointing ahead. When I looked through the paint-smeared windows I saw a rise in the ground, spanning the horizon, like a ridge, or a line of sand dunes. Was that the 'Trench'?

'Eric. What *is* this place?'

'Put all your preconceptions aside, Julie. Like nowhere else on this earth.'

15

In the Trench

Maps of the Martians' territory in England, as they possessed it at that stage in the Second War, are now readily available and familiar – not then! So you can imagine it as seen from above, from a Zeppelin, or a falling Martian cylinder. It would have looked like a tremendous archery target, I suppose. At the bull, you had the main group of Martian pits in the ruins of the Buckinghamshire town of Amersham, a complex still being busily extended, which had come to be called the Redoubt. From that centre, draw a circle of radius ten miles or so, to encompass Uxbridge to the south-east, and panning anti-clockwise past Watford, Hemel Hempstead, Princes Risborough, Marlow, Maidenhead and Slough. Use a thick pencil, for that was the line of destruction wrought by the fall of the 'dummy' cylinders at midnight of March 29, 1920, and the perimeter of the zone we came to call the Cordon.

Within that circle, the earthly kingdom of the Martians.

Outside the circle, two years later, had been constructed the most significant human response to the Martian incursion, called, laconically, the Trench. It was another great band around the perimeter of your target: a band of people and machines and watchtowers and weapons. Of course it was not a perfect containment, but it was the best we could do. And it was to the Trench that I was brought now.

Off the buses, we were met by a couple of NCOs, who formed us up into a rough column. We walked in our file the last hundred yards or so to that great earthen rampart I had seen.

Then we climbed. It had not been a dry winter and the ground, not yet bound by the new grass, was as muddy as you might expect, but there were paths to follow, of wooden duckboards pushed into the earth, and steps in places. Overhead there was a persistent buzz of aircraft, the hornet whines of aeroplanes or the deeper thrum of Zepp engines; the Cordon was continuously, if cautiously, patrolled from the air.

Eric walked beside me. 'Don't worry about the mud. You'll get used to *that*. And now, as we top this ridge, prepare for a marvel...'

It opened out slowly.

The ridge flattened out into a parapet reinforced with more duckboards. I found I stood on the lip of a tremendous ditch, a furrow in the ground. This inner face of the ridge was very steep, it cut down at an angle a lot sharper than forty-five degrees, and it must have been fifty feet deep, a gash in the English ground. Netting and wire had been flung down this great dug-out face, to stabilise it in case of rain I imagined, and there were rope ladders and rope-and-pulley arrangements reaching down the artificial cliff.

When I peered down into the trench to its very base, I saw people, all in khaki, making their way along a kind of narrow roadway, a path walled by sandbags and floored by duckboards. I would learn that the inhabitants called this deepest crease the 'gully'.

Beyond that tangled lane, I saw, a wall of earth rose up on the far side, mirroring my own side but riddled with detail, with walkways and ladders and shelters. That far side did not slope so steeply, and was broken up into terraces that spanned its length, to left and right as far as I could see, with shelves and steps everywhere. The vertical face itself had been dug into, to create rough caves, quite neat troglodytic apartments, faced by corrugated iron or wooden planks; the smartest even appeared to have glass windows. Here and there I saw the bright paint of red crosses. Men and women moved like maggots everywhere, across this face. A chorus of voices rose up, like the crowd in some strange amphitheatre.

And at the upper rim of this great complex there was a parapet of sandbags and spotting huts, with searchlights and what looked like Navy guns, and soldiers staring steadfastly away from us, to the west, into the Martian territory.

Glancing to left and right, I could see that this remarkable structure, this huge inhabited ditch, went on to left and right, sweeping to the horizon roughly to north and south – we had come on it from the east – with the slightest of curves visible in

191

the distance, suggesting a vast closed circle spanning the land. It reminded me of some relic of prehistory, a Saxon dyke perhaps, on a tremendous scale. But no nation of the Stone Age or the Iron Age had made this; I saw marks like the scraping of huge claws where digging machines had been used to gouge out the earth.

'There,' Eric said to me, grinning. 'Can you see the logic?' He pointed forward. '*That* way, to the west, are the Martians, and that's where they come from when they attack. So we built our cabins and stores into the east-facing walls, so there's some shelter when the attacks come, and made the west-facing walls steep so it's hard to clamber out, even for a fighting-machine. The Trench goes on in a great circle all around the Martian Cordon, an integrated defence system more than sixty miles long – which is the distance from London to Hastings, say. In fact it's the best part of two hundred miles of digging, for actually there are three diggings like this, one inside the other. We call them the "ditches".'

'*Three?*'

'Connected by a series of tunnels – you'll get used to tunnels here. This is the rear ditch, for supplies, training, medical support – you see the aid centres in the opposite wall. The middle ditch is for reserve troops, and the third, the innermost, is the front line. Anyhow that's the thinking, a kind of amalgam of the sort of trench-working we learned about agin the Boers, and developed by the Germans during the Schlieffen War.'

Lane grinned. 'And it works, I'm told. We can't do much about their flying-machines. But a fighting-machine, now – even a hundred-foot giant might trip over a fifty-foot ditch.'

'That's the idea, Sergeant. Make 'em think, at least, eh?'

I was still staring at the far wall, the swarming military humanity there – the detail of the workings, the shelters, the ladders and steps and galleries. 'It's like a cut-open termite nest.'

Ben Gray shook his head. 'Reminds *me* of the Amalfi coast, the sheer cliffs down to the beautiful sea, a town cut into a cliff face . . . Have you ever been to Italy, Miss Elphinstone? A rather more attractive populace there than a bunch of muddy Army types, though! Well, we'd better get on with it, we're holding up the line . . .'

Already I heard the NCOs calling to the newcomers: 'All right, lads, that's enough sight-seeing, and it's down you go. Old ladies and officers take the pulley lifts. The rest of you use the rope ladders; they aren't so bad, and the worst danger is getting your fingers stomped on by the lout coming down after you. But if you're a sportsman you'll take the slide.'

A woman's voice called, 'I'll show you boys how it's done!' It was a QA, a Queen Alexandra's nurse, I saw, in cape and skirt. She grabbed a bit of sacking, evidently left there for the purpose, sat down on it, slid on her backside over the crest – and then plummeted down the ditch face on a kind of slippery track, polished, I supposed, by the hundreds of backsides that had gone before hers. She whooped as she slithered, and finished with an undignified tumble at the bottom. But she got up laughing, and bowed to acknowledge the applause that broke out.

I was told we were to spend one night in the Trench before moving on in the morning, at seven a.m.

As I was attached to Eric Eden – a major, and something of a folk hero to troops facing Martians on the modern front line – I was privileged to be given a berth in a shelter on the ditch's second terrace up. The three officers who regularly shared this place called it a 'tamboo': English Army slang is full of Indian words.

Close to, I discovered the shelter was built on a frame of railway sleepers, the better, I supposed, to withstand blasts or landslips. It had a stove of its own, electric light run from a generator somewhere nearby, a table, chairs, bunk-beds, pictures pinned to the walls, a telephone – it even had a scrap of carpet on the floor. The washing facility and lavatory were basic, and connected to some system of sewerage that alone must have been a miracle of sapper ingenuity.

They had but a single room to share, yet the officers posted here, three calm young fellows, seemed used to hosting women 'day pupils', as they put it – yes, it did have the flavour of a public school lark about it – and they set up a system of curtains and so forth to give me privacy. Their conversation was banter, or Trench gossip, and all the officers were 'muffs'. They were very young men, and a little silly despite their experiences of war. It would not be quite true to say that they were perfect gentlemen around me. That evening, after a dinner of bully beef, potatoes and greens served by a batman, and the drink came out, a decent whisky, and the cards and the cigars, they rather forgot themselves and there was fruity talk about the nurses, and so on. But I, that bit older, with my short hair and trousers, did not seem to attract their attention in that way.

They did have an old Marvin wireless receiver, the worse for wear but serviceable, and we listened to the news from the government station. It was little more than the *National Bulletin* read out in sonorous tones. And they had a gramophone, which they wound up to play sentimental songs from musical-theatre shows I had not seen.

I got a little restless as the evening wore on, and when Eric checked in on me about nine o'clock I swallowed my pride somewhat and requested his permission to go for an explore. He frowned, and I am sure he would have preferred me to stay where I was, under his nose. But to my relief he put a call in on the telephone, asking if Sergeant Lane was free.

Then Eric bade me goodnight. It was an informal parting. I was not to know that it would be some days before I saw him again, in a transformed world.

Ted Lane turned up outside the tamboo not five minutes later, with an electric lantern and a torch.

'I'm sorry to drag you away from your free time, Ted.'

'Not at all, miss. Mind your step, now...'

We clambered down a ladder; he insisted on going first in case I fell.

I would not claim that the late spring twilight made the bottom of that ditch a magical place. That could hardly apply to a gully where a couple of dogs, whimsically called Lloyd and George, ran after rats with the inhabitants placing penny bets on their success, or where a 'sanitary man', an older soldier with a pronounced limp, worked his way along the duckboards, emptying brimming latrines into sump holes and spraying them with creosote and chloride of lime. But the lanterns hung prettily from the terraced wall rising steeply above me, giving it something of the look of Amalfi, as Gray, better travelled than I have ever been, had perceived. As the light faded, even the searchlights that raked the darkling sky, looking for Martian flying-machines above or fighting-machines on the march below, had an oddly jaunty air, I thought.

Heaps of stores sat in boxes and crates, waiting for sorting. I saw that some had come from Germany, and some from America – our transatlantic cousins were staunch allies in a pinch, disapprove of our accommodation with the Kaiser as they might. There was a kind of library, heaps of battered, much-read editions that included some classics and quality literature, not all of it William le Queux and other of the lowbrow entertainments you might have imagined – Ford Madox Ford was a particular favourite, I had time to observe. There was a post office marked by red and white flags; there were, it seemed, several deliveries a day, the mail from home being considered a cheap but essential boost to morale. And we passed medical stations – 'casualty clearing stations', they were called. We did not see many injured that night: with some days since the last contact with the Martians, we were told, those who needed better treatment had already been removed to stations behind the lines.

We came across groups of men in the gully, sitting together outside their shelters, patching clothing or writing letters and talking softly, even one fellow playing a mouth-organ, and a better performance it was too than my pet officers' gramophone records. These gully promenaders were mostly men, women being largely confined to the medical posts as nurses, or serving as cooks or clerks or drivers or in other support roles, even construction work – anywhere save the front line – and the men seemed inhibited by my presence. But they opened up to Ted Lane.

Of course the basic military hierarchy was in place. As one man explained it to me, 'You got your privates, which is *us* poor slobs, and you got your NCOs lording it over us, no offence, Sarge, and you got your officers lording it over them, and then your staff officers, and you got your generals above *them*. And every one of us complains about the sheer bleeding in-*com*-petence o' all the rest above and below, and it's a wonder anything ever gets done around here.'

'But it never does, Sid!' someone called.

However, cutting across this familiar ladder of rank were the specialisms. The Trench system itself had mostly been constructed by recruits with appropriate civilian experience, by agricultural workers, and 'navvies' and 'gangers' from the railways, and bricklayers and carpenters and concrete-mixers, all under the command of the Royal Engineers. I learned new bits of language. An electrical worker was a 'sparkie', the 'toshers' kept the rudimentary sewage system working, and every man had a 'banjo', a shovel, for the times when the rains came and threatened to flood or collapse the whole affair, and it was a case of everyone digging to save the day. Even on this calm night, I could see the task of maintaining the system continuing, with workers

195

labouring at the drainage of that lowest walkway, at the revetting of the walls, and repairing sandbag parapets.

Yet the military unity was something of an illusion. There were colonial troops serving in the Trench, especially Indian, and the latter had had to be kept apart from the British regulars, because of taunts of the 'It's your turn now, *sahib*!' kind. Meanwhile Ted politely steered me away from some less salubrious districts of that great circular city – such as a place they called 'Plug Street', semi-officially sanctioned brothels.

I tried to gather my impression of the place. 'This whole great earthwork is like – what? Like one vast body, this Trench curled like Ouroboros around the Martian canker, and these soldiers toil like antibodies in the bloodstream to keep the whole intact and healthy.'

Ted Lane pulled a face. 'That's a bit poetic for me, miss. It's the best we can do, that's all.'

I did wonder about the wisdom of the stratagem. If these Martians had come here to learn about us, then here we were providing them with a kind of idealised training ground, as we sat there and threw the best we had at them, and let them devise ways to counter it. But then, what else were we to do? As Lane had said, we couldn't simply wave them through.

On the way back to my tamboo I saw a man tending a row of pea plants, growing out of the earth under shoved-aside duck-boards. This was a Tommy garden, as they called it. When your eye got attuned, you saw them all over the face of the Trench, splashes of homely green.

16

A Tunnel Under the Trench

I had been told I would be roused, the next morning, by a bugle. In the event Ben Gray came in the dark and shook me awake. 'Get dressed.'

I pushed my way out of my bunk. The young officers were already gone; a half-drunk bottle of whisky and scattered playing cards stood on the table. Beyond the curtains of the tamboo's windows, I saw greyish daylight, and I could hear shouting and running footsteps. 'What time is it?'

Gray was gathering my gear and stuffing it without ceremony into my rucksack. 'Early. Not yet four a.m.'

'But we aren't meant to be travelling until seven.'

Gray looked me in the eye. 'The Martians have decided not to follow our plan. Get your boots on, empty your bladder, and meet me outside. That's an order.'

'Where's Eric Eden?'

'Fighting the Martians. Now come *on*.'

Outside the tamboo, boots and hat on, rucksack over my shoulders – I had lingered long enough to make sure Walter's packet of sigil sketches was safe in my pack – at first I stood astounded by the sight before me.

In the grey dawn light, the great ditch swarmed with activity.

Lanterns shone everywhere, and searchlights mounted on the parapets raked over this great linear hive. There was a barrage of noise too, whistles, bugle calls, shouts, though the human sounds were dwarfed by the great scale of the ditch. On the far wall, the steeper eastern face, I saw people clambering up or down the ladders, even scaling the stabilising netting, the main priority seeming to be to get off the face and to shelter. Loads

197

of materiel hung from the pulley cables, apparently abandoned. In the deep gully, and all across the terracing of my inhabited western face, people ran, some without their proper uniforms – some even barefoot – grabbing weapons and ammunition packs as they went, and dashing to their stations.

Now I heard the crack of an artillery gun, a huge pounding that shook the earth. All around me men stopped in their tracks, and looked up at the brightening sky, and pointed. I twisted my head, and looked up too, up, up past the terraces and the rows of tamboos.

And I saw it loom over the parapet of the western face, coming out of the Cordon: a cowled hood, a flash of bronze, tentacular appendages clutching what might have been a heavy camera.

'Down!' That was my own cry, I think; next thing I knew I had shoved Gray down and lay half across him with my hand on the back of his neck. That was the veteran in me.

And the Heat-Ray spat. I glimpsed the thread, the characteristic pale distortion of its guide-light in the air. It swept over the sheer eastern face, and where it touched, climbing men and women flashed to flame and vanished, human beings popping like pockets of flammable gas.

More guns barked now, from behind our lines. Shells flew over our heads. In '07 the Martians had come to an England where the most advanced weaponry on land was horse-drawn guns. Now we had motorised artillery, and were able to respond much more rapidly. But while some of the shells splashed against the face of the Trench, creating peculiar angled craters and adding to the din of noise, none reached the Martian.

Then, like a man stepping cautiously into a stream, the Martian folded its great legs, and pivoted, and stepped down *into* the gully. Once all three feet were down, it swivelled its cowl this way and that. Now that ghastly beam raked the gully itself, and the inner face of the Trench. I saw structures detonate and collapse across the wall, and people running like ants from a kettle of water. And the screaming began.

It all came back to me. Perhaps I froze, locked in memory.

Gray grabbed my hand and pulled me away, towards a ladder downward. 'Miss Elphinstone – Julie – we go now.'

'Where?'

'Into the tunnels, of course!'

*

Our port of call was what looked like a manhole cover, set in the duckboards of the gully. Ted Lane was waiting for me there, with soldiers – only a handful of men, armed with pistols, rifles and shovels.

I inspected the cover. 'That looks as if it came off a sewer, like the one we climbed down at Stratford.'

'It probably did. Let's get on with it.'

Lane and one of the soldiers hauled the cover aside, to reveal a shaft with iron handles set in the walls, just like at Stratford. That was where the similarity ended, though, as I discovered as I followed Lane down, with Gray right behind me. The tunnel we entered was deeper even than the great sewer had been, and faced with sapper-applied concrete, not neat Victorian brick. Electric lights had been fixed to the walls, along with cables and wires and copper pipes. And where the sewer had been half flooded, this tunnel was all but dry, with only a smear of damp mud at its lowest arc. All this, of course, had been constructed since the landing of the Martians.

At the bottom of the shaft, Lane grabbed a steel combat hat from a stack and jammed it on my head.

Then, without further ado, we ran for it.

The tunnel was straight and true, as far as I could see it, heading dead west. It was awkward work to run in there, for the rough-finished roof was too low for comfort standing up, even for shorter folk than me. Yet we were running, burrowing like big rats at the feet of the Martians, once again just as Bert Cook had predicted. And I, I was like a plague rat myself, scurrying off some ship into a crowded medieval port, my blood foul with disease.

Lane called back, 'We're passing beyond the Trench now. This passage goes on, at about this depth, all the way under the broken ground where the Martian cylinders landed.'

The soldier ahead of him called back, 'And tough work that was. Those blessed cylinders smashed up the very bedrock when they fell. You try digging all that out by hand while them Martians stomp about up top – it was enough to chill the blood.'

Ted Lane said, 'Pity you didn't make it big enough for a normal person while you were at it, mate, I keep banging my nut.'

'Huh. *That's* doing no harm, unless it's to my precious wall.'

Gray called forward, 'Shall we save our breath, lads?'

At length the NCO who was leading the sappers ahead of us held up his hand, and slowed. 'Rest area.'

We had come to a place where the concrete walls were wider, if only marginally; there was room to sit, a water tank with a spigot. On the floor I saw crushed cigarette stubs, what looked like empty food tins, and a covered hole for a toilet. The men stopped with grunts of relief.

'Just a breather, lads,' the NCO said. 'I know we just started, but it was all of a rush, and now's the time if you've got a boot on backwards or your corset's too tight.'

I, with Lane, walked through this area and just past it into the tunnel beyond, to make room for the rest. Gray, behind me, hung back, in the middle of the rest place. All of us were ducking our heads under the low roof.

I describe this quite precisely because our disposition at that moment was to determine life and death for all of us.

For the tunnel wall imploded.

I saw it come in from my right-hand side, the concrete shattering into a hail of blocks and rubble and dust that slammed across the tunnel and into the far wall. The noise was tremendous; my ears rang with it, and the grit got in my eyes – I suppose it was a miracle the electric supply kept working, so any of it was visible – but I saw how a couple of men were killed immediately, caught in this lethal wash, splashed like bags of crimson paint against the unyielding concrete. Despite my experiences in the First War, I had never witnessed such immediate and violent death before, not close to.

The surviving soldiers reacted faster than I did. Ted Lane grabbed me around the waist and pulled me back into the tunnel. The sappers formed up in rows, across the width of the rest area, with revolvers and rifles drawn. The NCO was yelling orders, and Lane was shouting in my ear as he pulled me backwards, but I could hear nothing but a muffled roar.

And then I saw the Martian, pushing in through the wall. Long tentacles came through first – metallic limbs, multiply jointed and flexible, with every appearance of life despite their surface artificiality. These limbs pulled at the broken wall, widening the aperture. Then through came one leg, two, long, insectile, power-ful. And then a broad body, like an upended saucer – like a crab but made of some metallic material. A third leg through, a fourth, a *fifth*. And riding that eerie carriage I saw a thing like a sack of leather, glistening wet and pulsing, with a scatter of concrete dust sticking to the moist flesh – very like the targets I had seen used for bayonet practice in the grounds of the house in Hampshire, but *alive*, visibly so, pulsing and quivering like a great lung.

This was a handling-machine, of the kind I had seen innocently manufacturing aluminium in the Surrey Corridor, with, on its back, a Martian. Later I would learn that this was the first time a handling-machine had been seen used in this way, as a weapon in direct conflict. But Walter Jenkins had foreseen it: as he had told me in Berlin, the Martians weren't likely to modify their machines, perfected as they were by a million years of use, but they were certainly capable of inventing new ways to use them.

And cradled in the limbs of this machine, as it clambered free of the hole it had made in the wall –

'Heat-Ray!' I tried to yell the warning, but could not hear even my own voice. 'Heat-Ray!'

The men stood their ground and fired. I could barely hear their shots; I saw the bullets splash off the metallic hide of the machine, but they could not reach the living Martian. Lane pulled me back further, and I did not resist; I had no weapons and could contribute nothing to the fight.

And the Martian wielded its Heat-Ray, at last. One man gone! Two! I heard their despairing cries as they died, and I could feel the waves of heated air, intense, shocking.

But the soldiers were not done yet. Gray grabbed the NCO by the shoulder, and I saw him show the man something he held in his left hand, a pellet small and dark. It was a grenade, I guessed. The NCO looked his officer in the face for one heartbeat. Then he moved back, yelling at his men until they followed him away from the rest area.

Gray waited until the beast had clambered fully into the tunnel. It was a big machine which barely cleared the walls . . .

Gray stood his ground, and looked at us deliberately, checking we had moved back . . .

He faced the thing from Mars . . .

He detonated his grenade!

In that confined space the shockwave knocked us like nine-pins, back along the tunnel. Whether the explosion itself damaged the handling-machine fatally I cannot say, but I saw the roof collapse, and a rush of earth and rock like a dark waterfall smashed down on man, machine, Martian and all.

And I saw the roof over my own head cracking.

'*Out! Out!*' That was the cry on Lane's lips, and on the sappers'.

So we ran along that tunnel, away from the Trench and under

the Cordon and on into the lair of the Martians; we ran through pulses of dust as sections of the tunnel collapsed; we ran on when the lights failed at last, ran through the dark by the flickering light of battery torches.

I do not remember the end of that terrible journey. Perhaps I was struck by a falling slab and knocked cold. I had Lane, I suppose, to thank for saving my life.

The next I remember I was lying on green grass, a pale summer sky above.

England, I thought. This is England. With such horror buried in the ground.

Ted Lane sat with me, looking down, his face smeared with pale dust, and a darker, crimson stain on his chin. When he saw my eyes were open, he helped me sit up.

I was in a meadow. Daisies nodded, irreverent. It was clear I had not been the only casualty of our flight: men in khaki lay scattered around me, their companions tending them. They were grey, dusty masses dumped incongruously on the green sward.

To my left I saw broken ground, a kind of rampart, dirt and rock crudely piled up like a stalled wave. It was the Martian perimeter, I realised with a kind of wonder, or the inner edge of that smashed ground. Where we had emerged, where our tunnel mouth was, I could not tell. But I was *inside* now; that was clear.

And when I looked the other way I saw Martians, fighting-machines, three of them, huge in the mist of distance. They picked their way to and fro across the fields like beachcombers collecting shells – their motions seemed peculiarly co-ordinated, even choreographed, and I thought of Walter's speculations of Martian telepathy. There was no sign of any human reaction or resistance. It was an almost casual vision, as if this was quite normal.

And I heard a car horn.

When I turned I saw a Rolls, bright yellow, bouncing over the grass. It made a sharp turn and skidded to a halt. The driver leaned out, doffed a leather cap and goggles, and grinned at me. A new scar on his face was livid.

It was Frank, my former husband.

'Parp, parp!' he called. My ears were ringing; I could barely hear him. 'But you never were one for Grahame, were you, Julie? Never mind. Welcome to Darkest England. Anyone need a lift?'

17

Inside the Cordon

Frank told me that when word had got to him that I was on the way in, he had insisted on meeting me in person, and here he was. But if he was to drive me away, Ted Lane insisted on accompanying me.

We left the surviving sappers with promises of transport as soon as it could be arranged. Still, I felt my heart would break as we drove away from those men, all so young, so many injured, who had seen their companions die in order that I should fulfil my mission: a mission of whose nature they could have no clear idea.

So Lane and I sat in the car side by side, covered in dust and mud, even splashed with blood. I felt grotesque. My ears rang too, adding to the sense of unreality. Frank told us there was a medical bag in the back of the car. We found it, opened it, drank from a flask of water, wiped our faces and hands, and applied antiseptic to our cuts. Concrete dust scattered from my hair when I shook my head. 'I must look a sight.'

'You look just fine, miss,' Ted Lane told me.

It was still very early morning; the countryside was bright and green. 'Is this real, Ted? Was *that* real? The handling-machine, the men who fell – Ben Gray—'

He took my hand. 'We're not out of the woods. This is Martian country. Put it aside for later. Like in a box, tucked deep inside, until you've got time.'

'Is that how *you*—'

'Keep thinking, miss. Just keep thinking.'

I nodded.

Frank did not look round. I had been married to him; I knew

he would understand, without needing details until I was ready. He, for one, was concentrating on the job of driving.

And meanwhile the Rolls fair rattled along a potholed road, leading us away from the heaped-up war zone behind us, and into a scene that was astonishing for its mundanity, all things considered, given what I had gone through to get this far. This was the English countryside, and on that mid-May day it was clad in that thick moist sun-drenched green you see nowhere else in the world. I glimpsed dogwood hedges, and houses of ancient-looking stone, and poppies and pimpernels, and thought I saw a yellowhammer, sat on a low twig and lording it over the world.

Compared to Germany it all seemed so *old*, and unplanned too, with field boundaries that might go back to Celtic times or earlier, buildings that might once have been barns or woodsmen's shelters now turned into garden stores or gazebos for a new generation of commuters. This was what you got when you had centuries of peace, so many slumbering generations. I had a sudden sense of age, of continuity, from Wat Tyler through Shelley to Darwin, to mention three of my own heroes – an England with a history that had nothing to do with these Martians – and I had a sudden determination that she had to be saved.

But if you looked closer things were far from ordinary.

There was no other traffic to be seen on the road along which we sped, for a start. Here and there one would see wreckage – cars driven off the road and abandoned to rust. The most startling sight of that sort, which we saw from a level crossing, was a crashed train. It lay along the line that had carried it; passenger coaches were smashed to matchwood, and freight coaches lay on their backs, with their rusting wheels in the air, like tremendous cockroaches, upended. It was not the train's destruction that affected me so much as the fact that it had never been cleared away.

A little later we passed at speed through an area that looked, from afar, as if it had been burned out, for a black dust, like soot, lay over everything: the road itself, the houses, the fields. I would learn from a grim-faced Frank that this was the aftermath of a Black Smoke attack. In the First War the Martians had rendered whole swaths of Surrey lifeless with the stuff. But *that* substance, evolved on an arid Mars, had been too easily laid by water and rendered into harmless dust. The Martians had tweaked the design – the stuff they had now was still more deadly – and the poison lingered, even in the English damp. The Martians had used that deadly substance sparingly in this War, Frank said, only as a 'punishment measure' when they encountered resistance. It was not their aim to exterminate us, after all.

And then, to add to the oddness of the day, there was the peculiar way in which Frank continually inspected the sky.

I noticed detail about him: the way his shirt collar was worn, the elbows of his jacket rather crudely patched with scraps of leather. That was not Frank's style; he was a professional man who preferred smartness. And his manner had changed; those upward glances told of a furtiveness, an inner tension. It was only later that he told me in detail of his experiences with the Army during the Martian landings – experiences that inevitably left scars – and he had since spent two years in an occupied territory. Even so, looking over his shoulder, I could see my ex-husband was enjoying the way the car handled. And perhaps he was glad to see me safe.

'Since when did you own a Rolls Royce?' My voice felt muffled in my own shock-blown ears, but I ignored the effect.

'Ah, if only I did,' he replied. 'Not mine; it belongs to the Dowager Lady Bonneville – the big cheese in this neck of the woods, you'll meet her – or more strictly it passed to her after the death of her husband some years back. Part of a collection.'

We were coming into a small village, unprepossessing, a row of shut-up shops and workers' cottages surrounded by fields. But it had a rail station, surrounded by rather boxy villas. The rail line itself was lost in green weeds.

'The widow kept the cars under wraps, so to speak, for some months. The Martians smashed up just about every vehicle they could see in the first hours or days, but *these* beauties were out of sight. Now, of course, they're proving remarkably useful – although one always has to be discreet.'

We pulled up before a rather dilapidated station building. He bundled out of the car, glancing again at the sky.

I followed him, as did Ted – sweating, blood smeared on his face and dust staining his crumpled uniform, staying steadfastly at my side.

The rear wall of the station building had been cut away, to be replaced by a hanging tarpaulin. Frank pulled on a rope, and the tarpaulin began to rise like a stage curtain. 'Help me, man.' Ted hurried over to take another length of rope, and I helped too, and we all pulled away.

The tarpaulin lifted to reveal a gutted interior. The window for ticket sales was still there, and a door to a lavatory gaped open, but otherwise the building had become an impromptu garage. Half of it was occupied by another vehicle, a small tractor, and there were tool sets, oily rags, and cans of oil and petrol lying around.

Frank waved us out of the way, briskly drove in the Rolls, and hustled out, dragging the tarpaulin down after him.

'Abracadabra,' he said dryly. 'As if it had never been. Looks rather strange, I know, but I think we can rely on the Martians not being *au fait* just yet with the fine particulars of late-nineteenth-century English railway architecture, and it's an effective cache. It's foot-slogging from here to Abbotsdale, I'm afraid, but it's not very far. Well – nowhere is very far from anywhere else in the Cordon, it's only twenty miles across, as you'll know...'

We walked on along the road, heading roughly north, and up a slight incline. I soon wearied. We were in the Chilterns, a landscape of chalk, of steep rises and hidden valleys: a country where a hill to climb is never far away, as I and my leg muscles were to discover in the days to come. But the peaceful quiet did us both good, I think, Ted and me, after our extreme experiences.

Indeed, after the shock, the sudden violence, this ordinary-looking country didn't seem real, not to me.

Ordinary-looking country. Not really, if observed closely even from the car, and less so now as we walked through it and saw the detail. The roadside hedges were untrimmed, bramble and holly both growing wild everywhere. A number of cottages we passed were evidently abandoned, some broken open or burned out. In places phone wires were down and lay where they had fallen. One poignant relic, for me, was a poster affixed to a tilted telephone pole for an agricultural show that would have been held in the autumn of 1920 – that season had come and gone, the show had never been held, but the poster, weather-faded, clung on.

Frank had brought his pack from the car, and he dug out water flasks. As we walked, Ted and I both drank thirstily.

Ted, coming to himself, was growing more observant, more curious in his practical way. 'Where do you get your petrol?'

'Stores from before the invasion.' Frank pointed to the sky where an aeroplane whined, a distant wasp. 'And we get drops. But the Martians have a good kill rate of the aircraft, unfortunately; we can't rely on that. There's a strict rationing system, for *everything* – you'll see. Eventually we'll run out.' He glanced at me. 'But maybe something will turn up before we get to that crisis, eh? They told me you were coming, but not what you're up to...'

I had known that some communication was possible with the interior of the Cordon; it was no great surprise to find Frank expecting me. I had always had a vague idea that as soon as I found Frank I would blurt it all out to him – even the deeper truth of my mission, the blood and the Lie – and rely on his judgement and strength of character, rely on his help.

But now that I was here, walking through this Cordon of his, with its patrolling Martians and stashed cars and so forth, I found myself peculiarly uneasy. In France I had lived in a country under occupation, and I had seen how individual lives and choices were distorted by that brute fact, how society itself was pulled out of shape. These were uneasy, nebulous thoughts – they made me uncomfortable even with Frank – but the upshot was that I decided to keep the secret of my true mission a little longer, until I understood what I had walked into. So I said nothing. Frank turned away.

We turned a corner, and came upon a tumbled cart with broken wheels, and the skeleton of a horse, the mighty bones jumbled in the traces. The bones had been picked clean; there was no smell, and it was a rather abstract sight.

Frank pointed. 'You can see the leg that got broken, and the bullet-hole in the skull where the driver put the animal out of its misery.'

Ted looked at him. 'What of human remains?'

'You come across some,' Frank said. 'In the ditches, in abandoned houses we break into for supplies – all under the mandate of the Vigilance Committee, you understand. We bury them decently. The Vicar at Abbotsdale comes out to say the words, and he keeps a note of names and dates, if they're known. Usually it's starvation and sickness that has taken them ... If it's the Martians, you see, there's no trace left. Come along – not far now – soon we'll be seeing our farmed fields.'

18

The Potato Fields

We came to a stream. The road crossed this by a small stone bridge, and here we stood and stared curiously. The water was a mere trickle, and it ran over a bed that was choked with dense crimson vegetation.

'I remember this red stuff from '07,' I said.

'I think we all do,' Ted Lane said. 'The red weed... But I thought that got killed off with the Martians.'

'So it did, last time,' Frank said. 'The Martians seem to have found a way to make the stuff immune to whatever earthly cankers did for it before, just as they evidently toughened up their own blood. Now here it is, surging into life wherever there's open water, or even heavy ground if the water table is high...'

I clambered down from the bridge for a closer look. I stood in mud that gave under my boots, and the weed sprawled and flourished around me. In that English stream bed I saw fronds and vesicles and stems and what seemed to be seed pods. In form it was reminiscent of cactus plants, with bulbous, prickly lobes sprouting from deep root systems. And all in that rich crimson, a deeper red than blood.

Much speculation had been vented on this biological novelty since the fall of the Martians in '07. Lankester of the Natural History Museum, for example, opined that a cactus-like morphology might be characteristic of an arid world such as Mars, where plants must extract and conserve what little water is available: digging deep with long roots, storing the treasure in vessels with leathery skins defiant of evaporation, and with prickles to drive off thirsty Martian animals – or humanoids. Now, not for the first time in my life, I discovered that comforting theories are one thing, but the reality of the alien, close to, is quite another, for the strangeness seems to drive out the analysis.

And certainly the weed seemed to have more about it than merely being niggardly of water. It was vigorous stuff. When I crouched for a yet closer look, I could see it growing. I mean that literally: I could *see* the leaves stretch and spread, the air blisters grow. How to describe that eerie development? It was faster than the imperceptible growth and movement of the ordinary vegetable world, slower than the fast oxygen-fuelled motions of the animal. Something in between. It was like watching an accelerated film, perhaps.

'Unearthly,' I said aloud.

'Indeed,' Frank replied. He reached down a hand. 'You'd better come out of there.'

When I stood up, I felt oddly giddy; I gasped for breath, and was grateful for his hand as I stepped back up onto the bridge.

Frank said, 'It's different when you see it on the ground, isn't it? The vicar I mentioned fancies himself as something of a naturalist. Once he collected beetles, he told me.'

I smiled, though I still felt queasy. 'A follower of Darwin, then.'

'Now he has widened his field of study. Where the Martian plants grow, he says, the red creepers and the weed, our native flora and fauna cannot compete. The green plants that once colonised this river bed, and on land the earthworms and the ladybirds and the flies and the spiders, and the birds who used to feed on them – all dying back. We are seeing extinction in action, he says. He references a French fellow named Cuvier, which means little to me. For all the strutting of the fighting-machines and the sinister shadows of their flyers, *this* is the real stranglehold that Mars is imposing on the earth; this is the cockpit of the war of the worlds. Nature versus nature.'

I took deep breaths. 'And the air? Why is it I feel as if I've run an Olympic steeplechase?'

'I've done some study on that myself, after my surgery was plagued by patients who complained of breathlessness after working the river-bed fields.'

'What river-bed fields?'

Ted Lane looked down the shallow valley of this stream. 'Perhaps like those.'

Glancing that way, I made out a number of figures toiling in the mud or the shallow water, perhaps a quarter-mile away. I thought some were soldiers, from the baggy clothes they wore

209

and a faint sense of discipline about them – and the fact that one or two of their number did not work but strolled about watching the work of others, as NCOs and officers will. But there were other, more enigmatic forms among them – different sorts of people, I thought, a taller, slender sort, and a squat, hunched-over variety whose bent backs appeared to bristle with hair. The oddest thing about *those* fellows, dimly glimpsed from a distance, was that they didn't seem to be wearing clothes at all... Curiosity sparked in me, even as a lingering sense of unreality deepened.

But after the violence of the tunnel, the whole day was like a dream.

Frank was still speaking, rather dully, of the changes in the air. 'I'm no scientist, but I've done some simple tests. Schoolboy chemistry stuff – you know. Over the weed, at any rate where it is densest, the composition of the air differs from the norm. I believe the nitrogen and oxygen from the atmosphere are being fixed in some compound in the weeds' root system, deep underground, just as some of our own plants will fix nitrogen. So the Martian plants are removing the dominant components of our air, leaving an apparent excess of the rest: water vapour and carbon dioxide and so on. Also I suspect there's a higher concentration of argon – as Rayleigh determined, argon is the next significant component in our air – but I'd need a more sophisticated chemistry set than I've been able to scramble together to establish that.

'It's a steady sequestration. Whatever other purpose the weed serves – and both sorts of Martian folk can eat the weed, even if we can't – it's a pretty efficient air extractor! And if you imagine that action scaled up to a field, or a few acres, or square miles...'

I looked at him. 'Martian folk? *Both* sorts? What Martian folk?'

Frank pointed downstream to the working party. 'Let me show you.'

We made our way in that direction.

Of course it was the soldiers Ted was most interested in speaking to, and never mind Martian exotica; we had to take a short detour and meet them. And of all the sights I might have expected to see in this confiscated corner of England, I would never have guessed at German soldiers tending potatoes.

It was all rather gentlemanly. One of the chaps strolling around inspecting the others' work turned out to be senior, though like the rest he wore a shapeless straw hat, shirtsleeves, and trousers with braces. As Frank introduced us he shook my hand, and Ted

Lane's. 'Newcomers, eh? Welcome to the madhouse. I'm Bob Fairfield, Lieutenant-Colonel if it makes a difference any more.' He eyed me with open speculation, and my dusty state, and I wondered what he knew of my mission – either the cover story or the true purpose. Uneasily I began to realise that I had no idea who I could trust here.

Ted, meanwhile, stood to attention and snapped out a salute. 'Sorry, sir.'

'Oh, at ease, Sergeant.' Fairfield glanced at his toiling troops, earthing up rows of potato plants with rusty spades, who looked upon us with a kind of resentful curiosity. 'Two years it's been since the great Martian curtain came down and trapped us all in here. We must keep up discipline; I've always been convinced it's the best way for the men – and as you can see, there's plenty of work to be done. We've long since exhausted the bully beef and beans we brought with us. I can always use an enthusiastic NCO, if you're up for it.'

Ted glared at the privates, who looked back at him, mud-streaked and sweating and resentful. Ted grinned. 'It'll be a pleasure, sir.'

'Meanwhile let me introduce you to my colleague. I'm sure it's well known outside that a number of Germans, fighting alongside us against the Martians, were trapped in here too. Damn good allies they were during the battle, and good companions they've proved in this big green prison camp. Their most senior officer is a Feldwebelleutnant Schwesig. Let's see if I can find him...'

They strolled off among the toiling men. Beyond this river-bottom field I could clearly see those *others* that I had seen before, the tall skinny ones, the squat hairy ones.

Frank was more interested in the potatoes. 'Actually it was my idea. Or rather Mildred Tritton's, and I took it to Fairfield and the rest.'

'Mildred?'

'Local farmer. Absolute brick; you'll meet her soon enough. We tried to get ourselves organised from the beginning, you know. The loss of the electricity and the telephones hit us on the first night; grub was the issue by the end of the first week. So we dug old ploughshares and the like out from the back of barns, and set to work opening up fields that hadn't been ploughed for twenty or thirty years. All back-breaking labour without machinery, of course, and we had a lack of horses too, but we got it done, and the soldier boys were a pool of muscle that needed application.

211

We resurrected other old skills as the months went by. We had to mend our clothes because we couldn't buy new. Some of the old dears remembered local cottage industries like straw-plaiting, and now you'll see English privates in straw hats like Chinese coolies. As for medicine, we've had drops of supplies of various drugs, and splints and bandages and the like. Anyhow that was how we got through the first year, with stores, and hard work, and good will.'

'And the Martians just let you do all this? Play Old MacDonald at the feet of the fighting-machines?'

He gave me an oddly furtive look – a look I would quickly come to recognise in the Cordon. 'If they're certain we are doing them no harm they let us be. We're survivors, Julie. Not warriors.'

'I'm not here to judge, Frank.'

'Yes, but—'

'And what of the potatoes in the river bed?'

'A challenge of the second year. Just when we were getting somewhere with the field clearances and such, the rivers started drying up. Look – you can see how the Martian weed is choking the stream, using up all the surface water. Bad news for us and our animals, of course.

'But look at the bed that's exposed. *That* we can use. That was my suggestion. Heavy river-bottom mud, when it dries a bit, is perfect growing ground for potatoes. We had to be cautious, because it meant coming close to the skinnies where they worked at the red weed, in the rivers.'

'The skinnies?'

He looked at me. 'I told you: Martians. Humanoids, at any rate, from the Martian cylinders.'

'I remember, from '07 . . .'

'All we found last time was drained corpses. *This* time—'

Despite my overwrought state, this news evoked wonder. 'Alive? Men from Mars?'

'Not men. And not just from Mars, either, it seems.'

I had to see for myself. Boldly, I walked down the river course, past the soldiers, towards those toiling others.

Others. They plucked and dragged and gathered the red weed, the leaves and sacs and pods and cactus-like growths, leaving the deeper roots intact. Much of this harvest they laid out on the river bank, as if to dry it. And some of it they tucked into their mouths, munching placidly as they worked.

212

I had concentrated on the task; some queer dread in me recoiled from looking too hard at those performing it. Now I made myself face them.

There were two sorts, both basically human – or humanoid, to use that odd, distancing word. The two kinds kept to their own groups.

One kind were tall, skinny indeed – taller than me at six feet or more, with odd round heads and big eyes over small faces, and pinched mouths; in fact their faces were oddly babyish. Naked they were, and all but sexless, the males with shrunken organs, the females with breasts that were almost flat. Many wore bandages of a crude kind on their legs and arms. Nude, pale, hairless, they looked fragile, and the work, light as it was, seemed an effort for them. They appeared quite incurious about me and Frank, and the sweating soldiers just yards away.

'They all seem to be adults,' I remarked to Frank, in a whisper – oddly I felt shy before these creatures even as I gawped at them.

'Yes, but there have been children born here,' he said. 'Since the landings in '20, I mean. They've been glimpsed. Of course we've had a few human babies too... *That* one,' he pointed at one female, 'appears to be carrying. Shows quickly on such an attenuated frame.'

'Many of them are injured.'

He nodded. 'Their bones are brittle, as you'd expect – meant for a lighter gravity than ours. They evidently have medicine of a sort, but it's crude. I've seen them at it. As if to set a broken leg is a habit so old it has become a matter of instinct, like a bird building a nest – not knowledge, or learning. D'ye see? I'd like to know if their skeletons are of the same siliceous sort discovered in the debris of the '07 landings. Of course none survived that trip, consumed en route between planets; we only found the remains, drained of blood. While this stock—'

'Are here to breed.'

'Yes. So we see a Martian ecology being established on the earth, Julie. There is the red weed; the humanoids consume that as our cattle consume the grass; and, just as we in turn consume the cattle—'

I shuddered. 'Do you think *they* understand how they are being used?'

'Perhaps. But so much of what they do seems instinctive, as I said; perhaps they have been slaves so long—'

'Natural selection has shaped them to the fate.'

213

'It may be,' he said bleakly.

As I watched the Martian humanoids toil I wondered if this was the future for those trapped in the Cordon – for all humanity. Would we too evolve into slavery, until we forgot the slavery itself?

'But those others,' Frank said, walking on, 'do not seem so adapted to their indenture.'

He meant the other sort of humanoids – perhaps a dozen of them, as there were a dozen of the skinny sort. These were shorter – not very short; they wouldn't have seemed out of place from that point of view in the poorer districts of London – and where the skin of the tall ones had been pale to the point of translucence, these were brownish, under a thick coat of body hair. Where the others' eyes seemed too large for the day and they turned habitually from the sun, these had small black eyes, and I would see them blunder into each other, as if the bright light of an English May day was not sufficient for them. And while they did not seem as stocky as a human, their bones not as robust, they were certainly heavier than the tall ones.

'Barely adapted at all,' Frank went on. 'As if they have been newly acquired.'

'Newly? What do you mean?'

'Well, look at them,' he said gently. 'The tall ones are from Mars – I think we can agree to that. So they are suited to the lower gravity and the dimness of the more remote sun.'

'Big eyes and fragile bones.'

'That's it. Whereas this new lot, of which specimens were *not* retrieved from the '07 wrecks, seem adapted to a brighter daylight than ours, and a gravity that may be only a little lighter than our own, not as weak as the one-third of Mars. And that coat of body hair—'

'It almost looks aquatic.'

'My thought exactly, when I first saw them,' he said. 'Like a water mammal, an otter or a seal.'

'Not much water on Mars.'

'No. But I don't think this lot *are* from Mars. It's a miracle they are able to subsist on the red weed, as the skinny ones do – or perhaps that's just another example of the Martians' biological manipulation.'

These toiling others, the hair on their legs caked in mud, looked back at us with a kind of furtive boldness. And I thought I heard them mutter to each other in an odd, high-pitched, almost gurgling sing-song. It occurred to me that I had not heard the tall humanoids utter a word to each other, and did not even know if they were capable of it; perhaps language had been bred out of them too by their monstrous masters.

'Then if not from Mars – where, Frank?'

'They're from Venus,' Frank said flatly. 'The Martians went to that planet, and brought them here to the earth. I think they're from Venus, Julie. Here in England!'

19

A Dinner Party

On our arrival at Abbotsdale, the de facto centre of the human administration in the Cordon, the first order of business was to organise transport to rescue our party of stranded sappers. Horses and carts were briskly dispatched; Ted Lane rode back with them.

Abbotsdale, I quickly discovered, was an odd place. Well, how could it not be?

I thought I could read the pre-Martian history of the village, such as it was, in the ruin of the ancient abbey that had no doubt given the place its name, a manor house, two venerable farmhouses which might have been eighteenth-century, and a couple of lanes of cottages built on what had been common land until only a few decades back – the cottages, I learned, had once housed brickmakers who had worked on the common, and whose trade was now being eagerly researched and recovered. There was also a scattering of more modern houses built here for commuting businessmen, as a kind of backwash from the nearby railway line. Sprinkle the dish with a couple of pubs, a school in ugly London brick, and a brace of nineteenth-century churches faced with flint, the architectural motif of the area, and you had a typical village of middle England of the time and the place.

Save that now Abbotsdale was a Martian colony. You could see it in the red weed that had infiltrated even into the heart of the village, and climbed all over one of the old churches like some gruesome ivy.

And, I thought from the off, you could see it in the faces of the people trapped there.

Frank had been given permission to move into one of the old cottages by the common, the middle one of a terrace – it was actually called 'The Brickmaker's Cottage', and the owners had been absent when the Cordon came down – and he quickly sorted out spare rooms for me and Ted Lane to sleep in. I unpacked such gear as I had in my small rucksack. Frank found a sensible trouser suit for me, borrowed from a fellow villager, which almost fit.

There was no running water – the wells in the village, long abandoned, had been laboriously dug out, but you had to pump the water up. I put my bloodied clothes in a sink to soak. I felt I could have enjoyed a long, deep, hot bath myself to soak out the concrete dust, the traces of cordite, the scent of blood and fear. But there wasn't enough hot water. Still, I found this domestic routine oddly comforting. Fragments of normality, assembling themselves around me after the vast shock of Ben Gray's terrible death, the bewildering presence of men from Mars and Venus, and all the rest of that extraordinarily long day.

There was no power, of course, no electric light, but the evening was mild, and light enough that a candle's glow was sufficient for me to see to brush my hair before dinner. Dinner, yes! For that evening we newcomers had been invited to sup in the home of Mildred Tritton.

I was shown briefly around Mildred's farmhouse. It was more than comfortable, I found, having shrugged off the loss of modern amenities like electricity and gas that had arrived so recently in its own long history; there was a big kitchen range, for instance, greedily burning wood. One room had been given over as a local library, where what books the villagers had had about them when the Cordon came down were brought and shared, with an accounts book as a kind of ledger of loans. Beside a bookshelf I found a Huntley & Palmer's biscuit tin within which was stored mail; I was to learn that there were fairly regular aerial drops of mail into the Cordon – and, indeed, of Huntley & Palmer's biscuits.

It may seem odd by the way that I had brought Frank no news of his wife and child, from whom he had been separated for two years. Well, I had had no contact with them myself, and no chance to pursue the matter in the rush of days since my meeting with Walter at Berlin. But as it turned out Frank himself had had messages from his wife, thanks to the mail drops. And through the radio communications and links through the tunnel systems I had followed myself, he had even managed to get word back out.

There was quite a guest list for that dinner: a mayor or two,

217

a priel of town councillors, a senior bobby with his jacket un-buttoned, the vicar whose broken spectacles had been fixed by a bit of tape, Frank who had become the local doctor. Bob Fairfield was there with his German friend, the Feldwebelleutnant whose name I quickly forgot – local potentates all. The most significant absentees, with places set for them at the farmhouse's long table, were the Dowager Lady Bonneville, lady of the manor (but she sent a boy with a note to say that her gout was troubling her), and the postmaster, a fellow called Cattermole, who sent no note, and whose empty place, I noticed, went unremarked.

The meal was a kind of buffet, essentially cold meat – rabbit – and potatoes, washed down with a couple of bottles of the village's diminishing communal stock of wine, and there was some chatter about how a Zepp might be persuaded to drop a crate or two to replenish the cellars – but none of that Teutonic hock, thank you! – at which our tame German soldier laughed politely. But anyhow the consensus seemed to be that if any luxury were to be dropped it ought to be cigarettes; the lack of tobacco was a persistent theme of conversation, the whole time I was in the Cordon.

Ted Lane seemed to be doing all right in this company. His Mersey accent alone was a curiosity here. For myself I felt oddly bewildered, oddly out of place – as if none of this was real – as if the only reality, in fact, was that peculiarly empty place at the table where the postmaster should have been sitting.

At dessert, Mrs Tritton somewhat bossily rearranged our seating places to mix up the conversation, and I found myself sitting next to the hostess herself, as I struggled to fork down stewed fruit.

There had been mention of a blood bank which Frank was maintaining with the help of his friend Verity Bliss, who turned out to be a VAD. Now Mrs Tritton brought this up. 'You must call by in the morning, my dear,' she told me. 'We all make our donations – you get such a feeling of satisfaction to know you may help save someone's life ...

'You'll find things aren't so bad here – well, I suppose you're as stuck here as the rest of us, aren't you? I was surprised how many of the soldiers are the urban sort – maybe I should have expected it. *They* have had trouble fitting in. Some of them, you know, they've seen men killed, but slaughter a sheep or a cow in front of them ... Of course we have these Martians stomping around. Oddly, they seem to be amused to watch the soldiers when they drill, as if we're clever animals. Like trained monkeys ...

'And it's still England, of course. In some ways it's been something of a pleasure to discard some of the new ways and go back to our roots. There's no government interference – no income tax! And with no foreign imports we've been thrown back on the way it was for our grandfathers. Why, we'll probably start speaking the old dialects again...'

As Mildred rambled on in this way, and as I half listened to other conversations at the table, I gathered glimpses of life within the Cordon. There was a regular trickle of suicides; not everyone was so jolly, it seemed, as these dinner-party guests. There could be visitors, some welcome – like doctors, parachuted in from outside or sent through the Trench as I had come – and some not. A dentist from Birmingham had been particularly lauded. There had even been adventurers, mostly from overseas, colonials out to 'bag a Martian' as one might bag a lion in the Congo. *They* were rarely seen again. And crime and punishment, ever necessary, was run on a 'common sense' basis, according to Mildred, in the absence of the usual 'chain of command' of the police and the courts. Later I heard of a case of a man, a would-be rapist, who had been left staked out for the Martians. I had no way of verifying the story; it struck me as authentic...

'Do you hunt?'

The non-sequitur threw me; I had no chance to reply.

'You must come,' she said. 'Especially in the winter. There's nothing like it. You're up in the morning mists, and off on the gallop. The cries of the hounds echoing, and then the hard riding, the eager horse under you – and then back home, hot and exercised, for a bath, a nap, and an evening of convivial conversation at a decent dinner party...' She seemed lost in memories. 'Better than life as a clerk in some office, eh?'

As soon as I could I made my apologies, pleading tiredness – which was half the truth, at least.

But Frank caught me on the way out. 'Well, now you've met the Vigilance Committee, or most of 'em.'

'Local worthies, all self-selected. Not much democracy, I imagine?'

'Somebody has to do it, Julie. Implement the rationing, for instance. There were cases of cannibalism, you know, in the aftermath of the First War. Can't have that. Oh! I recognise that expression. I can see your scepticism. Typical reaction from you, Julie! I admit there are a few who enjoy the chance to lord it over the rest. There always are. I'm just doing my best. But you must try to fit in.'

'"Fit in"?'

And he urged me to visit Verity in the morning for my blood donation, as Mildred had mentioned; Verity had been given the use of one of the pubs to run the operation, for it had a cool cellar.

'A blood bank,' I said mildly. 'I'm surprised it's a priority in a population as small as this. It's not a war zone – not an *active* one . . .'

He mumbled something about needing to cope with infrequent but traumatic injuries, then rather stumbled to a halt. Maybe he saw the suspicions gathering in my head before I was sure of them myself. 'Just do it,' he said, more harshly. 'It's rather the rule. We have to live with these people, Julie. We have no choice.'

'I need to see Albert Cook,' I said bluntly. 'Frank, it's important.'

'So is survival.' And he returned to the party.

So that long day was over, almost. Once alone in my room, I retired, and quickly fell into a dreamless sleep.

Only to wake in the dark, weeping.

Somehow Ted Lane heard; he knocked softly and, wearing an oversized dressing gown, sat with me.

'Ben Gray,' I said through the tears. 'It's taken all day for it to work through.'

'I know.'

'Silly fool. The kind of smiling privileged boy it's so easy to mock.'

'Brave as a lion. Let it out now.'

'Gave his life for us, Ted.'

'I know, miss. We've just got to make it count, that's all. Let it out.'

I think I fell asleep in his arms, like a child held by her father.

20

Verity Bliss

The next morning I called early at the blood bank pub, the White Hart.

Verity Bliss was there, opening up and giving the step a perfunctory sweep. She struck me as a sturdy, sensible woman in her twenties. She wore a kind of coverall, tough and practical in drab green, perhaps a farm labourer's work clothes. Her hair was cut even shorter than mine.

I introduced myself, offered a hand which was shaken.

She said, 'Your ex-husband told me you were here – warned me you might be coming to see me.' She smiled, but it was a wary expression. 'He said I needed to drag you from your bed if you didn't volunteer for the blood bank.'

'I'm told it is expected. What one does in this village.'

She looked at me closely. I immediately sensed there was a communication between us, under the surface. 'Look – no matter what our blessed Vigilance Committee says, whether you donate or not is up to you.'

'Why don't you show me this blood bank?'

She thought that over, and nodded.

To reach the pub's cellar we went through a trapdoor and down shallow wooden steps; Verity turned on an oil lamp which gave flickering light. With walls of flint, and I guessed that in this country the use of those glistening nodules on such a building was a sign of age and not affectation, the place was indeed cool, even in midsummer. Much of the space was given over to racks that looked as if they might have once held bottles of beer or spirits. Now they held flasks, slim, tall – each about the size of a

221

wine bottle, in fact, but without the neck – and fashioned of a silvery metal.

I plucked one flask from the shelf and hefted it. 'Heavier than it looks.'

'Aluminium. Each holds more than a pint of blood.'

I glanced around. 'There must be hundreds here.'

'There's more in other stores. Army issue, for battlefield use, left behind like the soldiers when the Cordon came down. They are derived from Martian technology; they are like Dewar flasks of an advanced kind – based on systems *they* used to store human-oid blood in their space cylinders.' She took the flask from me and turned it, showing a scribbled date, identity of donor, blood type. 'We're careful how we store it, and use it.'

I looked at her in the dim light. 'Frank said all this blood is needed in case of traumatic accidents. Happens a lot around here, does it?'

She said frankly, 'What do you think?'

'And how often must people donate, to build up such a store from such a small community? Once a month? More frequently?'

'Depends on the age of the donor, their health—'

'What happened to Mr Cattermole?'

'Who? Oh, the postmaster. Don't know him very well. What about him?'

'He didn't show up for dinner last night. His place was set; he sent no message. Next time – is this how it works? – there won't be a place set for him at all.'

We were eye to eye. She hesitated, then said at last, 'You're seeing it quicker than most.'

'The Martians must feed,' I said gently.

'Yes.'

'How *does* it work?'

'They come among us and they – *pluck* – as you might pluck a strawberry as you cross a field, and pop it in your mouth. You can run and hide, but—'

'You can't outrun a fighting-machine.'

'That's it.'

'And the blood?'

'It was Frank's idea, actually. That's what they're after, in the end. If we see them come, if we leave a stack of the donations in their way, it can distract them. Not always—'

'I imagine they prefer the fresh stuff. They did bring living humanoids in their cylinders, to top up their stored supply.'

'Yes,' she said. She looked away, as if ashamed. 'We've worked out a mode of living, you see – there's a certain rationality to it, for a live human can produce a pint of blood a month for ever, if you keep her alive, and I sense the Martians understand that – it's not communication, exactly—'

'You're *co-operating* with them.' I realised I had snapped; I was moved to touch her arm. 'I didn't mean to be harsh. You do what you must to survive.'

'Yes. And the blood store has saved lives.'

'But this place,' I said. 'The village. Mildred Tritton spoke to me last night of fox-hunting! As if—'

'I know.'

'They're too damn *comfortable*. Even Frank, perhaps – compromised, at least.'

She faced me squarely. 'Will you give the blood?'

I thought about it, thought about what coursed in my veins. Perhaps one donation would be enough to complete my mission, if the Martians took my blood as part of this grisly propitiation.

But I found I was not ready to commit that dread act, not yet. And I was deeply reluctant to participate, even dishonestly, in Frank's scheme of submission to the Martian lords.

My head was in a spin. I was reminded of France, again – of the compromise of occupation, of men who betrayed their own brothers to save themselves, of women I knew who had gone with German soldiers for the sake of a meal of military rations. This, though, a blood sacrifice – a literal one – so that one could go on living at the feet of the Martians – and Frank was complicit in it. I did not feel I could confide in him, about my deeper mission, any of it. And – *fox-hunting!*

I looked at Verity. 'We have only just met. But I feel as if I can trust you more than my own ex-husband.'

She shrugged. 'Frank's a good man. But that's families for you.'

'Have you heard of a man called Albert Cook?'

She pulled a face. 'Everyone's heard of him.'

'Do you know how I could find him?'

'No.'

'Very well. Are there *franc-tireurs*?'

She stared back at me.

'I mean, those who resist—'

'I know what it means,' she snapped. 'Yes.'

'I need to find them, I think.'

She was immediately suspicious. She had survived in this place two years; she had a right to suspicion. 'Why do you need to find *franc-tireurs*?'

'I have a mission.'

And I told Verity Bliss a partial truth. I told her of my cover mission, the drawings by Walter, the scheme to make a meaningful contact with the Martians, one lot of sapient beings talking to another – Walter's wistful project so cynically subverted by Eric and those who commanded him. I told nothing of the deeper truth, though I suspected I would be asking this woman to risk a great deal for me, and guilt stabbed even as I told these lies of omission.

'Will you help me?'

She hesitated a long time before answering. Then she said, 'There is a man called Marriott. I'll see what I can do.'

She had set up a meeting with 'Marriott' by the end of the day.

'How did you manage that?'

'Would you believe carrier pigeons? The Martians aren't aware of *them*.'

I wasn't sure I did believe it. This was a countryside full of secrets.

21

A Bicycle Ride

We set off the next day.

I had no idea if we would return to Abbotsdale or not. I wore the practical clothes I had travelled here in, complete with military-issue boots, and packed my rucksack with some essentials, and tucked Walter's leather satchel under my jacket. Verity took a small bag, and a kind of belt containing basic medical gear, for use on campaign – and a service revolver, and ammunition. I felt guilty not telling Ted Lane, at least, that I was going – terribly guilty, after last night! – but this was my mission, not his.

As for not telling Frank – I was ambivalent. Put it like that. I did not entirely disrespect his position here, but it would not have been mine. We were divorced, you will remember; we had differences of character profound enough for that. Certainly I felt no guilt.

And so we cycled off, Verity Bliss and I, on the back roads and the lanes, that sunny spring morning. The exercise did me good, I think, a loosener after days of sterner travel, and the horror of the tunnels which still haunted me.

It was a Sunday, and I heard distant church bells; evidently these, and the flocking of the human sheep to their services, did not disturb the Martians. But I remembered Albert Cook's bleak prophecy, as recorded in Walter's *Narrative*, of how in the domain of the Martians we would live in cages 'full of psalms and hymns and piety'. He was right! He was right!

And even in the bright daylight, with the birds singing as they had, I suppose, for a million years, in such a countryside on such spring days, Verity kept a wary eye out, and I learned to also.

'You'd think a ruddy great fighting-machine would be an obvious landmark,' she said. 'That you would see *them* before they see *you*. Not necessarily. It's motion that catches your eye, and when they're not moving they can have an eerie stillness about them. You might see a slender form from the corner of your eye; you think it a steeple, a flagpole, a wireless mast. No!'

'Mars is said to be a dusty world, and far from the sun,' I said. 'To come to a world like this – to a day like this – must be a glory of light and colour.'

'Or a dazzle, as a ski run is for us. Perhaps they wear sunglasses. Ha! That would be a sight to see.'

Verity said that the Martians generally didn't interfere with cyclists, not identifying that most democratic of vehicles with war-making capabilities. 'One can hardly carry a field gun on a safety cycle. Best not to go too fast, however. Speed seems to be another trigger for their attention.'

'Not much chance of that,' I said, gasping as we came to yet another rise.

'They are motivated to keep us alive, the Martians. Most of us anyhow. That is the horrible price we pay. But that latitude gives us an opportunity, just a chink. We must move around, we must *do* things – we must farm to feed ourselves and gather fuel to keep warm, and so forth. And we can use that freedom to move to serve our own purposes.' She tapped her temple. 'No matter how acute a Martian's eyes, he cannot see inside here, can he?'

In the end, we found Marriott by lunch time.

Having set off from one inn in Abbotsdale, Verity brought me to another, set on the crest of a hill on the road that runs southwest out of Amersham towards Wycombe. I thought it had been a coaching inn once; and, like many of the older buildings in the area, the inns and the churches, it was walled with flint nodules. I could see where a sign-board had been smashed off its bracket.

Outside, two men sat on a bench, lounging in the sun, dressed in grimy work clothes and flat caps, and with tankards at their sides. As we rode up the hill, they called out bawdy encouragement. 'Can you make it, love? Look at those thighs a-pumpin', Toby! You need a hand?' And they made lewd grasping motions with their fingers.

Verity glanced at me. 'Ignore them.'

I shrugged. But I saw that the liquid in the tankards was clear, like water; whatever they were drinking wasn't beer.

I took in the countryside. We were remarkably close to the heart of the Martian occupation here. From this height I could even glimpse the periphery of the Redoubt, the big main pit they had dug into the ruins of Amersham, a brown scar visible beyond the spring greenery. This was to our north-east as I saw it; to the north-west I made out an extensive but shallow flood from which trees and field boundaries and a few buildings protruded, running up a valley away from the Martian camp. I imagined the Martians' rough earthworks had damaged the local drainage, and such floods must be common.

As we dismounted the two men outside the inn got to their feet, staggering a bit, and comically doffed their caps to us. They were perhaps thirty, I thought, both tough-looking, their hair crudely cut and dirt smeared around their necks, and if their manner was drunken their eyes were oddly clear. Something wasn't right about them, I could see that.

One of them approached me. 'Welcome to the Flyin' Fox, missus. I'm Jeff and he's Toby.'

The other sniggered. 'No, you clown, I'm Jeff and *you're* Toby.'

'I'll give you a hand with yon jalopy.' He made a grab with his left hand for my handlebars – and with his right for my backside. 'Oops!'

Palm had barely made contact with buttock before I had got hold of his index finger, swivelled around, twisted the finger and forced him down on one knee, his arm bent backwards.

'Ow! Pax! Pax! I didn't mean no 'arm!'

Verity said calmly, 'I think you can let him go, Julie.' I saw that she'd set her bicycle on its stand, and stood with her jacket pulled back to reveal the service revolver in its holster at her waist.

The other man stood with his hands raised. 'Let's all calm down.' The country burr was still there but the drunken slur was gone.

I gave my miscreant's finger one last vicious twist, then let him go.

He got to his feet shaking his hand and tucking it under his armpit. 'I didn't mean no 'arm. Just keeping watch and playing a part, is all.'

'"Playing a part"? Thought so.' I got hold of one of the tankards and poured the clear liquid onto the ground. 'Well water? Even an idiot like you can't get drunk on water – Jeff, or Toby.'

'Neither,' he snarled, 'and you don't need to know.'

Verity let her jacket drop. 'It's all cover, Julie, in case the Martians are watching.'

'That's it,' said my assailant. 'They got used to seeing us drunk,

227

see, at a place like this. Rolling around and even laughing at 'em, when they come and stand over us. So long as you stay out of reach of them tentacles and nets ... I don't suppose they's so smart as to be able to tell a true drunk from a faker.'

'Got carried away in the performance, did you?'

'What's wrong with that? And where did you learn to hurt a man like that?'

'Paris, if you must know. I was caught up in the flight from London in the last lot, the First War, with my sister-in-law. We had to fight our way past men like you. After the War I learned how to look after myself properly.'

'Didn't mean no 'arm—'

'You deserved what you got,' Verity snapped. 'Now, Marriott's expecting us.' She pushed past the men and led me without further ado into the cool shadows of the inn.

22

'Marriott'

The man we knew only as 'Marriott' was in the inn's cellar. The Martians, of course, knew or cared nothing of human names, but I suppose the secrecy that surrounds such operations becomes a habit.

He was dark of complexion and dark haired, short, perhaps fifty, and he had a pronounced London accent. He poured us tea, made with hot water from a Dewar flask.

The cellar, which smelled faintly of damp, was lit by smoky candles that looked home-made, and most of it was taken up by the clutter you might have expected: stands with empty beer barrels, pipes and tubes, cartons and kegs, and bottles of spirit on a rack. But there were a few incongruous items: a stack of rifles, boxes of ammunition – even what looked like a Maxim gun. Maps had been pinned to the walls: good quality, ordnance survey. These had been extensively marked up in pencil, red and white, and stretches had been shaded blue, marking the flooded areas perhaps. And there was a kind of wireless receiver, on a side table by one wall.

Marriott sat in an office chair at a desk wide and handsome – a desk that had no place down here – while we sat on stools that must once have graced the bar above. There were papers heaped up on the desk, held in place with paperweights of flint.

'I'm sorry about the lads,' Marriott said when Verity briefly recounted our welcome. 'All part of the cover, of course.' He waved a hand. 'You can see why an inn is so useful. Even the Martians know that people come to such places at all hours. And an inn has a cellar, like this one, where we can get up to all sorts of mischief out of the Martians' sight. But it's all fakery upstairs, as – what did they give their names as?'

'Jeff and Toby.' Verity got up from her stool and roamed around, peering to see the maps in the dim light, to read labelling on the boxes and crates.

'That'll do,' Marriott said. 'But we ran out of beer on the second or third night. Ha! Didn't take us long to drink the place dry. And of course we don't have power or even running water. But we get by.' He grinned, self-satisfied in his little underground kingdom.

I was quickly deciding that I did not like this man, no matter how brave he proved to be, how noble his motives. With the aim of puncturing him a little, I ignored this speech and turned to Verity. 'How did you get in contact with these characters?'

'They approached me,' she murmured. 'Wish I could read these labels better... Since the first days, when Abbotsdale and its folk settled down to a routine, I have always felt – restless.'

'It's a foul business,' Marriott said, pushing his way back into the conversation. 'Living as we do with the Martians, and accepting – sacrifices. Better than the alternative, I suppose, when the Martians just swoop down like something out of Bram Stoker and *take* a fellow. But still it's all a brutal affair, and a daily demonstration of our humiliation. Yes, humiliation.'

'Hence this operation,' I said.

He beamed his pride. 'It's not much for now, although as it happens we have something of a spectacular planned for tomorrow. But one does what one can. And, yes, we're always on the look-out for new recruits. One gets a sense – a certain look – if a person isn't content to be one of the cattle.'

'Which is how you spotted Verity.'

'That's it.'

Verity was inspecting a dusty-looking revolver. 'I imagine much of this is a relic of the first days of the invasion.'

'Mostly from what the Army units trapped inside the Cordon had with them – there's a lot more out there, you can imagine, in one cache or another. That's where the ammo comes from too, most of it. They've tried air drops from the outside—'

'The Martians shoot them down,' Verity told me. 'They seem to be able to tell when there's weapons or ammunition and such. They let through drops of medicines and clothes and food – most of the time, anyhow; they seem to err on the side of caution. These crates – it is dynamite, isn't it?'

'Not military – there was a store here before for quarrying and demolition and suchlike. Even the farmers used the odd stick to clear deep tree roots, I'm told.' He grinned. 'We've been quietly spiriting the stuff here since the invasion.'

Verity frowned. 'Which was over two years ago.' She looked at the crates, again trying to read the labels.

'We've got more of it stashed all over, right up against the walls of the Martian pits in some cases. We had a quarryman on the team, and he showed us how to lay the charges so you get the result you want. Like sculpture, he described it, like sculpting the landscape, the very earth, and we all listened to him.'

Sculpting the very earth. That boast stuck in a corner of my mind, though I wasn't sure why, at the time. Perhaps in retrospect what I can only call my revelation was already stirring, like a seed in the watered ground. As I will relate in its place.

Verity said, more practically, 'And did your expert train you in how to keep dynamite?'

He ignored her. 'All we need is the word, and we're ready to serve.'

'You seem to have got organised quickly,' I said, at the risk of flattering Marriott.

'That we did. And that was all thanks to Captain Tolchard – an Army man, among those who got stuck here. Older chap he was, in his fifties; but he'd had some training in *franc-tireur* methods, back when they were still organising in case of an invasion of England by the Germans. Hard to think how it used to be, ain't it? All the things we were scared of that never came to pass, save for the biggest thing of all. Anyhow he got things set up sharp-ish so we could resist the Martians instead, and right from the kick-off. He made sure we got the weapons and so on squirrelled away. And he found a lot of willing followers; many of us had been in the Fyrd or had served before.'

'Where is he now?'

'Who, Tolchard? Taken by the Martians, would you believe. Just bad luck, that's all. I saw him myself, a man like Tolchard – he fought the Boers, you know – running like a rat before the catcher, just like a rat, before he got scooped up by one of those tentacle things—'

'So now you're in charge.'

'For my sins. I was in the Fyrd myself, a second lieutenant. But I was a bank manager. Cheapside branch of the London & Country.' He stroked his desk. 'Was out this way for a drive in the country, never been here before, this part of the world. Since my wife died, well, I hadn't been out much, but it was set to be

231

a fine few days. That was the plan. And then the Martians came, and that was that – I was stuck. Just luck, really.'

'A bank manager, though.'

'Not much need for those skills in here! But I got this desk from a branch in Great Missenden – well, it was going to waste. Got to have a good environment to work in, you know.' He tapped his head. 'Lots of planning to be done, and somebody's got to do it.'

Verity said, 'Those boxes of dynamite... *These* came from Somerset West, I can see that much, which is a factory in South Africa. I'm no expert, Marriott, but I've been around soldiers for the last two years – I can't find a date, but the boxes look weathered – they must be a good deal *older* than two years – do you turn these boxes?'

He waved a hand and said sternly, 'I have professional soldiers in this cadre and I leave all that to them, and I'd recommend *you* do the same.'

'Yes, but—'

'Perhaps you should come over here and sit down with your friend, and tell me what it was you wanted of me.'

She was clearly infuriated to be so patronised, and seemed reluctant to give up her pressing about the dynamite, but she nodded. 'Tell him, Julie.'

'I need to find Albert Cook.'

He scowled. 'That traitor.'

'Look, it doesn't matter what you think of him. The Abbotsdale folk have got their heads down. But *you* must know where Cook is. It's evident you have a wider knowledge of the country.' I got up and walked around the desk to the maps stuck to the wall behind him. The light was dim, but I could make out the names and places on the big, highly detailed ordnance maps.

'We got these maps parachuted in special,' he said with some pride.

I pointed. 'Here's Amersham – here's Abbotsdale – here *we* are.' The Cordon itself, the Martians' devastated perimeter, was a thick circular band shaded with pencil. 'I suppose the blue-hatched areas are floors. And these red spots—'

'The subsidiary pits, as we think of them. Where the cylinders came down away from the Cordon at the edge, and away from the Redoubt, the big central group at Amersham.'

I had not inspected maps of the occupied zone as detailed as this – I had barely got a glimpse of the chart in Eric Eden's office in Hampshire. But the pattern of landfalls was reminiscent of patterns that Walter had shown me before. Just as Walter had in Berlin with his old map of Surrey and London, now with the forefinger of my right hand, following the inner pit markers, I traced one loop, two, in a scrawled clockwise spiral, an integrated pattern that must have been twenty miles across, all contained within the dark band of the Cordon. I asked Marriott, 'And these lines you've marked that connect the pits?'

'Canals, we call 'em, but that's our joke – Martians, see – they're digging gullies between the pits. No water in 'em, however. No idea what they're for.'

But I saw it, inspecting his maps; the Martians were connecting their impact scars with lines and loops to make a sigil of just the kind Walter had discerned in unfinished form in the '07 landscape, and had predicted would be recreated now. He was *right*.

Verity said, 'And now you've had the word, have you? You mentioned a "spectacular" coming up tomorrow.'

Marriott got out of his chair and stood by me; he smelled faintly of cigar smoke and body odour. And he pointed to a blue-hatched area on the map. 'A particular opportunity we spotted. There's a kind of flood, a dam the Martians created for themselves, where a small charge might do a lot of damage – and we've had the go-ahead to try it. Don't do anything without orders, we're soldiers in here and not a rabble, just as Captain Tolchard left us.'

I broke in, 'Look – all I'm interested in is Cook. Do you know where he is or not?'

I could see pride and caution war in the man's small face. 'Yes,' he conceded at last. 'Yes, I know where he is. He's no friend to mankind, that I can see – from what's said of him. But at least he's his own man, I suppose.'

Verity said, 'Unlike the folk at Abbotsdale, you mean.'

'Yes – not just sitting around, munching on home-grown spuds and ordering people about.'

'Will you help me find Cook?'

He thought it over. 'Tell you what – help us tomorrow, and the day after that we'll get you to Cook. How does that sound?'

I exchanged a glance with Verity. We had no right to demand, I saw. 'Very well. But help you how? Shall we lug a few boxes of dynamite for you? As Jeff or Toby found out earlier, we're stronger than we look.'

But Verity put her hand on my arm. 'No,' she said firmly. 'Let's leave *that* to the experts.'

23

With the *Franc-Tireurs* of Buckinghamshire

We spent a not uncomfortable night at the inn. We two had to share an upstairs room that must once have been let out to travellers; it had its own wash-stand, and there was a chamber pot under the bed.

Oddly, in this period of my life I rarely had trouble sleeping. It was as if I had grown weary of being afraid, if you can imagine it. I saw it in my mother, when she knew she was dying of a lung condition. Nobody can be afraid all the time; it recedes to the back of your head, and your awareness fills up with the stuff of the mundane world, of the day. And I think I had wept myself dry over poor Ben Gray.

Besides, the bit of exercise on the bicycle had helped wear me out. It is odd that veterans of those years often speak nostalgically of the cleanness of the English air, with human industry all but shut down across swaths of the southern counties. The Martian Cordon was fine cycling country!

And in the morning, I woke relieved to find that nobody from Abbotsdale had tracked us down – not Frank, not even Ted Lane. The scheme was still on, then.

Over a breakfast of rabbit and potato, washed down with a decent nettle tea, we learned of Marriott's plan – and we found that during the night he'd revised it, to include our active participation. He brought up his maps from the cellar to the inn's lounge to show us. In fact I had already glimpsed the scene of the action which Marriott indicated now: it was that flooded area I had seen to the west of Amersham.

Marriott's pale bank manager's finger traced the lines on the map. 'This is the course of the Misbourne. Very minor, as rivers go; it rises in Great Missenden, here, and flows east-south-east

234

down the valley through the old part of Amersham, and eventually it joins the Colne near the Western Avenue bridge, *here*. Or it used to. When the Martians came down on Amersham, all unknowing they created a kind of dam with the earth their landings threw up.' He indicated a blue-pencil shading. 'The extent comes and goes with the rain and the seasons, but the result of the damming has been a flood, a permanent one, which has reached right back up the valley of the Misbourne, to beyond Little Missenden, *here*. And *here* is where the accidental dam lies right across the old river course.' This was at a village called Mantles Green, near the junction of the Wycombe road, on which our inn stood, and the main road that ran south of Amersham towards Uxbridge and London.

I remarked, 'And we know that the Martians are rather ignorant regarding water, which is a lesser element on their world, and long mastered.'

'You're right.'

Verity nodded. 'I get it. You plan to dynamite that dam.'

'Not I, but my men ... That dam has trapped behind it a great mass of water – which has, of course, three times the weight it would have on Mars. I am sure the Martians do not realise the implication, which is why they have left their accidental blockage unguarded and without any reinforcement. Even though, downstream, squatting in the ruins of Amersham and sprawling east towards Little Chalfont, you have the Martians' citadel – their headquarters in England, as far as anybody can tell – the Redoubt. We'll smash the dam, and drown the Redoubt. They won't know what's hit them.'

Verity nodded. 'I can see why you've had the approval to proceed. You could indeed do a lot of damage to the Martians,' and she glanced at 'Toby' and 'Jeff', 'while not risking much.'

One of the fellows, the one who had grabbed me, looked offended; the other, a more cheerful sort, blew her a kiss.

Marriott said, 'The Martians are suspicious of any moving vehicle, we know that. But if you take it calm they might not go at you straight away, at least. Which is where you two might be useful.'

Verity snorted. 'As cover?'

'Well, it seems to be a fact that the Martians can distinguish between men and women ...'

That was true enough, and a puzzle to the scientists who pointed to the sexlessness of the Martians themselves.

'And they seem to know that an attack is more likely to come from a body of men than a mixed group. You'll be two couples out for a joy ride, you see? Might buy us that bit more time. Especially if you act a bit merry, full of champagne, like...'

That was the scheme. As Marriott went over details with his men, Verity drew me aside.

I murmured, 'Seems to me we can't honourably refuse. Not if we want them to help us with Cook. And it's not actually a bad idea.'

Verity, with more military experience than me, was more sceptical. 'True. But, stringing along with this pack of idiots, a bank manager and a couple of lecherous pot-men – we'll do well to get out of this with our skins in one piece. Most likely the only harm we'll do to the Martians will be if they split their sides laughing at us... Do Martians laugh?'

'Scientific opinion is divided,' I said with mock gravity.

'I'm worried about that dynamite too. Look, just follow my lead...'

Within half an hour they had the cars ready – two of them.

And what cars they were! I had been impressed by the Rolls with which Frank had picked me up after my passage under the perimeter. Now I recognised a recent-model Mercedes, and another Rolls, a Silver Ghost, more treasured marvels. But their roofs had been removed, so the Martians could see the innocence of their passengers – and both cars had been disfigured by having slabs of iron or steel welded and strapped to the bodywork. And I could see that a box of dynamite had been stashed in the boot of the Rolls.

Needless to say all three of the men looked inordinately pleased as we looked upon these toys.

'I know what you're thinking,' Marriott said, almost bashfully. 'What a way to treat these lovely cars! Especially the Ghost. We had to cut up a lot of old boilers to get the plate for all this.'

Verity snorted. 'Why bother? The Heat-Ray would cut through this lot in a second.'

'Ah, but that's a second more than you'd have otherwise. We go whizzing by the fighting-machines, at their very feet. They can see us inside the car, nice and harmless. Then we pull out the grenades, and have at 'em.' He mimed driving, wrenching at the wheel. 'At their very feet. The Martians fire the beam – sizzle! We take

236

a lick, but with luck we live to fight another day, or another minute anyhow, and the armour has done its job. Whiz! Sizzle!'

He was a bank manager, standing in the morning sunshine, playing at soldiers like a small boy. But I was not one to mock him for it, for, even if he wasn't riding with us, he was showing more pluck than anybody I had met inside the Cordon, aside from Verity. And certainly it would take some courage to drive up to a fighting-machine in an open-top car.

He said now, 'You'd be better to ride with Jeff in the Rolls.' By 'Jeff' he meant the bottom-pincher. 'You'll see the Merc has a lot of clutter in the back. We hope to make a gun turret that will rotate, for the Maxim, you see—'

'We'll ride in the Merc,' Verity said firmly.

'Are you sure? But—'

'The Mercedes.'

Marriott shrugged, and instructed his men.

We shook hands one last time, with some feeling. Then we clambered into our respective vehicles, Toby driving the Merc in the lead, with myself and Verity riding with him, and Jeff in the Rolls following behind with its cargo of dynamite. It was this disposition which would save my life and Verity's – that and her foresight.

So we set off.

It was surreal, that first half-mile or so, the drive along an empty road through a deceptively peaceful scrap of English country-side. At least we got the sunlight. But the very smell of the car's interior was unusual, the customary fragrance of an expensive, well-valeted vehicle, of polished leather and carpet cleaner, replaced by a more industrial stench of welded steel, and the tang of cordite. I fretted a little that we had had to leave behind most of our few belongings in the inn – though Verity had her small first-aid pack at her waist, and her revolver tucked into the back of her trousers. And I had Walter's messages tucked safe in a pocket of my jacket.

We hadn't even reached the flood water before it all began to unravel.

Toby saw it first. 'Martian!' he hissed.

We could all see the fighting-machine, striding boldly over the open country ahead of us, off to the north-west. It was the sheerest bad luck; he must have been coming back from a patrol, and happened upon us. But there was no doubt he saw us; he

237

immediately increased his speed, using that strange loose-limbed gait to bowl along across the green towards us.

Toby immediately slammed his pedal to the floor, and the car lurched forward. 'Only chance is to get there before him,' he shouted. 'If we get those charges laid – even if we just throw the crate out of the Rolls—'

Verity and I shared a glance of horror; this sounded like fool-hardy madness to us. Better to abandon the car and take cover in a ditch than this flight *towards* our enemy! But we had no choice in the matter; we were not behind the wheel. And, glancing back, I saw that Jeff in the Rolls was following us, indeed more than matching our pace.

So we tore down the hill, and now I could see ahead of us the rough earthwork of the Martians' accidental dam, a mound two years old and thick with the bulbous growths of the red weed. The placid water behind, stretching off to our left up the valley, was itself choked with red and green, Martian and earth life mixed together. I saw no Martians moving there, and had lost sight of the fighting-machine that had spotted us.

But he had not lost sight of us.

I thought I heard a crack like an electric spark, smelled an electric tang – perhaps I smelled the plasma that the Heat-Ray makes of the air as it passes through – that was how close it came, but it missed us, by a fraction. The Heat-Ray's range is measured in miles, but its targeting is a matter of machinery, not miracles; even the Martians could miss.

That errant bolt of energy had, however, slammed into the road surface behind us. I glanced back and saw a crater, bits of tarmac and bedrock still cartwheeling in the air – and the Rolls following, with Jeff inside his box of steel, about to tumble into that new pit, with the dynamite crate in the back.

Verity yelled, 'Hold on!' And she ducked down, her arms over her head.

We pieced it together later.

Verity had always known the danger, but had despaired of get-ting through to Marriott when we spoke to him in his cellar. Guilt racked her, but that's all hindsight; he would not have listened.

Dynamite is not stable. It is three parts in four nitro-glycerine. Over time the dynamite will 'sweat'; it leaks its nitro-glycerine, which will gather in the bottom of a containing box. That was why Verity had asked Marriott if he turned his boxes; an old hand will turn such a store repeatedly. Worse, the nitro-glycerine can crystallise on the outside of the dynamite sticks, leaving the whole assemblage still more sensitive to shock or friction. Most manufacturers will tell you that dynamite has a shelf life of no more than a year, under good storage conditions. In that cellar Verity had found boxes at least two years old and probably more; and the storage conditions were anything but proper.

She told me later that even before the operation at the dam, if Marriott and his lumpen assistants had ever dropped a crate in that cellar—

I watched the Rolls tip into the crater—

The blast swept along the road and lifted up our car like a toy. I remember even in that instant a flash of concern about our driver Toby, but we worked out later that he, crumpled in the wreck of the car, must have been dead in an instant.

But Verity and I were both thrown through that open roof and out into the air, and bumped and banged as we flew helplessly in that cloud of debris. We both came down in the flood water itself – lucky!

I hit the water with a hard slap, and my fall was cushioned by the bed of vegetation which lay beneath the murky surface, some of it green and yellow, the colours of earth, but much of it that ugly crimson that is the palette of Mars. At first I did not struggle. Bewildered, I suppose shocked, I almost welcomed the softness of the swollen vesicles and thick leaves under me, as if I was being cupped in some vast hand. Oddly I could not feel the cactus-like bristles I had observed earlier, not at first.

I could see the surface above me, the sun's distorted figure – and then I saw the slim form of the fighting-machine, looking down on me through the air with a dispassionate calm, as a biologist might look at a tadpole wriggling in a pond. I took a breath, or tried to – I suppose the air had been knocked out of me by the detonation – and the water was like a cold soup pushing into my throat, dense, suffocating. Fear sparked, and at last I fought. But now I felt those bristles, digging into my clothing, even pricking my flesh; they gripped me, held me. This was more than vegetable; this was a lethal intelligence! And I was helpless.

My chest convulsed, but I could not empty myself of the water, and only dragged in more. I struggled against the grip of the red weed, but as in a nightmare the harder I fought the tighter it gripped me.

I stopped fighting. I was going to die there – I knew it for a certainty. I tried to relax, to submit. I remember that I did not pray, and nor did memories and regrets flood me, as I have been told is common in such situations – instead I hoped only that the pain would be brief.

And then I saw him before me.

Him – he looked human, despite the sleek hair that coated his nude body, and the webbing that stretched between the fingers of the hands that reached for me, and the bubbles of air that leaked from the flaps of skin at the side of his throat – were they gills? And, though the hair covered his groin, his chest, yet I knew, somehow, he was male.

He descended before me, upright in the water, swimming with the merest flick of his hands, his webbed feet. Even then I thought I saw a glint of gold at his chest: a cross shape – a crucifix? He took my face in his hands – cold fingers.

And he kissed me. I felt his lips on mine – cold again – and then air, thick, hot, poured into my mouth. It made me cough, and the liquid pulsed up out of me, into his own mouth; but somehow he kept those lips locked onto mine while I heaved and convulsed. Meanwhile I was aware of his strong hands pulling away the weed that bound me, frond by frond, barb by barb.

Suddenly I was free. He grabbed me under the armpits, flicked his feet once, and, with his lips still locked onto mine, we surged up into the light and the air, and I knew no more.

24

An Awakening

As I drifted upwards to consciousness, just as I had been lifted into the light from the murky flood, the world as it formed around me seemed normal, familiar.

I was in a room with a door, windows. I was lying in a bed, to the sound of rain on a roof. In the distance, thunder – not guns, not the detonations that accompanied a Martian advance, just a storm.

But I clung to sleep, and the absence of responsibility.

When I woke again the light was brighter but softer. Still the rain hissed, but the thunder was gone, the storm passed over. I became aware now that I was in an unfamiliar nightgown, all frills and tucks and more ornamental than comfortable, and that the sheets in which I lay were rather musty.

I rolled onto my side, and saw a figure sitting by the window, looking out. 'Verity?'

She turned, smiling. 'You're awake. You struggled once or twice, and muttered. You called for someone called Ben. I didn't want to disturb you. No, stay there.'

She came across, and I saw that she had one arm strapped against her body in a clumsily applied sling. The first-aid kit she had worn at her belt was open on a bedside table, amid dusty clutter: a clock that looked as if it hadn't worked since the nineteenth century, ugly ornaments, faded photographs in a silver frame.

She pressed a hand to my forehead, stuck a thermometer in my mouth, took my pulse, and listened to my chest with a lightweight stethoscope. Then she handed me a glass of water, which I drank gratefully. 'Don't worry, it's fresh – I set buckets out in the rain.'

'I should be nursing *you*.' My throat was scratchy, my voice hoarse when I spoke, and there was a vague ache about my chest. 'What's that, a broken arm?'

'I managed to crack a bone, but you were the one who was underwater. If not for the Cytherean who saved you—'

I remembered the incident in a flash now. 'Yes. *He* – was it a he?'

'Oh, yes.'

'Cytherean?'

'A man from Venus. That's what the educated types are calling them. I heard as much from the BBC, on a crystal set.'

'Almost an angelic figure, he seemed, in all that murk.' Another shard of memory. 'And he wore a crucifix, Verity!'

She smiled. 'Yes. Seems to be something of a fad among them. I blame the vicar at Abbotsdale. They are semi-aquatic creatures – well, that's obvious. Ideally suited to serve as swimming-pool lifeguards, I should think.' She touched her bad arm with her other hand, wincing. 'Not so cute when it comes to fixing broken bones, however. After all, our skeletal structures vary – it seems that the very fabrics of our bones differ.'

She was right about that. Studies on '07 specimens had already shown that on Mars the humanoids have siliceous skeletons, perhaps because silicon is one of the most common elements in the rock and dust of that arid surface. By contrast, as later studies would prove, the Cythereans' bone structure has a reliance on strong forms of carbon – long molecules, which give the bones a kind of springiness. Not so optimised for walking upright in heavy gravity, but ideal if you're flipping away through the water like a seal.

'The Cythereans have their own medicinal remedies, which involve a lot of licking and chewing and packing in mud. But I wasn't so confident that all that would work on my busted fin. So I resorted to more familiar techniques, a splint, a bandage. I did have Charlie set the splint for me.'

'Charlie?'

'The fellow who saved you – the one with the crucifix. I have a feeling he's spent more time with humans than some of the others.'

'Why "Charlie"?'

She grinned. 'No doubt he has a name among his own kind. I called him for Charles Daniels, who won all those swimming medals in the '04 Olympics – do you remember? Perhaps not;

the Games were in St Louis, and my sister and I travelled over with our father for a summer jaunt—'

'You had that *humanoid* put a splint on your broken arm?'

'It was rough handling, I admit. As if a bright orangutan did it – more strength than kindness. But he got the idea; they *are* more bright than the great apes, if less so than humans.'

'Good grief, Verity, it would have been bad enough if those buffoons from the inn had had to do it.'

'Both of them are dead now,' she said simply. 'The explosion – the dynamite – do you remember? You've been out for more than twenty-four hours.'

I glanced at the grey skies visible through the window. 'Long enough for a change in the weather.' I did remember, but not clearly; the jigsaw was jumbled in my head and we would piece together the sequence of events, as I have set it down here, later. 'People from Venus, though!'

She smiled. 'Even given the fix we're in – marvellous, isn't it? Would you like to see them?' She stood up. 'It's about time for a late lunch. We've fallen on our feet with this house. It was evidently abandoned when the Misbourne flood rose – we're on a sort of island here, as you'll see. There's a fair stock of tinned meat and such in the pantries, and we've the rainwater to drink, so that's safe. I stoked a fire in the living room so there's hot water, and I rinsed out your clothes – they should be dry by now . . . Would you like me to help you to the bathroom? I have had to keep you clean already, of course. Don't be shy! I am a nurse – well, sort of . . .'

I slept again, woke again.

Once fully awake, or so I thought, I fretted about time.

After all, as Walter and Eric had been well aware, the next opposition was due in the summer – the next wave of Martian cylinders might already be in space. Surely I needed to complete my mission before any possible landings. But I had no idea of the present date, let alone when the Martians might fall.

I got out of bed, a little groggily, and hunted for a calendar. No luck, but there was a diary, and I flicked through its pages, ignoring spidery elderly-lady notes about nieces' birthdays and the anniversaries of various dead relatives, trying to think it through. How would Walter have worked it out? You had the opposition, the closest approach of the planets, in June, and the landings, if they happened at all, would be three weeks and a day before *that* . . . But when was the opposition, exactly? I thought it was June 10, but I wasn't sure. And what was today, what was the date? . . . There was nothing in the room, no wireless set, that might let me find out.

I started to feel ill again, faint. I made my way back to my bed, determined to ask Verity for the date when I awoke again. But I forgot, I forgot.

I woke once more, nagged by another anxiety. I got out of bed and rummaged through my stuff until I found, sitting on a dresser, Walter's drawings in their leather packet, which had proved waterproof as well as robust; they were safe. I slept again.

25

The Villa of the Cythereans

When I woke again, later in the day, I felt much refreshed.

I rose unaided. It was a relief to shed a nightgown that felt as if it had recently been used by a lady several decades older than me, to climb out of sheets so musty that the dust I raised when I turned over started me sneezing. But I can't blame Verity for not trying to change a bed for me with her broken arm – and, it seems, her 'Cythereans', while willing to help, would not venture into the house. And it was a relief to wash, with Verity's help, and to dress in my own clothes.

Then I sat with her on a small veranda, gulping down Indian tea we found in a sealed caddy – delicious treat! – and corned beef and tinned peaches. The veranda itself, a paved area bounded by waist-high pillars and a couple of concrete lions, was the kind of pretentious but unremarkable feature you might have associated with such a property, a late addition to what I judged to have been originally some kind of gatehouse or lodge for a larger estate. The whole was quite ordinary – or would have been if not for the Misbourne flood.

On our doors and walls you could see the stains of surges, and you could smell a kind of rotting dampness throughout the house, the carpets and rugs uniformly mouldy. But the house was set on a slight rise, as many old properties are, so that when the flood had risen the house itself was left on an island, set in a new lake from which protruded hedgerows and telegraph poles, and the upper floors of other, less favoured properties. It was a strange, wistful, oddly peaceful scene, as if from a romance of some distant future when our civilisation had decayed and its remnants were slowly subsiding into a weed-choked marsh.

But the colours of that landscape were odd – peculiarly Martian, as it turned out. The open water was uniformly full of the red weed, which spread across its surface as would water lilies, while the ground, relatively uncolonised, retained the green of the earth, of the grass and the trees. Red lakes, green continents: just as the astronomers tell us they see on Mars.

And if the landscape was unearthly, so were its inhabitants.

As we sat there, for the rest of that day and into the evening, with faded blankets on our laps, eating tinned fruit and drinking tea, Verity and I watched the Cythereans at play.

They would swim languidly, or rest, rolling on their backs with their hairy bellies tipped up to the clouds. And then they would dart away, flashing down into the water and emerging with a mouthful of the red weed.

It was evident to me immediately that they had the power and quickness and acuity of senses of the natural hunter, but there was nothing palatable for them to hunt in the murky waters of the earth. Only the red weed, which had been brought with them in the cylinders from Mars, would fill their stomachs. But, oh! – what a sight it was to see those lean bodies flash through the water, so very like seals when they were swimming, but with those eerily human faces on their sleek, streamlined heads.

The young, too, for there were a handful of those, darted with abandon, and when their tiny forms surfaced with some prize from their play-hunting, a vole or a half-drowned rat, they would laugh with glee and clap their hands, and the two of us clapped with them – they were very like human children.

When they rested they would gather in small groups, in couples or bands of three or four. The children would snuggle with their parents, or they would clamber up on their backs and bellies; the very smallest suckled at their mothers' small breasts, and with teeth sharp enough for hunting that must have nipped painfully. I was tempted to label these groups as families, but the experts will tell you that one should not anthropomorphise.

Those who have not seen Cythereans in the wild cannot know how graceful they are in their unfettered, uncontained state – how elegant at play. And if I use the word 'play', it is because that is how they seemed to me, with every motion, every gentle interaction having a sense of fun, just as you will see with otters and seals and perhaps dolphins, the intelligent aquatic mammals of the earth.

Verity, having been a prisoner in the Cordon for two years, knew far more about her fellow captives than I did – and, of

246

course, more than anybody else outside the Cordon. In the years since, we have had time to study the Cythereans more fully, both in the wild and in captivity (in those nations where the imprisonment of evidently intelligent beings as laboratory specimens is tolerated), and it is the Swedish physical-chemist Arrhenius who has led a multidisciplinary study into the nature of these creatures, and their origins.

To begin with, we can be sure that the 'Cythereans' were indeed from Venus. The most convincing evidence for me is the anatomical. The strength of a Cytherean's skeleton is only a little less than a human's, thus evidently adapted to Venus's marginally lighter gravity. By comparison the skeletal structure of the Martian humanoids, adapted to a gravity one third of earth's, is enfeebled to the point of delicate. Nature makes us no more robust than we need to be. Meanwhile Venus is closer to the sun, and the brilliance of the daylight seems reflected in the smallness of the Cytherean eye, and a certain resistance of the skin to the sun's rays. Conversely, Mars is half as far again from the sun as the earth. To us, Mars would be twilit; the Martian humanoids have big receptive eyes and are easily dazzled.

Venus, according to Arrhenius, is warm and dripping wet: a world of swamps, full of water suspended in the sky, as well as on the land. It is not a world so much as a vast lagoon. The surface temperature is probably twenty or thirty degrees hotter than the Congo, and the humidity six times the earth's. This heat creates immense stacked clouds, piling up miles above the surface and laden with water vapour. We cannot see through the clouds to the surface of the world, and the Cythereans can never see the stars. But Venus is a bright world; seen from the ground, the sky must shine uniformly when it is day.

And the Cythereans are ideally adapted to this world. Their aquatic modifications are more than superficial – more than the webbed fingers and toes, the neatly streamlined coat of hair. They have strong voluminous lungs which can store air even when under the pressure of deep water. They have gills, which I had observed on my first encounter with Charlie. And, more subtly yet, they have *three hearts*, one to circulate the blood around the body and two supplementary organs which keep the blood flowing through the gills, where oxygen is extracted from the water to feed the blood. I am told the octopus on the earth has a similar adaptation.

(The commonality of the hominid form across the worlds

247

remains a puzzle, by the way. Some argue for a convergence of form to similar environments, just as a dolphin, a seabound mammal, has come to resemble a shark, which is a fish. Others posit older migrations, long preceding the Martians to the earth. Perhaps the Jovians – or even the inhabitants of lesser but still older worlds, Saturn or Uranus or Neptune – have visited our young planets before, and left a kind of imprint of design. But the deeper differences, such as the use of different structural materials for the skeletons, seems to argue against that. A wistful mystery! Are we interplanetary cousins, or not?)

So thick is Venus's cloud bank that the heat must be spread uniformly from equator to pole – and, say some of Arrhenius's followers, so must the vegetation and animal types be uniform; and on a world without geographic or seasonal variation, evolutionary innovation, they say, must be deterred. Venus may be a world of simpler, duller types than our own – fern swamps inhabited by slow-moving herbivores, perhaps. But others point to the evident intelligence of the Cythereans themselves – they are as intelligent as Neanderthal Man, some have opined. They are hunters and tool-makers, though the latter behaviour is inhibited by the available raw material; on Venus, stones that might have made Mousterian hand-axes are buried beneath miles of rotting vegetation in the swamp. Or perhaps they simply don't care for tool-making. Some commentators have suggested that they are essentially aesthetes: their intellect focused not on the striving that characterises humanity, but on the sheer athletic pleasure of the swim, and the competition and company of others.

Stapledon has even speculated that, so fecund and moist and warm is Venus, there may be other varieties of Cythereans, on scraps of dry land in that watery sphere perhaps, or even flying in the clouds, which are thick and dense and perhaps rich with aerial game – and if so, those happy flyers may have been beyond the reach of the Martian slavers when they came.

However, as I was to observe myself, some characteristics of the Cythereans' behaviour and their physical adaptations are reminiscent, not of hunters, but of prey animals. Their pregnancies are brief compared to ours; the babies emerge active and alert and fast-growing – ready to swim, and to flee predators attracted by the scent of birthing fluids, perhaps. And then there is the fear they will sometimes display before manifestations of the *large*: they will cower from Zeppelins, flee even from the shadows of gasometers. Perhaps great beasts like Owen's pliosaur patrol the swamps and oceans of that world. And perhaps it has been fear and flight that has driven their evolution to intelligence, rather than aggression: a need for co-operation with each other, perhaps, as was so evident in my brief witnessing of them.

Certainly the Cythereans became prey when the Martians invaded.

As Verity pointed out, 'Of course every adult Cytherean on the earth must have been brought by the Martians in their cylinders. Can you see how many of them are wounded? The fur hides it unless it's a grievous injury, but there are lumps and contusions and badly healed scars, and some have their ears bitten, or even fingers missing: injuries they brought with them from the cylinders – so we think, anyhow.'

'Injuries inflicted by the Martians?'

'Perhaps not directly.' She faced me. 'Imagine how it was! The Martian humanoids seem shaped by their slavery – they seem to have evolved to its conditions, so long have they been suppressed. Not so the Cythereans, squat, strong, stocky, and used to freedom – and with a will to live. If you were in that pen on the cylinder, suspended in interplanetary space – when the Martians came to bring out the next one for the crew's supper treat – would you not fight to survive? The battles in the dark of space, to *stay at the back of the pack*, must have been brutal and desperate.'

'Even so, some evidently lived to reach the earth.'

'And perhaps that was the plan all along,' Verity said. 'The Cythereans probably have a better chance of surviving on our earth than the spindlier Martian humanoids. So they have been released, to breed for the hunting in the future.'

I smiled. 'Like rabbits in Australia.'

'That's the idea.' She looked out at the Cythereans at play. 'But it's to be hoped that they don't prove as much of a pest as the rabbits, or the prospects for them on this earth – well, they won't get much of a welcome.'

The reader probably doesn't need me to emphasise how impressed I was with Verity Bliss. Frank later observed how far her natural intelligence had exceeded the education she had been given, and had expressed itself when it had the chance. No wonder the VADs gave her a supervisory role. Now, thinking of her acute observations of the Cythereans, I wonder if in some other world she might not have made a fine scientist. Her loss, as I shall relate, was keenly felt by both myself and Frank.

As the light of day slowly faded, the cubs napped, snuggling against their mothers. And the adults started pairing off. It was an unplanned process, a languid swimming to and fro, a matter of jostling, nudging with the nose, a caress with a webbed hand. Then, not yards from their neighbours – and within full sight of us – the coupling began. The most basic method was face to face in the water, with the male and female clinging to one another's upper torso to give anchorage, while the male thrust and the female pushed back. Sometimes they would go front to back, the male on top, the female's face lifted above the water so she could breathe noisily, and with an absent expression on her small face. And sometimes, before or after, even instead of a full coupling, they would play, exploring with their hands and mouths.

I dared not look at Verity.

She laughed at me. 'You get used to the sight. *They* are quite without shame.'

'Are we to regard them as animals, then, for all their cleverness? Animals have no shame because they can't conceive of it.'

'Not animals. They have a kind of language, you know – you hear it in the night sometimes when the world is quiet, a kind of continuous babbling, like a brook. Perhaps it's just that they haven't had thousands of years of priests telling them that their bodies are sinful.'

'And what of Charlie's crucifix?'

'As I said, you can thank the vicar at Abbotsdale for that,' she murmured. 'He has become rather obsessed by such speculations. Are the Cythereans fallen, as we are, or not? And what of the Martians? Was there a Martian Messiah, a Cytherean Christ? Or must the message of *our* Jesus, Christ the Man, be taken to these other worlds? Not trivial questions, you will agree. So the vicar tried to engage with the Cythereans on that topic. I saw him wade out into the muck of a mill-pond to give Charlie that crucifix! He liked the sparkly bauble, I suppose.' She looked out at the water, the shadowy shapes still gently paired, and winked at me. 'Between ourselves, I think our good vicar was rather too interested in the Cythereans' healthy sexuality than is good for him. Come on, I'm exhausted just watching them ...'

Exhausted perhaps, but I was also charmed. I admit that I always felt a certain repulsion at the sight of a Martian humanoid – not so much from the physical form as the evidently evolved abjectness of the race. The Cythereans were new to that game, and in them I saw something of the Noble Savage, I thought.

That is only my partial and prejudiced perception. The Cythereans were animals – *people* – with a cultural and biological heritage of their own, indeed as the Martians had once been, and had no need of my approval. But I offer these reflections honestly, for what they are worth.

We returned to the house. We banked down the stove on which we'd boiled the rainwater for our tea, and made our toilet, and retired to bed.

I think I slept well enough, once again. I don't recall that we'd made any specific plans for the next day. We had food enough, even tea, and we were both getting over the trauma of our arrival, and myself the strain of the days of travel even before that. I think we had vaguely intended to stay at least a day or two, to gather our strength and plot our next step – which would have involved getting off the island and out of the Misbourne flood, for a start.

Whatever we had intended, it never came to pass. For we were both woken in the small hours by the Cythereans' unearthly screams.

26

A Harvesting

In our borrowed nightgowns, we met in the gloom of the landing.

Verity said, 'You heard it.'

'Yes. We dress and leave.'

'Agreed.'

I hurried back to my room. Last night, luckily for me, I had been *compos mentis* enough to lay out my travelling clothes, a bag to hand mostly packed – it was a shoulder bag I had found in the house, for I had left my beloved rucksack at Marriott's inn. I threw on my clothes, crammed the rest of my gear into the bag, pulled on my boots, and even so I was out later than Verity, despite her broken arm.

We hurried downstairs and through the kitchen – even in that moment of peril I snatched the tea caddy from the table and shoved it in my pocket – and we emerged on our veranda, where we had spent the last evening. This faced west; the sky was clear, still grey before the dawn light came, and the swampy flood water stretched before us, its surface eerily still where the red weed lay on it in its lily-like sheets. And not a sight of the Cythereans, and their screams were no longer to be heard. It was as if they had never existed.

'Gone!' I said. 'But I suppose they had even less packing to do than us—'

'No.' She pointed with her good arm, into the murk. 'Look! There's one.'

I saw a swimming form, just under the surface, darting with remarkable speed and with scarcely a visible motion of hands or feet. This figure raced towards us, and then reared up out of the water, droplets spraying all around. I saw that it was Charlie, the crucifix still sparkling on his chest, just as before. Even as he rose he *yelled*, a weird ululation, and, in mid-air at the peak of his leap, he tapped his temple with his fist, and pointed beyond us, pointed to the east. Then he flopped on his back, hit the water, and vanished.

'Head,' Verity murmured. 'He was trying to say – *head*. He's warning us. For that is the Cythereans' word for—'

Then a long shadow cast by the dawn light swept over us, and I saw its detail spread across the mere in front of me: the peculiar shape of the cowl, the three long legs, the blunt gun, the dangling net within which something squirmed.

Head. What is a Martian, but a disembodied head? The Cythereans had it right, I thought. And they had it right to flee.

Now the fighting-machine itself rose up above the house, gaunt and black against the dawn sky. We could only stand and stare. It was in a mood for collecting rather than killing, I saw; people had already been gathered up into its net, where they lay like so many fishes, one on top of the other, some lying passive, others struggling, pulling at the net as if to rip it open. I could hear their voices, sobs and cries and yells of rage, from high in the air, faint.

And now I saw there was another net, a hundred feet in the air, dangling below the hood itself. Not a feature I recognised from previous images of the fighting-machines, it looked like a lobe of spittle, dangling from a drooling mouth.

I had a hunch about that second net. I tried to hold my nerve as the thing bent towards us, and one long tentacle uncoiled from the hood, metallic, glinting, supple, like no mechanical device made by human hands.

Verity raged, 'Stupid! Lazy! I've been here long enough to know. We should have kept watch, as the Cythereans must have; we should have taken it in turns. Well, no point running now. Unless you'd prefer the Heat-Ray to the exsanguination—'

I grabbed her hand. 'No. Wait.'

The tentacle descended further, as the Martian machine bent down with a kind of eerie grace; top-heavy as it was, it never looked like toppling. That tentacle! It was only yards over our heads now. I could see the rings that made up its articulated structure, the gaps between; there were faint puffs of green smoke as it reached for us, its sinuous gestures almost tender.

And I peered again at that lesser net that dangled from the hood. Now was the time to throw the dice. I yelled, as loud as I could, 'Cook! Albert Cook!'

Verity stared at me, astonished.

'Albert Cook!'

The tentacle stopped, ten feet above our skulls. The fighting-machine itself seemed frozen. Even those already caught in its net seemed distracted now; I saw them shift and squirm, curiosity working – perhaps they had a grain of hope, which my calls did not deserve to evoke.

That second net, the spittle-drop, began to descend now, silently, smoothly, on a lengthening cable. Soon I could see that a single man rode in it, and not cast in like a landed fish; he sat in a cushioned seat, like the pilot of a biplane in his cockpit. He wore peculiar garments: what looked like an expensive leather coat, a white wig like a judge's, and a heavy gold medallion like a mayor's around his neck.

As he came closer, he could see my face, and I could see his.

'You!' I said.

'You!' said the artilleryman.

27

A Fighting-Machine's Passenger

'What are you doing here?'

I shouted up, 'I might ask you the same question.'

Verity must have been as terrified as I was to be so close to the Martian machine – feet away! Yet she stood there with one hand on hip, her bad arm in its sling, defiant. 'Julie, aren't you going to introduce me to your friend?'

Cook glared down at her. 'Don't get lippy with me. I know *you*. You're with that crew at Abbotsdale, aren't you?'

'What if I am?'

'You want to be more respectful. Or else, the next time I'm a-striding across the country on my fine steed here, I might attract his attention to you, rather than make him look the other way.'

'I don't believe you have that much control – though you've evidently sold your soul for that seat.'

He shrugged; he seemed genuinely indifferent to that barb. 'Believe as you like. *You*, though,' and he turned again on me, 'I haven't seen you since – when was it? That dead astronomer's gaff, before the cylinders started falling again. Came to find me, did you?'

'Yes,' I said bluntly, and that layer of truth held up, at least. 'I've got a message.'

'Who for?'

'The Martians. You evidently have some kind of – relationship with them.'

He grinned at that. 'Well, given as how they haven't killed me yet, or sucked out my blood, I suppose you could say that. A message? From who?'

'From Walter Jenkins.'

And from a grin, his face twisted immediately into a snarl. 'That liar.'

I had to suppress a laugh, incongruous as it might seem in such a situation. Here was a man dangling from the cowl of a Martian killing-machine, and he was still smarting at slights delivered in the pages of a book, years ago. 'Are you that petty, Bert? Even now? Even *here*? Maybe we deserve to lose this war if we're all so small as that.'

'Oh, we deserve to lose the war all right – or most people do. Walter Jenkins does, anyhow. He's such a weak fool. All that stuff about utopias, and a cleansing of society, before "moral advancement" becomes possible. Can't you see, *this* is what he longed for? And other comfortable fools like him. An apocalypse to smash everything up. Well, I'm not so soft. I don't dream of golden cities of the future full of – full of *fairness*. I embrace the apocalypse. It's not a phase, it's a destination. It's an end. *I* live in it. I inhabit it.' He grinned. 'I'm here, now, ain't I? Look at me!'

I couldn't deny it. 'But will you help me? I've come a long way for this, Bert – all the way from Berlin, if you want to know. To see *you*.'

He grinned again, his mood mercurial as ever, and adjusted his judge's wig. 'Fine. You want to talk, we'll talk. Do you know West Wycombe, the caves?'

'I do,' Verity said.

'Very well. Go there. You'll be on Shanks's pony, for I can't offer you a lift. This Martian's hardly a London cabbie.' His joke seemed to amuse him, and he cackled. 'I'd cut across country if I was you, and keep to the hedgerows.' He jerked a thumb at the fighting-machine above him. 'The lads are hungry, and they're on the prowl for fresh blood – well, as you've seen. That's why we came here. Them fish-men like the flood, nice big stretch of open water for them to frolic about in. Easy pickings, and there's always a fat old beggar amongst 'em who's got too slow to swim away . . .' He glared at us. 'How did *you* get here, anyhow?'

I looked at Verity. 'Can't be any harm telling him. Marriott won't try it again for a while. Bert, we came because the local *franc-tireurs* thought they could blow the dam and flood the Redoubt, the big Martian pit.'

He glanced around with a soldier's eye, sizing up the landscape from his elevated vantage. 'Hadn't thought of that. Not a bad idea, if it had worked. What went wrong? Well, it doesn't matter. You're right, though, they won't get close again; the Martians will figure out what they were trying to do and will keep a watch.' He tapped his head. 'Smarter than us, they is, and you always have to remember it.

'As for you, keep to the shadows, as I say. Watch out for the fighting-machines. And when you get to West Wycombe, wave a handkerchief or something and call out that Bert sent you. Got that? My Mary is a crack shot, or getting to be.'

'Mary?'

'You'll see – if you live.' He glanced at a wristwatch. 'Oh, and keep the noise down. Baby'll be having her afternoon nap by the time you get there.'

I glanced at Verity, who shrugged. 'The day could hardly get any stranger,' she said.

'Meanwhile, I got work to do. Them human rabbits won't chase themselves.' He grinned, a complicated, unpleasant expression. He had a tool, a heavy, rusted spanner, tucked under his seat; he rapped with this on the cable from which his net cage hung. 'Piccadilly, driver, and don't spare the horses!'

The cable reeled in, silently, smoothly, and he was whisked into the air. I remember him vividly in that seat, evidently purloined from some crashed aircraft, with his absurd garb, that legal wig, grinning down at us as he rose, until he was a detail against the tremendous structure of Martian technology above us.

And then the fighting-machine walked on, the cowl lifting, one great leg passing mere yards over our heads. The folk in the basket at the machine's back grew agitated, and began to call to us. Hands even reached through the net. Perhaps they imagined we had somehow been negotiating with Cook for their release. It made no sense, of course, yet had I been trapped in that net of death I too would have begged and pleaded for my life.

In only moments the machine was too far away for us to hear their calls.

28

In the West Wycombe Caves

We headed roughly west, passing villages like Holmer Green and Hughenden and Naphill, before dropping south into West Wycombe, which is on the main road west out of High Wycombe. We took Cook's advice and avoided the roads and open country; we skirted fields, stuck to the shadows of hedgerows, passed through clumps of trees. We saw few people. It was a countryside where folk routinely hid away.

We made a hasty lunch of canned meat and rainwater in the shade of an ancient oak. Our walk that day must have been seven or eight miles; it took us until mid-afternoon, and felt longer. We were both fit enough, but I was still recovering from my near-drowning, I suppose, and I think Verity's arm hurt her more than she cared to admit, especially when we had to scramble or climb over walls. We got through it.

The caves themselves were not hard to locate. West Wycombe Hill is a local landmark, topped with a mausoleum and a church whose tower was once capped by a golden ball – it had been visible for miles around. Verity said she thought it was a folly, a reminder of somebody's Grand Tour to Venice. But when we came to it that day the church was tumbled and scarred, a ruin no doubt created by a careless swipe of the Heat-Ray, and the tower was a jagged splinter with the golden sphere vanished. All this was irrelevant unless we could get inside those caves safely.

The caves, I would learn, were themselves relics of a couple of centuries past. During a series of crop failures the local family, the Dashwoods, had showed uncharacteristic heart by employing local villagers to quarry chalk from the hill. The material was used to construct the road from West Wycombe into the main town – and, being a mercurial sort, the current Dashwood had made something of a monument of the resulting holes in his hillside ...

We found a sort of courtyard. It was open to the sky but walled, with the doorway that was evidently the entrance to the caves themselves set in a flint façade with stained-glass windows. The setting, eccentric, had something of the feel of an old ruined abbey, with the roof collapsed and the interior open to the rain. We came into this place with the caution you would imagine. We waved white handkerchiefs and kept our hands in the air, and we walked in the bright afternoon sunlight, keeping away from the shadows. We even called ahead: 'Bert sent us! We're friends of Albert Cook! Mary! We're women and unarmed!' The last word being a lie.

As we reached the middle of the courtyard, a rifle shot cracked out. I could not help but flinch, but we stood our ground.

Verity was made of sterner stuff. 'We're alone,' she called. 'Just the two of us. It's true what we said, Mary. We met Bert—'

'Dead, is he? Rifled his pockets?'

'Not that,' I said. 'He found us – he was riding a fighting-machine.'

Verity managed a grin. 'The Buffalo Bill of Mars.'

'That sounds true enough.'

'Can we come forward, then? Really, we mean no harm. Julie here knows Bert. She's in the Jenkins book too! Mary, we know you've a child to protect. Bert warned us you'd be cautious, and rightly so.'

She hesitated. 'All right, then. Keep your hands where I can see 'em. One bad move and I'll plug you. If anyone follows you trying to catch me on the hop I'll plug *them*, and then you. I got all the angles covered here.'

Verity nodded. 'Bert has trained you well, I can see that. We're coming in now.'

We crossed the courtyard and got to the door. There was Mary, short, dark, solid-looking, dressed in a kind of coverall of blue serge. Behind her I saw a candle-lit tunnel, arched. She had been wielding a rifle, but she had propped that against the wall behind her, and now held a revolver: a better weapon in close quarters and another sign of a bit of training. 'Don't come close. Turn round. Hands against the wall. And drop your packs, I'll look in those too.'

I glanced at Verity, and she at me, and we turned round as ordered.

Verity sighed. 'I have a revolver in a holster at my waist. You'll find that.'

'So you lied.'

'Wouldn't you? Safety's on, though, but it's loaded. More ammo in my pack.'

'Fine.' She rummaged in Verity's pack, and took the pistol and ammunition.

'May I have it back when I leave?'

'Have to see what Bert says. *If* you leave.'

Somewhere, echoing, I heard a baby's cry – an incongruous sound when you are braced against a wall having a conversation about guns.

'I'll take you to the Hall.'

I asked, 'The what?'

'You'll find out. Walk ahead, side by side, where I can see you; there's candles and lanterns lit. I'll holster my gun but I got it right here and I've been practising.'

'You don't need to worry,' Verity insisted.

'It's you who should be doing the worrying. Go ahead, now,' she said, as if commanding a pair of horses.

So we went ahead.

If you think about it, a cave is a natural shelter from a Martian.

It is a blind spot for them. The Martians, it is suspected, do not understand cave systems. Caves in middle England are 'solutional': that is, the product of running water acting on rock that is already in place. On Mars such spectacular effects of plentiful water, so obvious on the earth, are comparatively unknown. Save for the odd volcanic formation, caves must be an exotic mystery on Mars – but not on the earth, indeed not in Buckinghamshire. I would learn later that across the country systems of natural caves had been exploited by the authorities to provide concealment from the flying-machines, and cover in case of any Martian advance.

Cook's cave, of course, was not natural, but it was not the rough quarry I had expected. For the most part we followed a neat tunnel, with flat floor and vertical walls rising up to an arched roof over our heads. As Mary had said, the way was well lit with candles and smoky oil lamps; the light was good enough for me to see the marks of individual picks in the walls – the signatures of workers already two hundred years dead, I supposed.

This tunnel opened out into a couple of chambers, one of which had subsidiary passages going on out of sight, like a maze. Then we turned into another, still larger chamber. This cave turned out to be called, locally, the 'Hall'. And here it was that Cook and this Mary had made their home, their nest.

There was no bed, but a mattress heaped with sheets and blankets lay on crates – I imagined the labour of hauling down a decent bedstead. A robust table and chairs looked like the fold-out type people brag about being meant for use on campaign. Clothing hung from coat racks or lay heaped in open trunks. There was no facility for cooking, though there was a kitchen range closer to the entrance to the caves, where a chimney had been improvised. Water stood in buckets, and I would learn there was a kind of chemical toilet. The heating came from a stove fed by bottled gas, with a kind of vent set in the wall above to carry away the waste fumes. Since we were three hundred feet underground at the cave's deepest point, I had, and still have, no idea how Cook had managed to arrange for this bit of ventilation – perhaps via some natural crevice. But he had been in the horse artillery, I remembered; such men develop practical skills. Still, it must have taken hard work to survive down here, I realised at once: lugging water in and waste out, digging shafts for the air. Cook must have thought the concealment worth it.

And the reason for all this care and attention to detail soon became obvious. A small child sat in a cot, in the middle of the chamber, raised up above the cold floor. The little girl could not have been one year old, but when she saw us approach she grabbed the bars of her cot and tried to stand.

'Oh, how adorable.' Verity took a reflexive step forward.

'You keep off of her.' That was Cook.

I turned, startled; he must have been only paces behind us as we came down the corridor. Now he stood at the entrance behind us, dimly lit, revolver in his hand.

Verity raised the hand that was free of the sling. 'Look – I'm not a nurse, but I'm a VAD, trained as such. *You* know what that means, Bert. And I've had to learn fast about the care of children and infants since I got stuck in Abbotsdale.'

'There's nothing wrong with Belle,' Mary said defensively.

'But it can't do any harm to let me look.' Verity glanced around at the cave. 'Are you down here all the time? I mean, I don't suppose she sees much of the sunshine – or of doctors. There might be vitamin supplements which—'

'You leave us be!'

Cook was more placating; he holstered his revolver and walked forward. 'Now, Mary, don't take on. I don't believe she means any harm.'

'That's true,' I said. 'For she's only here by accident. It's me who's been trying to get to see you, Bert – poor Verity's just been dragged along in my wake, so to speak.'

Verity grinned. 'Nice way to speak of someone who helped save your life.'

'You know what I mean.'

Cook rubbed Mary's back. 'If she wants to look Belle over – well, let her, she might do some good. People are there to be exploited; if they volunteer for the purpose, then use them.'

I shared a glance with Verity. I had not expected to find he had a secret family, but that remark about 'exploited' was the authentic Bert Cook.

'But not just now, eh?' He began to strip off his outer garb: the coat, the legal wig, the mayor's chain. 'Mary, isn't it time for her feed? You see to that, and I'll rustle up some supper.'

Somewhat resentfully Mary took the baby from her cot and walked past us, deeper into the cave complex and out of sight. The baby, wide-eyed, stared at us as she passed in Mary's arms.

Bert Cook tried to be a host, in his own extraordinary way. 'Sit there,' he said, pointing to the fold-out table. 'Now, if I turn my back to prepare some grub, can I trust you two not to pull any tricks?'

'Oh, don't be ridiculous, Bert,' I said wearily as I sat down. 'You know me, at least. None of us are story-book heroes.'

'Very well,' he said, though he sounded cautious. 'And I suppose I should remember my manners. We don't have guests for dinner very often, as you can imagine.' He cackled. 'The odd rat, but Mary sees to them with a spade or a broom.' He started digging out packets of food and tin plates from one of the trunks as he spoke. 'Funny sort of place, isn't it? The caves. Read up on 'em once I acquired 'em. Chap who dug 'em out supposedly ran satanic rituals down here. Nah, I don't believe it; he was a traveller, a rake, a bit of flash; I think he was cocking a snook. Good story though, eh? And besides, what could be more devilish than the Martians? And *they're* no legend.

'Are you thirsty? The water in the buckets is clean. As for grub, it's bacon and spuds and beans.' He leered at me. 'From the farmers. They pay me to keep the fighting-machines away. Leave offerings, like. Of course, some are more compliant than others. We get it all cooked up – we do it in batches on the range that's out by the door – we cook when it seems safe, then scoff it cold, with a mug of tea.' He set a kettle on the gas stove. 'Your brother-in-law did feed me that night on Maybury Hill, all those years ago, in the middle of the First War. Albert Cook pays his debts.'

So we sat and ate cold meat and bread in the cave. The food made us calm and relatively companionable, as a shared meal always will – a bit of common humanity. I even made Cook a gift of the caddy of Indian tea I had taken from the villa; he accepted it without comment.

I asked tentatively, 'How did you come to this, Bert? And Mary. Why do you hide away?'

'Wouldn't you? If you did what *I* do.'

'I'm not sure *what* it is you do.'

He turned a knife, casually, but point first at Verity's chest. '*She* knows. If I let you go, you'll skedaddle off back to Abbotsdale and tell all them soldiers and nobs where I am, and maybe they'll tell the authorities outside, the soldiers and the government, and next thing you know they'll be flushing *me* out like a rat. And *that* won't do, will it?' He eyed her, more calculating. 'The only option being for me not to let you skedaddle out of here at all – ain't it?'

Verity looked at him with contempt and, I thought, some courage. 'I'm not going back to Abbotsdale – not for now. I'm going to stick with Julie, and *she* wants to go on into the Martian pit – don't you?'

In fact we'd never discussed such plans, not so bluntly, Verity and I, not since we'd been thrown together.

Bert raised his eyes at that. 'And?'

'And she thinks you can get her in there. Because you come and go, Bert, you come and go.'

I forced a smile. 'Come on, Bert. Tell us the tale. There's nothing you like better than to talk about yourself, I know that much.'

He looked at me, startled, and a disarming grin spread across his face. 'You know me better'n I know myself, I think. Ha! Very well, then. But if you ever write it down –' now he pointed the knife at me '– make sure you have it true, *this* time.'

I promised I would, and it's a promise I have endeavoured to keep in these pages.

29

The Artilleryman's Tale

'I was here when the cylinders fell. Two years back. You know that much, I was with your husband Frank, *then*, with the sojers who'd been sent to greet 'em. When everybody else ran away from the Cordon, I ran *in*. Because I knew that's where the Martians would be.

'In the beginning it was just like '07 over again.' He sounded nostalgic, as if those terrible days had been the finest of his life – and perhaps they were. 'Just like '07. Refugees on the roads going this way and that with their babbies and old folk and carts of luggage, but most of 'em too dim to have grasped that we were already in a big cage with invis'ble bars that cut across every single road you might try. I saw the soldiers fighting back, and generally they put up a better show than in '07 – they was brave enough, and we had learned something from that matinee performance, but it made no difference in the end.

'But while they was running around, *I* was watching, and listening, and calculating. Straight away I could see what the Martians was up to – well, they started with the same routine last time. They was knocking out the soldiers and the rail lines and the telegraph lines and the cars on the road and anything else that might pose a threat – they did the same in '07; they understand that we organise, see, they know we're civilised to a degree, even if we're a rung or three below *them* – but they were letting the people go free. Well, it makes sense, doesn't it? We *know* what they want us for. And if you came on a flock of sheep with a machine gun, what would you do? Why, you'd knock out the gun and settle down to a feast of mutton, that's what. And that's exactly what the Martians were doing.'

'Hunting us down,' Verity said.

'Hunting now. Farming in the future, perhaps.'

Verity and I exchanged glances at that chill remark.

'And I hid out as the days went by, and I watched 'em do it. How they'd swoop down in their fighting-machines on some sheep-fold like Abbotsdale, and they'd scoop up the slow and the lazy and the stupid and the weak, and drop 'em in those nets of theirs, for the consumption of, later. And I watched the people who skedaddled at their feet, *turning their backs* on those who had been taken. As if they'd never existed. For that's a way to cope with it, see, if the other fellow is taken and not you, and you go on living, to pretend like he never were at all. People become accustomed. As if they was being trained.'

I remembered the dinner party in the farmhouse in Abbotsdale, when Mildred Tritton had told me country-life anecdotes, and we had all ignored an empty place at the table. 'You're right, Bert,' I said. 'Though I hate to admit it.'

'And not for the first time, eh?' He grinned. 'Well, now, I sees all this, the healthy sheep running and leaving the lame sheep behind, but all of them *sheep*, and I thinks, these folks is worthless, miserable, pointless. The stock is *improved* if they're cut out of the bloodline. In a way they're doing their duty to the race by letting themselves be culled. Do you see? But not me – not men like me. *I* was roaming around, alone, trying to figure the angles. How I could profit from the set-up.'

'Profit?' Verity sounded disgusted.

He shrugged. 'They was going to die anyway. Well, one day I got my chance. I was foraging in a village outside Chesham, not much more than a pub and a farmhouse – when here they come, the fighting-machines, one, two, three of them bowling along with their keep-nets dangling – quite a sight of an autumn afternoon! . . .'

As he told us this story he continued to eat his meal, cutting up the bacon and mixing it with cold spud, steadily consuming his food with the discipline of the habituated soldier.

'Well, I saw them – a handful of sheep – they was bolting down into this inn's cellar, and pulling down the delivery hatch behind them. So I dashed over and got my fingers under the hatch – just! – and begged for 'em to let me squeeze in. It was a crowd down there, and they was pushing and shoving and complaining. Well, they let me in. I got inside and I was near the top of the pile, by the hatch, and through a crack – it was one of those big metal lids – I could see a fighting-machine bowling down the road, heading towards Chesham. Well, thought I – Bert, here's a chance.

'And I pushed open that lid, and I hopped out onto the road, and I took off my hat and waved at the machine and the Martian who rode it, and I yelled and pointed. Who knows what the Martian made of it! But he saw me, and bent down – and for a moment I was braced for the Heat-Ray myself, or the caress of a tentacle – and the fellows in the hole behind me were pulling and banging at the lid to get it closed again, but I kept it propped. Well, I suppose the Martian saw the easy meat inside that cellar. So he bent down, and opened that lid with a metal tentacle, delicate as a surgeon—'

Verity couldn't hide her disgust. 'You gave up your fellow humans to the Martians.'

'You can put it like that. *But they'd have died anyway.* D'ye see? If not that day, then the next, or the next. For the Martians only take a tithe – even then I think they were trying to keep breeding populations intact. Better off dead anyhow, that sort.

'That was how it started, see. The Martians can see a lot from up on high, in their aircraft and their fighting-machines. Oh yes, a lot. But this isn't their world, not yet. And a man on the ground, with a trained eye, can spot a lot more. Places people are hiding, for instance.'

'A man such as you,' I said. 'You became a scout for the Martians.'

'You can't talk to a Martian,' he said. 'Leastways, I don't know how. But you can – *communicate*. I do this for you, you leave me be, and the next day I'll do it again: that sort of show. I started to wear my gear, the chain and the wig and so on – colourful rubbish I found – for the Martians must have trouble telling us one from the other, I reasoned, so let me make it easy for 'em to spot *me*. And when they saw me they would know they could rely on me to root out a nest or two for them, no trouble. Eventually they fixed up for me – well, you've seen it – my spotting seat on a cable so I can travel with 'em. Took some guts to climb into it the first time, I can tell you.'

Verity said coldly, 'But if you are obvious to the Martians, you must also be to the people in the regions you cover.'

'That's so – but I try to be discreet – all *you* ever heard of me is rumour, I bet?'

I said, 'But it's rumour that's spread outside the Cordon, Bert. Which is why I'm here in the first place. You ought to take care.

Somebody might take a pot-shot at you in your sling. And if the authorities ever got hold of you—'

He just laughed. 'You know as well as I do, Julie Elphinstone, that the only authorities that count on this world, now and for the future, are the Martians.' The kettle began to whistle. He turned and yelled, 'Mary! Tea!'

She came through briskly, and poured hot water into a big battered pot, sluiced it around and served us tea in tin mugs.

Verity watched Mary with a kind of disgust. She said now, 'And what relation are *you* to the great survivor? A trophy?'

Mary slammed a mug down on the table and slapped Verity across the face, hard. 'Don't you speak to me like that, you stuck-up cow. You don't know nothing about me – nothing. What do you think I am, some tart?'

Verity, shocked, held her face. 'I didn't mean . . .' But she let it tail off, for I suspect that that was exactly what she had meant.

Mary pointed at Bert. '*He* saved my life. I was with friends – we're from Chorleywood, we was workers in the munitions factory, and we was on a couple of days out in the car. I grew up around here, see. And we woke up one morning and the Martians had come, and we was stuck, and when the petrol was gone, well, we was like vagabonds. We lasted for a bit – nobody helped us, nobody, but the soldiers made comments, like *yours*. About what we could do if we wanted a share of their rations. *You* know. Then down came a Martian one day, and we scattered and the Heat-Ray was firing, and I lost my friends, and I was under the Martian and I thought I was a goner. And then *he* came.'

'I managed to distract it,' Bert said. 'Led it to a barn full o' farming folk. Come, Mary, sit down, let's eat; don't let *her* bother you.'

'He saved me,' Mary said stubbornly. 'Where the government and the Army and that lot did nothing. I didn't have to come with him, but I did.'

Bert grinned. 'Couldn't get rid of her.'

'And now here we are, like this. Living. With a baby. Some day we'll get it properly done – I mean, married. But for now we're surviving. As to the rights and wrongs of what *he* does, I don't know. But I don't see many others being brave and bold about these Martians, do you?'

'No,' admitted Verity. 'And I'm sorry I jumped to conclusions. We're all doing what we can to stay alive, that's all. I hope you'll let me look at little Belle for you.'

For a moment we ate in silence.

Then, cautiously, I essayed, 'But if you're right, Bert – what's your long game? If we never can get rid of these Martians—'

'Ah, but that's what I don't accept, see. Never have. I just don't think we're going to do it with guns and Zepps and such. The government's no use in here, nor the Army. And now there's another opposition due, and I just bet there's more cylinders on the way – why, given the dates, they might be hanging in the sky above us now, for all the gov'ment tells us – and pretty soon it will be as if a Cordon's being thrown around the whole blessed world.' He belched and picked a bit of bacon from his teeth. 'And where will we be then – eh? It'll be just the Martians, and us, and we'll be a world of rabbits. That's what we are – not sheep, not rats like I used to think – rabbits. For what are rabbits but vermin when they're in the vegetable patch, but you'll pot the odd one for supper, won't you?'

'Then you're a rabbit too, Bert.'

'True. But I'm the smart rabbit. The rabbit who's got close in with them, who's seen how they work their equipment, the fighting-machines and the handling-machines. I'm the rabbit who's learning, about *them*. And soon enough I'll find others of a like mind, and we'll come and go in the very face of the Martians, until one day – *bang*. We'll make our move, all unexpected.' His voice was softening, his expression growing dreamy.

Mary scoffed, fondly. 'He does like to dream. Should see him playing at fighting-machines with little Belle – Zip! Sizzle! Stamp! It's a fair spectacle.'

And, looking around at that hole in the ground, I wondered if Bert Cook was any closer to realising such dreams than when my brother-in-law had given him up as a fool and a fantasist on Putney Hill, in the First War. But that wasn't my concern.

I leaned forward. 'Bert, I want you to get me into the Redoubt. The big Martian nest.'

30

A Strange Negotiation

Cook regarded me steadily.

I pressed him, 'Can you do it?'

'Yes,' he said bluntly. 'Why do you want to go *there*?'

I told him the surface lie. 'It's Walter's idea. My brother-in-law—'

'*Him* again.'

'He thinks there are ways to communicate with the Martians. Well, you've proved that, in your fashion. I've brought images to show them – drawings Walter made himself. They might mean something to the Martians. And even if not, if we can show we're at least intelligent enough to try to speak to them, then perhaps they will spare us.'

He forked up more spud. 'Waste of time,' he said around the mouthful. 'A sheepdog *communicates* with its master, but it's still just a dog. Spouting poetry wouldn't get it sent to Eton or Harrow! – just a beating, and back out into the fields. Walter Jenkins always was a dreamy idiot.'

'But it was he who suggested you, Bert. Knowing of your exploits in here. You're the one man who might build a bridge, make it work – or give us the chance to try, at least. The world's at stake, Bert. The future. You might think Walter a fool. But isn't it worth a try, at least?'

'Hmm. What do you think, Mary?'

She shrugged. '*I* want to know – what's in it for us?'

He nodded, and eyed me.

I was at a loss. 'I don't see what I can offer you that means anything. Money, treasures—'

'One thing.' He glanced across to the passage leading to where the baby slept.

I guessed, 'You're concerned about Belle? Her future?'

'Concerned she might not *have* a future.' He looked at me intently. 'Listen. I ain't seen it with humans yet, but it'll come. But I seen 'em with the fish-men.'

'The Cythereans? Seen what?'

'When the Martians hunt. They're not simple predators. A Martian isn't a lion. He won't go just for the weakest of the group, and let the strongest get away. He's smarter than that. He's *husbanding*, see. Some day he wants to be a farmer, a herdsman, not a hunter.'

Verity said, 'You mean they intend to domesticate the Cythereans. Domesticate *us*.'

'Look what they did to their own stock, the human types from Mars! Not a flicker of defiance left in any of them wretched creatures. *That* is what they want in the long run.'

I nodded. 'And so with the Cythereans—'

'They cull the weakest. You may as well, easy pickin's. *But they cull the strongest too.*' He tapped his forehead. 'That's what I've seen, and I've worked it out. Don't want that powerful blood being passed on down the line, see. Selective breeding. So they watch, see who fights back the hardest, is the most ingenious escaper.'

I began to see it. 'And when it comes to us—'

'I think they'll be more systematic, like, in the future. Maybe they'll pit us against each other, make us fight like dogs or cocks – like gladiators. How about that? Those Martians with their big eyes around the pit, hooting and braying and laying bets on the winner, for all I know. What a spectacle! Or maybe they'll set us to hunting each other down. Either case they'll keep the winners fattened up as long as they're entertaining or useful but *they won't let them breed*. Eliminating the strong from the blood-lines, see. Now, to the present: of the human pack in this great Buckinghamshire warren, who will they see as the strongest?'

'Ah.' Verity nodded. 'You've certainly brought yourself to their attention. You fear they'll let you live, but they'll extinguish your bloodline. Which is why you're hiding your baby down in this hole in the ground. It's not just hiding from people. You fear for Belle.'

'Wouldn't you?' He looked me square in the face. 'I'll do what you ask. But in return I want you to promise me that you, or whoever is backing you, will get Mary and Belle safely out of here.'

If anywhere *is* safe, I thought.

Mary grabbed his hand. 'No, Bert! Not without you.'

'I'll survive,' he said with that grin of his. 'You know me. But this—' He gestured at me. 'What a gift, to drop into our laps! And if we can get our little girl safe . . .'

Verity and I talked it over in private, briefly.

'That's Bert Cook for you,' I said. 'Likes to make everyone dance to his tune. But there's a certain truth to his speculations, don't you think? A brutal rationalism. There always was; Walter saw it in him.'

'But I wonder how the military and the politicians will regard him. The traitor who seems to have exposed hundreds to the Martians . . . What charges could be brought if they got their hands on him? They'd probably have to invent a whole new category of law. Crimes against the species.'

'Verity, do you think we should do this? Deal with Cook, I mean.'

'If it will get you into the Redoubt.' She smiled. 'And it's in the little girl's interests to get *her* out of here. Everybody wins.'

'Agreed.'

We went back to Cook and Mary. Verity asked bluntly, 'Bert, do you have access to a telephone? . . .'

Of course he did.

It took twenty-four hours to set up.

The scheme involved a Zeppelin sortie over the Cordon area, close to where we were, while Bert set up a diversion in the north, hopefully to distract the attention of the Martians. A squad of marines would drop from the Zepp, retrieve Mary and Belle from the caves, and lift them away. That was the arrangement. It took most of those twenty-four hours before Cook was happy with the promises he'd received, including a personal assurance from Churchill himself.

Of course neither Cook nor Mary, nor even Verity, knew the true purpose of it all – knew of the weapon I carried in my veins. No doubt Mr Churchill was aware, but he didn't drop it into the conversation.

For our second night in the caves, as he had the first night, Cook offered us heaps of blankets, and suggested we tried to nap. I for one did not sleep.

We left the caves at midnight. It was, I would ascertain later,

May 19, a Friday. Cook assured us it was safer for us to come upon the Redoubt in the small hours, for the Martians were calmer at dawn than at other times of the day.

We carried weapons as we crossed the countryside, but would stash them in a ditch before we reached the Martian base, at Cook's advice; we would not be allowed to carry in guns. I had with me, however, Walter's pictures, in their battered leather case, carried all the way from Berlin.

So we walked through the silent dark towards the pit of the Martians. With every step closer I felt a gathering dread, as I had for twelve, thirteen days already as I had travelled. And in the silence and the dark I thought I could feel the agent in my blood, the poison. If the Martians were a canker in the earth, there was a canker in my own blood, as if my body were a mirror of the whole infected planet.

We arrived at the Redoubt a little before four a.m. Albert Cook grinned at us in the grey light, and it was as if he had read my thoughts. 'You've heard of Darkest Africa. Welcome to Darkest England, ladies.'

31

Into the Redoubt

Two years after the fall of the cylinders the Martian base at Amersham was in essence a tremendous earthwork perhaps a mile across. Its beginning had been the infall of three ships close together, whose overlapping impact craters had since been greatly extended and deepened by the patient work of the Martians' excavating-machines. Now it was one vast bowl surrounded by an earthen rampart.

We climbed this rampart, Verity and I, with Bert Cook at our side. And at the crest we stood on a frozen wave of broken tarmac and brick and shards of glass, and we looked into the Redoubt.

It was the space cylinders that first drew my eye. They were like great tilted pillars stuck in the ground: three Pisas of heat-scarred metal, in the grey dawn light. And even from here I could see, at the very centre of the earthwork, a shadow in the earth, enigmatic, dark. I knew this was a deep shaft, visible to spotter planes, that the Martians were cutting straight down into the ground. Similar efforts had been started in the pits they had excavated during the First War, especially at Horsell Common, site of their first landing, and on Primrose Hill. That was the essential layout – the three great cylinders stuck in the ground at the corners of a rough equilateral triangle, with that deep shaft at the centroid. Fighting-machines stood tall and inert, looking a little like the water towers you see in some American states – dozens of them, in loose groups.

All around these tremendous monuments, the Martians and their lesser machines worked, glistening and rustling in the gathering light, emitting soft hoots, and hisses where the green smoke escaped from limbs and apertures. There was motion everywhere, looking oddly insectile.

And even from here I could see people – what looked like several groups of them – sitting passively on English soil, or in the foundations of ruined houses. Perhaps they were recent captives, yet to be processed.

'Don't move,' Cook said softly.

My attention snapped back to my own situation. Now I saw that a handling-machine had, all but silently, clambered up the inner face of the rampart on which we stood.

The machine stopped dead before us. Evidently we were being inspected.

The machine had five articulated legs, as they all do, and long manipulative tentacles composed of the usual metal rings, and a set of fine specialised tools fixed to its front. I wondered what delicate task it had been pursuing. The Martian riding it was a leathery sack, from a distance rather like a bear curled up to hibernate – but there was no fur on that glistening hide, and those gruesome hands, with their long, supple fingers, were folded beneath the carcass.

And so I faced the Martian, at last. I had seen pictures; I had read accounts, including my brother-in-law's. I had not been so close to any Martian before, save for the pickled specimen they had put on display in the Natural History Museum – and save for the beast that had attacked us in the perimeter tunnel, and then there had been no time for cold contemplation. It gazed back at me now with those huge, oddly bright eyes, set in that enormous smooth head with the disturbing, lipless beak of a mouth – a head fully four feet across. I knew there was a logic in this strange morphology. From ape to Neanderthal to human you can see a progression, a growth of the forebrain, a regression of the protective brow that shelters the eyes, a shrinking of the jaw and the great muscles used to chew coarse food. In this Martian those trends had been progressed to their limit. But it was not evolutionary logic that struck me in those moments of encounter. That strange round head with its small features, that pinched mouth, the eyes widened as if in perpetual surprise: it had the look of a monstrous infant, which shard of familiarity made it all the more repulsive.

I have always regarded myself as rational, but a wave of intense antipathy broke over me at that moment. I longed to destroy this thing, to expel it; it did not belong on our earth, and I wanted it gone, down to the very cells of my being. More than disgust, it was a deep visceral revulsion – and a stab of savage despair too.

Verity's good hand grasped mine. 'Welcome to hell,' she murmured.

Cook grunted, 'And call me Virgil. Ha! Two snobs like you don't expect a bloke like me to start quoting classic literature, do you? Just keep still. He wants to check you over, that's all. Oi, pretty boy. It's me!' He held up the mayoral chain around his neck. 'Good old Bert! You know me. Go on, you tell your bosses... They do it all by thought, you know. Reading minds.'

I said softly, hardly daring to move, 'You believe that, do you?'

He snorted. 'Not a question of *believe*. It's obvious if you watch 'em for a bit, as I've done.'

Now, with grace but sudden speed, one of the machine's handling tentacles uncurled towards us.

'Hold still! I warned you – they're checking you over! Hold still!'

I was first. I stood there while the arm swept over me, its tip, its cold flank, running over my body. Its motions were smooth, clean, mechanical. I cannot believe it searched me merely by touch; perhaps it relied on some effect analogous to Roentgen rays to perform a deeper inspection. In only a second it was done, and I breathed again. Then it was on to Verity, and she held my hand tight, especially when the Martian probed her broken arm with its splint.

Then, with sudden abruptness, the machine backed away, turned, and walked off with its usual liquid grace, returning to whatever task it had abandoned to come to us.

Bert said, 'There you are. You're in. I come up here every now and again to let 'em have a look and make sure they don't forget who I am. And I told you to leave your weapons behind. For if you hadn't, they'd have been found and it would have been the drips for all of us.'

'The drips?' I asked.

'You'll see. Come on.'

He led us down the inner face of the perimeter rampart. The low, multi-legged Martian machine had passed down this rough slope easily, but we bipedal humans had to pick our way more cautiously.

On the floor of the Redoubt we walked forward, through a scene of industry. All around us excavating-machines, big, mole-like, dug into the earth and shaped it into pits and galleries, tunnels and canals around that deep central shaft. These secondary dimples were huge excavations in themselves, in some of which, amid puffs of green smoke, I saw handling-machines working on the familiar process of the extraction of aluminium from the clay of the earth, as well as less recognisable tasks. And in other pits I saw machines working on the construction of *more* machines, handlers and excavators, working in pairs like surgeons, or midwives. In one great cavity I even saw them assembling a fighting-machine, the heavy handlers crawling over the great bronzed cowl, the articulated legs laid out in sections.

Picture it! Martians and their machines, moving everywhere, in the low dawn light, in near silence.

Unexpectedly Cook made us pause. 'Wait a minute. They won't interfere with us unless we do something stupid. Just *look* ... Sometimes I stand on spots like this and sort of half-close my eyes, so it gets dim and indistinct. It's all industry, I suppose, but it ain't like human industry, is it? Just stand here and take it in. Think of it not as a kind of factory or a quarry, but as a landscape ...'

I stood, and strove to set aside my fear – and that instinctive loathing of all things Martian – and tried to see it as he had suggested.

It has long been remarked that all Martian machines have a certain living quality, thanks to their ingenious electric musculature, in sharp contrast to our own crude arrangements of wheels and gears and levers and rods. Now I saw that quality evident all around me. Excavating-machines ploughed in a group through the broken earth, as dolphins will dive through the waves of the oceans; and a herd of handling-machines, of all sizes gathered together, crossed an open area, en route from one task to another, the dawn light shining from their metal hides as if from the backs of migrant beasts. And I saw a brace of fighting-machines on the move, off in the distance beyond the far rampart of the pit, tall, elegant, striding through the dusty air. Over it all hung the faint tinge of green, of the smoke that was emitted from joints and fixtures by Martian machines on the move, and from the pits they dug in the ground, like a mist.

'*I've* never been to Africa,' Cook murmured now. 'Not even to Boer country. But I've seen pictures. When I look at it like this, I don't see industry. I see a kind of savannah. They're like animals on the move, big and small, individuals or in herds.'

'Yes,' Verity said, sounding surprised. 'You're right. I see it now. It all has that quality of life. The handlers like horny-backed herbivores, the fighting-machines like great giraffes perhaps – no! They are too aggressive for that.'

'Like tyrannosaurs,' I suggested. 'Striding across some Creta-ceous plain.'

'Something like that, yes.'

'See, I've read the books, or some of 'em,' Cook said. 'Some say there *must* have been animals on Mars, once. Because you wouldn't get humanoids, and then Martians, just showing up on a world without a whole *zoo*, plants and animals and such, evolving together. And others say that's all gone now, because Mars is too dried out. The Martians have had to turn the whole world into one big city, or a factory, where there's nothing but the canals and the machines and the pumping houses, I suppose. Like the whole of Mars is a giant Birmingham – ha!

'But what about the animals? Well, in *my* lifetime I'm seeing animals being replaced by machines. I trained in the horse artil-lery, and now the nags are being swapped out for motor-wagons, for better or worse. A lot of us miss having the beasts at our side. And maybe the Martians feel the same, see, and they've done something about it. Maybe they've got a few old bones in the museums, up there, a few of the last specimens in 2005, as we'd have. But they've gone further, see. A motor-lorry ain't much like a horse – a horse doesn't have wheels for a start. But Martian machines have legs, like animals . . .'

'I see what you're getting at,' Verity said now. 'Maybe the Martians modelled their machines more closely on their animals than we ever did.'

'That's it,' said Cook. 'As if we made mechanical horses and elephants and such.'

'So what we're seeing is a kind of diorama – it's how Mars used to be. Impressionistically, at least. And it's this way because the Martians, for all their apparent brutality, didn't want to lose their own past. How – romantic.' She sounded reluctant to say the word.

It was a fetching thought, and I grinned at the old artilleryman. 'Bert Cook, you *do* have an imagination, don't you?'

But he retreated into his shell of customary resentment. 'Got no education to speak of – no respect from the toffs. But, ho yes, I always had imagination. I imagined all *this* back in '07, when the rest of you thought we was done with the Martians. *I* kept thinking. Now then – you two come with me and I'll show you things that will beggar *your* imagination.'

We walked on.

And he led us to the cage of the Cythereans.

32

Prisoners of the Martians

It was not much of a cage, in fact. To hold their captives from Venus, the Martians had dug out a kind of tank, a shallow cylinder lined with some rubbery, impermeable material, and filled with water that was stained faintly crimson, the colour of the Martian weed. A containing net of a silvery mesh was stretched over the pit, and firmly fixed by a solid band anchored to the ground. This mesh was hexagonal, the holes the size of pennies, perhaps – enough to let in the sun and the rain, not enough to allow out a Cytherean, nothing larger than a digit on those webbed hands. But we could see the Cythereans, and they could see us, with their small black eyes set in those smooth faces.

A handling-machine stood by, motionless, like a guard, but without a controlling Martian riding it.

We crept closer, to see.

My life had been saved by a Cytherean, and I had spent some time with them, but I could scarcely claim to be an expert in their psychology. Their mood was not hard to read, however. Most of the wretched creatures just lay in the water, floating, on their backs; some, heartbreakingly, had infants basking on their bellies. One big male swam back and forth, back and forth, just a couple of firm strokes with hands and feet taking him from one side of his enclosure to the other. It was as you might see a tiger pace in a too-small cage in a zoo. And another adult, a female, was working at the net, picking at it with her fingers, gnawing at it.

Cook grunted. 'She'll get nothing but a broken tooth for her trouble. Can't blame her for trying, though – *I* would.'

'The water is stained red,' I observed. 'Are they given food?'

Cook shrugged. 'You get that where you dump a Cytherean in clean water, I think – as you get greenish slime in a stagnant

278

pond. They aren't held for long before they're hoiked out and taken to the blood bank, or the drips.' He did not elaborate on these terms. 'The Martians can't be bothered to feed 'em, but they like to get value out of their catch. Don't want 'em turning skinny. So this lot will probably be gone by tomorrow, one way or another, and a fresh batch chucked in. Before they take 'em the Martians will pass a shock through the water – a kind of electric shock I think – it makes 'em malleable, but they're still awake.'

Verity the VAD grimaced. 'Are they aware of what becomes of them? Do they experience pain?'

Cook shrugged. 'They aren't held for long,' he repeated.

I shook my head. 'I hope none of these are from Misbourne.'

'Makes no difference,' Cook said brutally. 'Nothing we can do for them – never was. Come on now...' And he led us on, deeper into the Martian complex.

In the next pit there were people.

One must be analytical about it. One must describe what one saw, not how one felt about it. But there are times, even penning this memoir, when I envy Walter Jenkins his self-proclaimed detachment from mankind!

In general terms, you must imagine, the arrangement was similar to the holding of the Cythereans: the pit in the ground, the mesh net enclosing it anchored by a peripheral band fixed to the earth. This pit held no water, of course, and it had been dug deeper. Again an empty handling-machine stood by, like a prison guard.

And as we peered down, we saw faces looking back up at us, like coins shining at the bottom of a fountain: human faces this time, pale, dirty, some defiant, some fearful, some tear-streaked. I believe there were about a dozen people in that pit. Such was the arrangement of shadow, and so grimy were the occupants, that I could see little of their bodies. Only the faces stood out in my vision – and in my memory now, as I think back on it.

They saw us approach, silhouetted against the dawn sky, I supposed, as seen from their point of view. They became agitated, naturally enough, and the calling started. 'You – who are you?' 'Can you help us?' Some of the voices were quite cultured. 'Please take my little girl, she's only three...' I saw the child held up into the light.

'Don't worry,' Cook murmured to us. 'They can't reach you.

The Martians dug this deep – they learned. We humans are wilier than Cythereans, and are more ingenious at doing damage. So they put the mesh out of reach of those clever monkey fingers.'

Verity seemed to have retreated into a shell of brittle self-control. 'It's not myself that I'm concerned about, Cook. There are children in there.'

He looked at her, and laughed. 'Well, you need to toughen up. There's nothing we can do. And they won't suffer. It's the same as the Venus-men; they won't be held long. They'll get the same treatment – paralysed, if not stunned, and pulled out like big floppy fish.'

I glared at him. 'How can you be so heartless, Bert? Even you.'

'What choice is there—'

'Hey, it's Bert Cook! You monster, you betrayed us! Let's do it, lads—'

And now there was a kind of surge from the depths of the pit. I saw one man, two, swarm at the earthen walls, and a third man climbed over the backs of his fellows and managed to reach the mesh, where he clung on. It was a rehearsed move, I think, and the rage at Cook was the trigger to try it. That third man, the climber, was rough-shaven, grimy – but I thought he seemed fine-featured, with a scholarly aspect: I may be snobbish, for looks are deceptive, but he looked like a thinker, a lawyer, a teacher, a writer. Yet that face was twisted in gut hatred, and I imagined he would tear apart Bert Cook with his bare hands if he got the chance. But he could do nothing but shout insults from beneath the mesh.

The guardian handling-machine, alerted, rumbled forward. But Cook, nimbly, got in the way of the machine, standing between it and the pit. He dug a handful of black stones out of his jacket pocket, and began hurling them into the pit, aiming them at the climbing man. 'Back in the hole, you brute. Back, I say!' Some of his shots bounced off the mesh, others fell harmlessly into the dark – but one caught the climber fair in the forehead and he fell back, howling. Once again the yells of rage came, and more of those entreaties too, growing ever more desperate as Cook drew us away, and we passed out of their sight.

Verity grabbed my hand, squeezing it too tight for comfort.

Cook was grinning as he walked, evidently pleased with himself. 'There's more yet. You haven't seen it all.'

'Those pebbles you threw,' I said to him.

'Not pebbles.'

'Can I see?'

He glanced around, as if to be sure no Martian was about, then dug his hand into the pocket again. The stones he withdrew were black, gleaming, shaped.

'Flints,' I said.

'Not just any ol' flint. Look at them. Look at that edge...'

Verity took one. 'That's been knapped.' She looked at Cook. 'By you?'

'Not by me. I tried it – after all, flint is lying around in the ground in this peculiar part of the country – and all I did is smash my thumb. Maybe some day. No, I swiped these from the museum.'

'The museum?' I looked again. 'These are ancient, then. Prehistoric. Hand-axes and arrow heads.'

'That's the idea. Tried it one day, carrying one in, under the noses of the Martians... They'll stop you with a weapon, something obvious. Even a bow and arrow, once, a kid's thing from a toy shop, tried that just to see – they took it off me. But the stones, see, the shaped stones. They don't recognise *those* for what they are.'

'As tools,' I said, wondering. 'As weapons from the Stone Age. The only tools we had for almost all of our history.'

'Huh. More recent than that. My Mary's mum was a local girl, and Mary says her grandfather had tales of when he was a boy, and even then the workers, the woodsmen and such, would think nothing of picking up a flint, breaking off a slice and knapping it, if they wanted some job done quick and didn't have a knife to hand. One old fellow even shaved with them, so it was said.'

'But the Martians don't recognise them,' Verity said. 'Not as artefacts.'

I nodded. 'Perhaps they have retained something of their own past, in the forms of their machines, the odd artificial ecology they make up. But they've forgotten their own Stone Age—'

'If they ever had one, on Mars, if the geology permitted it,' Verity said. 'And you, Bert. There you were loudly complaining there was nothing to be done about the plight of the human victims here. And yet you're chucking them flint blades, under the eyes of the Martians!'

'It's little enough,' he said. He seemed almost embarrassed by the revelation. 'It won't cut that metal netting stuff – I know, I've tried, nothing we have will cut it.'

'Then I'm confused,' I said. 'What use is it, in that case?'

Verity said patiently, 'The flint won't cut metal. But it would cut human flesh, Julie.'

And I saw it.

'Better way out,' the old artilleryman said. 'For them that's got the guts to take it. Or to save your kids. Them that's got the guts. I'm setting 'em a kind of test, see.'

I found this hard to absorb – maybe I am not as imaginative as Cook was, or indeed Walter. 'You're doing a good thing, then, Bert,' I said.

''S much as I can do.'

'You do have a heart—'

'Don't spread it around.'

'*I* wouldn't have seen it.'

He looked at me coldly. 'The Martians can't see it either, but maybe they will, eventually, and that little game will be up. They're trying to understand us. They're *experimenting*. You say you're here to talk with the Martians. Well, then, you need to see what they're up to – all of it. Then you'll know what's what. And that's what I'm going to show you now.'

33

A Laboratory

He led us to a part of the compound where quite deep circular pits were set out in orderly rows and columns. Over each stretched the metal mesh, and beside each a handling-machine stood on guard, a motionless, tireless sentry. And I heard now a kind of whimpering, a weary crying – not from one voice, but from many.

I hung back again; I could not help it. I think I might not have gone further if not for the strength of Verity beside me – and if I had not been unwilling to show weakness to Bert Cook, or indeed to the Martians all around us.

In the first few pits, however, there was nothing unusual to be seen – nothing, that is, but the ghastly sight of people, men, women and children cast down together for a few hours of imprisonment, before a worse fate. But these pits were arranged in arrays, almost as if they were part of some vast game board. I have learned since that our scientists will run experiments with similar layouts. If they wish to test for the effects of varying combinations of factors – different mixtures of ingredients in experimental drugs, perhaps – they will create a matrix of combinations, set out physically in the laboratory, in a grid of the kind I saw dug into the ground.

And, Bert said, this was indeed a kind of laboratory. What the Martians were studying was the human soul.

'As I see it the Martians don't have families as we do. Or family ties. Oh, they give birth, they bud, but once the little beast is skedaddling around it will go to any one of the adults for attention. And they don't suckle, by the way; if the Martians were ever mammals, they ain't now; it's straight on the old claret for a young 'un as soon as it's split off from the parent.'

'Claret' – a ghastly joke!

'Of course they are loyal,' Bert went on, 'to each other, to the race as a whole. Well, we learned that, didn't we? When they crossed space all that way and came again to England, they had other things to achieve – they wanted to learn how to beat *us* – but they came back for those they left behind before, or at least their bodies, for what remained.'

I nodded. 'Walter predicted the return to England based on that very observation.'

But Bert Cook would never be interested in anything Walter Jenkins said or wrote. 'The point *is*,' he said now, 'here they are, watching us. And they see that *we* are loyal to each other, in family groups, to our parents, our siblings – 'specially our children.'

A ghastly awareness was creeping over me. 'And what has this to do with these rows of pits?'

'Well, they're testing us. Mixing folk up. *I* don't know the detail. But in one corner you might have a family group, parents and offspring. In another, strangers chucked in together, adults with somebody else's kids. Those two extremes, and everything in between. Now – you might sacrifice yourself for *your* kid, but would you do it for another's child? Or one further removed, a nephew or a niece or a grandchild ... If I offered you the chance to save two nephews in exchange for one daughter – or a dozen, I don't know – would you do it? *That's* what they're testing for – that's what I think, anyhow. I seen 'em come at it, day after day, chucking in new specimens, while the children weep for the mums they've just been ripped away from.'

'They're experimenting with human emotions, then,' Verity said. 'Experimenting with our capacity for love. And *methodically*.'

'I'll tell you what I saw once,' he went on, more darkly. 'Parents and one kiddie – only young, they were. The parents gave up the kiddie, when the Martian handling-machine came to collect; cutest little blonde girl you ever saw. Pushed her into the clutches of the machine, they did, jus' like that. And you know what the Martians did? *They released 'em*, the parents. I saw it with my own eyes. Opened up the pit, and let them climb out, and they emerged blinking and grimy and a bit bewildered, and I had to tell them which way to go to get out. Laughing my head off I was, they was crying so hard – but, crying or not, off they went. Probably still out there somewhere now, growing spuds and having dinner parties.

284

'Because *they're* the sort the Martians want to preserve. More selective breeding. Do you see? They want the meek, the controllable – the selfish, disloyal sort. And that's what they're selecting for. Submit and you live – and breed more like yourself.'

Verity shook her head. 'That's monstrous, Bert.'

'Plausible, though,' I murmured.

'And that's just the start,' said Bert Cook. 'Some day, when they've bred us into the strain they want...' He held up his hands, as if framing the scene. 'I got this vision of the future. People being grown in rows like plants in a big field, all passive and waiting their turn. And the fighting-machines walking up and down the rows, just plucking them when they're ripe.' He laughed at us. 'Still squeamish, are we? All this too tough for you to take? It's not over yet. *Look* at what I brought you to now.' With a dramatic flair – he had been a showman, after all, peddling his stories on stages around the world – he pointed down into yet another cage, another pit. '*Look* down there...'

Verity looked more closely than I did at what lay in the pit, but then she had been a VAD, a nursing assistant, and had seen worse before than I ever had. I could not look for long; it was a glimpse, a vivid horror.

The woman was young, I would judge, no older than twenty-five. She was naked from the waist up; her lower body was covered by a coarse blanket; she lay on her back in the shadow of the pit. A man sat beside her, older, looking at us warily, resentfully – almost possessively. And the thing that grew out of the side of her belly was a head – a recognisable human head – it looked like the head of a child of perhaps nine or ten. A crumpled face, eyes closed, a sketch of a nose, no hair on the scalp. Fingers, long and skeletal, were gathered around the mouth. And that mouth had a pointed upper lip, like the letter V. That was all I saw, before I had to turn away.

Verity asked, with eerie calm, 'Who is he? The man with her.'

Cook shrugged. 'Doctor of some kind – or pretending to be. It's another kind who gets spared; if you show yourself to be a doctor or a nurse, or with those sort of skills, they'll keep you, for a time anyhow. What better than to have a sheep playing the vet for the rest of the herd? This isn't the only experiment they've run. On reproduction, I mean. They're interested in all that. They like to examine the stages of a pregnancy.' Mercifully he went into no detail. 'And the children growing up too. Take a few kiddies away from their parents and set 'em in a pit on their own. Maybe they want to see how we would grow up feral. Would we work out our own pack structure, like wolves? Would we work out a language from scratch, or do we have to be taught it? ... I suppose that's what they're interested in. Whether we're more or less biddable.'

Verity said, '*This*, though—'

'Gen'rally they don't last long,' said Bert Cook, almost casually. 'The bud seems to drain the mother's body of too much blood, too fast. I say *bud*. I say *mother*. Not sure whether those terms are the right ones, I ain't no Huxley.

'Some say the Martians were like us – once. Ain't that so? Humans, or human-shaped – like the wretches they bring with 'em to eat during the voyage. But they evolved away, or rather sculpted themselves away from that form. Eugenics: the betterment of a stock by surgery or fiddling with the germ plasm – *I* don't know, all I know is what I read, and I don't even understand half of that.'

'And now they're trying it on us,' Verity said, joining us, her face closed with disgust and rage. 'Seeing if we can be made Martian, like them.'

I whispered, 'Whatever it is, I wish—'

'You could end it? Myself also. Put an end to this House of Pain!'

Cook said coldly, 'You still ain't seeing it clearly. The Martians, you know, would say they are doing us a favour. Lifting us up, as if we made a chimp smart as a college per-fessor. And who's to say, by their lights, they are wrong? And – pain? What of it? You clever-clogs keep telling me the Martians are above us mere mortals. Perhaps, with their heads detached from their bodies, *they* are above pain as above pleasure. And what need they care about the pain they inflict on us? Any more'n we care about the pain of the animal in the slaughterhouse – or the tree we cut down. To recoil from this is hypocritical – d'ye see?' He grinned at me, mocking. 'And, seeing this, do you still think you'll be able to communicate with 'em? Still think they'll be impressed by you being able to prove Pythagoras's theorem, or whatnot?'

I saw that even an imagination as dark as Bert Cook's had not guessed at the truth of my mission, at what I carried in my veins, even now, as I completed these last few steps of my long journey, seven hundred miles from the bright civilisation of Berlin to this, the centre of evil – no, not of evil: of the unbearable inevitability of cosmology, and intelligence, and Darwin's chill logic.

But perhaps Bert was right. By the Martians' lights – *and perhaps in the view of our own descendants of the far future*, they who would have to deal with the cooling of the sun, and the freezing of the earth, as the Martians have done on their world – the Martians' ghastly treatment of the young mother in the pit, our own first step to a greater evolution, was the noblest gift they could have given us.

In any event, what Bert Cook said to me now was: 'I think it's time you saw the end of it.'

34

The Drips

So we were brought to the very centre of that mile-wide pit. From here the bordering rampart could be glimpsed all around, and the sun, I saw, was soon to rise over the wall to the east – it was still very early. Before us the great fallen cylinders protruded from the earth like megaliths; it was a Martian Stonehenge. We were close to that tremendous central shaft in the ground, too; from here I could see the excavating-machines toiling under its lip, widening and smoothing the walls, and I could hear a great pulse sounding from deep underground – *boom, boom, boom* – like a tremendous engine, or a beating heart. You must imagine this monotonous, oppressive rhythm as the background to all that followed.

And there, in a shallow arena, the Martians sat together.

They were out of their machines, and resting on a carpet of their red weed. They were flattened balls, as if deflated, their skin creased. I imagined that was an effect of our earth's heavy gravity. Again I saw those strange faces clear and close to – the immense dark eyes, the lack of a brow ridge, the V-shaped lip, the lack of a chin, the brow huge and sweating: not unlike the brow of Walter Jenkins, I thought! Occasionally one would pluck at a vesicle of the weed or a fatter cactus-like growth, lift it with those long, flexible fingers and push it into its mouth. They regarded each other with those great eyes. And they hooted and honked, like broken-down steam engines. Huge, flaccid, ugly, they would have been almost comical, I think, if not for the equipment arrayed around them.

That equipment...

Imagine a series of hanging brackets, like scaffolds, with a handling-machine settled at the base of each. A human being hung from each of these scaffolds, by the feet, inverted, the arms loosely strapped to the sides. These captives did not struggle, but they were conscious throughout. Later anatomical examinations proved it: the Martians used electricity to render their selected specimens flaccid, incapable of physical resistance, but it seems clear they were awake through most of it – and, probably, capable of sensing pain. All of them happened to be adults, and for that I am forever grateful; the images burned in my memory might have been so much worse yet if children had been among the victims. Dangling people, then. Eyes closed, their faces flushed with blood – their hair loose and fallen, the skirts of the women draped in an undignified way. Some were well dressed, in fact; it made no difference now.

And a tube, crimson, protruded from the side of the neck of each of these victims – the left side, I remember vividly – attached to a valve set in the jugular vein or carotid artery. Each tube snaked down to a rack among the group of Martians. These tubes, and the racks they were lodged in, had peculiar markings which Keynes, an authority on blood transfusion, has since speculated might be related to human blood types; a Martian may prefer, or be compelled to take, human blood of a particular type, and the tubes were coded as necessary.

For this was the feeding, of course.

The last stage in the process was simple, technically. Using the long fingers of those strange hands, a Martian would take one of the tubes, insert it into a kind of cannula attached to its own flesh, and turn a tap, so that the blood ran directly from a human being into its own body. There were young in the Martian circle, like the adults in every particular except their size, and I saw one adult, almost gently, use its long fingers to adjust the feed tube to the inlet on the flesh of a confused infant. It seemed an almost touching moment.

'Sometimes they'll feed in a kind of frenzy,' Cook murmured in my ear. 'Then they can't get the victims in quick enough, handling-machines or no handling-machines. Your Martian needs a lot of blood through him, from time to time. Why? I'm no sawbones, but I'd say it's the need to flush out the waste from the bloodstream. How else are they to do it? Never seen a Martian on a lavatory – I bet you never thought about that, did you? Or sometimes they just bleed the victims out into big refrigerated stores, like blood banks.

'And other times, like this, it's more leisurely, sort of in-between.

Like a tea party, don't you think?' He laughed. 'Almost polite. Sometimes they'll empty you in one feed. Or sometimes they'll turn you right way up and hang you in a kind of store, and keep you for later. Eventually you're used up, of course.'

I said bleakly, 'And then?'

'And then you're no more use.' He grinned coldly. 'The crows are allies of the Martians, at least. You two ladies have done well – thought you'd pass out or run away long before this. So, now what? Going to give 'em your geometry lesson?'

'Let us talk,' I said, and walked away from him with Verity.

Her face was pinched with anger and disgust. 'If I had a Zeppelin and an immense bomb, I would drop it and erase all trace of this blemish. It doesn't belong on our earth.'

It was time to tell her the truth. If not now, when? 'I don't have a bomb, Verity, but I do have the next best thing...' And I told her, quickly, of Eric, and Porton Down, and the concoction in my blood.

I would have been consumed with resentment at this dishonesty. But Verity was made of better stuff, and, as I have said, intelligent beyond her education; once she grasped the idea she immediately saw the opportunity. 'Will you use it? Here we are at the heart of it all – Cook seems to roam around with impunity. If we could get to this blood store he speaks of—'

'No.' I pulled away. I turned round. Confused, distressed, I was acting on pure instinct now, but my instinct was not to poison. 'A grim old pathogen from the heart of Africa – if we use *this*, are we any better than the Martians? And even if we succeed, it won't be enough. For even if we poisoned this lot, they would learn to safeguard against it, and more would come, and more...'

She looked helpless. 'Then what must we do?'

And in a flash I saw it.

'There was a reader of my memoir,' Walter Jenkins once told me, 'who criticised my account of the end of the Martians on the earth, in their '07 adventure.'

I had replied, 'You mean, their slaying by the bacteria? Criticised how? It was a fair and accurate account, as far as I know.'

'But I think this fellow was considering the dramatic qualities of the incident. The literary quality of my book, if you like. After all our struggles against the Martians, it was a *deus ex machina* of a resolution. Out of nowhere, so he said, the germs came to our rescue and it was a case of happy ever after, the end. As if I had cheated in the telling. As if it was *my* story! A mere fiction!'

'This wasn't the Year Million Man again, was it?'

'Not him this time, though *he's* been trouble enough. I had to point out to my amateur critic how carefully in fact I had foreshadowed this final revelation, if you read the text – right from the opening paragraph, where I speak of the Martians watching us as "a man with a microscope might scrutinise the transient creatures that swarm and multiply in a drop of water". Then I took care to point out how the blights struck at the red weed and other Martian vegetation, before the bacteria got to the Martians themnselves... And so on and so forth! It's germs from the off, and all the way home.

'And, more deeply, I tried to tell the fellow how he had missed the point of the piece. This wasn't a novel, this was a history; and the emergence of the bacteria at the resolution of the conflict was logical, it was necessary – historically, biologically necessary. It's all about context, Julie. This was never a war waged by Martians against humans. We were only in the way – or rather, only a part of that which was invaded. This was a war of Mars against the earth, of Martian organisms against a billion years of terrestrial evolution. And the resolution was no *deus ex machina*. The earth won...'

Now it was as if Walter whispered in my ear, as I stood there in that pit of horrors. Of course the demon in my blood wasn't the answer; no weapon wielded by a human hand could be, not like this. And Frank had seen it too, as he had observed the red weed choking terrestrial life into extinction – there in the ground the true war was being waged, a war of the soil, of the essence of life.

It was the strain, the shock of it all, of the last few days, I suppose. Or perhaps it was the memory of Ben Gray, in that tunnel: the way, the last heartbeat before he detonated the grenade and destroyed himself, he had checked, calmly and methodically, to be sure that I and the others were safe. If he could think on such a plane, could I not?... Whether that was an influence or not, I dedicate what follows to Gray's memory.

For, standing there, for the first, the only, time in my life, I thought like Walter Jenkins! As if a window had been opened up in my mind. I thought I saw it through to the end – *I thought I saw the solution*. I carried it with me, in fact – not in the lethal sludge they had forced into my veins, but in the battered leather satchel I had brought all the way from Berlin, at poor Walter's behest.

Or rather, I saw the necessary solution in the grander ideas that had framed Walter's project, ideas that had been used as no more than the basis of the Lie by Eric and his commanders – ideas of which even Walter seemed to have lost sight.

This was a War of the Worlds. And that was how it must be fought – and won.

Eager, I grabbed Verity's hands. I had to make her see my revelation.

'Look around, Verity! This is England, and there are beings from two other worlds here – from Mars and Venus. It is an interplanetary war, as Walter saw, and that's how we must handle it, and no bit of petty sabotage is going to resolve it one way or another.'

In retrospect, I can see that she was quite baffled; I must have seemed deranged. She asked, 'How, then?'

I was still thinking extraordinarily quickly, and the shape of a scheme formed in my mind even as I spoke. *That* was when I thought of Marriott and his boast of earth-sculpting, and I laughed out loud.

Verity looked at me strangely. 'Julie?'

'I know what we must do. But we have to get out of here.'

'Very well. And then?'

'And then we have to contact Eric Eden, and Marriott with his bombers ... Remember how he bragged of how his explosives could shape the very ground? Well, let's see if that's true. We've work to do, Verity. Work to do!'

It was then, I think, that I saw the green flash in the sky.

Verity looked around, distracted too. A gleam of the sun showed on the rampart wall to the east.

I grabbed the girl's shoulders. 'Verity – what time is it?'

She checked her watch. 'A little after five a.m.'

'And the date?'

'The date? Why—'

'The confusion – I was unconscious for so long—'

'It is Friday. May 19, I think ...'

I was chilled. I remembered now, the faded diary, the old lady's bedroom. *This* was the date I had computed in my addled brain, assuming I had remembered June 10 correctly as the opposition: three weeks and a day before that astronomical encounter. The date of the landings, if they were to come this year. And here were the fireworks, right on schedule!

Another flash in the sky, a green streak, like a crack in heaven, heading west.

I shook Verity. 'The cylinders! Did you see that one?'

'The next wave – it must be. And stop shaking me!'

'Perhaps if we had been outside the Cordon we would have known, the government must have announced the sightings of the cannon fire on Mars by now...'

But she looked confused. 'I don't understand. The Martian cylinders – they always fall at midnight. It's nearly sunrise—'

'Midnight at the target site, though,' Cook said bluntly, staring at the sky. 'Midnight *there*, not here. Here's another one, look. And another! Whoosh, whiz!'

And even as we spoke, and the Martians hooted languidly as they fed, more cylinders fell across the sky above us, and more. They were all heading west, I saw, towards the Atlantic.

Towards America. Where, on the east coast, in Washington and New York and Boston and Miami, it was midnight.

And I knew I was right. Even if I successfully infected the Martians in England, the other nests would adapt, and the war would be lost anyhow. Our only hope, and a fragile one, lay with Walter and his 'graphic geometry': mankind's only defence lay in my mind, not my blood.

'Told you.' Bert Cook raised his arms to the sky. 'Come down, you beauties!'

293

BOOK III
Worlds at War

1

The House in Dahlem

On the day the lightning fell across the earth, Walter Jenkins was in Berlin. And from that powerful city his view of that world-wide catastrophe far exceeded my own perspective at the time, trapped as I was in the Cordon in England.

Walter had taken a rented home in a village called Dahlem, south-west of Berlin proper. I later visited the house, out of curiosity, during a trip to the city in the aftermath. Dahlem is (or was before the Martians came, and will be again) an opulent place, green and leafy – indeed a corner of the Grünewald Forest laps over its boundary – a community of wide avenues and spacious villas. As Walter told me later, he had chosen to move away from the 'laboratories' of central Berlin, where Freud and others continued to examine his prototypical disorder of the mind, his 'gun-dread'. Here he had privacy, and space, and the quiet to think – and, crucially, the means to observe the invasion which he anticipated.

To that end – and long before the attacks were due – he had installed additional telephone wires, even a telegraph receiver, and wireless sets of impressive power. All this was at not negligible cost, but, as I have previously mentioned, thanks to his *Narrative* Walter was not without means – and, he seemed to have decided, if the Martians were on their way in force then soon money might not mean very much anyhow.

And the Martians *were* on their way: of that he was as certain as any individual outside the scientific, military and government establishments.

It's hard to recall now how total was the secrecy blanketing the astronomical project at the time. But Walter had resources and contacts. He listened to whispers and words and speculations from friends within the world-wide astronomical community, many of whom, being bull-headed scientists, had little time for official blankets of silence. In short, they leaked, if discreetly.

So it was that Walter eventually learned that the Martian cannon had indeed begun to fire again, as early as April 8 – that is, even before I had visited him in Berlin in May, though he had not known it at that time. It was just as in '20 when news had reached him so late of the coming of the Martian fleet.

And as Walter tried to analyse the available information, the numbers of these new blasts soon became clear. In 1907 there had been a mere ten cylinders launched from Mars; in 1920 ten times that number, a hundred falling in formation in central England – and now, the astronomers privately estimated, another tenfold increase would bring a *thousand* Martian ships to the earth.

Where would the Martians land, though? The cylinders seemed to be flocking in space, gathering in flotillas as latecomers joined the interplanetary armada – just as had been the case with the invasion of Britain. But because the Martian pilots repeatedly adjusted their trajectories as they crossed space – their rocket-like devices flared green even as their cylinders fell across our sky, as I myself witnessed from the Amersham pit – for many days the pattern was unclear.

So Walter had collected world maps of all kinds – he even had a cheap schoolroom globe – as well as astronomical tables, and a variety of mathematical manuals. Even a slide rule! Walter was a philosophical journalist, never a mathematician, but he had long ago learned that mathematics was the language of the astronomer. And it was the pattern of those assemblings that he slowly puzzled out as the astronomers' observations of the approaching cylinders and projections of their flight became more precise.

The core of it was simple. *The Martians always landed at local midnight.* They would come out of the dark, he saw, falling into the shadow of the earth. He imagined the view from an approaching cylinder in the first cluster, with Europe – London, Berlin, Paris and all – already carried into the light of a new day, but the Americas blanketed in the midnight dark, the cities laid out like jewels along the coasts and on the courses of the great rivers. Blanketed in dark, and helpless. Then the Martians would land.

And after that, as the world turned, as the midnight line crossed the land, so the following Martian battle groups would fall, again and again.

'I told you so,' he muttered to himself (as he subsequently recounted), a man alone in that house in the German dawn, in pyjamas and dressing gown, eyes no doubt dark with fatigue, sheets of his spidery scrawl covering tables and walls. 'I told you so. You *damned* fools.'

And meanwhile in America—

2

On Long Island

As midnight approached, Harry Kane thought that the atmosphere in the Bigelow mansion was agitated. No, that was not the word. Feverish, perhaps. Or on the borders of hysterical. Everybody knew that if the Martians were to come to the earth at this opposition the landings ought to start tonight – or rather the day that would begin at midnight, Friday May 19, the regulation three weeks and day before the opposition itself. Anybody with a calendar could have worked that out, even if the Hearst papers hadn't been ardently telling them so. Well, if the astronomers had seen anything it hadn't been released to the public.

But even so the atmosphere at Bigelow's party was quite something.

Perhaps it was the drink, or the pills, or the rag music from the apparently tireless band, or the giddy excitement of being young and rich and utterly free to indulge yourself as you chose ... Or perhaps it was the sheer privilege of having been one of the lucky few (well, lucky few hundred) to have been invited to this party, at this cusp moment when, maybe, the world itself was about to come to an end – at least according to the gloomier prophecies in the papers ...

And how to capture this wild, glittering fragility in a word, a phrase?

As I have mentioned earlier in this memoir, my good friend Harry was a journalist for the popular New York city papers, a regular contributor to the *Saturday Evening Post* in particular – and, under another name, a pulp novelist. Well, we all have to make a living. He had a nose for news, which was why, as it would turn out, he ended up at precisely the right location on that dramatic night. But he lacked the other half of the true reporter's

300

skill set, in that he struggled with the words themselves, always uncertain allies at best for poor Harry. And that distracted him, for he would stand bewildered before the jewellery heist or the train wreck or the car crash, while lexicological fragments drifted behind those handsome blue eyes. I told him once that he could have been a great writer if only he could write.

But he did have an eye for detail; when he came to write down his own account of that night he would remember that as midnight approached the band was playing 'The Sheik of Araby'.

Restless, he pushed his way through the ballroom of the Bigelow mansion, ignoring the Japanese panelling and the rich flock wallpaper and the Parisian chandeliers that adorned that brilliantly lit room, and through the wide French windows to join the crowd out on the veranda and under the open sky. He would remember the drink he carried; it was a highball, not his first – he would remember many details of that night.

There, as he wandered across the veranda, he took in the scene. If the Bigelow house itself looked as if it was a wing of the palace of Versailles, carved off and carried over the Atlantic to Long Island, the gardens were scarcely less spectacular. The lawns, studded with lilac trees and hawthorns and plums, many in blossom, were strung with coloured lights. The garden's centre-piece was a swimming pool, a disc of brilliant blue light across which girls swam like dolphins – all of them in proper bathing costumes, but that would change as the night wore on and things got rowdier; it was always so. As you looked further out from the house you saw the jetty, a couple of small boats, the dark waters of the Sound, and the lights of Manhattan on the horizon, a misty blur.

And people drifted through this scene like pretty ghosts, drinks in hand, the women in expensive creations of beads and chiffon, the men in dress suits and patent leather shoes like Harry's own, or – probably the Long Island natives – in white flannels and sneakers. Purple seemed to be the colour that year – or just that month or that week – and every woman wore her hair tight in a carefully shaped bob. Bigelow's guests looked alike, Harry thought, all but indistinguishable unless you made out the care-fully selected detail. Thus the convergence of fashion and money: lots and lots of money.

While he was people-watching in this way, of course, he was missing the real news of the evening. Slowly he became aware that many of those pretty faces were turned upwards, to the sky.

301

It was only then that it occurred to him to look up too. It was a clear, cloudless night, a late May night, with just a tang of chill in the air after a warm day. The lights of the party were so bright that no stars were to be seen.

But Harry saw the streaks across the sky, off to the east. They came and went, splinters sporadically visible.

Harry was a country boy, from Iowa; he had seen meteor showers before, and this had something of that look. But these streaks all ran parallel to each other, and they were crowded together, dense in the sky: evidence of co-ordination. And no meteor he had ever seen flashed green.

Of course he knew what this meant; the detail was just as the more irresponsible newspapers, including most of those he wrote for, had predicted. Harry had never been to England, had never seen a Martian or its works close to, save filtered through photography or flickering cinema images. It was one thing to play with the ideas of bogeymen from the red planet – and he had written lurid potboilers about the Martian threat himself – and quite another to have it become *real*.

The house's many clocks chimed midnight, in a jangling discord.

Then, a short time later, Harry saw flashes, as if from distant explosions, and heard what sounded like thunder, coming from the east.

He stood back in the shadows, keeping to himself.

To the people around him, these midnight events seemed extraordinarily exciting; they shouted, pointed, yelped and whooped; some broke into spontaneous dancing; some even started to applaud. It was giddiness, thought Harry, as ever searching for the right word like a squirrel for a lost nut. The over-excitement of the party and too much chemical stimulation was now laced with this cosmic terror, as if sherbet had been thrown into a glass of champagne.

A girl he knew slightly grabbed his arm. 'Dance with me, Harry! Isn't this just the *end* – the end of the world party? They say Guggenheim's here, and Eddie Cantor, and Jack Dempsey—'

'And P. G. Wodehouse.'

'Who? Oh, let's dance, Harry, what's wrong with you?'

He smiled, shook his head, gently disengaged, and let her whirl away.

He walked out from the brighter lights and down towards the

jetty. He heard car engines gunning, vehicles driving off – sight-seers, he supposed, off in search of Martians, the latest sensation. And he remembered from Walter's account how the very first cylinder to fall in England, at Horsell Common, had similarly attracted flocks of gawping visitors.

He reached the jetty. By the water he spotted a man and woman in the shade of an awning, calmer than most, watching the sky, quietly smoking. Harry hung back a moment and observed; they were two silhouettes wreathed by cigarette smoke. Harry sensed they were not a couple, and would not object to his approaching them. (If vocabulary was his weakness, Harry was always sensitive to emotions.)

He walked up. 'Mind if I join you?'

They turned. The woman smiled, a little distantly, and the man shrugged, but stiffly, as if in mild pain. He was in uniform, Harry saw now, and he wondered if the fellow was some military veteran.

Harry politely offered fresh cigarettes. 'Quite a night.'

'Thanks to the Martians, yes,' the man said. 'Coming down on cue, according to the astronomical timetable – though not quite where the military analysts said they would.'

Harry stuck out his hand. 'Harry Kane, by the way. I work for the papers.'

The man seemed indifferent, but he shook Harry's hand. His grip was strong, but Harry observed how he winced as he flexed his shoulder. He was perhaps forty, dark and heavy-set; he wore the uniform of a junior army officer. 'Name's Bill Woodward. Captain, if you can't read the uniform.'

Harry took a stab, erring on the side of politeness. 'Retired?'

'Not quite. Sick leave.' He tapped his shoulder. 'Took a bullet in the Philippines six months back. Wouldn't mind if I weren't pretty sure that bullet was German-made. Recuperating well enough. The Army's good enough to be paying my bills, though the place I rent, not far from here – nothing like *this*. No family to mop my brow, as I was explaining to Miss Rafferty here.' His voice had a southern twang, Harry thought.

Meanwhile the woman was studying Harry closely. She held out her hand and introduced herself as Marigold Rafferty. She was perhaps thirty, with a Boston accent or so Harry judged, and she wore riding habit: boots, long skirt, sensible jacket. Harry would one day tell me she looked a little drab against the background of the glittering party-goers, and a sight more adult.

'Harry Kane,' she said. 'I know your face, I think, but it doesn't fit the name. Do you also write books, by any chance? . . .'

Harry coloured. 'I'm afraid I do, Miss Rafferty—'

She snapped her fingers. 'I knew it. *Edison versus the Canal Builders* – that was one of yours, wasn't it?'

'It's something of a side-line. It can pay pretty well, given the serialisation rights and such. But I see myself as a serious journalist—'

'Edisonades, eh?' Woodward grinned. 'Tales of the exploits of the great inventor of the lightbulb. I read a couple of those. *Edison and the March of the Kaiser* was my favourite. Was that one of yours?'

'No—'

'Always thought *that* one, at least, had a certain plausibility. Those Germans ain't exactly forgiven us for taking the Philippines and Guam and Cuba from the Spaniards. Edison against the Martians, though – that's a stretch!' He glanced at Marigold Rafferty. 'I did always wonder how the great man felt about his starring role in such works.'

Marigold gently punched the soldier's good arm. 'Come now, Bill, not only have we two just met, but we just met this poor young fellow too; let's not guy him. Harry – or "Mr Jarvis X. Kendor", wasn't that your *nom de plume*? – if you want to know how Thomas Edison feels about starring in one of your stories, you can ask him yourself.'

'Edison? Quite a name-drop, Miss Rafferty! I imagine he's in New Jersey, at Menlo Park.' This was where Edison had his research establishment at the time.

Marigold shook her head. 'Not a bit of it. *He's right here*, Mr Kane. Here on Long Island. In fact, a little earlier, he was at this very party! But he tires quickly – well, as you would; he's pretty sturdy, but he is seventy-five years old.'

'Edison, here on Long Island? Why?'

Marigold said apologetically, 'I should explain. I work at Menlo Park too; my technical background is in telephonic circuitry, but for the last couple of years I've been something of a personal assistant to Mr Edison himself. Mr Edison has taken the predictions of Martian returns pretty seriously at every opposition since '07, and habitually takes himself, and his family, out to what he hopes will be a safe refuge, if they do come. Away from the immediate vicinity of New York anyhow, which you would think would be a target in any wider strike. As it happens the company, and indeed the federal government, have been happy to support him in this.'

Woodward grinned. 'There you are, you see, "Jarvis". You hit on a truth in your pulp novel—'

'I'd hesitate to call it "pulp"—'

'Edison's no superman but he is a pretty valuable national asset. As it happened they rented him a villa next to mine. Me, a neighbour of Thomas Edison! What are the odds, Mr Kane? What are the odds?'

Harry said to Marigold, 'You say the government lends a hand. Is the old man really so important?'

She shrugged. 'You need to ask? *You* wrote about Edison inventing super-weapons to defeat the Martians.'

'That was just fiction. In real life—'

'In real life, Edison has been inventing super-weapons to defeat the Martians.'

Harry Kane could only stare.

But he thought he saw the argument about safe havens from the Martians; he'd worked through some of the logic himself. Hypothetically, if the Martians *were* to attack New York, surely they would come down on the mainland for ease of movement, and for access to the continental interior. So Long Island, pro- tected by the Sound, a barricade of water, might be bypassed, for a time at least. Yes, this was a sensible place to stash a national treasure like the brain of Edison.

And that was why Harry himself was here, for many of the city's rich seemed to have come to a similar conclusion. There had been a veritable flight to the Island's resorts in the last few days, and Harry had come to observe that expensive flocking.

Harry had enough of a sense of history to understand that the recent floods of new wealth in America were based on genuine economic growth in the country; you had the opening-up of huge mineral assets – silver from Nevada, copper from Montana – and the exhilarating expansion of modern industries such as telephones, movies and photography, electricity, cars. But in the cities, especially in Manhattan – thanks to financial speculation, and services like bond trading, the dealing of long-term secured loans – you could get very rich very quickly, and perfectly legitimately. And also, of course, illegitimately; prohibition had created a major black market all by itself. That extraordinary wealth found expression in the hedonistic, hectic culture that underpinned this very party.

Against this background, trouble overseas meant little. So what, if the Germans had whipped up a storm of flags and guns in Europe? These were remote problems that could be dealt with in the future. Even the Martian attacks on England seemed fantastical and distant – something detached from the normal processes of the world.

But now had come the drizzle of predictions of a new wave of Martian invaders. What if they came to Boston or New York this time, not London? Harry suspected that most Americans rather looked down on the British response to the invasion of 1907, and even that of two years ago. Surely the American military would have put up a better fight than the British; surely the American character, tested, would have fared better. It was this intuition about his native culture that had prompted Harry to pen his own Edisonades, about heroic resistance and jut-jawed counter-invasions of Mars. His sales told him, and his publisher, that he had hit a nerve.

Tonight, though, Harry, picking up on the gossip and chatter, had looked for an unusual angle. If the Martians *did* come to America there would be a million eyewitness accounts of military manoeuvres and the defence of the cities and the fleeing masses – but who would tell the story of the privileged rich? What would *they* do? Long Island would be something of a refuge, he had figured, where you could watch the Martians be wiped out in Manhattan while you drank champagne... and then return to the ruins, like so many precious birds. *Martians of the Jazz Age*: that was the book he'd write about this some day. He'd publish under his own name too.

Now, it was no comfort to Harry that his story instincts had been good. Because the Martians weren't playing ball.

Now Marigold gasped. 'Look! Up there! *More* of them...'

Woodward looked up and nodded, his lips pursed. 'Green flashes. A second wave?' He glanced at his watch. 'In England a couple of years back they came in two waves, but a day apart – midnight to midnight. It's not yet one in the morning. Is this a new tactic, the second wave an hour after the first?'

He was right, and perhaps the first in all the world to see it; this was the strategy that the Martians would stick to through the rest of their coming assaults, that night and in the coming day.

Woodward said now, 'I'm no expert on Mars, but I have been under artillery fire. And it sure looks to me like those shots are

306

heading for a spot on the Island. *Here.* And a spot not so far away from where we stand. Not Manhattan at all.'

Marigold said, 'So much for a safe refuge. I think I'd better call Mr Edison.'

And Harry saw more flashes, and he thought he heard more thunder, from the east.

3

In the Bigelow Mansion

Inside, the house was a cave of light. Harry waited with Bill Woodward, both of them smoking, while Marigold went in search of a phone to call Edison's residence. The band was playing, right now a rather sad waltz that Harry recognised, called 'Three O'Clock in the Morning' – badly timed, it was only a little after one a.m. There were plenty of people still here, plenty of champagne and claret still to be poured, plenty of noise from the bright chorus of voices. And yet, it seemed to Harry, there was a certain brittleness about the scene. Harry accepted a mint julep from a passing waiter – but then he caught Woodward's eye, who nodded, and Harry thought it was as if an unspoken message passed between them: *We stay sober.* Kane took one sip of the drink and set it aside.

Woodward asked softly, 'You have a car?'

'Not here. My house is a short walk away.'

'I have mine here. Beat-up Dodge, but it does the job; I don't hold with this habit of changing up every year just to keep up with the fashion in interior colour schemes . . . Maybe I ought to go check up on it, there was a lot of traffic a little earlier.'

'I heard it, after midnight. A lot of drunken drivers, gone to see the Martians, I suspect.' Harry found himself looking for Marigold, a little anxiously, as if the three of them had formed a bond, a unit. 'Let's think this out, Bill. We figured the Martians wouldn't come to the Island because it's a dumb place for them to land. Right? And yet they came anyhow. Why?'

'I can think of two reasons,' Woodward said. 'One is just to do precisely the opposite of what we would expect, to catch us wrong-footed. A human general might think that way; you don't walk into the other guy's punch. But, from what I've read of

308

them – which isn't much aside from those Edisonades – I don't think they care much *what* we do or think, we just can't hurt them enough. Or we haven't so far.

'So my second possible reason is that it *suits* them. Given the accounts from England, they're less vulnerable in that period just after landing than they were, but must still be somewhat; even a few minutes to get your weapons out of those cylinders is an opportunity for your opponent. My guess is they looked at the local geography, saw the Island as a place where we'd give them no trouble for the first few minutes or hours – and then they can march on the mainland, the city, in good order. Anyhow, whyever they did it, I guess it worked. We don't have much to oppose them on the Island. The National Guard, the police – maybe the guns from a couple of Navy boats if they can be brought in fast enough.'

'Soldiery isn't my line. We're going to stop them – right?'

Woodward eyed him. 'Look, Harry, the US Army isn't the force you might think it is. After all, most of the fighting we've done since the Revolution has been small-scale stuff against the Indians out west, or in Mexico, or against the Spanish in '98. We don't have the kind of big conscript army you get over in Europe, the Germans, the Russians – even the British since the Martians came. The only time *we* had millions in uniform, they were the conscripts from North and South during the Civil War. Maybe if we'd gotten involved in that big European war in '14 it might be different. As it is, I believe we have a hundred thousand regulars right now, plus the Guard and the state militias. And most of those are nowhere near the east coast. Or the west, come to that.'

Harry didn't like the sound of any of this. 'Then where are they?'

'In our garrisons on Puerto Rico, Cuba, the Philippines: the possessions we won in the Spanish War. Keeping the Germans and others at bay. Some on the Mexican border. And a lot of the rest are out west – the old Indian country. Of course that threat has subsided now, but the Army bases are all out that way for historical reasons.'

'Historical reasons. Holy cow! It's a shame the Martians ain't coming down in the wild west, then. Maybe Hopalong Cassidy could save the day.'

'Take it easy,' Woodward murmured gently.

'Sorry. But the federal government must have prepared for the Martian threat. They must have got some warning from the astronomers, even if it wasn't released to the public.'

'Sure. But how do you plan for an attack that might hit you anywhere, on the continental US and beyond – an attack coming down from the sky? Anyhow don't ask me. I'm injured and on leave, remember?'

'Hey, can you hear cars? Sounds like they're all coming back ...'

4

An Exodus

Out front of the house, the traffic noise had got a lot louder.

The driveway was, Harry supposed, one of the Bigelow mansion's more elegant features, long and brilliantly lit by electric lamps and carpeted with crisp pink gravel – imported from England at huge expense, the gravel was the same stuff they had used on the Mall in London, or so rumour had it. When Woodward and Harry walked out, the driveway was still crowded with cars, Dodges and Fords and even some station wagons. There was one magnificent Rolls Royce with a green leather interior.

'You're salivating,' Woodward said.

'One day,' Harry said. 'One day.'

'Keep writing those Edisonades. In the meantime, for a journalist you ain't so smart at spotting what's important, seems to me.'

'Hm?' Harry looked around. 'Oh – you mean that empty garage over there.'

'That's where Dan Bigelow, our host, keeps his own car. His latest is a Daimler, I think.'

'*He's* gone, then,' Harry said. 'I never noticed.'

'Did you meet him? . . . Nor did I. I suppose, with a party like this, the host isn't the point. And I suppose it's possible that as the house-owner he might have gotten the news earlier than we did.'

Harry felt chilled. 'Wouldn't you warn your guests?'

'What, and risk the roads being clogged up before you made your own escape? I don't think men like Dan Bigelow get where they are in the world without a little ruthless calculation.'

That traffic noise rose to a roar. They turned to look out at the road, beyond the wrought-iron gates of the mansion. More

Dodges and Fords and a few grander cars were barrelling past at speed, coming out of the east and heading west, Harry realised, west towards the bridges, and Manhattan.

'The sightseers,' Woodward said. 'On their way back through.'

'Right.' Harry glanced at his watch; it was not yet half past one in the morning. 'So at midnight they go pouring out to find the Martian landing site.'

'They find it. Maybe they're still sightseeing when the second wave comes down. And now—'

'They're back and fleeing in terror. The pits can't be far from here, then – maybe a half-hour's fast drive east – twenty, twenty-five miles?'

'Look out—'

Woodward pulled him back as one car took the turn into the gateway at speed, nearly clipped a post, and skidded to a halt on the pink English gravel. 'Help me! Help me!'

Woodward and Harry were among the first of the revellers to get to the car, and among the more sober. They found that a young woman had been driving, inexpertly. 'It's his car! Not mine! We just went for a drive! We just thought we'd go see – it was supposed to be fun!'

In the passenger seat was a man, almost as young-looking, crumpled over; his white jacket and flannels were stained with blood. A dozen pairs of hands grabbed for him, but Bill Woodward took control. With a peremptory snap he ordered everyone back, and to Harry's bemusement they obeyed. That was military command for you.

Woodward knelt by the young man, feeling for a pulse. 'He's breathing. Pulse feathery. I don't know if he's conscious. Hold in there, son; I've seen men survive worse.' He glanced around at the party-goers, who looked to Harry like curious, faintly horri-fied peacocks. 'You may come forward *only* if you are a trained nurse, or a doctor. *Only* if.'

After some hesitation a young man in a slightly distressed morning suit came out of the crowd. 'I'm a student. Will that do? I'm in my fourth year at—'

'Shut up and take over.'

The boy came forward, knelt down, and immediately began to work with the injured man.

Woodward, with Harry, hurried round to the far side of the car. A couple of women were trying to soothe the driver, the girl.

'I did my best! I never drove in my life! . . .'

312

'You did fine. Was it the Martians, though?'

She nodded, dropping her head. She said that the Martians had come down near Stony Brook.

'The whole town was there, it felt like. Looking at those darn pits and all the broken ground. And then about one o'clock more of them came slamming down – what a sight! And they came out of their shells, those Martians, just as soon as they landed. Well, the Guard opened up, and the police. But the Martians just – the Guard and the cops, they just – *burned*. And the big machines rose up on those stilts of theirs, like some kind of circus act, and everybody started to run away. We all ran back for the cars. But Simpson fell, I think he twisted his ankle, and I tried to help him up. But we were in the road, and a car came, and it just *hit* him, it just *knocked him aside*, like you'd shove a baby deer out of your way, I'll swear it was deliberate . . .'

'How did you get him to the car?'

'My dear, have some brandy, just a nip to calm your nerves.'

'This other car. You get his number? The police will want to know about this, Martians or no Martians . . .'

Woodward plucked Harry's sleeve. 'Nothing more we can do here. Let's get back to the house.'

They walked back up the drive, to a house that was still brightly lit. But now the guests seemed to be streaming out, and Harry heard more cars starting up and crunching over the gravel and out of the drive, all heading west.

Inside the house the band was, remarkably, still playing, a jazzy number now, that Harry recognised as 'Beale Street Blues'. Waiters and other staff circulated; there was still drink to be had if you wanted it – and some did, evidently intent on partying to the end – but there was coffee too, and Harry and Woodward both grabbed cups gratefully.

Woodward kept glancing at his watch. 'We probably still have a few hours' grace. In England a couple of years ago, they landed at midnight – just like here – and they seem to have waited until dawn before moving out in big numbers. I know the way the waves came down was different this time, but even so—'

'Hm. But the longer we wait the harder it's likely to be to get off the Island.'

Woodward grinned. '"We". Are we a team now, sport?'

'I reckon I'd be a better driver than you with that busted shoulder of yours.'

313

Woodward nodded grudgingly. 'You're probably right. You say you live close by. Your car?'

'A Model T.'

'Hmph. What are you, a hobbyist? We'll take my Dodge. But—'

'But we wait for Miss Rafferty.'

'Marigold, yes.'

Harry glanced around. 'Maybe we can find out what's going on. There must be wireless sets around, away from these party rooms anyhow.'

'You're supposed to be a reporter. Can't you call your newsroom? They should know.'

'Hey, that's a thought. I could even file a report.'

Woodward stood up. 'Another day, another dollar, huh?'

It was a long night of waiting, for Harry and Woodward.

They stayed close to a radio set. There was little news coming out of the landing sites on the Island. Harry considered calling his family, his parents in Iowa. He figured he'd only scare them to death, being called in the middle of the night for no good reason.

At around three a.m., they learned from the newsroom of the *Post* that President Harding had announced a second Martian landing, in the hills outside Los Angeles. It had been local midnight there, just as at Long Island.

There was no doubt about it. America was under attack from Mars.

At around four a.m. a servant circulated through the house, calling for Woodward; there was a telephone call for him. It was Marigold Rafferty. She'd found Edison and his staff at his rented villa. After a brief discussion it had been decided to load the old man on a power-boat and take him across the Sound to Manhattan. There hadn't been room to take everybody, and despite Edison's vigorous protestations Marigold had got left behind. She was waiting on a ride back to the Bigelow place, but everything was very disorganised. Woodward told her they would wait for her, and Harry, despite his growing anxiety at being stuck there, nodded agreement.

Five a.m. came and went.

At six came the first reports of the Martians moving out of their pit at Stony Brook. To nobody's surprise they were heading west, parallel to the Sound, towards Manhattan. The Island's authorities could mount only minimal resistance, and were anyhow more concerned with organising evacuations.

At ten past six Marigold Rafferty was at the door.

The three of them ran to Woodward's car, and with Harry behind the wheel they fled the residence, heading west, soon joining a slow river of cars and people funnelling down the length of the Island. Glancing back, Harry saw that even now, in the gathering daylight, the Bigelow place was glowing with light. Somewhere in there, he suspected, the band was still playing.

5

I Arrive at Thornborough

It had been at five a.m. (in Britain, midnight on Long Island) that Verity and I, in the Martian Cordon, had demanded of Albert Cook that we be taken to Eric Eden.

Cook responded immediately, and quite impressively. He got us out of the Redoubt, made a phone call from a concealed station to the Army contact he'd been using to negotiate his terms, and then took us to a heavily camouflaged car of his own and raced us across the Cordon. He assured us the Martians wouldn't touch him, but I was never confident about that.

At the perimeter we were met by a couple of taciturn soldiers in unmarked camouflage gear and with dirt-blackened faces, and led to a bolthole in the ground. I had to fight an intense, phobic fear about going down into a tunnel once more – it was as if I saw Ben Gray in the shadows, as I looked into that hole – but I went through with it.

This time the Martians did not detect our passing under the Trench, or interfere with it.

On the far side, out of the Cordon, we were met by a junior officer – a Lieutenant Hopson – waiting with a car, armoured and camouflaged, with a woman driver, a heap of blankets and flasks of coffee. Not for the first time I was impressed by the efficiency of all this, of the management of operations that spanned the Cordon from the huddling countryside outside to the zone of suppression within.

Through Cook we had asked only to be reunited with Eric Eden, who I thought of as my principal conduit to the Army's chain of command. It was Verity, in fact, who, as we drove away, first asked precisely where we were being taken. It was only then that we heard we were heading for Thornborough and the 'landship base'. I don't believe I had heard that word before: *landship*. When Verity asked what it meant, the officer would not reply – or could not.

So we were off again. I was content to huddle with Verity in the back, and clutch clean-smelling army-issue blankets around me, sip strong but rather stale coffee, and listen to the competent murmurings of the officer and his driver as they called ahead by wireless to their command stations.

And I tried not to look up at the sky.

Thornborough turned out to host an Army base, a couple of miles east of Buckingham – and so perhaps thirty miles north-west of Amersham and the Martians' Redoubt.

It was hard to see much as we were passed through the base's fence, for of course the Army wished to stay out of sight of the Martians. Every building, every vehicle was painted or draped with camouflage green and brown. But still the landships, pointed out by Hopson, were unmistakable, as we drove past them – unmistakable, if unclassifiable. They were lined up in rows, enigmatic mounds of different sizes, the smallest perhaps twenty feet long and ten tall – I guessed immediately that these were bulky vehicles of some sort – but the largest was immense, more than a hundred feet long and with turrets at front and back perhaps three times my height. It looked like a ship, in fact, though we could not have been further from the sea. All this merely glimpsed, the profiles obscured by camouflage blankets and netting.

Verity's hand crept into mine. 'What frightful things.'

I squeezed her fingers. 'At least *these* monsters are on our side.'

We were escorted into the base by our tame lieutenant.

The place was busy, bewilderingly so. It appeared to be disguised as a series of rambling farm buildings, all connected by tunnels of canvas and plywood so as, I imagined, to be invisible from the air. Outdoors, in the 'farmyard', soldiers in heavy combat gear were forming up into groups of four or six or twelve, talking softly. They were equipped with the customary tin helmets and gas-masks and small arms, but, unusually, they also carried tools: bags of spanners and wrenches and the like.

We were hustled past and through a doorway. Inside was a series of crudely partitioned rooms, where we could see huddles of officers in discussion, and walls covered with maps, and plates of stale-looking sandwiches and cold cups of tea standing around.

317

Meanwhile, uniformed staff were literally running along the tunnels between farmhouse and outhouse and stables and barns.

'As if we've stepped into a wasps' nest,' Verity murmured to me as we were hurried through all this. 'But the Martians aren't coming down in England again, are they?'

'No, they're not, according to the astronomers and the spotters,' said Eric Eden from a doorway just ahead – at last we had found his office. Like the soldiers we'd already seen, he was in heavy combat gear, evidently preparing to take part in some mission. 'But we've already heard of landings elsewhere ... Come, we don't have much time.'

He chivvied us into his office – everything was in a hurry that morning – and I, exhausted already and sleepless, found it difficult to cope. I glanced around at the charts on the walls. One of them was a world map, Mercator style, with two ugly Mars-orange markers pushed into the sites of New York and Los Angeles. It was now after eight a.m. The meaning was clear.

'That's the point of our own operations this morning,' Eric was saying now. 'The fact that we're in the middle of another wave of landings, I mean. Today, as a new wave of cylinders comes down – and the analysts are saying they expect landings all around the planet through the next twenty hours or so – surely the British complex is the nearest the Martians have to a command and control centre. And we intend to do something about it.'

Verity nodded. 'With those – cockroach things outside.'

He grinned. 'The landships, yes. We've been saving them for a special occasion. When, if not now? And I, for my sins, am in command of the HMLS *Boadicea*, the nastiest cockroach of them all. So: while I'm very pleased to see you two safe and well, I'm far from impressed that you failed to fulfil your mission of the contaminated blood, Miss Elphinstone. But I'm sure the intelligence people will want to pump you dry of all you learned inside the Martian Cordon. Now, if you'll excuse me, I really must find my crew and get on—'

I grabbed his arm. 'Eric – we came here to find you, remember – you need to listen to me.' We had not met for some days, since I had been delivered to the trench. I can imagine how I looked to him, still in the clothes I had worn in the Cordon, grimy, perhaps blood-splashed, smelling of mud and dirt and sweat and sheer fatigue. Wild-eyed – but, I like to think, determined.

'I really don't—'

'Sigils,' I said.

A junior officer called him. 'Major Eden, we're ready to load up . . .'

He made to pull himself away. 'Julie, I have a battle to fight.'

'And I can tell you how to win the *war* – or at least, to end it.'

He hesitated, clearly torn. 'Sigils. This is the Walter Jenkins stuff, isn't it? The "messages" we were using as cover for the blood scheme. Are we back to that? All rather eccentric—'

'Not eccentric, Eric. Look, I'm probably more sceptical than you are. But the things I saw in the Cordon . . . This isn't like another war against some portion of humanity, the Germans or the Russians—'

'Actually it's generally been the French,' he murmured with an irritating smile.

'*This* war is interplanetary. It's just as Walter has been saying all along – ever since the *Narrative*, even. And if we're to prevail we have to think on that scale.'

'And we do that with drawings, do we?'

'Not the drawings, but their subject – sigils – symbols. Graphic geometry, Walter called it.'

His junior officer coughed, one communication that wasn't terribly subtle.

But Eric hesitated for one more second, and I held his gaze.

'All right. Barker, take the crew to the *Boadicea*. God knows Hetherington will be able to take you through the start-up; it's his bloody design. I'll be with you shortly.'

'Sir.' The man hurried away.

Eric turned back to me. 'You've got five minutes and counting, Julie.'

'Then shut up and let me talk.'

I hastily summarised Walter's theories of interplanetary signalling. Eric had not been interested in thinking this through before, other than as a cover for his own scheme, but now I made him listen.

'It's an old idea, after all,' I said. 'You know there was a mania for signalling to other worlds decades before the Martians showed up and *proved* that there are civilisations elsewhere. People proposed digging Pythagorean triangles in the desert and setting them alight with oil to make them visible to Martian observers – that sort of thing. In the end, they were right!'

Eric, to give him credit – and with the huge distraction of the forthcoming battle no doubt foremost in his mind – seemed to be working it out. 'It all seemed a lot of silly nonsense, I suppose,' he said. 'But then, after the '07 war, there were those luminous markings the astronomers spotted in the clouds of Venus. "Sigils" – the word Jenkins used in his book, wasn't it?'

'Yes! This was in 1913. And at the same time, *similar markings were seen on Mars*. Now we interpret that as a marker of the Martians' successful invasion of Venus.'

He nodded slowly. 'Very well. But even if I buy all that – what's it got to do with the Martians in Buckinghamshire?'

'Everything. These are communications between worlds, Eric. *And communications we can manipulate*. Do you have a map of the '07 landings? And maps, or aerial photographs, of the '20 landings . . .'

It took a minute of my five for him to retrieve relevant maps and photos from the clutter in his room, and another minute to find a thick wax pencil with which I defaced said maps and photos. Without needing to refer to the documents I carried, I remembered what Walter had shown me; with the pencil I connected the Martians' landing pits, in Surrey in '07, and in Buckinghamshire more recently – connected them with looping, sinuous swirls. I made these marks without comment, and let Eric make the last leap of induction.

He held up the '07 map, disfigured as it was. 'But this symbol – it is the same as the astronomers saw on Venus.'

'Exactly. You see it. *It is the Martians' brand of ownership*, like a stock handler's, burned now into the flesh of England herself. Over and over again. That was what they were building here even in '07, but had no time to finish. And they're doing it again, in Bucks – Marriott for one has maps that show exactly that, if you know how to look.' I tapped my battered leather case. 'These are Walter's drawings of those sigils. He wanted me to show them to the Martians as proof of our intelligence.'

'It was only to be a cover story; I didn't pay much attention to the detail. But this set of symbols is what you wish to manipulate – is that the idea?'

'Yes! But it's not the *Martian* sigil that's important here . . .' And in a few words I sketched my idea, the what and the how and the why.

Eric mused. Then he grinned. He did have an imagination; I knew him well enough for that. 'It's outrageous. It's insane!'

'I know. Even Walter Jenkins didn't think this big, and that's saying something. It might work, though. Look, I know you've been feeding explosives and weapons to the resistance units inside the Cordon. I met one contact – this "Marriott".'

He looked uncomfortable at that.

'And you have hundreds of soldiers, trapped in there since the day of the invasion. I *know* you're in touch with these people. What we need to do is to get to those groups, to tell them how to use those resources in a once-and-once-only exercise – to set their charges, to make some precise modifications on the ground—'

He eyed me. 'You realise you'll have to do this yourself. I can control the Army element, but you'll have to convince them – Marriott and his kind – as you've convinced me. Well, half-convinced – and then see it through. *I* couldn't do it. It's your vision.'

I'd been expecting this, if not dreading it. 'If I have to go back into that hell on earth—'

Verity grabbed my hand. 'I'll be with you.'

Eric considered. 'What a war this is – what dilemmas you pose for me!' He glanced at his wristwatch. 'I'm not saying I buy all this, and at some point we'll have to have a discussion about why you didn't carry through your orders about the contaminated blood. But, in parallel with our more conventional efforts, it's worth a shot, and won't cost much. Your five minutes is more than used up.' He looked at me. 'Very well. We'll give it a try. But I'll tell you this – if you're to go back into the Cordon today, the only way you're travelling is with me, in the *Boadicea*. I'll take you via stores; you'll both need to be kitted out. I hope you're adept at lacing up your boots on the run...'

6

At Los Angeles

Accounts of what has become known as the 'Lightning War', the Martians' global attack, are multitudinous, but variable in quality and authenticity – most penned, if I am any judge, by 'observers' who were far behind the lines, and based on eyewitness accounts, if at all, only at second and third hand. What one needs to get to the truth is an account set down by a witness close enough to have seen the action, yet lucky enough to have survived the carnage of those May days – *and*, of course, a witness honest enough to tell it as she or he saw it, without spicing up the truth for the sake of sales or self-aggrandisement.

Luckily for me and for future historians, such witnesses do exist.

One such was Cherie Gilbert, then aged 24, a famous name now, who at the time of the Martian landings near Los Angeles was employed in Hollywood as a personal assistant to a director of the Paramount movie company. Cherie's skills already extended well beyond the clerical, and such was the chaotic nature of the industry in those days that Cherie soon found herself used in a variety of roles, some of them quite technical. She had even served as a camera operator in the shooting of Griffith's *The Kaiser's Lover* in 1921, when influenza had laid waste to the workforce.

'And that's why you got to come with me,' said Homer Girdner, as, panting, he led Cherie up Mount Lee, the green-clad hill that stands above Hollywood itself, and then higher into the San Gabriel Mountains.

In LA it was only just after six in the morning of the Friday (it was early afternoon in England, and I was stuck in the carcass of a crawling landship, as I will describe). But the breeze, blowing off the land and towards the sea, already bore a faint tinge of burning, Cherie thought. They hadn't climbed high enough yet to get a good view to the east. But everybody knew that was where the Martians had come down: inland, in the direction of San Bernardino. And the evidence of war was already apparent.

It was just as in New York, it turned out. The cylinders had landed in two waves, the first fifty-odd being dummies that had smashed a lifeless cordon into the ground, preparing the landing sites of the second wave an hour later, which carried crew and their war-machines. This would be the pattern repeated around the planet, in the next few hours. In Hollywood, it had seemed like everybody had stayed up to listen to scratchy accounts of the initial fighting on the radio stations; units of the National Guard and the regular army had met the Martians as they emerged from their cylinders, to no significant effect. Then, a few hours later, at around dawn – again, just as they'd done in New York – the fighting-machines had broken out of their cordon of smashed ground and begun their advance.

And now, on that fine early summer morning, high in the hills, just six hours after the first Martian cylinder had landed in California, there was a smell of burning.

Homer led the way up the trail, panting and sweating, his words broken by breathlessness – even though it was Cherie, she wryly noted, who was having to carry the damn camera itself, while he merely lugged a batch of film cans.

'I knew you'd come,' he said now.

'You did, did you?'

'Come on,' said Homer. 'You're the bravest guy I know. Figuratively speaking.'

'Kind of you to say so.'

'I mean it. It was you who kept filming on the *Nero* set when it caught fire for real, and everybody else had high-tailed it to the bar, and the footage you got was great. And I saw how you punched out the last actor who grabbed your butt.'

'I almost got canned for that,' she said ruefully, panting herself now as the trail steepened. 'Lucky for me the make-up covered his split lip.'

'He deserved it. Listen, Cherie, we're going to witness history today – hell, we're *making* it. We're the ones who are going to film the Martians as they come to LA. It will make a doozy of a picture, and some day they'll make a movie about *us*.'

'I suppose we'll be starstruck lovers, in the story.'

He had his back to her as he led the way up the trail, but she was pretty sure he blushed. Homer was a script editor with ambitions to make his own movies – hell, everybody around here had that ambition, if it wasn't to appear in one – and she knew, too, that he had a crush on her. He said now, 'Either way we're going to make a pile of money.'

But Cherie was distracted, as that smell of burning on the breeze intensified. And she thought she heard something, carried on the morning air: a distant bellow, of triumph or rage, like a vast animal: *'Ulla... Ulla...'*

She kept climbing. What else was there to do but see it through?

At last they reached a spot Homer thought was going to be suitable; he'd scouted it out in advance, he said. While Cherie fixed her camera on its tripod, Homer dumped his film cans, unloaded the lightweight radio receiver he'd carried in a rucksack, and began elaborately tuning around, looking for a signal. They both rummaged in the rucksack for bottled water.

And Cherie took a look at the view.

It was indeed a fine spot. Los Angeles sits in a bowl cradled by mountains to the north and east, and from up here, high in those mountains, Cherie's lens took it all in: she could see the brash glitter of Hollywood below, and the grey sprawl of downtown LA itself, and directly beneath her was a pretty green splash that was Pasadena, a suburb of lawns and roses and climbing geraniums – she'd long fostered a dream of moving there some day. Off to the west, beyond the cityscape and still grey with morning mist, was the immensity of the Pacific Ocean. This morning the ocean was littered with ships, small boats, what looked like passenger liners, and sleek grey shapes that might be warships.

The roads out of the city seemed crowded too, though she was so far away that the grandest of automobiles looked like crawling ants. She thought she heard the screech of a train whistle, almost as eerie as those unearthly cries coming from the east.

Overnight, as the precise location of the Martians' midnight landing, a few miles out of LA, had at last become clear, most people she knew in Hollywood had announced their intention to pack up and get away. If so, where would they go? Down into the city for sure, and then out of town – mostly north, probably, towards San Francisco, using the better roads and the coastal rail tracks. She wondered if the newsreel companies would have

324

cameras out in the train stations and along the roads to catch that great American exodus, a parallel of Long Island, indeed of London twice before.

Well, Cherie had a picture to shoot. She got her camera set up and loaded, and cranked a few frames, an establishing pan shot. And she turned to focus on Homer, squatting on the dirt ground, headphones on his ears, tinkering with his radio.

'Shit,' Homer said now.

She frowned. He wasn't one to swear. 'What's wrong?'

'The Martians... I'm listening to KDZF.' He was a radio buff. She knew that was one of his favourite stations, and, run by the Automobile Club of Southern California, one of the more authoritative. 'Also I got a couple of the police bands.'

'What about the Martians?'

'They cut the aqueduct. The Owens River... Once they broke out of their pit, they sent a party straight over.'

She knew about the aqueduct, a mighty canal that brought LA its water across a distance equivalent to the span between Washington, DC, and New York. A civic monument, gone, just like that. 'They know what they're doing, then,' she mused. 'They've cut our throats. So where are the Martians now?'

He listened again, and his eyes grew wide. He took off the 'phones, stood, looked around, and pointed east. *'There.'*

And the fighting-machines casually walked over the hills behind them.

'Jesus,' said Homer.

'Help me.'

'What?'

'Help me get the camera turned around. Feed me film. Come on, Homer, damn it! This is why we're up here...'

As she cranked the handle she watched the Martians through the camera's small viewfinder. She saw five, six, seven of them, spreading out along the crest of the hills. She panned and zoomed, trying to catch the essence of their motion. Seen in the grey of distance they were less like machines than lithe animals, she thought now: tall, leggy animals like giraffes, moving past each other as they sought good positions.

Five years back, in her home town of Madison, Wisconsin, she had watched Griffith's *Martian Summer*, the tenth-anniversary epic of the first English war, over and over. Starring Charlie Chaplin as his trademark lovable Cockney gunner, with Mary Pickford playing the American girl he rescued and fell in love with, it had been one of the great spectacles that had drawn her to Hollywood in the first place. Now she had the feeling that the scenes Griffith had shot of stiff, tottering fighting-machines downed by plucky Brit troops (led by even more heroic American volunteers) weren't going to turn out much like the reality.

There was a crack of thunder, coming from the bay, that made her jump. She lost the shot, the camera wavering.

Homer grabbed her shoulder and pointed. 'Look! The ships are firing their big guns!'

Cherie saw puffs of smoke along the flanks of those low grey silhouettes on the ocean. She couldn't make out the shells in flight, but soon she saw splashes of dirt on the hills held by the Martians, heard the crump of explosions. And again the great guns shouted, and again. She hastily got her camera cranking again.

Homer clenched his fist. 'Yes! Smash those devils! See, the first volley fell short, and now the second is going long – they are bracketing the target – and with the next shots—'

But the Martians were adjusting their positions, and Cherie saw them wield those terrible projectors that looked so like movie cameras, but were not. Some seemed to be firing on the incoming Navy shells, which popped harmlessly in the air. And the other Martians marched down the hillsides, apparently oblivious to the danger of the long-range shots which continued to crater the ground around them. She said, 'I think—'

Homer gasped. 'Pan, for God's sake. Pan. Look at the city. Look at the city!'

She turned, still cranking.

And she saw that the advancing Martians were already firing on Los Angeles. The Heat-Ray beam, as it cut in a dead straight line through the air, was all but invisible – certainly it wasn't caught through her crude lens, and probably not on film – but its effects were all too dramatic. The city had lain still in the morning light, but now, at scattered points, buildings simply exploded into flame, and palls of smoke threaded up into the air. After a couple of minutes Cherie thought she could hear the clang of fire bells, and, perhaps, a distant screaming. She zoomed out instinctively to capture the panorama.

'Jesus,' Homer said. 'It's like 'Frisco after the quake. And where's the damn Army?'

'Going the way of the damn Navy, maybe.' She pointed out to sea. One of those grey warships was burning, listing in the water.

'Jesus, Jesus... What's the range of that Heat-Ray?'

'The English thought miles, at least. Homer, were you thinking we'd get shots of the Martians marching into downtown, the National Guard bravely holding out? They don't need to do any of that. They can just stand on the high ground and pick us off—'

Now there was another immense detonation, less like thunder this time than a tremendous footfall, and Cherie wondered if she felt the ground itself shake.

Homer pointed north, excited. Huge plumes of black smoke rose up. 'Look at that! They're going for the oil, the refineries!'

Again Cherie panned and zoomed. 'First the aqueduct, now the oil.'

'Those aeroplanes they flew out of England,' Homer said. 'They went all around the world. Did their spotting pretty smart. They know what to hit.'

'Yeah,' Cherie said. 'The city will die of thirst because they cut the aqueduct, and pretty soon we won't be able to fight back at all because there'll be no oil.' She looked around. 'They're moving again.'

The great machines strode through the clearing mist, heading purposefully down the slope, and now their invisible rays struck at suburbs closer by, in the lapping hills. When the Heat-Ray swept over Pasadena, Cherie turned the crank steadily as green lawns crisped and fried, and fine houses exploded like cheap props.

Homer said, 'We need to get out of here.'

'I'm doing what we came to do. Filming until we run out of stock.'

He plucked at her sleeve. 'Cherie—'

'Load me up or leave me alone.'

He hesitated. Then he bent to open a fresh can.

And meanwhile, in England, I was going into battle myself.

7

HMLS *Boadicea*

Close to, His Majesty's Landship *Boadicea* was magnificent. But her designers must have been insane.

That was my overwhelming impression when I first properly saw her in the full morning light, as we hurried out with Eric Eden, commander of the craft, and the last to come on board thanks to my distraction of interplanetary communications. She was stripped of her camouflage blankets now – though her hull was painted with splashes of white, black, and light and dark green – and her form was clearly visible. She was a ship of the land indeed. Imagine a broad, low-slung body, with a command tower rising up from the heart, and heavily armoured gun turrets, two in the bow, one in the stern. The guns were Navy issue, in fact, each turret having a pair of four-inch guns on steerable platforms. And now imagine all of this planted on a great wheeled framework – a tricycle, with two immense wheels in front and one behind. Immense, yes: each of the wheels was no less than forty feet in diameter, the height of six adult human beings standing on each others' shoulders; the wheels alone were big enough to look like elements of a circus ride, and wrapped around by a kind of tread with thick ridges.

She was the greatest of the landships, though *Boadicea* was in the van of a whole fleet of lesser vessels that looked like mutated variants of the basic design, all bristling with armour and guns and caterpillar tracks. The technology was still experimental, the design not fixed, and the different vehicles, as they had emerged from the proving grounds in remote, well-concealed areas of Scotland (as I would learn), were more or less hand-crafted.

As we ran up to *Boadicea*, many of the machines had already started their engines, and we were surrounded by a growl of mechanical noise, and plumes of exhaust, and engineers running everywhere, servicing these behemoths even as they made ready to move. It was as if we were waiting for the off at a race at Brooklands, and from the laughter and backslapping I saw among the crew and engineers, perhaps they had some of the competitive camaraderie of men who engage in such events. A cold part of me wondered if the Martians would be impressed.

Eric, being Eric, observed our reactions even as we approached our ironclad. 'Quite something, isn't she? She's faster on the road, of course, though she chews up the tarmac. But she makes good speed across country too, and given her size she'll tolerate few obstacles.'

Verity, who had a practical eye, grunted sceptically. 'Why a tricycle? I had a trike when I was a little girl. I never imagined seeing it scaled up to this monster size!'

Eric grinned. 'The one rear wheel makes her easy to steer. Simple as that.'

'She *looks* impressive,' I gasped as we hurried to the monster. 'But what's to save her when the Martians offer a dose of the Heat-Ray?'

'Ah.' We had reached the machine now. With a gloved fist he rapped hard on the metal, and then scraped at the camouflage paint to expose a little of the yellow-white metal that lay beneath. 'Recognise that? Over a frame of aluminium, we've used one of our most precious resources of all: Martian cylinder hull-metal. We've never managed to manufacture the stuff, so this is all stripped from the Martians' own cylinders, as landed in Surrey fifteen years ago. Designed to protect a cylinder's occupants as it comes hurtling into an atmosphere at interplanetary speeds, you see – not even the Heat-Ray can cut it, and teams in the universities and on the military ranges have spent years establishing that fact. Indeed the armour has already been tested in battle.'

I noted he did not say where; even now Britain's involvement in the Russian front was officially a secret. 'I'm glad to hear it,' I said.

We came to an open port, round-cornered like a watertight door on a ship, with a short stepladder reaching to the ground. It seemed to be the only breach in the hull, save for slit windows and weapons platforms contained in sponsons, great bulges on the flank of the hull large enough to host a gunner or two. But I saw periscopes jutting up from the hull – the 'ship' was like a submarine in some ways, then.

Eric hastily waved us aboard.

We clambered up the ladder, each of us with undone shoelaces and leather helmets not yet on our heads. Clambered up and into the belly of the machine. It was a space we were to share with the engines, I immediately discovered, which dominated that compartment: two huge, gleaming monsters that I would learn were Sunbeams, diesel engines designed for submarines. Gigantic differentials and cross-shafts spanned the rest of the interior, delivering the motive force to the tremendous wheels. Every wall and floor surface had been painted white, and the whole was brilliantly lit with electrics – I could not see a scrap of daylight. It was a complex space of compartments and bulkheads, and gangways and ladders to the gun turrets and the bridge tower – cramped, but geometric and orderly: even the rivets were white-painted. I felt like a mouse under the bonnet of a car.

And it was extraordinarily cluttered too, like a mobile ammunition store, with every wall fixed with racks that held shells for the big guns and bullets for the small arms. In underfloor lockers there were caches of various specialised tools, as well as access to the vehicle's mechanisms. In the few spaces remaining were heaps of other useful items, such as towing cables, water flasks, grease guns, protective clothing, hard hats, gas-masks and goggles.

Then the engines started up, the noise a howl in that confined space, and the whole shook and shuddered.

'No room for the crew!' Verity protested, yelling over the noise.

'We find a way,' Eric shouted back. 'Look, don't worry, you're in the best possible hands; our drivers are Stern and Hetherington themselves, and it's all their fault!'

I could barely hear either of them. Later I would observe the crew communicating in a kind of improvised sign language, and even by slamming spanners on the pipes.

Eric yelled, 'Now, look, you two, make yourselves useful. Julie, we're one crew member light, so get up into this sponson – there's a door in the hull just there, see? You can be a spotter even if you can't work the gun; we have telephone links throughout. I'll be up on the bridge. And Verity –' He moved a heap of spare clothing to reveal a first-aid box, painted with a red cross on white; it was alarmingly small, I thought. 'You're a nurse, aren't you?'

'Just a VAD.'

'Better than what we had before, which was nobody. But when

330

the action starts, just keep out of the way! Oh, and stay away from the engines. Every surface in there gets hot enough to fry bacon...'

So I clambered up into my sponson, which was a blister barely big enough for a kind of reclining chair into which I wedged myself, with the controls of a tremendous gun in front of me. With my legs up, my head bent forward on my neck, and barely able to move around the weapon, I was soon stiff and sore and increasingly uncomfortable.

Then the landship moved forward, with a crude jerk that I imagined was something to do with the gigantic gearing, and with a ferocious rattling thanks to the lack of any kind of suspension.

We were underway! The crew cheered, and I clung on for dear life.

8

Into Action

Our pilots, Stern and Hetherington, were, I learned later, significant figures in the short history of landship development – I suppose we were lucky to have them aboard.

Captain Albert Stern was a civilian given a volunteer commission, and Commander Tommy Hetherington of the 18th Hussars a dashing cavalryman with a vivid imagination. The vessel we rode, it seemed, had started life as a sketch on a napkin made by Hetherington, at a dinner with Churchill at a London club. At the time our greatest war machines had still been ocean-bound, and had proven little use against the Martians. Churchill could see, as few others did, that this was a way of bringing that powerful technology to land combat.

And only Churchill, one might think, could push such mad visions to actuality. The great engineering concerns of the north of Britain had been involved, under the emergency government's orders, in the development and construction of these beasts, from Metropolitan Cammell of Birmingham to Mirrless Watson of Glasgow. Churchill had taken a key interest in the project throughout, and had inspected training exercises on a military range in the Highlands, although many trials had taken place on the continent, I learned – and some of the smaller models had indeed been tried out in battle, in the bloody secrecy of the Germans' Russian front.

Once we were underway I explored my lumbering metal prison. I located the sighting slits, gaps in the hull from which I could draw back rather stiff metal covers. These gave a view out to the side, and a limited view ahead. I had a small periscope, too, through which I got a narrow view, front and back and to the sides.

By these means I could see the countryside across which we rolled, and the vehicles that followed us, a fleet with *Boadicea* at the crest: landships small and large, though none so large as us, proceeding in billows of exhaust smoke and with the soil of English fields being thrown up around their tracks, so that we left an ugly brown scar that stretched back the way we had come. The clumsy vessels reminded me of lungfish, creatures of the water crawling painfully over the land. Smaller vehicles, cars and motor-cycles, darted around us, and aircraft flew overhead, bright little insects in the morning sunlight, whose noise was quite drowned out by the engine roar of the advancing land armada.

But we made progress slowly. Our top speed off the road was only four or five miles an hour, and there were a lot of break-downs and other delays. The cars and 'cycles could make much greater speed.

As the journey wore on I took breaks from my small prison. Every so often I needed to bend my spine back into something resembling a natural posture. And, so that she need not leave her station, I brought Verity cups of water from a spigot that ran increasingly hot as the journey wore on.

Hot – the whole of our living space was hot, noisy, oily, cramped and crowded, and we were jarred with every rabbit hole we crossed. The crew, wearing face-masks and goggles, laboured at their engines, continually tending the clattering pistons and hissing valves. At least the air we breathed seemed fresh enough; I imagined there must be some circulation system to stop the build-up of exhaust gases. But I thought we might all melt in the rising temperatures, as that long morning wore on.

The crew of the landship, however, despite the heat and clamour, worked steadily. They were technical, highly trained, competent, efficient young men. Despite their khaki fatigues they had the air more of naval officers than soldiers – indeed, they called their commander 'Captain'. They might have been tend-ing some tremendous power generator, perhaps, as opposed to a weapon of war. I wondered if this was a vision of the war of the future, of calm young people working their precise controls and dispensing remote death. Perhaps we were becoming like the Martians after all, I thought, who made war on the earth with a similar lack of passion.

The lavatory was a hole in the floor covered by a metal hatch. I used it once; there was no partition, but in the circumstances modesty was hardly an issue. We were dehydrated, I think, and I could not remember when we had last eaten a decent meal.

It would take us all morning and more to reach our destination. And while we lumbered through the mud, as I learned later, the Martians were devastating Los Angeles, and had landed in Melbourne, Australia.

It was with some relief that I realised we were approaching the Cordon at last. It was after two in the afternoon, I think.

The support vehicles fell away now, leaving only the landships, the vehicles of serious intent. I could hear a dull booming, like thunder, coming from directly ahead of us. This, I learned, was an artillery barrage; guns many miles away were targeting Martian emplacements close to the site where we were aiming to breach the Cordon perimeter, softening up the invaders before we fell on them. We were rolling into gunfire, then, and the battle had already begun.

Through the telephone in my sponson I listened to Eric and his crew. Now there was none of the joshing that had characterised the camp at Thornborough; there was only the calm reading of instruments, and routine reports from the engine room, and Eric's quiet voice counting off the distance remaining: 'Half a mile to the wire, boys, not long now...' I knew that men going to war would pull back into themselves, and think of their homes, of their wives and children, or their own mothers. They had to be dragged back to the reality by their officers, like Eric. 'A quarter-mile more – keep it steady – two hundred yards – I can see the sappers pulling back the barbed wire for us, and I'm tempted to chuck out a bottle of whisky for their pains, but I won't... Here comes the Trench.'

And the landscape changed. Where before we had ground through a leafy countryside which, if untended, if lacking sheep and cattle in the fields, was pretty much indistinguishable from how it might have been on any day in mid-May in any of the last dozen years, now the land was bare, the buildings ruined, fences knocked down, even trees smashed or burned. The ground itself was churned up by the passing of wheels, and pocked by shell craters. I saw other signs of combat – a smashed gun emplacement, the metal of the maxims melted like toffee – and, a gruesome sight, the white of bone, a skeletal hand protruding from the dried ground. I had not seen this hinterland of war before, for

I had travelled to the Cordon through the underground passages. But in truth the Heat-Ray left few relics.

'Now, Mr Stern, if you please, give me all she's got!'

The engine roared, and we lurched forward, and tipped up as we climbed a steep ramp – and the prow of the landship dipped as if we had fallen into an immense well!

I would have seen it better if I had been an observer outside the hull of the great ship. Of course, such an observer, unprotected, would not have survived the battle long.

To penetrate the Martian Cordon, we had first to get through the Trench, a triple ditch system deep enough to trip a fighting-machine. It was into the first such ditch that our ironclad of the land now flung herself, with an uncharacteristic burst of speed. The trench was perhaps fifty feet deep and as many wide – but the *Boadicea* was a hundred feet long, and had been designed for just such purposes. After climbing that short ramp to the parapet she simply hurled herself over that great gash, and before she could tip into the depths her huge forward wheels engaged the far side wall. With engines screaming, with clods of earth being dug out by the treads – and with everybody aboard yelling encouragement – the wheels did their job, the prow rose, and she scrambled across this, and then the next two ditches of the Trench, smashing through the last barricades.

We were the spearpoint. Behind us the sappers made the breach permanent, with pontoons and bridge sections hastily flung across the triple ditches. The lesser vehicles behind us poured across and up the ramp we had created, and closed up behind us as we advanced.

And the Martians came out to meet us.

I only glimpsed them as I peered timidly through my periscope: the great tall legs, the bronze cowls, the projectors of the Heat-Ray being brought to bear. We drove straight at them, into that forest of legs, and even over the engine's roar I heard exultant yells from the crew.

But now the Heat-Ray splashed on us, coming from all angles.

I seemed to feel it like a physical blow, each jolt of heat, and men screamed with each punch. The great Martian hull-plates would resist the heat, but they had been fitted into the landship's frame by imperfect human engineering and there were gaps and seams, so that where the beam hit, sprays of molten aluminium showered the interior of the craft, slicing into the clothing and the flesh of the crew. Verity was kept busy at her medical station. But despite the casualties, despite deep scoring wounds to the structure of our craft itself, still we advanced, into the teeth of the fire.

Now we approached that barrier of supple, metallic legs. I abandoned my periscope and huddled over on myself—

We hit with a *clang!* There was a scraping over our roof, and a crash and smash and a kind of explosion behind us.

A glance through my periscope, when I dared uncurl, showed me what had happened. We had scythed through the legs of not one but two fighting-machines; both had tumbled over, and the cowl of one, it seemed, had detonated on impact with the ground. Other machines quickly clustered around the fallen, as was the way of the Martians. And now I saw that armada of lesser vehicles coming up behind to engage the Martian group. Many of their crews would die today, I knew – die in the next few minutes, in fact – but they would take Martians with them.

In the midst of such a battle it may seem odd that Eric Eden yanking open the door of my compartment should make me jump, but it did. His face was blackened by smoke and soot, save for his eyes, where he had removed his goggles. And he was grinning, his teeth white. 'That was quite a stunt, wasn't it?'

'Two fighting-machines at once – I'll say.'

'If you tried that on a soccer field you'd be penalised for taking out your man. Well. The battle is closing behind us, but we, and a few more vehicles, are pushing on. The primary purpose of the expedition is to try to disrupt the Martians' command and control, and so we're making straight for the central Redoubt at Amersham. But you, madam, get out here.'

I clambered out of my cell, stiffer than ever. Within the hull, Verity, I saw, was working frantically, treating four wounded men, all of them horribly burned, on face, neck, back, legs; all seemed groggy with morphine. A fifth man, himself limping from a burn to his leg, was helping Verity as best he could. The air was murky with smoke, and rich with the stink of cordite; the engines roared, the gears screamed. But still the crew worked with frantic energy; still the landship advanced.

Eric said to me, 'I'll give you a young officer. Lieutenant Hopson – the chap I sent to bring you in, if you remember. Smarter than he looks and he knows the Cordon, been on a number of infiltration operations before. He'll get you to Marriott.'

'And Verity?'

At the sound of her name, she looked up from her work, distracted. 'Leave me here.' And she turned away, before I could acknowledge her.

I would not see Verity Bliss again; she did not survive the engagement. Of all the folk I met in the course of the Second War, it was Verity who seemed most to have grown into the part she was asked to play – as if it had all been a paradoxical opportunity for her. In the end she gave her life on the front line, and died very young. I knew few soldiers braver.

Eric tapped me on the shoulder. 'Come, then. The sooner I can get rid of you the sooner I can regain control of my ship; Tommy Hetherington's a marvellous chap but a touch on the reckless side . . .'

The great landship did not even come to a full halt before depositing myself and Hopson; it had too much momentum to be wasted on the likes of us, and we had to jump down and roll in the broken dirt. But we made it in one piece.

Hopson was the first to his feet, and he dragged me to cover behind a fragment of scorched, broken wall. Already the *Boadicea* was moving on, and that huge flank slid past us as if she were a great liner leaving a Liverpool dock: an extraordinary sight.

As it turned out she would reach Amersham that day, leading the remnants of her land-borne flotilla, and engage the Martians, and do a lot of damage. The question of whether that great incursion made any difference to the Martians' execution of their global Second War remains controversial in the eyes of many historians. In my judgement it was worth the try, at least. But the *Boadicea* herself would not survive; her monumental wreck is, today, the centrepiece of a museum.

Hopson gave me a minute to breathe. Then he said, 'Now to find this scallywag Marriott and his chums. Ready?'

'Always.'

He sat up, glanced around to see if the coast was clear, and led me out into the open.

And in the hours that followed, even as we progressed across the Cordon seeking our co-conspirators, the line of midnight swept across continents and oceans, more Martian fleets landed, and everywhere the fighting intensified.

9

Escape from Long Island

The Martians had begun moving in earnest from their huge pit in the ruins of Stony Brook at six in the morning, New York time. They headed relentlessly west, sweeping along the Island towards Manhattan, driving before them a great wave of people in cars and trucks and on motor-cycles and bicycles, and many, many on foot, heading west towards the bridges to the mainland.

And Harry Kane, after stoutly waiting for Marigold Rafferty, had made a late start.

Driving Bill Woodward's Dodge, and with Marigold tucked in the back, Harry joined the main drag heading west. But he found himself slowed to a crawl from the gitgo, not so much by the traffic as by pedestrians, dusty people limping along dusty tracks, adults burdened with luggage and infants, miserable children tottering on skinny legs, old folks and the disabled in bath chairs. Every time he had come to Long Island Harry had been struck by the extremes of wealth and poverty to be encountered here. Only a few hundred yards from an emblem of supreme wealth like the glowing Bigelow mansion you would come to some dirt-poor post-industrial community of broken-down factories, warehouses and jetties, maybe a dismal hotel or boarding-house and a bar – always a bar, Prohibition or not – and shack-like dwellings strung out along the road. This morning it seemed fitting that rich and poor should be fleeing together along this dirt highway.

Meanwhile, most of the stores were closed that Friday morning; those that were open were mobbed, and a couple looked to have been looted. The worst hold-ups were at the few gas stations that still had stocks. They spent a half-hour stuck in a jam outside one station that was still serving, and a couple of burly guys stood by with shotguns as ragged assistants laboured to fill up one car after another from dusty red-painted pumps.

'Wow,' Marigold Rafferty said, peering out. 'The free market in action, right? I wonder what prices they're charging.'

Woodward murmured, 'We have more than half a tank. Also there's a spare can in back. As long as we shut the engine down when we're stuck, we'll have the gas to get us to Manhattan – it's not so far after all. No, running out of gas isn't going to be our problem.'

Harry stared glumly out of the window. At times the flow of people was such that the car was entirely surrounded by bodies, shuffling by. 'This happened in England in 1907, and again in 1920. Though not so many cars in '07.'

'And in the European wars,' Woodward said sternly. 'Whether you're a Russian peasant or some deadbeat garage hand on Long Island, I guess it doesn't matter if it's a German armoured truck or a Martian fighting-machine that's coming after you, guns blazing.'

'No sign of the police, by the way,' Marigold said. 'Or the Guard. Damn. And it's my fault. You two could have got away hours earlier. You shouldn't have stayed for me. We didn't even know each other twenty-four hours ago.'

Woodward laughed. 'It's this way on the front line. When the action cuts in and the units get mixed up, you find yourself fighting for your life alongside some guy you met twenty-four seconds ago, never mind hours.'

Marigold said, 'I've never been to the front line.'

'You have now,' Woodward replied softly. 'Gap in traffic; we can move.'

The sun rose steadily in the sky. And Harry, looking north towards the Sound, thought he saw the light glint from the carapaces of fighting-machines on the move. They could be striding out in the shallow water, close to the shore.

'Smart guys, beating the traffic,' Woodward said sourly, when Harry pointed this out.

They approached the city around noon.

10

The Bridges of New York

Woodward's tactic was to cut through Queens, and then cross to the island of Manhattan by the Queensboro Bridge.

But long before they got to the bridge it was apparent that driving all the way wasn't going to be possible. For one thing everybody else had the same idea; all the traffic, wheeled and foot, was funnelling towards the few crossing-points on the East River, including Queensboro, and there was a solid, unmoving jam everywhere, long before they reached the waterfront.

And for another, Queens was in flames. Even before they got out of the car the stink of smoke was obvious, and there were ominous glows on the horizon, bright even on an early summer day.

Before they abandoned the car, Woodward put together light packs of their remaining water, beer and food, and handed out heavy driving gloves and scarves from a small trunk in the back. 'To save your hands from the fires. Pull the scarf over your mouth to keep out the smoke ... And here, take these.' He handed out pistols, one to each of them.

Harry inspected his. 'A Colt Automatic.'

'Ten years old. Kicks like a mule. Some day I'll give 'em back to the Army. Here's a couple of clips each.' He eyed them. 'I'm going to assume you both know how to handle a gun.' He showed them the basics, reloading, the safety. 'I got no plans to kill any Americans today. Think of it as a magic wand that you can wave when you *need* people to get out of the way.'

Marigold said, 'You seem prepared.'

'Hell, no. Making it up as I go along.' Before he left the car he carefully locked it, and left a US Army parking permit in the window. He winked at Harry. 'Won't save it from a Martian

Heat-Ray, but you never know, I might yet be back to collect it.' Harry noticed that as a final preparation Woodward tucked a tyre-iron into his jacket. 'OK, we're going to get over that damn bridge or die trying.'

So they pressed on into the urban landscape of Queens, which struck Harry as a tangle of warehouses and factories and blocks of rough housing, fronting onto the river. And, today, the refugee flow from at least half the length of Long Island, all the way back to Stony Brook where the cylinders had landed, had poured into a burning suburb where the local population was already looking to flee. There was chaos, panic, crushing, the streets blocked by abandoned or burning vehicles, or by shoving masses of people.

Through all this, they steadily made their way west towards the bank of the East River. Woodward tried to keep them away from the worst of the big blazes; you could see where the fires were, from the plumes of smoke that rose up into the sky. And both Woodward and Marigold proved smart in finding ways through, by ducking down alleys, climbing over walls and hurrying through empty yards – once they even cut all the way through a house, through an open front door and out the back. To Harry's relief, they avoided confrontations; better to evade than to pick a fight.

And Harry's journalistic eye picked out details: the old woman fumbling to lock a door as smoke billowed around her; the little boy sitting with a toy wooden battleship on a stoop, crying his eyes out; a woman who seemed to be going into labour, right there in the middle of the street, with a few folk gathered around her, trying to help, and others pushing impatiently past. There was an old man who just *died*, clutching his chest, right in front of Harry, almost without warning: fell down and died. Harry wondered who he was. Harry was sore tempted to dig out the notebook and pencil that sat in the breast pocket of his jacket, but every time he stopped to stare Woodward or Marigold shoved him in the back. 'Keep moving, you ass!'

And then Harry saw a glint of bronze, high in the air. It was the hood of a fighting-machine, high above Queens.

He would tell me that the sight gave him an extraordinary thrill, as if of exhilaration; none of it seemed real, as if it were all a huge movie set. That's youth for you.

At last they broke through to the river front, and by a miracle of Woodward's navigation right at the entrance to the Queens-boro Bridge.

Harry, coughing from the smoke, was dazzled by the sudden brilliance of the open panorama. There was the bridge; below it the river on which lay the low grey profiles of warships, and smaller specks that looked like ferries, bravely hauling off handfuls of refugees from the Island. And ahead of him was Manhattan, a great reef of buildings. As far as he could see the air above the city was clear – no sign of unusual smoke, not yet. Looking back, though, he could see that over in Brooklyn an immense, smoky fire burned, and Harry heard the crump of a distant explosion; he knew that Brooklyn was dense with heavy industries, refineries and shipyards, which would no doubt be targets for the Martians.

And the Queensboro Bridge itself was a solid, unmoving mass of vehicles and people.

'The Martians haven't crossed yet,' Marigold said. 'So we're still ahead of the game ... All we need to do now is get across that bridge. Shit.'

Harry grinned. 'Hey, language! You're not in Menlo Park now, you know.'

Woodward pressed forward. 'Come on. And now's the time to use your magic wands.'

He led the way, pushing through the crowd by main force, and Harry and Marigold did their best to follow. Woodward's pistol was indeed only a back-up, a symbol; he made most of his progress through firm shoving, and snapping out orders that people obeyed without thinking – he got through, Harry thought, mostly by showing a kind of unswerving belief in his own right of way.

And, inch by inch, yard by yard, they made the crossing.

The bridge passed over Blackwell's Island, on which stood grey, utilitarian buildings: hospitals, a prison. Harry saw that people were decanting there, apparently exhausted, or maybe thinking that this mid-river scrap of land might provide a safer refuge than Manhattan itself. But the island was already full, and what looked like prison guards were lined up with nightsticks and revolvers to turn people back.

At last they reached the Manhattan side. Here people spilled off the bridge and out into the neighbouring streets, which were crowded but nothing yet to compare to the crush on the Queens side, or the bridge itself.

Woodward drew his party together. They were all three breathless, dishevelled. 'Everybody OK? Now we go find the US Army.' And, boldly, he led them west, along East 60th Street.

11

Central Park

The Army, it turned out, along with units of the National Guard and the state militia, was bivouacking in Central Park. Woodward left Harry and Marigold waiting at the corner of 59th and Fifth Avenue while he went into the Park to find an officer and figure out what was going on.

Around Harry, Manhattan still felt like Manhattan. Traffic still flowed, if heavier and faster than usual, and with more military trucks; there were still cops at the interchanges. Harry, dusty, sleepless, felt like a vagabond who had just wandered into the city. But even here there were people hurrying along the sidewalks with suitcases in their hands and rucksacks on their backs – little kids being dragged along, bath chairs for the elderly, just like on the Island. And they all seemed to Harry to be streaming north.

From here Harry could see the Plaza Hotel. He sighed.

Marigold raised an eyebrow. 'What's your beef?'

He looked down at the ruin of his dress suit. 'Look at me. I haven't changed since I got ready for the Bigelow party, oh, twenty hours ago. I sure could use a couple of hours in one of those suites in the Plaza: a shower, a glass of champagne, a cigar, a heap of newspapers...'

Marigold, by comparison, looked at ease in her riding habit, practical and serviceable, which seemed to show barely a mark. She shrugged. 'Good luck with that. As for the papers, we came here running *from* the news; we know it better than any editor in town.'

'Ain't that the truth? And nobody knows if we're alive or dead...'

With that thought, on impulse, Harry looked for a phone box, and ran over to make a call to his parents. It felt odd to find the lines working. His family, in Iowa, were safe but concerned and following the news; Harry promised he would come home as soon as he could, and he meant it. When Marigold tried to follow his example, the line went dead. It would be many days, he would tell me, before Harry was able to make another call.

Woodward came strolling up, hands in pockets. 'You should see what the Army has done to the Park. Jeez. I dug better latrine trenches in my first week of cadet training.'

Marigold raised her eyebrows. 'So, are our brave troops ready to smite the foe?'

'I wish. Patton wishes.'

'Who?'

'Oh, a friend of mine. For better or worse there aren't many officers in the modern US Army with combat experience – but George has, he was involved in the Pancho Villa expedition back in '16, and now he's got himself in charge of the operation here, on the ground. *And* got himself bumped up to Major.' He grinned. 'Smart guy all round.'

Marigold looked distinctly unimpressed. 'Enough of the back-slapping. What is Patton going to *do*?'

Woodward shrugged. 'Work out how best to use his forces to counter the imminent Martian threat, and protect the civilians. Right now he's in a fierce debate with his commanding officers about when to blow the bridges from Brooklyn and Queens.'

Harry was astounded. 'Like the Queensboro? But they're all crammed with people – and aside from the ferries, that's the only way off Long Island.'

'Sure. But, in the eyes of the brass, that's also the only way off for the Martians too. If we can keep them bottled up —'

Marigold was growing angry. 'Are you serious? *Bottled up?* Have none of you soldier boys read the briefings from England? The river won't hold them!'

Woodward held his hands up. 'Don't shoot the messenger. Meanwhile, they are setting up evacuation routes off the island. You can go west to New Jersey – the trains are still running for now, and there are the ferries and bridges – or you can head north and over the bridges to the Bronx.' He glanced around, and spoke more quietly. 'Patton's been ordered to detail some men to see to the shipment of the bullion stores off the island. Don't spread *that* around.'

Harry thought it over. 'So, they're sending people west and north.'

'Right. My problem with *that* is, that's precisely the way the Martians are going to progress, after they've taken Manhattan. That's the way to the mainland, after all.'

'We go south, then,' Harry said, working it out. 'We'll still be stuck on another damn island—'

'But we won't be in the war zone.' Woodford grinned at Harry. 'Anyhow, you're a reporter. You'll want to be on the spot, right? Martians in New York! It's the story of the century. Listen. Make for Battery Park, which is about as far south as you can get. Keep away from the fires. If I can, I'll come find you when things stabilise. *If.*'

Harry felt alarmingly exposed to be losing Woodward, like a child abandoned by his father. 'What about you?'

'I'll go back to the Park.' He tapped his shoulder. 'Broken wing or not, I've still got more fighting experience than half the bozos in there combined, and somebody needs to keep George Patton's feet on the ground.'

Now a soldier came running from the direction of the river, looking for officers to report to, yelling about some new development. Woodward stayed with them long enough to figure out what was happening now.

So much for cutting the bridges.

The Martian fighting-machines were simply *wading* across the East River, in a broad crescent formation, between the Queensboro and Williamsburg bridges. The river was only some forty feet deep – no obstacle to the hundred-foot-tall fighting-machines, a fact which, as Marigold furiously pointed out again, should have been apparent from the British briefings. And meanwhile, they would learn later, smaller, squat handling-machines, at the feet of their tripedal big brothers, were scuttling *under* the water and clambering out on dry land, their aluminium chassis glistening, dripping river mud and weed, Heat-Ray projectors ready to wield.

Now, looking down 60th Street, Harry saw them come, their bronze hoods visible high in the air between the faces of the buildings: Martians, in Manhattan. Already artillery was coughing from the emplacements in Central Park.

Harry and Marigold exchanged quick handshakes with Woodward, and ran west and south.

And around the world, still the cylinders fell.

12

How the Martians Came to Melbourne

On the morning the Lightning War came to Australia, so Luke Smith believes, he was fourteen years old. At the time of my writing this account Smith is an educated young man in his late twenties, trained as a lawyer, and with a passion to defend the rights of his own people. He has a clear memory of the events of those astonishing days, and when he finally overcame his illiteracy he wrote down what he had seen.

But 'Luke Smith' is not his name, and was not when the Martians landed. He had been separated from his family, in upstate Victoria, at a young age. Given the name of a Gospel writer, he was raised in a Christian mission until the age of ten, and was then 'loaned' – he remembers the word being used – to a sheep farmer near Bendigo. There he was abused. He is vague on specifics. The culprit may have been one of his own people. At twelve he ran away, into the bush.

And he headed south to Melbourne, a city he had heard of but had never seen. He learned that a city is like a vast machine for producing enormous amounts of waste, accessible to those clever enough. By the age of fourteen he had joined an underclass of young Aborigines, despised and even more invisible in that urban setting than were his people in the countryside.

He was a clever if entirely untutored child, with a poor, rough-accented vocabulary. Still, from conversations with others, and from comments made by white folk in his hearing – I imagine they believed he would not understand – he gained an impression of the plight of his people. He seems to have formed a determination to survive, at a very young age.

Luke always felt he was effectively alone.

Then the Martians came.

The cylinders landed at Fairfield, north-east of Melbourne, at local midnight of Saturday, May 20 – it was Friday afternoon in England.

Luke had been sleeping in Luna Park, which is an amusement resort at St Kilda, on the shore of Port Phillip Bay, to the south-east of Melbourne itself. When he woke, some time after dawn on that fateful Saturday, the place seemed deserted. He had heard movement during the night of motor vehicles rolling – he even heard the growl of animals – but it had not disturbed him; there were such noises every night, in the Park. It was a sprawling, casually policed place, much of it on the edge of criminality anyhow, and there was a plethora of hiding places for a boy like Luke to tuck himself away and sleep in safety.

When he emerged from his hiding place, though, there was nobody around.

He walked through the Park, past the stalls and stands and attractions, some of them locked up, others simply abandoned. Even then it occurred to Luke that he could break into one of the abandoned food concessions, but cautious habits drew him to the garbage pails as usual. He did notice that the rats seemed bolder.

After eating, following an instinct he would not later be able to understand, he left Luna Park to walk the few miles into downtown Melbourne.

He passed through the Albert Park area, making for South Melbourne and the river. His sense of direction had always been good; after a couple of years he knew the city's geography pretty well, even if he had trouble reading the street signs. These suburbs were not entirely deserted, but almost. He saw a few people in shut-up houses, peering fearfully through north-facing windows – looking out for a menace Luke still knew nothing of. Here and there late-goers fled, mostly on foot. Electric trams stood silent on their rails, useless. A few shops had been broken into. Abandoned luggage littered the streets.

And Luke saw, a couple of times, a sight he had never witnessed before: the dead bodies of white folk. They had been killed in the stampede to flee.

He crossed the Yarra by the Queens Bridge. Now he was in a grid of streets, the expensive part of the city. In those days Melbourne was still a young town, and later he would learn something of its history: the Gold Rush money on which it had been founded, the banking crash of '93 that was still talked of in hushed tones three decades later.

With an instinct driven by a never-assuaged hunger he made for the Queen Victoria Market, a sprawling development with craft and clothing stalls crammed in among the food vendors. Luke knew this place; on market days it was crowded with a miscellany of folk, from gowned academics from the colleges to black-robed Italian grandmothers pushing carts. Rough types came for the petty thieving; Luke had often come here for the waste, and a bit of begging if he had to. Today, as elsewhere, the place was mysteriously deserted. But the bins behind the stalls offered rich pickings, of cold meat, stale bread, half-eaten sugary cakes. Luke considered finding a bag and filling it; he might never have a chance like this again. But you couldn't run if you were burdened. He decided he would come back to the market later, and fill his belly when he needed to – if his luck held.

In the meantime, he was free, even of hunger.

On a whim, he made his way a short distance across town, to Swanston Street, and the State Library of Victoria. He knew that this was a building full of books, and he even had a dim idea of what books were *for*, despite his own reading being barely enough to pick out his own name. What interested him about the Library was the tremendous dome that topped it – supposedly, he had heard people say, the largest concrete dome in the world. (In fact that wasn't quite true, a local's boast.) Luke liked the idea that he could stand here and just *look* at something that couldn't be bettered anywhere in the world.

It is an image that appeals to me: the ragged Aborigine boy, in the deserted street of that white folks' city, illiterate, unwashed, abused and ignored, standing on that sloping lawn before the pillars of the front portico – alone, and yet inspired by a monument to knowledge.

That was when the Martian fighting-machine appeared, over the Library, there at the heart of Melbourne.

Luke would later be surprised how little fear he felt. But then for a boy from the outback everything about the city was astonishing: the great buildings of the business district, so tall they looked as if they might topple over at any moment; even the Ferris wheel at Luna Park, as tall as a Martian, was more alarming than a fighting-machine at first glance.

For a moment the Martian simply stood there, as if gazing down at the boy, as he gazed up at it. But then glittering tentacles writhed about the Martian's cowled superstructure, and it wielded a device like a heavy cannon. Luke had seen guns before. He turned and ran, fast and hard.

But he was curious enough to glance over his shoulder.

The Heat-Ray made the Library's dome explode in a hail of concrete shrapnel, and the incineration of the precious books began with a tremendous flare of flame.

Luke had overheard white folk talking of their justification for taking his ancestors' land and driving them towards extinction. When the Europeans had landed in Australia it had been a *terra nullius*, they said, a land belonging to no one, a land as empty in law as if the native people did not exist at all. And the victory of the Europeans had been the result of a war of steel against stone. Now, thought Luke, even as he ran, whatever that tremendous machine was – he wondered if it might be Japanese, for he had heard the gentlefolk of Melbourne expressing fears as to the territorial ambitions of those foreigners – now this country was seeing the waging of a new war: not with steel this time, but with heat.

He ran and ran, laughing.

13

In Peking

If Luke Smith slept through the invasion of Australia, when the Martians came to Peking – they landed a couple of hours after Australia – at first Tom Aylott didn't believe that there was an extraterrestrial threat at all. 'That was China for you in the Twenties,' he told me years later in Sydney, when I met him after the launch of his own book on those times. 'You wouldn't have thought it could get any madder. But *then...*'

He had been shaken awake at around six a.m. by a friend, a Chinese student called Li Qichao. 'You come! War! You see!'

Li, an ardent disciple of Sun Yat-Sen and a visionary of a future Chinese democracy, was barely twenty-one. A bright, ambitious boy from the country, his education disrupted, he had come to the city to learn as much as he could of the realities of power and diplomacy. While waiting for destiny to call he survived by means of various part-time clerical posts – and he had fallen in with Tom Aylott.

But he was prone to be excitable, and Tom tried to turn over. 'Yeah, yeah. Wake me when the house is on fire, Qichao...'

Tom himself was only twenty-two, but he was making a name for himself as an energetic correspondent for *The Times* of London. That morning Tom was having trouble surfacing from another riotous night with other young westerners in the bars of the Legation Quarter, as it was known, an area within the walls of the Inner City itself that had long been claimed as a protectorate by western governments and companies.

And after all, in those days war was no novelty in China. The Boxer Rebellion against foreign meddling had been only twenty years in the past; the last Qing Emperor, a boy called Puyi, had abdicated just ten years before; there had been a breakdown of order in the country since the death of the first strong-man President, Yuan Shikai, in 1916. Peking was still the residence of the internationally recognised Beiyang government, but in practical terms much of the country was in the hands of one warlord faction or another, or else prostrate under foreign control.

But here was Li shaking Tom vigorously, with his English disintegrating as it often did under stress. 'War coming, Tom!' he insisted. 'War coming!'

And now Tom thought he could hear it: a distant crump of explosions, the sound of running feet, women and men shouting – and the wail of frightened children, a sound that was all too familiar in Peking.

Tom's first thought was: *story*.

He forced himself fully awake. He was already in his shirt, underwear and socks; he grabbed trousers, jacket and shoes. Despite Li's protestations he used the small bathroom – his bladder was too full to allow any other course.

'You come! War close!'

'Sure, Qichao, sure,' he called over his shoulder while buttoning up. 'Who is it this time? The Zhili, the Fengtian – where the hell is my Kodak? The Kuomintang, even?'

Li grinned, wildly excited – as, Tom was already mature enough to reflect, only the very young can be, stirred by the coming of war. 'Come see!'

So they dashed out of the apartment, into a daylight already so bright it made Tom wince. And led him directly south, towards the walls of the Inner City. The air was thick with smoke and the smell of cordite, and a coarser stink of burning.

The heart of Peking, Tom told me, was in those days a place of nested rectangles, each with its walls. You had the Inner City, a domain of aristocrats, officials, soldiers – with, in recent decades, the grudgingly admitted foreigners in the Legation Quarter – and within the Inner City lay the Imperial City with its extensive water gardens, and within that in turn the Forbidden City, protected by a moat and three sets of walls. There was also an Outer City appended to the south wall of the Inner, a tremendous annex stuffed with enormous temples. Of course since the fall of the Qing even the Forbidden City was forbidden no more, but every foreign visitor knew that the best view of Peking, and the countryside beyond, was from the city walls.

And it was onto those walls that Tom and Li climbed now. As

he breathed deep from the climb Tom found himself coughing in smoke-laden air.

They soon made the top of the wall. The city as seen from up here was always an odd sight, almost a sylvan scene rather than urban in the western sense, with the green of trees punctuated here and there by the egg-yolk yellow of the domes of palaces and temples. Peking itself seemed at peace. But the countryside was not.

When Tom and Li looked east, into the rising sun, they saw the fighting-machines, silhouetted, their slim shadows long before them. It was a sight Tom immediately recognised from images of the British landings. Tom says he was struck by the sheer animal-like grace of the great machines, as are many observers on their first encounters with Martian technology. It was remarkable to see them suddenly superimposed onto this Chinese landscape, a world away from England.

And there were many of them, the machines marching in what looked like a grand crescent, heading for the city. Li tried to count them: 'One, two, three, four ... eight, nine, ten, eleven ... *many.*'

There were attempts being made to resist the Martians' advance, Tom saw. Weapons fire sparked around their footfalls, and shells burst close to their hooded carapaces. That was no surprise; Tom imagined that aside from the Germans' front in Russia, this must be one of the most militarised places on the planet. And he wondered if the warlords were co-operating, for once, against this common enemy.

Even if so, they were doing no good. Just as was seen around the world that day, the Martians applied the lessons they had learned in England about the danger of our artillery, and simply shot the shells out of the air. Tom could see military vehicles, cavalry units on stocky horses from north China – even men riding camels from the Gobi – all scattering at the feet of the advancing Martians. And here and there men and animals and vehicles were incinerated in silent bursts of flame, Tom saw, appalled.

Meanwhile, behind the machines a kind of corridor of smoke was rising, as the countryside the Martians had already crossed began to burn.

'We must get out of here,' Tom said. But even as he spoke he raised his camera and captured hasty images.

'Magnificent sight.'

Tom glanced at his friend; Li's face was shining. 'You sound as if you are enjoying this.'

'China flat on her back,' Li Qichao said. 'Foreigners every-where. Russians want Mongolia. British want Tibet. Japanese want Manchuria. Americans – Americans just *sell* stuff. Govern-ment a joke, country full of warlords. And yet, and yet, China still a great country. Even Martians see that!'

'They're attacking you, and you see it as an endorsement?'

'New age starts,' Li said. 'I, I will go east and south, find the Kuomintang. Sun Yat-Sen. It is said the Emperor will join us.'

'What Emperor? Puyi? He's just a kid.'

'Let Martians drive out foreigners. Then Chinese drive out Martians. We survived Genghis Khan. Will survive this. Now we have the foreigners' railways and telephones and guns. And *then...*'

But already the Heat-Ray, with a range of miles, was licking at Peking, and buildings in the outer suburbs were flashing to flame.

Tom closed up his camera. 'OK, Qichao. But for now let's just make sure we live to see some of that future.'

Li grinned. 'Come!'

They made their way around the wall parapet, away from the Martian advance, as the destruction of the city began in earnest.

14

The Martian Invasion of Manhattan

The dawn of Saturday in Peking had been around midday of Friday in New York. And through that long Friday afternoon, Harry Kane and Marigold Rafferty watched the battle for Manhattan unfold.

They could not have had a better view, Harry reckoned, than from Battery Park, the end point of their flight south, if 'better' was a word to use on such a day. The Park itself was on a rise – and to get an even more favourable observation platform they had managed to break into the Park's Monroe Tower. Dating back to 1910, such towers had been set up all along the Atlantic and Gulf coasts at a time when German aggression had appeared to threaten the US itself, as well as to breach the long-held Monroe Doctrine of non-interference by European powers in the Americas. The Towers, intended for spotting warships at sea, had seen no use in anger, and had quickly become obsolete as aeroplane surveillance techniques had advanced. But the Battery Park Tower still offered an unparalleled viewpoint over south Manhattan, and had become a popular tourist spot.

Of course that morning it was locked up; it had been the work of a moment to break in, and it took only a little longer for the two of them to scramble up a spiral stair to the spotting platform, an electric elevator being out of action.

And there was Lower Manhattan laid out before them, with its excrescence of tremendous buildings – like trees in a forest, Harry thought idly, competing for the light. The complex fretwork of docks and wharves around the island's shore added still more organic character. It was magnificent, the windows of the buildings sparkling in the sun, the elegant, rectilinear simplicity of the street plan – the sheer vigour of it all, the newness – though you could see even from up here the extremes of wealth and poverty, tall palaces a short walk away from the darker warrens of a deprived polyglot population.

But now an interplanetary war had come to Manhattan.

The fighting, in fact, had begun even as the Martians waded across the East River, dozens of them coming across from all along the Brooklyn shore. The Navy had tried to hold a line at the river; a handful of destroyers bore down on the wading fighting-machines. But even before they closed the Heat-Rays had wielded their invisible energies. Several ships, their hulls melting, their stores of fuel and armaments exploding, were turned to helpless hulks. Even so, some of the shells hit their targets; with the naked eye Harry had seen fighting-machines stagger and fall, each like a man shot in the eye – and each casualty took others out of the fight, for, just as had been observed since the Martians' first incursion into England, when one Martian fell, its fellows would retrieve it.

But with the brief naval battle won, the remaining Martians had landed on Manhattan's eastern shore unimpeded.

As they began to make their way into the island's interior, they were skeletal figures glimpsed between the buildings, the sunlight glittering from their cowls: 'like medieval visions of death', Harry wrote down in his notebook. And they deployed their scythe, the Heat-Ray. The towers of central Manhattan loomed even over the fighting-machines, but the beams swept the faces of the great buildings, as if mining the walls of a canyon. Concrete and steel buckled and smashed and melted, and glass rained down. Harry glimpsed the people fleeing in the streets; he saw them not as individuals but as swarms, like ants before men with flame-throwers.

Soon battle was joined by the military forces on land. Harry saw and heard the big guns in Central Park open up in earnest, and the clatter of small-arms fire; he imagined Woodward and his buddy Patton leading brave charges against the advancing machines. One large Martian battle group lingered over Central Park, where, it seemed, much of the city's armed forces were still concentrated. But more were soon moving northwards, just as Woodward had predicted, no doubt in search of easy pickings on the mainland, in upstate New York and beyond.

And, Harry was dismayed to see, a third group marched south through downtown, heading straight for the Monroe Tower, or so it seemed. The slowness of their progress, Harry thought, had nothing to do with human resistance but was a product of the sheer density of the buildings, the number of targets available. The labour of destruction.

Harry grunted. 'So much for our theory that they wouldn't come this way.'

Marigold said, 'They have the machines to spare, I guess. At least we'll get a good view.'

She sounded remarkably unafraid, Harry thought. And yet he himself felt little fear; perhaps it was simply exhaustion, or perhaps his capacity for fear was overwhelmed.

As the southern group advanced, a pack split off and veered left along the waterfront, some making for the navy yards on the East River, others pushing into the crowded tenements of the Lower East Side. There were no tall buildings there. The Martians dominated, the Heat-Ray played easily, and whole blocks were blown apart by the fire.

Meanwhile a central group reached the financial district. Harry himself saw the destruction of City Hall; with the smashing of the seat of the city's government, he supposed organised resistance, what there was of it, would begin to crumble. The Woolworth Building, still the world's tallest building almost a decade after it was completed – nearly seven times as tall even as a fighting-machine – seemed to attract particular attention. Marigold had binoculars – a small set like opera glasses that she carried in her jacket pocket – and she loaned them to Harry now so he could see handling-machines swarming up the sides of the building, rapidly reaching its upper levels, where they began its demolition floor by floor, working their way downwards, so that rubble cascaded into the streets below.

'It almost looks beautiful as it falls,' Harry said. 'Like an opening flower.'

'They seem to have targeted it. Maybe they could see the Woolworth from Mars. They might think it has some military function.'

'I've drunk coffee in there,' Harry mourned.

'We'll build it again – bigger and better.'

But, after all he had seen that day, Harry wasn't so sure about that.

At last the lead Martians approached the southern tip of the island. Now the big military forts at the mouth of the harbour, Fort Tompkins on the New Jersey shore and Fort Hamilton on the Brooklyn side, added their own firepower to the fight. But it seemed that yet another detachment of fighting-machines had walked down the Brooklyn shore and were already lashing at Hamilton with their Heat-Rays – and the weapons had the range to take on Fort Tompkins too.

One fighting-machine, Harry saw, waded out to Liberty Island, and climbed up onto the dry land. For a moment, perhaps a third the height of the statue, it rested there, and it appeared to look around at the battles underway on land and sea. Harry heard its eerie cry: '*Ulla!*' Then, evidently having decided the statue was not worth the trouble of demolishing, it waded away.

Marigold touched Harry's arm. 'We must go. They'll be here soon.'

'*Ulla! Ulla!*...'

Harry imagined that same cry echoing all around the world, that terrible evening. Dazed, he allowed Marigold to take his hand and lead him to the stairs to ground level.

'*Ulla! Ulla!*'

15

Walter Jenkins in Dahlem

Eighteen hours after the Martians had first fallen on Long Island, Walter Jenkins was still at his self-constructed monitoring station in Dahlem – by his clock it was after eleven p.m. He assuaged hunger and thirst with flasks of coffee and packs of biscuits, assembled before the vigil had started. He had been sleepless for more than twenty-four hours already. And yet, he hoped, his concentration and powers of analysis had not faltered.

Walter thought he was seeing the strategy. As the cylinders had continued to fall, a rain of aluminium and fire around the world, his attention had turned from the astronomical to the geographic, from the reaches of interplanetary space to dispositions on the ground. He referred frequently now to a big Mercator-projection world map on which he had marked, in vivid red ink, the fall of each cluster as it was reported. It was clear by now, of course, that just as he had predicted the Martians were making each first landfall at local midnight, wherever they fell, inert missiles first with the crewed ships to follow. He pictured those cylinders still out in space, hanging over the earth as it turned beneath them, like a stream of bullets from some tremendous machine gun.

But those volleys had clearly been planned to land, not simply according to a geographical pattern, but at key human targets. The Martians seemed to be making for all the world's major inhabited landmasses, from Asia to Australia. And in each assault they came down close to a key city. The first wave of dummy cylinders would smash down to sterilise the terrain, within an hour the second wave would come, and within six hours the battle groups were out, mounting large-scale, co-ordinated, lightning-strike assaults on the cities and their supporting facilities, fuel stores, transport links. And, by means of this brutal decapitation of human society – wrecking capital accumulated by an industrial civilisation across centuries – it seemed the Martians might be striving to win their war quickly.

Yet it was a war Walter knew that mankind could not afford to lose. For, with the whole world smashed as England had been over the last two years – with stores depleted, manufacturing capacity gone, governments dissolving – we would soon lose out capacity to resist, and would never be able to assemble the resources for another chance. The massacre of mankind as an independent species would be completed in this generation. And for the children of the future – like the wretches in the Martians' cylinders – only a million years of slavery.

But the battle was not lost yet.

Walter concentrated on the immediate situation. The first landings had been scattered, at New York, Los Angeles, Melbourne, Peking, Bombay – one per midnight band. Now, though, in the last hour – and even as he had listened to wireless reports of the devastation of Peking – the pattern had changed, with no less than three targets at the same longitudinal meridian being selected: St Petersburg in Russia, the Ottoman capital Constantinople, and Durban in South Africa – the latter the first Martian footfall in that continent.

Then, through his window, Walter saw a flash of green light in the darkened sky. He glanced at a clock. In Berlin, it was midnight.

He waited for the sound of thunder.

16

A Shadow Play

'*Ulla! Ulla! ...*'

In the strange, lonely dawn of Saturday, Emre heard that eerie cry echo over Constantinople, even drowning out the muezzin calls.

Emre Sahin was, by inclination and training, a soldier. A decade before, in the wars against the Balkan League, a Greek cannonball had neatly detached his left leg and the lower part of his right. He had been just twenty years old at the time. Now Emre had become an accidental journalist, and he would leave one of the more compelling accounts of the Martians' action in Constantinople, for the benefit of myself and other historians.

But as it happened, in the days before the Martians came, Emre, anticipating the ending of Ramadan a few days hence, had been preparing a shadow-puppet play.

Emre had always enjoyed the end of Ramadan: the three-day celebration that followed a month of fasting, when family would visit to exchange gifts of sweets and tobacco and perfume and porcelain, and there would be happy gatherings in the coffee houses, and in the open spaces there would be a *bayram*, a fair with amusements for the children. And Emre, after his injury, with time to fill, had got in the habit of mounting shadow plays: his own adaptations of traditional stories for his nephews and nieces and their neighbourhood friends, and bawdy shows for the adults. His art was simple but his storytelling good, and the work gave him and his family a good deal of pleasure. And it had become a key part of how he had rebuilt his life.

Emre had perforce come to spend much of his time in the home of his parents, deep in the heart of that ramshackle part of Constantinople south of the Golden Horn which foreigners then called by the archaic name Stamboul. Life after the injury was difficult, of course, but there were consolations. Emre was blessed with loyal brothers and one sister, all older than he was, and a rising generation of nieces and nephews. That was how the writing began; as well as making up shadow plays, he assisted the children with their own school exercises, and wrote out the stories he made up for them. Some of these he placed with a Stamboul newspaper, whose editor encouraged him to do more. His mother, who had survived her husband, probably thought it a foolish endeavour and a waste of time – but then her crippled son, largely bedridden, now had nothing *but* time, and why not let him waste it?

Emre could hardly be a roving reporter. But he soon discovered he could journey in time, with the help of books his family bought or borrowed for him. He wrote topical pieces on aspects of the city's history, and later graduated to better-paid work for guide books for the foreigners who swarmed through Constantinople: visitors so eager, in recent years, to prove themselves friends to the Ottomans and not foes, thanks to the oil.

Emre, helpless, followed the news. The Schlieffen War had threatened to destabilise the already crumbling Ottoman empire almost as much as it had the Russian, but it seemed to Emre that in recent years the situation had grown calmer. The Sultan had been restored, to no great enthusiasm. The British insisted on their 'protectorates', to ensure access to the Suez canal and the oil of Mesopotamia, but otherwise kept themselves to themselves. The Germans, meanwhile, had proved themselves useful allies at least in the short term – fighting to fend off Russia's ambitions to own Constantinople itself. Allies in the short term: perhaps you could hope for no more than that.

But now, in the middle of this complex swirl of history and ambition, the Martians had landed.

Constantinople was almost unique in the Lightning War in that the first cylinders of the Martians' invasion party fell within the bounds of the city itself, landing in that more modern part of the city north of the Golden Horn known dismissively by the locals as *Frengistan* – 'Foreigner Town'. Hotels, business centres and embassies had been flattened indiscriminately, and few of the surviving Turks mourned.

Soon, though, the Martians had been ready to move.

They advanced through the districts of Pera and Galata. And then the fighting-machines simply waded through the waters of the Golden Horn, north of the new German-built Galata Bridge, and into the old city. Centuries before, the ancient Roman city walls had been no defence against the Turks with their gunpowder weapons; now they proved no obstacle to the Heat-Ray. It is to be wondered if the Martians sensed anything of the antiquity of the quarters into which they probed, the cowls of the fighting-machines over the dusty houses and bazaars, and the ancient, glittering mosques. But then, I suppose, to a race as antique as the Martians, even Constantinople is as evanescent as a traveller's pitched tent.

The Martians' advance into Stamboul was a shock to the inhabitants; communications in much of the empire, even the older parts of the capital, were still primitive in 1922. When the fighting-machines came an alarm had been sounded, the local police running from house to house and ringing bells. One of Emre's brothers, dragging his children behind him, had come to the door to collect their mother.

It was unfortunate that Emre was missed, and left behind. In his room at the back of the house, a wounded soldier too stubborn and proud to call out, he stayed where he was.

So it was that when the Martians came to his neighbourhood, Emre was entirely alone.

The first he saw of them was a kind of slim pillar passing his window. He realised later that he had seen the leg of a fighting-machine, picking its way through the dilapidated neighbourhood, as an adult might step cautiously across a carpet strewn with toys.

Emre had a vehicle of his own, a kind of low cart made for him by one of his brothers – practical, but hated by Emre, for it was like a beggar's chariot. Still, now he used his strong arms to lift himself down from his bed and onto the cart, and rolled through the deserted house to the front door.

Something was coming down the street.

Emre saw a thing like a swollen metallic spider, so huge it all but filled the narrow street, side to side, but its five limbs carried it over the cobbles with uncanny grace. As it passed, tentacular limbs probed into the houses to either side, through the open doors and windows. And what Emre thought was a sack of leather was riding on its back. This was the controlling Martian. It was a standard tactic in some parts of the world: the Martians sent in their handling-machines to explore densely inhabited neighbourhoods, in advance of destroying them – or perhaps in search of feedstock, a fate that, fifteen years before, had so nearly had befallen Walter Jenkins and the curate in the ruined house in Sheen.

The Martian seemed to spot Emre. It stopped, freezing to an eerie stillness. Emre too waited, sitting on his cart, as the Martian sat on its own machine. They were strange shadows of each other, Emre thought, each dependent for movement on a mechanical aid.

Afterwards, Emre would always wonder how the encounter would have worked out, if not for the child.

It was a boy, barefoot, aged no more than five or six – Emre wasn't sure if he knew him – somehow left behind in the evacuation. Now he stumbled from a doorway. He looked around, and then started running towards Emre, presumably the only adult he had seen all morning.

Emre reacted quickly. He waved his arms. 'Get back!'

But the Martian was almost as fast. Emre saw, from the corner of his eye, a metallic limb hold out a cylinder – it was a Heat-Ray projector – and sweep it through the air like a wand. Walls exploded, windows shattered, wooden frames burst into sudden flame.

And the near-invisible beam brushed the child.

Emre was not the only Turk to encounter Martians that day. After the invasion of England in 1907 the great Islamic empire had studied the Martians as a potential enemy, for, among much other damage, they had destroyed the Shah Jahan mosque in Woking, the first mosque in Britain, and the Sultan had sent aid to that community. Even now a brave young officer called Mustafa Atatürk was leading a force in defence of the ancient and glorious Ayasofya – and later this heroism would be a platform for Atatürk, rehabilitated under the Sultanate and encouraged by the Federation of Federations, to achieve great things on a world stage. Constantinople itself was resilient; it had survived invasions, the fall of empires, earthquakes, fires, and in recent decades coups and counter-coups. It would survive even an invasion from another world.

But at that moment Emre knew none of this. He was alone against the Martians – but not powerless.

Emre had been crippled for ten years, but he was only thirty years old, and still strong in his upper arms. Enraged by the wanton murder of the child, paddling at the road's cobbles, he used all his strength to hurl himself at the Martian. Perhaps he could smash a hole in that great fleshy lump in the top of the machine before he was killed.

But the Martian coolly regarded him, from lidless eyes. Then it turned and receded from his view, effortlessly outrunning him, before Emre had to give up, exhausted.

It was some time before Emre had the courage to seek out the remains of the child. And he found, in a peculiar irony, a strange shadow play. So rapidly had the Heat-Ray passed – and perhaps it was on some reduced setting for the safe use by its controlling Martian in such an enclosed space – that it had incinerated the child entirely, but had merely scorched the surface of a wall behind.

And so a kind of inverted shadow of the child remained, caught running in his final moment, as if painted on the darkened wall.

17

Above Durban

'*Ulla! Ulla!...*'

The Martian cry was heard around the world, in the Americas, in Australia, in Asia – in Africa.

It was in the early morning of that Saturday, on a foothill of the Drakensberg Mountains, high above Durban – and with the Martian machines still ravaging the city below – that Gopal Tilak came upon the Zulu woman. She sat alone, a small pile of belongings at her side, the morning light on her rather expressionless face.

I met Gopal Tilak much later, when I was visiting the ruins of Bombay, only to happen by chance upon this eyewitness to the destruction of Durban. By the time I met him Gopal had become a prominent lawyer advising a newly independent Indian government on the proper application of the human rights legislation imposed by the Federation of Federations in Basra. In the calm environs of a very English tea shop on the outskirts of Bombay, Gopal would tell me of that dreadful morning, and his accidental meeting in the foothills.

He had judged the woman to be perhaps thirty years old, more than ten years younger than himself. She did not seem to have noticed him coming. The world was quiet, up there; the detonation of the buildings and the screams of the people of the city were whispers on the wind. He could still make out, however, rising from a dozen places, the ugly, discordant cry of the Martians: '*Ulla...*'

He coughed, so as not to alarm her; the sound seemed magnified in the silence.

She turned her head, glanced at him, turned away with no apparent interest.

He said to her, in English, 'May I join you?'

'I do not own hill.'

'Quite so.' In fact, he knew, the native folk were allowed to own land in only seven per cent of the territory of the Union of South Africa. And here he was thinking like a lawyer, even now; on such a morning as this, surely it was only common humanity that mattered.

Moving stiffly, he sat beside her. He wore a suit, dusty now and the tie long loosened, and his patent leather shoes, meant for carpeted city offices rather than rough hikes, were badly scuffed. He was not unfit, he played a little cricket, but he was new to the way of life of the refugee. This woman, he instinctively felt, presumably after a life of toil, was more sturdy than he.

'I have water,' he said.

'I too. We share. Water is scarce just here.'

'Thank you. And food? I have some biscuits...'

'Are you hungry?'

'No.' He sighed. 'Though I should be, I suppose, it is a long time since I ate.' He carried a satchel; long emptied of books and other weighty objects, now it held little but the identity papers which had to be carried throughout the British Empire, a few biscuits, a flask of water. He took the flask, sipped from it, and offered it to the woman. 'I was on a train coming into Durban. I have been advising on employment rights for the Indian population here. I have been trying to leave this country since the news of the Martian attacks in America. I wished to travel home, to Bombay, but the Martians fell *there* some hours ago. And now the Martians are in Durban too!' He laughed bitterly. 'I am a lucky man. Before we reached the city my train stopped, the crew wished to turn back. But I need to get to the coast, to the ships...'

'You walked.'

'Yes,' he said. He hesitated. 'My name is Gopal Tilak.'

She nodded. She said her name was Nada, and a surname that he would later not recollect.

'"Nada". Is that an unusual name?'

She shrugged. 'My mother, worker on a farm. The farmer's wife, she give me name. Nada. Name from a book. Means "nothing" in some tongues. Thought that was funny. Later I read book.'

'You speak English—'

'Afrikaans better.'

'You read and write.'

'And count. Family workers on farm, in the country. I work in a company in the city. Exports diamonds.'

Diamonds, and the gold of the Transvaal, Gopal reflected: the huge mineral wealth of this country that flowed out into the world, mostly benefiting the British who owned the mining rights.

She said now, 'When Martians came—'

'You decided to walk home? Just like me. It's just that we're walking in opposite directions.'

She looked at him. 'Know Durban?'

'Not well. My work mostly took me inland, to the towns, the villages. That's where most of the problems are in this strange stitched-together country, of Afrikaners, Indians – and Zulus like yourself.'

'Zulus here first. Now everything taken away.'

'I know,' he said with some passion. 'Ten years ago, more, I worked with Mohandas Gandhi. Do you know of him? English-trained lawyer who led campaigns for the rights of the Indians here. Passive resistance – that was his tool; we call it *satyagraha* in our language. You just down tools and refuse. But even as we won our small victory, a much greater injustice was being legislated into existence – I mean, the institutionalised discrimination against the native majority.' He regretted his rather complex language, but she seemed to understand.

'Gandhi? Where now?'

'Went back to the Raj, to advance the rights of our countrymen on our own soil.'

'In Bombay?'

'I hope not.' He closed his eyes then, and tried to imagine Bombay as it must be now. Gopal came from a well-to-do family from Delhi, but as a young man he had moved to Bombay for the commercial possibilities of a city that had grown huge under the British, and he had come to love it: the sprawling old quarters, the giant cotton mills of the industrial zones, even the great administrative buildings of the British. And then there was the scent of it, of the spices of cooking, of the sandalwood burned at the festivals. Well, more than sandalwood would be burning in Bombay this terrible morning.

'Can't fight Martians,' Nada said now. 'Just wait until go away. What was word?'

'What word? Oh – *satyagraha*.'

She repeated it with relish, syllable by syllable. '*Satyagraha.* Wait until go away. Then take land back.'

She was right, Gopal thought. But even if the Martians could be beaten, they would leave human affairs everywhere stirred up, as if with a giant spoon. Nothing would be the same, anywhere in the world, he supposed.

Nada stood. 'Now I go home.'

He stood with her. They scrupulously shared out the water they carried between them, then shook hands rather gravely, and she walked away, deeper into the hills.

Gopal waited until the Martians' main attack seemed to be over. Then he worked his way towards the outskirts of Durban.

As it happened the Martians themselves withdrew before Gopal reached the city. And he was intrigued to learn later, so he would one day tell me, that they had been seen heading north, a great ambulatory army of them, making steadily, it seemed, for the forested heart of Africa.

18

Outside St Petersburg

'Ulla! Ulla!...'
Heard in every continent, that day, from east to west, and south to north – from southernmost Africa to the far north of Russia...
'Ulla! Ulla!...'

At midnight the Martians had landed at Tosno, some thirty miles south-east of St Petersburg. In retrospect Andrei Smirnov would reflect that Martians coming to Mother Russia ought to have been strange enough. But, for him, it got stranger.

In his barracks in the city, Rifleman Smirnov had happened to be awake, and had seen for himself the cylinders pass across the sky, streaks of light like so many green shooting-stars. Most of the men in the barracks, sleeping as best they could, had missed it. Even when the word got around, and those who woke were told the strange news, most of them didn't care. Martians were England's problem; Germans were Russia's.

St Petersburg, Russia's capital, sat on a fat isthmus between Lake Ladoga to the east, and the Gulf of Finland and the Baltic to the west. In this eighth year of a long war the German divisions had pushed through Finland and come on the city from the north, evidently intent on taking the capital at last, in a bold and demoralising coup. But the Imperial Army had responded well. The Germans had been held north-west of the city, at a line that had since solidified in miles of trenchworks and wire and artillery emplacements, backed up by rougher ditches and wooden barricades assembled by civilian squads. But they were German invaders stuck like a knife deep in the belly of Russia.

This particular night the men in Smirnov's unit, on a rest

rotation, had been holed up in what had been a school hall a few streets behind the Pushkin Theatre. They were far behind the lines, in fact inside the city itself, on the southern bank of the Neva, the river that bisected St Petersburg. And when morning came the men, summoned by the bugle, formed up in a yard where no children had played for many months.

Once they were outside the barracks, a sense of general urgency was apparent to the men. Smirnov heard church bells ringing, rousing the population. Something was up.

They soon learned that Smirnov's unit was not being mustered to march back north to meet the Germans, but to go south to face Martians.

Smirnov could feel the fear sweep along the lines, like the passing of a ghost. Andrei Smirnov was a conscript soldier, one of many millions – some said as many as *five* million – mobilised since the Germans' declaration of war. He had seen little action, even since being posted here, to St Petersburg itself. Was he to be spared a German bullet, only to face an interplanetary death?

As it turned out, not that particular day, not for him.

A lieutenant, in a crisp staff officer's uniform, walked along the lines, briefly inspecting the men. He stopped by Smirnov, tapped him on the shoulder and beckoned him away. 'You'll do. This way.'

And in a moment Smirnov's life had changed, and he was set on a path that would lead me, one day, to write to him to ask about his memories of this day.

For now he was just confused, and wary, for no soldier likes novelty; novelty gets you in trouble, or dead. Smirnov looked over to his corporal, but the man shrugged. Smirnov had no choice but to follow the officer.

The lieutenant looked him up and down. 'Your name?'

Smirnov told him.

'Can you ride a motor-cycle?'

'Yes, sir, I—'

'I am an aide to General Brusilov.'

Automatically Smirnov stiffened to a kind of attention.

The lieutenant handed Smirnov a packet of papers, and a small white flag. 'Here are your orders. You are to take a message to the Germans. Am I keeping you awake, soldier?'

'No, sir. I mean – sorry, sir. The Germans, sir?'

'You may have heard of them. Ugly sausage-eaters with pointy hats.'

'Sorry, sir.'

'Naturally we've been trying to get through to them by other means, telegraph, wireless. We do need to communicate from time to time. Probably the wireless will work. *You* are something of a last resort.'

'Very well, sir.' He stood waiting for details.

The lieutenant, who didn't look much older than Smirnov, waved his arms impatiently. 'What are you waiting for, man, a push?'

'But how should I—'

'Ride through the city to the German lines, and wave that bloody flag before the Germans shoot your balls off, and make them read the letters. All right? . . .'

Of course it wasn't as simple as that.

The first part of the assignment was easy enough. On his requisitioned motor-cycle, he took a direct route north-west through the most picturesque part of the city, through Palace Square, across the Neva – from the bridge he had a fine view of the Peter and Paul Fortress, the oldest building in the city, now a prison, and scarred, like so many of the city's landmarks, by the Germans' shelling. Granted, that morning the streets were filling with confused and frightened civilians, so more than once he had to gun his engine and wave to clear a path. Evidently the news was out that the Martians had landed to the south, and of course one would have an impulse to flee – but where to? The north was the obvious route, but the Germans were to the north, they had not magically gone away, and a German bullet would kill you just as effectively as the Martians' Heat-Ray.

By the time Smirnov reached the north-west suburbs, nearer the front line, he was passing along streets that were much more badly damaged, and all but deserted.

Once outside the city proper, he first had to produce his packet of papers when he got to the rear trenches of the Russian line.

He was stopped by a sentry, then taken to a corporal, and then another lieutenant, who read a covering letter with apparent amusement. He looked Smirnov over. 'Sooner you than me carrying this, on such a fine morning. I'll assign a couple of men to cover you – and, Corporal, find him a bloody big stick to wave his flag on, will you?'

So Smirnov found himself disarmed, and sent out through a string of communications trenches to the front line. Then it was up a short ladder and out of the trenches – after the muddy enclosure of the trenchwork, to be out in the sunlight again so suddenly felt like being born – and he was led out by scouts through a gap in the wire.

After that he was on his own, marching through churned-up mud, waving a flag that seemed ever more pathetically small the further out he got. He had been to the front before but not beyond the trenches—

'Halt.'

The word was given in Russian, coarsely accented. A man stood before him, in grey field uniform, mud-splashed as Smirnov's was. Smirnov did not know German insignia well enough to be able to read a rank. His heart hammered. But he said cordially, 'Good morning.'

The man laughed. 'And to you.'

'You speak Russian?'

The German sighed. 'I studied it at university. And my reward is this, a conversation with an idiot, in a position where I am likely to get my head blown in by one of your snipers at any moment.'

'As I by yours.'

'That's true. But you started it. What do you want?'

'Nothing. I come with a gift.' Smirnov held out his pack of papers, now slightly mud-splashed. 'This is for your commanding officer.'

'Ah. A message from the famous General Brusilov, no doubt.'

'As a matter of fact, yes.'

'Who are you, his boyfriend?'

'Just a messenger.'

The German took the papers, and eyed him shrewdly. 'I think we both know what this is about. And what do you think Brusilov has to say, Private?'

Oddly, Smirnov hadn't thought that through. 'If I were the General, I would suggest that you Germans lower your arms and join us in a fight against a common foe.'

The German nodded. 'Just so. Because it will take them mere minutes to burn their way through your peasant army. Together at least we may slow them a little longer – is that the calculation?'

'I'm just the messenger.'

The German considered the papers. 'If it were up to me,' he

said, 'I would join you, for two reasons. One is our common humanity. And second—'

'Yes?'

'We have heard – it is only rumour, here on the line – that the cylinders have fallen close to Berlin, too.'

'Ah.'

'Germans and Russians, two mighty hosts. If joined together, perhaps even the Martians would find us formidable opponents. Do you think?'

'Maybe.'

The German looked over Smirnov's shoulder. 'Russia is unimpressive. It is only – what, sixty years? – since serfdom was abolished in your land. Sixty years! Your Tsar still rules—'

'He answers to the Duma now. The convention of 1917—'

'Is that the one where they locked up all the Bolsheviks?'

Smirnov's grasp of politics was poor. 'Who?'

'And as for your army, you have millions of men in arms, but they are poorly trained, poorly equipped...'

'So poor are we that our city is not yet named "Wilhelmsburg", as your Kaiser boasted it would be years ago.'

The German laughed. 'I give you that. Even if we fight together, the Martians may defeat us. Then what?'

Smirnov grinned. 'Then we retreat, as before Napoleon. No conqueror in history has taken the whole of Russia. It is impossible. As the Martians too will find.'

'Hah! Well, I must take your letter to my commander, who will give it to his commander, and then to the generals, who are probably speaking by field telephone to Brusilov already... I look forward to marching down the Nevsky Prospekt side by side with you, my friend.'

'What is your name?'

'Voigt. Hans Voigt.'

'I am Andrei Smirnov. Farewell, Hans Voigt.'

'Farewell, Andrei.'

They saluted each other, each in his style, turned on their heels, and parted.

19

The Advance From the Elbe

By the time of Smirnov's meeting with Hans Voigt, the Martians had indeed fallen on Berlin, or close to it.

Walter Jenkins, making telephone calls and listening to the wireless, huddled in his nest of charts, maps and calculations, took some time to establish that the Martians had come down on the north bank of the Elbe, near the town of Dessau, some seventy miles south-west of Berlin itself. Walter did not drive – he had always felt, he said, that his nerves were not up to it – but, having been a refugee once, he travelled with a motorist's pocket atlas of local roads tucked into his overcoat pocket. A glance at this was sufficient to show that the Martians' obvious line of attack on central Berlin would be a straight advance to the north-east – which would bring them close to Dahlem, or even through it, and other suburbs at this south-western corner of the conurbation.

Therefore Walter had to flee.

He washed his face, splashing cold water to try to induce wake-fulness. Part of him regretted now his lack of sleep for so long.

He did not leave in a panic, as he might once have done; he always said he remembered the lessons of his time with Albert Cook fifteen years earlier, when the two of them had sought to cross a Martian-infested Surrey. Having tidied away his notes in a stout fireproof box, he donned his coat and cloth cap and heavy walking boots, and he filled his pockets with his various medicines and creams, and with bread and cheese, and matches, an electric torch, a pocket knife – and a pack of cigarettes with which to win friends. He had his pocket atlas, and a German phrase book to back up his own faulty grasp of the language. And he had a notebook and pencils; he never travelled without a means of recording his adventures, or more specifically his inner musings.

An outside observer would have thought him leisurely over these preparations. It will always be a puzzle to me how conscious Walter was or not of his own decision-making at such times – for, of course, every hour wasted brought peril closer to his door.

He scribbled a quick note to the villa's owners and left it on the kitchen table, weighed down by an empty coffee mug. Then he glanced around with some regret at his maps and calculations and logs.

It was seven a.m. by the time he emerged from the house, under a clear sky. He locked the door carefully behind him, pocketing one key and hiding a spare on a lintel. Then he dug his bicycle out of its shelter at the side of the villa, near the potting sheds. This was a Raleigh, a solid English make which he had had imported at considerable expense; only two days before he had oiled the chain and checked the tyres.

Here was Walter Jenkins, caught for the second time in his life between an advancing Martian force and a vulnerable human city.

It was already an hour since, to the south-west – if they had kept to the timetable that they had used around the world – the Martians had left their pit, and they must already be on the move; already humans must be dying as they flung themselves in the face of that advance. If he were rational, he knew, he would get out of the way altogether – head west or east, to Wustermark or Schönefeld perhaps. But if Freud and his disciples had taught Walter one thing about himself, it was that whatever drove him at times like this was deeper than the rational. Once he had walked straight into a London he believed the Martians still occupied. Fifteen years later, so it must be again. In that German dawn, curiosity and dread warred in him; not for the first time, curiosity won. To the heart of Berlin!

He told me he grinned as he climbed aboard that bicycle, and pedalled away.

He headed towards the Rheinstrasse, one of the great highways that leads to the centre of the city.

Long before he got to the junction with the main road he was panting, his legs and backside aching. When the Martians had first come to England he had been forty-one years old; now he was in his late fifties and he felt a lot more used up. But he pedalled grimly, sweating inside his heavy coat.

He saw nothing unusual about the morning, at first. Cars and motor-cycles passed in an orderly fashion, and people came and went, many of them in smart office clothing. This was a suburb of commuters; people would travel by motor-car, tram and bus to jobs in offices and department stores in the centre of the city. Perhaps the Kaiser's government was still giving out reassuring messages: *Work as usual! – the menace will be contained.*

He came upon the first soldiers at the junction with the Rheinstrasse. Walter got off his bicycle to see better.

Trucks and armoured cars and motor-cycles, and a few small artillery pieces, had been gathered at the side of the road. *Landsers* – German tommies in grey greatcoats – stood around smoking and talking quietly, while field wireless sets crackled. In a small park opposite, others were digging, hastily constructing a complicated earthwork. It would be a star-shaped formation surrounded by a trench, with machine guns placed at the corners, and a big Howitzer at the centre.

Walter approached a couple of men beside a battered-looking artillery piece, drawn by a couple of patient horses. Walter chose these men because they weren't smoking; now he produced the pack he had brought for this very purpose. In his clumsy German, he asked, 'You are going to meet the Martians? I heard they landed near Dessau.'

One of the men took Walter's cigarette with no apparent interest in conversation. The other was a corporal, smaller, darker, more shrewd-looking. He said, 'That's what we heard. Waiting for more units to get their backsides out of bed and form up here, and then we advance south-west. Air cover as well, we're promised that.'

'They're on the move, then. The Martians.'

'Out of the Dessau pit, yes.' The German word he used for 'pit' was *Adlerhorst*, 'eagle's nest'. 'We already put up some resistance at Treuenbrietzen. Quite a force coming, apparently. Nobody knows *quite* how many. The scouts were too busy running away to count, probably. But it's said that some of the Martians have peeled off to head for Brandenburg and Potsdam.'

There was a droning noise, high in the sky. Walter glanced up to see a brace of high-flying aeroplanes, heading back the way he had come: scouts, perhaps. 'Soon there will be better information.'

'Yes.'

'Stop them before they get to the city. That the plan?'

The corporal eyed Walter, taking in the residual burn-scars on his face. 'You English?'

'Is it obvious? My German is poor, I know.'

'You seen anything of the Martians over there?'

'Some. Especially the first lot.' He gestured at his face, his gloved hands. 'I got this fleeing from their advance. But I was never a fighting man.'

'Even so,' said the corporal, 'even so, to see them up close... No doubt I'll have the privilege before the day is out.'

'They are overwhelming.'

Again a glint of shrewd intelligence in the man's eye; this was a veteran who would take nothing for granted, and not under-estimate his interplanetary enemy. 'What about you? Where will you go?'

'Into the city.'

The corporal eyed him again, then shrugged. 'Suit yourself.'

There was a revving of engines, a stirring among the men. Walter had seen enough of the military to understand: some-where orders had been issued and received.

The corporal nipped out his cigarette and stored the stub behind his ear. 'Thanks for the smoke. Now you'd better get out of here before my lieutenant requisitions your bicycle.'

20

To the Capital

From Dahlem to central Berlin was only a few miles, but Walter made slow progress. As he neared the centre the roads were increasingly crowded, with motor-cars, buses, even a few horse-drawn vehicles – and with pedestrians: fewer office-worker types by this time, more of them now with the familiar look of refugees, families on the move with children, old folk, suitcases, all heading away from the expected Martian advance. Walter was forced to dismount and push his cycle through the crush. Just as in London in 1907, there were boys selling newspapers, literally hot off the press, bearing the latest news of the coming of the Martians. Every so often, too, an official car would come by, military or police or government, perhaps a black Mercedes with official flags fluttering, and the civilian traffic would squeeze out of the way. There were soldiers everywhere, and police – in short, Walter reflected dryly, a plethora of uniforms.

If the Dahlem commuters had not entirely grasped the signifi-cance of the day, by now Berlin was waking fully to the impli-cation of the extraplanetary force that was approaching. And yet – so far at least – there was none of the sense of the rapid breakdown of society that Walter had observed in London in those dreadful June days of '07. Perhaps he should not have been surprised. Of course, if the Martians came, they would come to Berlin, and of course the Germans would be ready. Nonetheless he was astonished to see a cleaning truck come by, toiling along the gutter, brushes whirling. On such a day! That was Berlin for you.

But even as the truck passed he heard a sound like distant thunder – coming from the west and south, this was surely the sound of guns, big ones – and then came a stink of burning

379

on the breeze. The crowds stirred. There was a greater sense of urgency as the pedestrians pushed on, the motor-cars began to bunch up at blockages and sounded their horns, and soldiers and police shouted commands.

Walter reached Potsdamerplatz, which he thought of as Berlin's equivalent of Piccadilly Circus. Here the traffic was chaotic, the pavements even more crowded. But the brilliant electric advertising panels still glowed brightly in the May morning, and many of the shops and department stores were open, Walter saw, somewhat bemused.

And then, quite unexpectedly, Walter glimpsed a fighting-machine.

Faintly misty in the air it was, rising above the buildings to the north and east of his position – the exact opposite direction from where he would have expected it. He saw that bronze cowl, unmistakable, there and gone, moving out of sight as its animal grace took it away. A brace of aeroplanes tore over the city in that direction, very high.

His first Martian since London! Electrified, Walter began to battle his way north: where the Martians were, *that* was where he wanted to be.

21

With the Martians in Berlin

Walter reached the Ebertstrasse, which runs along the eastern edge of the Tiergarten, the city park. Here, Walter found, by now, people were mostly heading south, away from Martians to the north, and he had to battle to make way – and, after a hundred yards, regretfully, he finally had to abandon his bicycle.

He tried to understand how it was he had seen the Martian machine off to the *north-east*. He had after all been running ahead of their advance from the *south-west*. In the two advances they had made on London, in 1907 and 1920, they had driven more or less directly into the heart of the city. But the fighting-machines were fast, and it was evident that the Martians had become more flexible in their tactics – and indeed, it would be shown retrospectively that the Martians' tactics varied around the planet in this war, responding to differences of geography and human resistance. Perhaps this assault group – which might number hundreds of machines – had split into packs, which were now probing into central Berlin from west, east, even north, as well as directly from the south. This would bring chaos to any evacuation of the city, if all possible escape routes were cut off... And if surrounded, Berlin would presumably be turned into a ghetto by the Martians, and a gruesome larder. Some fate for the capital of Prussia, Germany and Mitteleuropa!

But such thoughts were for the future. For now the great narrator continued to drive himself straight towards the centre of events.

In the park itself – to Walter's recollection mainly memorable before that day for its extensive collection of VERBOTEN signs – civilians had been excluded, and soldiers laboured at trench-works and artillery emplacements. Walter thought he recognised

381

anti-aircraft weapons, even big naval guns, as well as field artillery pieces. But he had no time to pause and study this frantic build-up as he pushed on against the flow.

He reached the Unter den Linden near the Brandenburg Gate. And here, to Walter's surprise, people were marching. Walter saw no old folk here, no children, no invalids in bath chairs; these were not refugees. And nor were they military or police; Walter made out only a handful of uniforms, shining brass helmets, standing back from the crowd warily. These marchers were the ordinary folk of the city, mostly young, male and female alike; they were heading steadily east along the great avenue, they carried the flags of Prussia and Germany, as well as crude weapons, poles and clubs, and they sang as they marched, Germany's anthem, which shared the melody of Britain's own: *'Heil dir im Siegerkranz, / Herrscher des Vaterlands! / Heil, Kaiser, dir!...'*

Walter consulted his traveller's atlas and understood. At the eastern end of the Unter den Linden, over a short bridge onto Museum Island, lay the Stadtschloss, the Kaiser's city palace. Was Wilhelm in residence today? With Berlin under threat, of course he was. And where else would the people gather but at the palace of the conqueror of France and Russia? It was just as crowds came to Buckingham Palace on great days in Britain.

'Fühl in des Thrones Glanz / Die hohe Wonne ganz, / Liebling des Volks zu sein! / Heil Kaiser, dir!...'

On impulse Walter joined the marching throng, heading east. The sun was high now, and, over the heads of the crowd, beyond the rows of leafy trees, the palace was already visible, a blocky mass on the horizon. Walter had always thought he had a side susceptible to persuasion, especially when under stress; he had never forgotten how he had fallen under the spell of Bert Cook, as, on Putney Hill, that undistinguished artilleryman had laid out his plans to defeat the Martians single-handed. Now Walter had to try hard not to lose himself in this marching, singing crowd, in their mass defiance – their mass delusion, he thought, as if a little shouting and a few thousand waved fists might deter an interplanetary invasion. But he had to admit it was a stirring moment.

And then a Martian rose up beyond the palace.

It was clearly visible, silhouetted against the sky, poised over the building like a man standing over a doll's house. And then another, and another, and more beyond, which Walter saw as shadowy, complex pillars. Cowled heads turned this way and that, as if looking around, curious.

As the Martians were spotted, there were shouts, and cries of dismay – and, yes, more yells of defiance, even insults. The procession stumbled to a halt, the crowd compressing, pushing.

And the lead Martian manipulated a cylinder – even so far away, Walter seemed to see every detail: the tentacular appendages cradling the instrument, positioning it carefully.

Of course Walter could see nothing of the Heat-Ray itself, at this distance.

The heart of the palace exploded, a shower of brick and glass and marble.

More fighting-machines stepped in their eerie triple-legged way through the burning ruin, waded easily through the shallow strait that separated Museum Isle from the mainland – and then strode boldly, and with remarkable speed, straight down the Unter den Linden.

The crowd broke, lost its shape, turned into a mass of individuals fleeing or fighting to flee. The uniformed soldiers and police who had been supervising them turned and ran too. At last, Walter thought, pushing his way out of the crush, at last this was the social liquefaction he had seen before, the inevitable collapse of all human organisation before the overwhelming might of the Martian machines. Yet even now one or two resisted the receding tide; they sheltered behind trees and aimed weapons at the advancing Martians, or struggled to improvise barricades from fencing and other debris.

But the Martians came on relentlessly, bowling through the crowd. People were scattered and crushed just by the touch of those mobile, electrified limbs. And the Heat-Ray projectors played, deployed with unerring accuracy and ruthlessness: people flashed and burned, gone in an instant. The screaming began now, the cries of the injured, those whom the Heat-Ray beams had touched more carelessly, scorching off a limb here, turning a back to a crisped cinder there. And now came too-familiar smells: of burned brick, of melting tarmacadam where the Heat-Rays touched the road surface, of roasted flesh.

The guns in the Tiergarten started to speak at last, a rumbling thunder, and bangs from the big Navy weapons shook the very ground. Walter could see the shells rise, threading through the air. One smashed the bronze face of a Martian; the machine staggered and fell – a few in the fleeing crowd saw this and yelled in triumph – and two of its neighbours gave up the pursuit of the human crowd to bend over it, like soldiers solicitous over a fallen colleague. But as always most of the shells were shot out of the sky by the Heat-Ray, far short of their targets. The gunners had to try, Walter realised, the Germans now like the English before them – and, through this last dreadful day and night, like the Americans and Chinese and Russians and Turks – they had to try.

Things worsened rapidly. The recoil from the Martians soon became a stampede, those forward shoving into those behind, and the crowd compressed and became chaotic. Errant shells were landing in the trapped crowd – it seemed the Germans were killing more of their own than were the Martians.

And Walter himself, so the deep-buried survivor part of him pressed now, had to save his own much-abused skin.

He thrust himself into the crowd, pushing back down the Unter den Linden, heading west once more. If he could get past the Brandenburg Gate, which stood before him already, he might yet reach the Tiergarten. There the crowd was fanning out, he could see, keeping away from the military emplacements, making for the shade of the trees. Walter had hidden from Martians before, underwater, in wrecked houses; he could do it again. But the crowd was dense, and the Martian machines, scattering all before them, were coming up behind much too quickly, and the Heat-Rays spat. Walter pushed at the backs of those ahead of him, squirming through the crush.

And now a new noise erupted, coming from beyond the Gate, directly before Walter, a kind of thunder bellowing down from the sky. Shocked, people screamed, ducked, scattered. 'Is it the Martians?' 'More of them?'

Walter, his progress blocked once more, broke out of the crowd and scrambled for shelter under a chestnut tree, whose upper branches were already singed by a lick of the Heat-Ray. There he huddled, his knees against his chest. That shattering noise still poured down from the sky.

And then Walter saw them, through the branches of his tree: aeroplanes, human machines, not Martian.

The centre of the group was an immense bomber, it must have been forty feet long, with four pulsing propeller engines; its course, parallel to the avenue below, was so low it seemed it must clip the top of the Brandenburg Gate, and as it passed over Walter's head the noise from those engines battered at the ground in heavy, thrumming waves. This behemoth had a retinue of smaller planes, fighters, much faster, that darted high in the air or close to the ground, already deploying weapons with a clatter of automatic fire. Later, Walter would learn that the bomber he saw was a Gotha V, the fighters were the nimble, robust craft called Albatros – planes of the type that more than once had crossed the Channel to strike at the Martians in London. German air power had developed out of all recognition in the great crucible of the Russian war. Now these craft flew over the heart of their own capital.

Walter had to see it all, of course. He came out of what little shelter the chestnut tree afforded him, and pushed his way to the edge of the fleeing crowd.

And he saw the fighters duck nimbly through the air, their weapons clattering as they launched themselves at the hoods or limbs of the Martian machines – but their bullets appeared only to bounce off the sturdy bronze hoods of the Martians' carapaces. One by one they were touched by the Heat-Ray, almost tenderly it seemed, their fragile structures crumbled, crisped and burned, and they fell from the air.

But now the big bomber rose up – Walter saw it – and disgorged a load of munitions that rained heavy on the pack of Martians. The Martians fought back, the Heat-Ray projectors swivelled and snapped, but so plentiful was the load of the bomber that some of the munitions got through. The hoods of two Martians, three, four, exploded in dazzling flame. And as fireballs burst around their feet, more Martians staggered and fell, their forward march disrupted at last. The scrambling crowds cheered deliriously.

The bombs used that day were in fact incendiary weapons, called D-class Elektron fire bombs, with casings of magnesium and Martian-manufacture aluminium that burned at a thousand degrees: another product of the eastern front, and tested on hapless Russian flesh. Well, the seals and linkages even of Martian machines were not immune to such temperatures. And even as the first bomber passed on, its load discharged, a deep thrumming announced the approach of a second craft, heading for the line of the Unter den Linden as had the first.

But, as Walter watched, a handling-machine scurried through a fast-scattering crowd to the foot of the Brandenburg Gate. Somehow this machine had dashed ahead of its fellows, even as the taller fighting-machines had been targeted by the aircraft. Now, without hesitation, the handling-machine swarmed up one of the Gate's pillars, like an outsized beetle clambering over a model.

Walter could clearly see the Martian riding the machine, a pulsing grey sack. With apparent ease the machine reached the plinth, and reared up alongside the crowning sculpture, the goddess in her chariot pulled by its four horses. And the Martian raised a bulky cylinder: a Heat-Ray projector.

When the second bomber came over, it seemed to fly straight into the path of the heat beam.

One wing was sliced away, and fuel tanks detonated inside its structure, even as the great craft's momentum carried it on, lumbering over the heads of the crowd. And it began to fall, twisting as its one remaining wing grabbed at the air. The surviving Martians trained their Heat-Rays and the craft burst apart, raining hot shrapnel on the crowd.

Before the last remnants of the bomber reached the ground, Walter was gone and running, past the Gate, away from the triumphant Martian machines and the scattering crowd, and into the shadows of the Tiergarten.

22

A New York Edisonade

In Manhattan, as night had fallen on that very long Friday, though they descended from the Monroe Tower, in the end Harry and Marigold had not dared venture far from Battery Park. The two of them found what appeared to be an abandoned gun emplacement, a grassy pit. Here they huddled under their coats; they drank water and ate biscuits they had brought. At least the night was not cold, and Harry thought he slept a little, though the drifting smoke made him cough.

Once he got up and clambered out of the pit to see the progress of the war. The night was almost pitch dark, and he wondered if smoke obscured the sky, rather than cloud. Much of Lower Manhattan was blacked out, though here and there a building still shone brightly, an isolated jewel – a hospital, perhaps, with its own electric generator. A hulk was burning on the river, perhaps one of the brave battleships slowly dying, casting gaudy reflections from the water.

And on the Brooklyn shore, illuminated by the light of fires which burned unchallenged, he saw fighting-machines at work. They moved cautiously through the ruins now, as if more circumspect. Every so often he could see a slim silhouette bend down, almost gracefully, and those metallic limbs reach out to pluck something from the ground – something wriggling, something screaming perhaps. Just as it had been in England before, here were the Martians harvesting Americans for their grisly repast.

He wondered what the hell else was going on around the world, this terrible night.

He returned with heavy heart to the gun emplacement, huddled against Marigold's warmth, and tried to sleep.

*

He was shaken awake. Suddenly it was daylight. A blackened face loomed over him, grinning.

Harry struggled, but a hand was clamped over his mouth. Beyond, Harry saw Marigold, sitting up, pulling at her tousled hair.

Cautiously, the hand was removed from his mouth.

'Bill Woodward?'

'The very same.'

'I – what time is it?'

'About six in the morning, Harry; you were sleeping pretty deep.'

'Six. On Saturday?'

'Yeah, it's Saturday. I guess we're all exhausted.'

'You went off to Central Park, the Army units...'

'I spent the day killing Martians. Or trying to. We took a pasting,' he said grimly. 'They outnumbered us, two hundred to twenty thousand. But we made damn sure they knew we're here. And the evacuation's proceeding, maybe we saved a few lives. The radio says Babe Ruth got out safely.'

'Well, that's something!'

'And then, towards the end of the day, we had a delivery. Parachute drop. Very brave, very risky.'

'A delivery? Of what?'

Marigold leaned over. 'From Menlo Park, Harry.'

Harry saw now that Woodward had dragged a kind of cart with him, covered by a green Army blanket. Woodward pulled back the blanket to reveal three metal cylinders. He reached over and hefted one of these: perhaps a foot wide, four feet long, wrapped in leather. It looked as if it might be an engine component, or some heavy gun.

'Think you can manage this? It's the latest fruit of Mr Edison's ingenuity.'

'Edison? What are we going to do, throw light bulbs at them?'

Marigold said, 'Oh, rather more than that. Menlo managed to produce fifty of these, and ship them over. Mostly untested, probably half won't go off at all. But if even a fraction of them work we'll have struck a mighty blow. After all we think there are only around two hundred and fifty fighting-machines in the area, so taking out even one—'

Harry sat up and reached for a cylinder. 'Show me.'

Marigold slapped his hand, 'Whoa! Hold your horses, Hopa-long, there's high explosive in there.'

Woodward grinned again. 'We've got work to do. Get up, empty your bladder, eat something – I have coffee—'

'You have *coffee*. In the middle of the end of the world?'

'Not that yet.'

By seven a.m., led by Bill Woodward, the three of them had infiltrated the Lower East Side. It wasn't difficult. There was no power, no traffic moved in the rubble-choked streets, and in some blocks fires burned unchallenged. Martian fighting-machines stood around the precinct like prison watchtowers, but just as in the Cordon in England, it seemed that individual humans were allowed to move to and fro without hindrance, so long as they offered no threat to the Martians.

No *visible* threat.

Woodward led them to a site – Harry believed it was on Allen Street, but it was hard to be sure so extensive was the damage – where the Martians had already begun the construction, in the light of that first morning of occupation, of one of their characteristic redoubts. The excavating-machines had dug a great crater in layers of shattered masonry, cutting through broken-open cellars and stores, even gouging into the granite keel of Manhattan itself. Fighting-machines stood over this pit, some of them empty of their drivers, and busy handling-machines had already begun their efficient processing of American dirt and rock into fine aluminium ingots, preparatory to the construction of new machines and structures. In the shadows individual Martians lurked, shuffling in their heavy, leathery way, and hooting to each other as they avoided the morning sunlight – they were creatures of a colder world than ours. Ruins looked down on this scene, gaunt and eyeless.

And at the centre of the pit were people: men, women and children, perhaps thirty of them, sitting in a huddle. They seemed unconfined, but Harry had no doubt that had they tried to escape they would have been struck down quickly. Instinctively he began to pen character sketches in his head. Most of the captives looked as if they had been inhabitants of the wretched tenements that had stood here: tired-looking women, grimy men, wide-eyed, shoeless children. But there was one soldier, apparently wounded, as helpless as the rest, and a woman in the uniform of a nurse. One mother was trying to speak to the nurse, as if asking for help for the child restless on her lap. But the nurse turned her face away.

The rebels peered at this scene from behind a broken wall.

Woodward growled, 'Livestock to be consumed. Americans! Well, not today. Here's the plan...'

The tactics were simple. Woodward and Harry would take the three bombs to a hole in the ground Woodward had spotted, close to a cluster of machines, probably a blown-open cellar. The bombs themselves would be ignited simultaneously by a wireless signal, sent by Woodward. And while the Martians were hopefully paralysed and confused, Marigold, on the opposite side of the great pit, would call to the prisoners and lead them to freedom.

That was the plan. They quickly got everything into position.

Then, with a feral grin, Woodward counted down. 'Three, two, one—'

It almost worked.

What Edison and his boffins in Menlo Park had come up with was a new kind of bomb. It came out of research into Martian technology, at least of a secondary kind. I suspect Harry never understood it fully, but then, neither do I.

It was, and is, believed that the Martians' energy cells – used to power the Heat-Ray, for example – are based on the extraction of energy from the nuclei of atoms. Einstein and others have shown that in principle the compression of matter to sufficiently high densities will cause it to *fuse* to a secondary state of greater density, a different elemental combination, with tremendous energy being liberated in the process. It is as if, says Einstein, some of the very mass of the fuel has been transformed to energy. This process itself was not well understood before the Second War, and indeed is still not under our control; investigations into the phenomenon dating back to the aftermath of the First Martian War caused terrible accidents, in Ealing, South Kensington and elsewhere.

However, by 1922, it had become clear that the Martians achieved this enormous compression of matter with the use of very powerful electrical and magnetic fields. And our investigations of these comparatively familiar technologies had advanced our own capabilities in these areas by, some would say, decades.

Edison's bomb was called an 'explosively pumped flux compression generator' – a flux bomb, to the soldiers who used it. Its purpose was simple: to produce, for but an instant, in a restricted area, extremely powerful electrical and magnetic fields.

It achieved this by exploring a quirk of electromagnetic physics (a quirk to me! – a miracle of theorising and practical application to the physicists, I dare say). If you have a magnetic field, and surround it with a conductor – say, a band of copper wire – and then you *contract* that band, the magnetic flux through the conductor, contained by the wire, will stay the same strength – but its *intensity*, you see, the density of that power, as it is squeezed, must become much higher. It's as simple as that, and you can demonstrate the principle with a schoolroom experiment, using an electromagnet and a few bits of wire.

Now scale it up. Wrap your conductor and your magnetic field in a few packets of high explosive. Set that off in a careful design so that the explosive forces push inwards – and the compression of the magnetic field becomes enormous, if only for an instant, before the whole thing blows itself apart . . .

The point is, as Edison realised, that Martian machines depend on electrical fields for their operation. The great legs of a fighting-machine, for instance, have what Walter Jenkins once described as a 'sham musculature' comprised of discs inside a sheath of elastic. When an electric field is applied, these discs, polarised, are drawn together or pushed apart. The result is the smooth and remarkably graceful motion of any Martian machine, from the march of a fighting-machine to the finest of the manipulative tentacles of a handling-machine – and all of it controlled by electromagnetic fields. But if those fields were disrupted, by a sufficiently powerful electromagnetic pulse nearby . . .

I am told, by witnesses from Menlo Park itself, that the devices Bill Woodward brought to Harry and Marigold, packages each easily carried by a single person, could produce pulses in the tens of terawatts and the millions of amperes: that is, more powerful than a lightning strike. Once Bert Cook had described the use of human artillery against the Martians as 'bows and arrows against the lightning.' Now, in the course of the defence of New York, humans at last turned the lightning on the Martians.

The detonations themselves seemed overwhelming to Harry, huddling by a wall. They left him with a ringing in his ears that persisted for days.

When he emerged from cover he found that only two of their bombs had worked. But those two had done tremendous damage to the Martians. Even as Harry watched, one of the great fighting-machines fell like cut timber, legs stiff as wood, and crashed down into an already ruined house. The other machines seemed paralysed, the busy excavators and handlers frozen in their tracks. The living Martians, stuck in their machines, tried to scramble out, and hooted to each other in dismay, and Harry wondered what messages of fear or rage were passing telepathically between them.

Marigold picked up a rock. 'They're helpless. We can kill them before the machines recover – if they do.'

But Woodward held her arm. 'No. Some of the machines survived, you can see that. All it would take would be one working Heat-Ray gun... We've done what we came to do. Let's get those civilians out of there.'

As the human party hastily left the pit, they saw more fighting-machines converging, travelling down the rubble-strewn streets to come to the aid of their fellows. It was evident that despite the blow they had struck, and the detonation of similar bombs across the occupied territory, Manhattan still belonged to the Martians.

'But it's a start,' Woodward said grimly. 'Americans fighting back, at last. A start!'

23

A World Under Siege

Having no better plan after the Martian triumph in Berlin, Walter Jenkins joined the ragged crowds fleeing from the centre of the city, and out into the suburbs and beyond. From there Walter retraced his steps – and, somewhat to his own surprise, made it back to his rented house in Dahlem.

It was still only the early afternoon of that extraordinary Saturday.

By now Walter was a veteran of such situations. He made for his study, gathered up equipment, and hauled it down to a cellar used only for storing coal, firewood and a rack of wine – he even managed to drag a telephone receiver down there, its cable stretched along the cellar stairs. He made one last foray above ground for water and food. Then he retired to his improvised bunker, listening to a battery-powered wireless set, trying to make calls on the telephone, and making obsessive notes by candle-light.

Thus, through the Saturday night and into the Sunday, Walter renewed his witnessing of the Second War.

He learned that by noon of that Saturday – noon London time, that is – urgent reports had been received via the transoceanic telegraph and telephone lines of the Martians' attack on Buenos Aires. Their strategy had followed its by now customary course, with a landing at local midnight – that is, in the small hours of Saturday morning, London time – some distance inland along the valley of the Rio de la Plata, and then at local dawn an advance on the city. Images later returned were particularly vivid: of the Martians smashing the huge grain elevators that lined the banks of the river, of fighting-machines standing proud over the vast La Negra slaughterhouse, of the rich elite crammed aboard the

393

frigorificos, the giant refrigerated ships within which Argentinian beef is exported. And the poor had to fend for themselves as the poor always do. (A romantic tale, by the way, of a band of gauchos riding out and using their *bolas* to trip fighting-machines turned out to be just that – a tale.)

So much for the Argentine capital. But this was the last of the Martian incursions; since the first landfall on Long Island, a twenty-four-hour cycle of landings and assaults had been completed.

By midday of the Saturday, then, the earth was stitched about by pinpoint Martian attacks – knots and scrapings of fire that could surely have been seen by an observer on Mars itself – with ten landings having occurred in the Americas, Africa, Europe, Asia, even Australia, and comprising a thousand cylinders in all. Human attempts at organised resistance had proved all but futile, just as they had been in England in '07 or '20. Such innovations as the Americans' flux bombs and the Germans' incendiaries might have enabled humanity to take the war to the invaders a little longer, given time.

But to Walter a rapid disruption of human civilisation and organisation seemed assured, and the unending domination of the earth by the Martians inevitable.

The next day, everything changed.

24

The Revenge of the Martians

In New York, around nine on Sunday morning, Harry Kane, Marigold Rafferty and Bill Woodward sat in Battery Park, where Harry and Marigold had been camping for two nights now, and surveyed what they could see of Lower Manhattan and Brooklyn. Some fires still burned, the rivers were still littered with wrecks. They were eating German sausages from cans looted by Woodward, and drinking coffee they had boiled up in a saucepan over an open fire. It was another fine, bright day, the weather belying the state of the city.

Marigold was using her binoculars. 'I still see no fighting-machines. Maybe your squawk-box is telling the truth, Bill.'

Woodward had purloined an Army field-wireless kit from the corpse of a signals officer, and had been trying to follow the progress of the war. 'Well, they are still moving. As Patton predicted, they broke out of Manhattan to the north and are already in Connecticut. Reports say they've got as far as Peekskill on the Hudson, and Danbury on the Housatonic. They may not go much further north; the land is bad up there. The intelligence guys think the Springfield Armory in Massachusetts must be a target – biggest in the country, and we know they did their scouting before the landings. One group looks as if it's considering an advance to Hartford, maybe even to Boston.

'And there's another group heading south-west, maybe making for Philadelphia, Baltimore, Washington, DC. The Army set a trap at a place called Grovers Mill, New Jersey, and they've been held up there. But—'

'But wherever else they are, they withdrew from Manhattan.'

'Thanks to Edison's bombs,' Marigold said with a grin.

Woodward nodded. 'If you think about it, they reacted just

395

as they did before, in England. I read the history. In Surrey in '07, the first time an artillery shell knocked one of them over – I bet they weren't expecting us even to be capable of that – they rescued their wounded and withdrew to their pits for a while. Just as here. We bloodied their non-existent noses and they pulled back.'

Looking into the east, Harry thought he saw something in the sky, over Brooklyn and Long Island, like a cloud perhaps, in an otherwise cloudless heaven. No, it was too dark to be a cloud, and moving too quickly. If not a cloud, then what? A Zepp?

Marigold said now, 'Fighting-machines or not, I haven't seen much in the way of rescue work and such.'

'You will,' Woodward said. 'It takes time to move resources on this kind of scale; you got a whole city down here . . .'

Not one cloud but three. Black as night, solid. And they seemed to be scattering some kind of dark rain below.

Approaching fast. Not clouds at all.

'Oh, damn.'

Marigold raised her eyes comically. 'Harry! Not in front of the US Army.'

But Harry wasn't about to smile. He pointed. 'They're coming back.'

Marigold shaded her eyes from the sun.

Bill Woodward got to his feet, fumbling for his own binoculars. 'Flying-machines. Spotters always say they're bigger than they look, and further away, and faster than you think.'

Marigold said, 'They'll be here soon enough. And that black stuff they're scattering – it looks as if it's pooling on the ground, like the smoke from dry ice. Swirling around the buildings.'

Harry nodded. 'The British call it the Black Smoke. A new variant, resistant to water. You can slaughter whole populations with the stuff, easier than the Heat-Ray. But it's only been used on a limited scale over there, this time anyhow. They want to knock us out of the fight, but not to kill us all, it seems. But, the British found out, if you resist, you get whacked.'

Marigold said grimly, 'New York resisted. And here's our reward.'

And Harry Kane felt true fear, for the first time in the war – perhaps in his life, he would say. All he had experienced so far, even in the midst of the fury, had left him exhausted, wrung out, but oddly untouched. Somehow he had always believed he would come through this intact, no matter what happened to those around him. As if he were invulnerable and immortal. Perhaps all young people have such illusions.

The coming of the flying-machines changed all that. For Harry, the Black Smoke, an approaching wall on that Sunday morning, was like the advance of death itself, implacable, unavoidable. Harry thought he was doomed, the earth itself lost.

Well, he was wrong, as Walter was. For I had fulfilled my own mission.

25

A Player of the Game

On the Friday afternoon, after debarking inside the Martian Cordon from the landship *Boadicea* with Lieutenant Hopson, I had quickly got in touch with Marriott once more, and through him his network of resistance fighters. Meanwhile, following Eric's orders, the surviving underground telephone lines into the Cordon had been fizzing with new instructions to the troops stranded there.

I have never been sure if Marriott believed my hasty account as to *why* I wished him to use his stock of explosives in one great earth-shaping exercise. He may have had his pompous side but he was a hard-headed, practical man, and determined to take the fight to the Martians as best he could, and good for him; now he cavilled at the fact that this operation would not be hitting the Martians directly. But I think, paradoxically, he liked to be given an assignment from authorities to which he still believed himself accountable, and loyal. He relished the thought of such a technically complex set-up, being part of an operation that included many of the regular troops trapped inside the Cordon with him. And, more than that, he liked the sheer symbolism of it.

After all – what a gesture! A communication intended to be seen across space!

Whatever he was feeling, after I persuaded him to my cause Marriott and his scattered army immediately got to work. It took them much of the rest of the Friday to plan it – I had found him late – and much of the Saturday to move the explosive caches into place, all across the Cordon, all beneath the gaze of the Martians. Still, everything was ready by the morning of the Sunday. After some final checks, and with a last co-ordination with the military authorities, Marriott, by phone, sent the messages to his *franc-tireurs* to detonate at noon.

So it came to pass.

That Sunday lunchtime, all across the Cordon – and even within the Amersham Redoubt itself – the Martian earthworks were disrupted by a series of blasts, carefully placed. It could never be complete, never perfect – there was not the time, some of the bombs failed, and the explosives were placed under conditions of extreme peril, whether by regulars or the *franc-tireurs*, and so the accuracy of placement was never faultless. What was done was good enough, nevertheless, and the stratagem was effective. Aerial photos taken before and after the blasts show it clearly.

That morning the Martians' earthworks, as imaged at eight thirty a.m., had undeniably sketched a set of sigils, some miles long, incomplete but near-perfect copies of that sinuous marking humans had first perceived on the faces of Venus and of Mars, after the Martians' invasion of the younger planet – and that later, through the scholarship of Walter Jenkins, had been made out in the unfinished pattern of pits the Martians had dug into the ground of Surrey in the year 1907. This was the Martians' brand of conquest. But in the afternoon, by the time the dust and smoke had cleared, these sigils had been disrupted, blasted apart – and they had been replaced by *circles*, on all scales, far from perfect but the intent clear. At noon on Sunday, then, we humans replaced that Martian brand upon the earth, not with a symbol of our own – *but with a Jovian sigil*, the circle, that figure of infinite symmetry which the astronomers had seen burn in the clouds of Jupiter itself.

And a couple of hours later the Martians began to respond.

In Battery Park, meanwhile, in those last moments, as the flying-machines approached, the three companions stood in a line and held hands, Woodward and Harry to either side of Marigold.

Marigold said, 'Old Bigelow will never know what he started when he invited the three of us to that party – was it only on Thursday night? It seems a different world.'

'Do you regret it?' Woodward asked. 'Resisting, I mean. The flux bombs. We probably could have got out of here...'

'Hell, no,' Harry said.

Marigold smiled. 'Ditto,' she said firmly. 'And, you know...'

And then something changed.

The fall of Black Smoke stopped abruptly.

The flying-machines broke formation. Huge dishes in the sky, they swept round in wide curves, and receded as quickly as they had come, growing smaller, vanishing into the mists of morning – gone in minutes. The last of the Black Smoke, dispersing, blew harmlessly out over the water.

Harry felt a surge of emotion, of relief; he would say he had not understood the depths of his fear until it receded. But he felt utter bafflement at still being alive.

'What just happened?'

26

Armistice

At that point it was around three p.m. in Berlin. And Walter Jenkins, huddled in the cellar of his house, was immediately aware of a change in the Martians' behaviour. It was a silencing of their movements, he said, a kind of slithering withdrawal. That cry, '*Ulla!*', heard all over the planet that terrible day, now seemed more plaintive – and receding.

He pushed out of his cellar and – heart thumping, for he could not be sure of his deductions – he emerged into the light of a German afternoon. Other people stood by, in the wrecked street, dusty, bewildered, some injured – all watching. And Walter saw the fighting-machines, tall and graceful, receding steadily from the city – heading north. All this in his first glance.

In that moment I think he guessed what must have been done – what *I* must have done – emulating my own intuitive leap. Well, it had started out as his idea, even if I had thought it through in the end. And he even guessed correctly at the timing of its completion: about noon British time.

He hurried home to his cellar to try to verify his theories, praying that the telephone would be working.

Of course it was all guesswork, in the end – about how the Jovians might respond. Educated guesswork, though.

What did the Jovians want? When the Martians invaded Earth and Venus, had the Jovians set up the circle sigils in their own clouds and moons as a warning to the squabbling races that Jupiter must remain inviolate? And, worse, to ensure their own future survival, must the Jovians one day fight a war to dislodge the destructive, meddling, expansive Martians from this earth, and even from Venus?

My intent, when I imagined creating those great signals of dirt and explosive, was that with one bold gesture we would proclaim this earth *an ally of Jupiter*, in that epochal combat to come. And evidently, in response, the Jovians gave the Martians some warning, or instruction, and the invaders had no choice but to withdraw. Thus, for once and only once in my life, I had thought in terms, not of a ground war, but of an interplanetary context – and that was how I sought a solution. Call it a *deus ex machina* if you wish, like the bacteria which had slain the Martians in '07. This time, *I* summoned down those gods from their machinery!

My signal was created at noon, London time. The Martians did not withdraw until two p.m., roughly. Why the delay of two hours? – a lag which caused many of us intense anxiety as we lived through it, as I can testify.

Walter, so he told me later, would have predicted some such pause. Jupiter is five times further from the sun than the earth; the distance between the planets is never less than some four hundred million miles at the closest, never further than six hundred million miles at the furthest. And so it would take a ray of light never less than thirty-four minutes to cross from the earth to Jupiter, and thirty-four minutes back again.

Walter, for one, is convinced that the Jovians, whose capabilities must vastly exceed even the Martians, must scrutinise our earth and our own comings and goings in great detail – and not remotely, as if through some vast telescope, a view to which the Martians seem to have been restricted, but close up. I imagine a swarm of invisible, artificial eyes peering down at our world; surely it is more subtle than that, as unimaginable to us as the mechanics of a microscope would be to swarming life forms in a drop of water.

But how are those observations to reach Jupiter itself? Einstein has proved that nothing in this universe can travel faster than a ray of light. Whether God could surpass the speed of light I will never know, but even the Jovians have limitations! And therefore any Jovian response to our signal, our violent scrawling of Jovian sigils in the English soil, could *not* have been expected to come in less than an hour after we had created the sigil. For it takes that time, you see, for any signal to travel from our earth to Jupiter and back again.

But, delay or not, it had worked; the withdrawal of the Martians seemed to prove it. We had intervened in a conflict on an interplanetary scale. We had called in the Jovians, as a bullied schoolboy might call in an uncle to save himself from a beating.

It had worked.

When he came back to England a few weeks later, and we met, Walter cackled with pride at the thought of it – he gave me full credit for the inspiration, but of course the well of it had been his own deep thinking – and the next minute he all but wept at our temerity, *my* temerity. I think actually he was a little afraid of me. For – what had we done?

What had *I* done?

I had brought humanity, irrevocably, into the grave awareness of Jupiter. The Jovians are older than us, and, we must deduce, immeasurably more intelligent, immeasurably more wise. We may *hope* they will be like a kindly celestial uncle. But, Walter says, even if so, there is no reason to believe that what *they* see as benevolence will translate into what we may experience as kindness, even mercy. Thus a child weeping over a sick mother could never imagine the moral choices that confront a battlefield doctor in triage.

Yet on reflection, Walter still felt we had had no choice. The Jovians *might* spare us; the Martians certainly would not have.

And still, on that fateful Sunday and in the days and weeks that followed puzzles remained.

The hostilities ceased immediately; the Martians everywhere withdrew. They left their Cytherean feedstock behind, along with any surviving human victims, but they seem to have taken their own native humanoids with them. Just as it had been in England in '07, the slow, sad work of recovery began.

And slowly, too, parties of military and scientists and various officials approached the great Martian earthworks. They were empty – the Martians gone – and stripped this time of technology, of the cylinders and all they had brought, all that had been manufactured.

Yet the question remained – for we knew, as I will relate in due course, that only a fraction had left this earth – *where had the Martians gone?*

And then, what of our still greater neighbours? They had saved us, if indirectly – but how? It was evident that the Jovians, alerted by our crude sigils, had sent some kind of commandment, to the Martians. But how? What had been sent, what received?

In the end, the answer to that became obvious. At that time, late in May 1922, the moon was a crescent, dwindling towards a new moon. *And the moon had changed*, as even the naked eye could see. In the darkened sector of the disc, a fine line could be made out: an arc, within the perimeter of the moon's face. As the days passed, and the new moon came, the truth became apparent for all mankind to see – as our unwelcome Martian guests had evidently made out more quickly. The moon bore a tremendous circle, silver, perfect, a thousand miles across, shining somehow in the sunless shadows of the new moon's darkened face. The Jovians had written their sigil on the face of the earth's own satellite.

And it is evident for whom the symbol was intended. That great design was observed to persist, as the moon waxed and waned, through the coming months – through a year, and then most of another. Then it vanished, as suddenly as it had been created. The date was April 7 1924.

It was Walter who first computed the significance of the date. 'It is just as the Martians timed their attacks to *our* day-night cycle, and they landed at *our* midnight,' he said to me. 'The lunar sigil persisted for two years less forty-three days. Allowing for the leap year, that comes to six hundred and eighty-seven days that the sigil was in existence.'

Which is precisely one Martian year.

BOOK IV
Mars on Earth

1

A Telephone Call

It was in the autumn of 1936, fourteen years after the Second War, that Carolyne Emmerson called me.

It was quite out of the blue.

I had been living in Paris, more or less contentedly, with my sister-in-law Alice close by. I had spent the intervening decade rebuilding my career as a journalist, and I was continuing to work, rather slowly, on drafts of the narrative history you are reading now. Under strict military instructions – even in the age of the Federation of Federations secrecy is a habit when it comes to the Martians! – I had kept silent about my own role in the withdrawal of the invaders. (By the time this memoir is published, by my sanctions-defying American publisher, I will no longer care.) I was forty-eight years old. With the poisonous plague removed from my body by a full-blood transfusion, I believed I had put my own Martian entanglement behind me. Call this narrative itself a final flushing of that poison.

And, I am ashamed to say, at first I did not recognise the name: Carolyne, having divorced Walter Jenkins before the Second War, had never remarried, but had eventually reverted to her maiden name. Nevertheless it was Walter she wanted to discuss with me.

'I'm concerned for him,' she said, her telephonic voice a whisper. 'He's never stopped being engaged with it all, you know. As soon as the Second War was over he plunged straight into the Basra conferences, and made a public ass of himself on a number of points. Now he's wangled access to the Martian pits at Amersham, and spends his waking life there. He's as careless of his health as ever he was.'

'I see the papers are using his articles again.'

'Only for the shock value, I think. You know how the public temper is changing as the opposition approaches . . .'

She meant the next perihelic opposition, due in 1939; another set of close approaches of Mars to the earth, more opportunities for invasion fleets to cross – an alarming prospect if you believed the scare stories put about by old warhorses like Churchill. And if the Martians followed precedent they would make their first crossing in the opposition before, in 1937, only months away. Indeed we had already passed one possible opportunity; the 1920 invasion had come *two* oppositions before the optimum in that particular cluster. It was disturbing that there seemed as little astronomical news available to the general public under our glorious new world order as there had been under the old.

And this time the speculation was spiced by much fearful renewed guesswork about where those Martians who had come to the earth in the twenties might be hiding. They had not been observed since the end of the Second War, but, as far as anybody knew, they were still here. It all made for a horrible lack of resolution.

'The mood is souring,' Carolyne whispered. 'All this talk of the Germans and the Russians and the Americans rearming, despite the Federation treaties. And so, of course, there's Walter all over the place, arguing against rearmament, the newspapers' pet apostle of peace! Some are even calling him a traitor to humankind.'

'You fear for his mental stability.'

She laughed, sadly. 'I have always feared for his mental stability. It's not just that, Julie. Now I fear for his life. Since the assassination of Horen Mikaelian . . .'

It had happened two days before; I too had been deeply shocked by the murder of that patient architect of peace and unity – a murder inflicted by those who feared a new war with the Martians, or, perhaps, longed for it.

'Walter has already been on the BBC condemning the act. Of course I agree with him; of course he must say what he feels. But—'

I sighed. 'But as we've seen ever since '07, he will go charging into danger without a thought for his personal safety.'

'Please go to him, Julie. See that he is safe.'

'But, Carolyne . . .' The Jenkins' marriage was an old, long-tangled mess, which poor Carolyne had survived with dignity and kindness. Yet I knew that Walter had never lost his tenderness for

408

his estranged wife. As she had once remarked herself, you could read about it in his books. 'Carolyne, it's you he needs, not me.'

'I cannot,' she whispered. 'I cannot.'

That was family for you.

Of course I could not refuse to help – and I agreed, in fact, that Walter probably really was in danger given the shocking precedent of Mikaelian. Of course I would go to him. Even if it meant, I realised, the publisher of my own narrative of the Second War would have to wait even longer for a finished draft.

I tried to make contact.

In the event I did not have long to wait before I received an invitation from Walter himself, over the signature of our old friend Eric Eden, to visit that Unreliable Narrator at the Martian pits at Amersham.

2

Aftermath

When Carolyne phoned, I admit, I was rather out of touch. From the relative sanity of a liberated Paris, I had been content to watch the recovery of a wounded world as if from without – a very Jenkins-like perspective.

Everything had been so different after the Second War!

The Martians' global assault was over in a few days, but the immediate aftermath was as painful as ever: the search for survivors, the clearing of the dead, the beginnings of reconstruction – the unseemly scramble for scraps of Martian technology. And after that the longer-term problems had started. The Martians might be gone, but the banks were still not issuing loans, the stock exchanges were not trading, and in America as in London and Berlin even the bullion reserve was not secured. As global trade ground to a halt, after a couple of weeks the food shortages began, and the power cuts, and the water supply failures – even in cities that had never glimpsed a Martian – and soon after that the plagues.

Then came the riots.

And then the revolutions, in Delhi, in the Ottoman provinces, even in France against the occupying Germans. Things might have disintegrated altogether, as some feared.

These early days of emergency, in fact, had been the inducement Mikaelian had used to call her parliament of the desperate to Basra.

Horen Mikaelian was an Armenian nun who at the time of the Second War had been in Paris, a refugee from persecution under the Ottomans. Her emergence as a key figure after the war was remarkable – as was her capacity for persuasion, which had fuelled the first tentative efforts to construct a new post-Martian world order. Indeed, one of Mikaelian's first achievements had been to broker a hasty armistice between the German and Russian empires. The fact that the two nations' armies had co-operated in resisting the Martians at St Petersburg and elsewhere had helped with that.

Then, with that achievement behind her, Mikaelian had called presidents and emperors and monarchs and ambassadors, and scientists and historians and philosophers, to gather in Basra, an ancient city at the heart of the world's first civilisation (and from which the British occupying presence had been hastily withdrawn). At that first conference, emergency aid packages were immediately agreed, an international bank quickly set up to aid relief efforts, and longer-term infrastructure projects begun – institutions that had later become the pillars of a new order.

At first Mikaelian's 'Federation of Federations' was little more than a patchwork of agreements over trade, spheres of interest, and guarantees of mutual support. But at least all this 'Turkish parley-voo', as Churchill had wryly called it, might enable mankind to govern itself with a little more sanity than it had managed before.

Walter Jenkins, that notorious utopian, had been invited to the Basra summits. Age had not mellowed him. He wrote of the impressive celebrities he met – Gandhi for one, a representative of a newly independent India, and Atatürk, the Ottoman ambassador – but Walter's principal memory seems to have been one of irritation that he had been largely outshone by a long-standing rival: 'You know the fellow, the Year Million Man, with his alarming novels and scattershot predictions, forever falling out with some socialist or other, and the whiff of extra-marital scandal ever clinging about him, and his damn squeaky voice . . .' We may have been all but prostrate at the feet of the Martians, but we humans continued our own petty wars regardless. Oddly that gives me a certain hope for the species.

And I should note here that the efforts of Walter's 'Year Million Man' to lobby for a declaration of human rights to be a centrepiece of the new Federation's constitution will long be remembered, with gratitude.

Well, it seemed to be working. The institutions for which Mikaelian had argued, and which had seemed so utopian before – global transport networks, resources such as mineral rights held for the common good, international interventionist financial institutions (Keynes argued for that) – had quickly proved their worth. Even the somewhat sceptical and isolationist Americans had been glad of the new order when global aid poured in to alleviate the effects of devastating floods on the Mississippi in

411

1926–7, and again when the collapse of an overheated Wall Street almost caused a global recession. The invasion of China by Japan in 1931 had been another test for the Federation's councils. The restored Chinese Emperor Puyi had argued eloquently for help; concerted international pressure caused the Japanese to abandon their adventure. Even the old empires were evolving towards a looser, more democratic form of federalism: relics of an age of conquest and despoliation, now mutating into agents of the peaceful coexistence of peoples.

Meanwhile the Cythereans, our unwilling guests from Venus – those who had not been spirited away by the Martians when they withdrew – were the subject of international and interdisciplinary study, in reserves and zoos and biological institutions across the planet, a study the public followed avidly in the newspapers and newsreels. I suspect, in fact, that their very presence on the earth, their very strangeness, inspired a subliminal sense of unity in mankind. Some, indeed, said that we should be housing these visitors, not in reserves, but in their own embassy to the Federation of Federations. Such troubling questions are for the future, perhaps.

As for myself, I had ventured to Basra, anonymously, for the great ceremonies on April 24 1925 when the Federation's constitution had been signed. And I admit I came to London to celebrate the independence of Ireland and India in 1927, and the granting of the vote to women – at last! – in 1930…

But I always scuttled back to Paris. Something in me, I think, had been *changed* during the War. When I saw people around me, especially in anonymous masses, I could find it hard to see the spirit beyond the flesh and bone – as if they were no more than plastic receptacles of blood, ready for the emptying at the whim of a Martian. A touch of the Jenkins Syndrome, you might say. In London I had found greater consolation, in fact, at the Tomb of the Vanished Warrior, before an empty coffin, than in the company of the living.

So we had enjoyed an age of hope and unity that had raised the spirits, even if Walter Jenkins grumbled endlessly about the details. An all too brief age, it seemed; already tension was on the rise, thanks to the wretched astronomical clockwork of the solar system that was bringing Mars swimming once more towards the earth – tension that had already taken, at the hand of some deranged protester, the life of that apostle of peace, Horen Mikaelian herself.

And here I was, about to plunge back into the maelstrom.

412

3

By Monorail to England

Despite a rivalry between France and England that dates back a thousand years, the straight-line distance between their capitals is a mere two hundred miles. And in the late autumn of 1936 it would take only two hours for me to travel from one city to the other. Two hours!

Though I was not yet fifty, I felt like a relic in this new age. The Paris-London monorail, for example, was a miracle given us by Martian technology, an application of their mastery of electromagnetic fields (a technology now globally shared through Federation science institutions, as opposed to being monopolised by the British as in the past). My carriage, propelled by the invisible energies of electricity, was balanced on its rail on a row of *single wheels*, its mechanical intelligence keeping it upright like a circus unicyclist, so I clung to the cushions of my seat as the train rocketed along, smart and silent. When I was a little girl, I reminded myself as if I was some crone in a rocking chair, we didn't yet have motor-cars – and now *this*.

I did comfort myself with the fine views, as my train rode the rail on its elegant stilts, green and blue, high above the rooftops. Paris itself, as I am certain most Parisians would have wanted, had been changed little by the tumultuous events of the early decades of the twentieth century – in fact the city had suffered more at the hands of the Germans than from the Martians. The grand old city was a fine sight to see in the low September sunshine. And yet it was a new addition, one that I could not see from the train, that was the most significant location of all in the modern city: the embassy of the Federation of Federations, all glass and Martian aluminium in the Place de Fontenoy. This modest building had been accepted into the venerable Parisian skyline, but would always be dwarfed by the Eiffel Tower, expensively restored for the 1924 Olympics.

And as we rode along I saw that the weather was changing, with heavy thunderclouds streaming in from the east, soon to blot out the autumn sunshine. I cursed my luck, though that was scarcely fair to the fates. Across the northern hemisphere, the climate had been worsening for a decade, with an excess of extreme events, notably storms of rain or snow or hail, and bloody-minded winds that had done nothing to help humanity's efforts to recover from the Martians' assault. The elderly, in which category I now tentatively included myself, dreamed of what in retrospect seemed idyllic late-Victorian times: days before the Martians, the summer days of childhood. But then, perhaps everyone felt that way about the past. So I mused then; I was, of course, to be proved wrong about that.

Beyond Paris my train soared across the countryside of north-west France, passing without stopping through Amiens and Boulogne – and then, in utter silence, as if on invisible magnetic wings, we sailed over the Straits of Dover, with the sun bright above us once more and the Channel waters glittering below, and the slim monorail towers a chain of mighty new Eiffels.

During the Channel crossing coffee was served by calm bilingual stewards. That, I thought, was just showing off.

At Dover our service swept through a Crystal Palace of a new station, and on, striding on more stilts over the pretty towns of Kent, with the North Downs a great wave of greenery. And very soon we came to London.

Such was our speed as we raced towards Waterloo that I only glimpsed the damage that had been done to the city by the Martians in their years of occupation of England, and the rebuilding since. But in places I saw what looked like handling-machines and excavating-machines busily scraping and digging, with the eerie puffs of green smoke that always characterised Martian technology. Meanwhile, in the more expensive districts, in Chelsea and Kensington and along the Embankment, grand new buildings were rising up, skyscraper blocks and terraces that gleamed with Martian-manufacture aluminium. They seemed grand to me, anyhow; I had not been back to America for a time, and had not seen a restored Manhattan that Harry Kane told me 'would make you eat your hat'.

But even so London was transformed. After the invasion of

'20 London had been systematically pummelled by the Martians for years, and had got it worse than any other city on earth, with every landmark you can think of targeted. It had been like the Great Fire, I suppose, a chance for a rebuilding. So some modern Wren had erected a new St Paul's on the site of the old, crowned not with a dome but with a shining needle of Martian aluminium, topped by a crucifix. And I knew that many of the new structures were as extensive underground as above, with cellars, bunkers and dormitories. The government was digging huge bunkers under its ministries – it was the same around the world. Some commentators said that, fearing a Martian return, we were becoming as subterranean as the Martians themselves.

We came into Waterloo, and I was delighted to see the figure who waited for me on the platform. It was Joe Hopson, nearly forty years old now and his hair a rather startling grey, but as dapper as ever in a crisp, clean uniform. After the operations we had been engaged in during the Second War, we had gone through a few 'debriefings' together, and we had kept in touch since – with Christmas cards, at least.

He made to embrace me, but I recoiled. My blood has long since been scrubbed clean, but still I find I flinch from physical contact. Instead, I mockingly gave him my best attempt at a military salute.

'At ease, soldier,' he said with a grin. After a brief struggle, his old-fashioned manners warring with my sense of independence, I allowed him to carry the small rucksack that was as usual my only luggage. 'Come. We have a car waiting.'

'So you're a captain now,' I said. 'If I'm reading your stripes correctly, that is.'

'Afraid so. Didn't get terribly far, did I? My cadet instructor at school, old One-Ear Crookswell, would be mortified. And also I'm retired – well, semi. I'm a sort of reservist now – most of us veterans are. Even on a salary, if a small one. The Second War was so brief in the end that those of us who had the luck to do the actual fighting were pretty few, and those who survived are even fewer. So it's worth keeping us old warhorses in the stable and feeding us the odd handful of oats, so we can give the shiny new generation the benefit of our experience. Staying match fit in case the Martians decide to have another go, you see. I run into Ted Lane sometimes at such bashes, and *he* says he still hasn't forgiven you.'

I pulled a face. 'Well, he's a right to be aggrieved.' He was talking of the time I had slipped out of Abbotsdale with Verity Bliss to find the Buckinghamshire *franc-tireurs*, without so much as a word to Ted who had followed me across the North Sea in the role of protector. 'I suppose keeping match fit, as you say, makes sense – if you think the Martians are likely to come back.'

He glanced at the sky, apparently involuntarily, which I have observed is a tic among those who went through those days – no doubt I share it myself. 'Well, that's always possible,' he murmured.

We came to his car, emblazoned with a military flag and parked in a premium spot. I suppressed a pang of alarm that it was one of the modern designs that, like the monorail carriages, was carried on single wheels. Somehow this thing kept its balance *even standing still*.

I entered this vehicle with some trepidation, and I was whizzed across London.

When we reached the desolation that had been Uxbridge we came to barriers of various kinds, manned by police and military. I was reminded of the old Surrey Corridor.

Hopson guided me through all this with a few calm words. He had seen more of the fighting than me, and he had been a very young man at the time. He was always one of those who hid his real feelings, in his case beneath a layer of faux public-school innocence, but every so often you would glimpse greater depths, as if a shaft of sunlight pierced murky water.

Beyond Uxbridge, we drove to the relic of the Trench, the huge and complicated fortifications thrown up around the Martian Cordon. A way through the perimeter had been brutally cut, and I peered up at earthworks that now looked like artificial hillsides, covered by sparse grass and rosebay willowherb. To see all this again, empty of the soldiers who had swarmed everywhere all those years ago, was very strange for me. Then we passed into the Cordon itself – through that cratered annulus smashed up in a few seconds when the Martians' dummy cylinders had fallen, and still a lunar plain all these years later.

Stranger yet was to drive into the countryside beyond, through towns and villages and the undulating green of the chalk country of the Chilterns, even now comparatively unscathed. This was the region that the Martians had 'farmed', in the jargon of the military analysts, with trapped humanity as their stock. So you would see a village with a couple of inns open for business beside

416

a church whose steeple was melted to slag. And I saw cattle in the fields and sheep, with that season's healthily grown calves and lambs.

But I knew that this area, everything within the Martian Cordon, was still under the direct military rule that had once been imposed on the whole country. For here continued a very secret process of weighing guilt: of determining who among the residents could be charged with active collaboration with the Martians. Of course it was fourteen years in the past now, and I knew that many of those guilty, or at least fearful of being found guilty, had quickly fled. The last I had heard of Albert Cook was that he was living under an assumed name in Argentina, with his partner and the daughter I had once met – Mary and Belle – and I found it hard to begrudge that brutal but clear thinker a retirement of peace. I was glad that ex-husband Frank had been cleared of collaboration charges, but he had since disappeared from my view – he was pursuing front-line medical work in communities still recovering from the War, as far as I knew. 'Marriott', by the way, got an O.B.E., much to his smug satisfaction.

Thus, at last, we came to Amersham.

4

Back to the Redoubt

Once again, not without trepidation, I entered that mile-wide fortress.

I had last seen the Martian pit itself with Albert Cook, while the Martians were still in residence. Now there was a kind of patina of humanity over the whole thing, with metal walkways and steps and ladders, and small huts set up on the beaten earth, and heaps of equipment here and there. People were walking around in coveralls and helmets of various hues. It all reminded me a little of some tremendous archaeological dig – Schliemann at Troy, perhaps. Yet the whole was penned in by barriers of steel and barbed wire, and soldiers patrolled – and, I saw as we got out of the car, a Navy airship swam overhead, the lenses of huge cameras glinting.

I tried to ignore all this, to remove the people in my mind's eye, and to replace them with Martians and their machines. Yes, I thought, that peculiar terracing might have been created by an excavating-machine. That mound of chalky earth, glistening with flints, might have been raw material for a handling-machine as it industriously produced its ingots of aluminium. And that flat place, cut like a cave into the wall, might have been where the Martians themselves would gather, emitting their eerie hoots, to feed. Over it all would have been standing, not bored sentries, but fighting-machines.

And under all this activity, I reflected, still lay deep buried the ruins of old Amersham itself, together with its unlucky inhabitants, smashed in an instant when the cylinders fell, a Boadicean layer of destruction.

'All this security – better safe than sorry, I suppose,' I murmured to Joe Hopson as we got out of the car.

'Indeed,' he said, as he led me, on foot now, deeper into this knot of mystery. 'After all, *we* would leave behind minefields and other booby traps. Why not the Martians? Not that anything of the kind has been discovered so far. Also there's talk of keeping it intact, more or less, as a monument for future generations, like Woking...'

'I wonder if that's wise.'

This was Walter Jenkins.

He stood waiting for us. He did not look well to me: gaunt, his face shiny with medicinal cream, his hands swathed in bandage-like gloves. But then he was seventy years old.

'Nice to see you, Walter,' I said dryly.

'You wonder if *what's* wise, old bean?' Hopson asked pleasantly.

'To make a monument of this symbol of oppression. Such things confer power. Look at the Tower of London – the corner of a Roman fort, the relic of one occupying power, later reused as a bastion by another, the Normans. Well, the Romans left of their own accord, and so did the Martians, but we never got rid of the Normans, did we? Some dictator of the future using this place as his seat, calling on the mythic authority of the vanished Martians? No thanks. Let's fill it in and let the grass grow.'

Hopson only grinned. 'The Normans? You Welsh are all the same. It's been eight hundred years, you know. Live and let live.'

'Oh, I am deadly serious,' Walter said humourlessly.

As Hopson led us deeper into the complex, progressing slowly, I took Walter's arm. 'Now, play nice, Walter. You invited me here, remember. I've come a long way. And you know that Carolyne set all this up in the first place, don't you?'

He seemed to find it difficult even to hear his wife's name. 'Have you seen her?'

'Not recently. It was a phone call.'

'Of course *this*,' he said, 'is only a waystation. A teaser.'

'Ah. We're talking about the Martians, are we? A safer subject? Very well. A waystation en route to what?'

'*To the place the Martians went, of course.*'

I glanced at Joe Hopson, and he at me; this was evidently a revelation to Joe too.

Now Walter glanced at the sky, where that airship still patrolled. 'Looks like rain again – so much for the sunshine. But of course, that is all part of the problem. A *symptom*...'

'What's the weather got to do with it?'

'Come, then, the guided tour. If you would be good enough to stay close by, Captain Hopson, and keep flashing those credentials, we should not be impeded; the security people here know me well enough by now...'

'You always had the most infuriating manner, Walter. Dribbling out your clues, your bits of information...'

We were two old relics in this museum of war, bickering as before. Yet we walked on, through a series of fences, and over ramps and duckboards, into the very heart of the Redoubt, where, at the very centre, a deeper shaft gaped in the earth.

As we approached, I remembered the noise of this place as it had seen before: a *boom, boom*, the relentless noise of subterranean workings. That at least was silenced now. And a kind of pulley system had been set up on a frame over the shaft; two bored-looking soldiers stood beside it, smoking. The victory of the mundane, I thought.

Walter was watching me. 'Intrigued? You should be. Follow me. Tread carefully, now...'

That pulley system proved to be a crude elevator. It looked rickety to me, and it had an alarmingly large wheel, implying an alarmingly long length of cable to be paid out.

'Oh, it's tried and trusted technology,' Walter said dismissively. 'The kind of gear they use to wash windows in New York – *you* must have seen them, intrepid fellows with mop and bucket suspended high above Fifth Avenue... We won't be going very deep. Only six hundred feet or so.'

Evidently this too was all new to Joe Hopson. 'Six *hundred*...'

'Come, hop aboard!'

There was a rail to which I clung, and with a nod from Walter to the military men controlling the pulley, we began our rickety descent. The disc of daylight above quickly receded, the heads of the soldiers silhouetted against a sky bright and out of reach. Electric lamps lit up on the gantry we rode, and I was soon grateful for them as the dark closed in.

Joe said nervously, 'No deeper than six hundred feet, you say.'

Walter smiled again. 'They put a net at that level – the military – telescopic poles jammed against the walls, just in case anybody falls, though six hundred feet would doom you anyhow... The shaft as a whole is some half a mile deep.'

Now it was my turn to parrot his words. 'Half a *mile*!'

'The depth is necessary for this shaft's true purpose. Or one of them. You have any idea what that purpose is, Captain Hopson?'

Joe looked at him. 'How wide is this thing?'

'A little over thirty yards, as you suspect, don't you?'

'Mr Jenkins – *is this a cannon?*'

I leapt on the idea, seeing it at once. 'Of course. *That's* where the Martians went!'

'The British party, at least,' Walter said.

'So they built themselves a cannon—'

Hopson said, 'And refurbished a space cylinder or two—'

'And shot themselves back to Mars, the way they came!'

Walter grinned. 'The launch was observed, in fact. Visible from over much of southern England, though most people had no idea what they were seeing. Well, nor did any of us until the images were analysed, and it's all been kept thoroughly classified ever since. Did you ever notice that even under our new united-world government, old Marvin's DORA act of 1916 was never repealed? . . .'

Hopson was frowning. 'But hang on, old bean. How deep did you say this shaft was? Half a *mile*? But that's not nearly deep enough. I remember at school we read Verne's book, Americans to the moon, *you* know, firing themselves out of a great cannon, and we soon calculated that the accelerations and so forth would have mashed the travellers to a pulp—'

'Quite right,' Walter said, sounding grudgingly impressed. 'But the projectile's motion as it came flying out of the cannon mouth could be measured from the images, chance observations by spotter planes and from the ground. It must have been driven out of the gun with an acceleration of about ten times the earth's gravity – that is *thirty* times higher than the Martian, but not, perhaps, unsupportable, if you suspend your bulk in fluid, or brace with supporting equipment. And the secret is that the cylinder continued to accelerate even *after* it left the muzzle of the cannon. Observers saw green flashes, and there appears to have been a tremendous plume of hydrogen emitted from the base of the craft. If the acceleration rate remained the same, a continuing thrust up to perhaps four hundred miles from the earth would have been sufficient to hurl it free of the planet. And thence, to Mars!'

Hopson seemed awed.

With a rattle of cables, the elevator was slowing, and I saw that there was a doorway, neat and circular, cut in the wall of the shaft.

'We have almost reached our stop,' Walter said.

I looked at him. 'A stop at what?'

'The city of the Martians,' he said. 'Be careful when you climb off the platform.'

5

The Martians' Underground Lair

We walked, hesitantly. It was a city indeed, or a warren at least, far beneath the ground of England, now lit by electric lamps strung up by the sappers: a network of cylindrical tunnels and spheres, and with a geometry that eluded me though I was assured it had all been thoroughly mapped.

Aside from the silvery metallic fabric of the tunnel walls, I saw no Martian equipment. But there were traces of humanity everywhere: telegraph wires taped to the walls, a chemical toilet, caches of battery torches and candles in case, I supposed, the electrical power failed – even oxygen bottles and masks.

'But these are a mere precaution: the air stays fresh,' Walter said. 'There are several shafts to the surface, and a breeze flows, apparently naturally, though I have my suspicion there is technology involved somewhere in the process – something subtle, not a pump as we would use, a kind of osmosis perhaps, or a capillary action . . .'

We came to a big spherical chamber – one of several, I was informed. The floor was terraced with concentric horizontal platforms, like broad steps leading down from the sphere's equator where we had entered. All this was seamlessly moulded from the same metallic substance as the walls of the tunnels. A couple of soldiers stood on guard, watching us warily, one with a field telephone at his side.

Walter Jenkins sat stiffly on a step, and we followed his lead.

'Of course all the Martian gear has been removed – mostly by the Martians themselves, save for a few relics retrieved by the first humans to penetrate the place. One can only imagine how it was when the Martians themselves were here! It would have been rather dark to human eyes, but as you know Mars's sunlight is dimmer than ours. And the Martians, scattered through this chamber like great leather sacks, hooting and puffing as they did, those strange finger-tentacles working... But still one can deduce a great deal about the Martians and their society even from the basic layout of the place.'

'Oh, really?' I asked, in a mood to be sceptical. 'Such as?'

'Just compare *this* to any human structure you ever saw – consider what's *missing*. You have the passageways, and the communal areas, and that's it. There is nowhere for privacy, for the Martians evidently don't desire it. And there's no evidence of status. Nobody has a grander room than anybody else. So we can deduce their social structure is flat! No hierarchies! They must make their decisions by discussion and consensus. They share everything – we see no evidence of anything like private property. They are supremely loyal to each other, too, as we know. And remember, I have strong reason to believe the Martians are telepathic. They could not *lie* to each other. Have you considered that? Imagine how human society would be transformed by that one simple adjustment! Why, even these common areas have a kind of democratic symmetry. One must sit and talk in the round.

'We found one exception, a chamber with a peculiarly dimpled floor. The best speculation is that this is where the young are kept, after they bud from the parents, when they are small and dependent.'

Hopson seemed to like the idea. 'Just like being sent away to prep! Didn't do me any harm. A Martian at Eton? Well, he'd be good at table tennis...'

'This is how the Martians live on their own world, I surmise. After all, what do we see when we look at the planet? You have the snow and the ice, the oceans, the vegetation, the canals. *Nowhere do we see a Martian city*. Not a single building. Not even at the most complex of nodes in the canal network, like Solis Lacus. It's all industry. Where do they *live*?'

I saw what he meant. 'They must have retreated underground – into warrens like this.'

'That's it. It's logical, isn't it?'

Hopson wasn't keeping up. 'But *why* would one choose to live in a warren?'

'For protection. For breathable air, as one's atmosphere thins and collapses. *For warmth* – for even when the sun dies, you know, the interiors of the planets will retain their heat, and in fact the earth more so than Mars because of its greater mass. This may be *our* destiny some day, when the sun becomes cold: to huddle underground, kept alive by the planet's residual heat.'

'But there's nothing here,' I mused, looking around at the blank walls. 'Not just an absence of sunlight – what would one eat?'

'Life in the subterranean cities would be one of technological advancement rather than biological complexity,' Walter said, rather pompously. 'The end of the game in which the Martians are already engaged. The Martians rebuilt their world as they rebuilt themselves, in a great simplification, just as they discarded the wasteful lumber of gullet and stomach to become little more than a brain and a blood circulation system. Consider their ecology: there is the red weed, and the humanoids that feed on the weed who provide blood for the Martians themselves. Everything else – extirpated! Discarded!

'One day the Martians will surely go further yet, leaving behind altogether all this messy business of biology. Imagine a machine that could take rock, and raw energy from the sun or the planet's heart, and turn *that* into food – for all the elements one needs can be found in the minerals, you know. The ultimate efficiency – the most exquisite simplicity – nothing but sunlight, and rock, and brains. *That*, I believe, is the ultimate technical goal of the Martians.'

I sniffed. 'You sound as if you envy them. Isn't that what the psychologists said of you, Walter? That you're half-Martian yourself? Anyhow now they're gone – *this* lot at least. So where are the rest? The ones who landed in New York and Los Angeles, and Peking and Berlin... Even you must be aware of the disquiet that mysterious vanishing continues to cause. Do you have some new notion about that?'

He smiled. 'In general terms, it was always obvious.'

I glowered; he could be infuriating. 'Obvious, was it?'

'Most of the earth is too hot for them. So they will have migrated to where it's *cold*. And as most of them landed in the northern hemisphere—'

'The north,' Joe Hopson said, interested now. 'That's always been clear, yes; they would seek the coldest lands. But the Arctic, the roof of the world – Canada and Asia – it's a damned big place. *Are you saying they've been found?*'

He answered mildly, 'I'm saying there have been reports to that effect. There's an expedition planned next year. Weather

425

permitting. Julie, fancy a trip? There we can confirm what the Martians are doing up there – or rather, what I believe they've been doing...'

To the Arctic, searching for Martians! Well, I wasn't about to say no. Would you?

6

The *Vaterland*

That winter passed slowly for me, in a daze of expectation.

Then in early March 1937, I boarded the LZ-138 *Vaterland*, at Murmansk. We would be travelling in the late Arctic winter, about as inhospitable a time and place as our dear old earth offers you, although, as Walter Jenkins never tired of pointing out, to a Martian it would be like the balmiest of summers. We privileged few, however, a multinational party, would travel in a flying hotel.

We gathered in a chilly aerodrome outside the city. The snow was not falling, but we saw it heaped up in tremendous banks beyond the apron. Here was Walter himself, seventy-one now, frailer than ever. Joe Hopson was with me; he had kindly volunteered for the trip to serve as a general companion, assistant and guide. Like most military veterans he was a supremely competent chap, and I was glad to have him with me.

And Eric Eden was there too, aged fifty-five, now officially retired from the British Army but still serving as a paid advisor to various government departments on all things Martian – he bore his own burn scars, and he was another survivor whose presence reassured me.

All told there were fifty passengers of a dozen nationalities, most of whom were scientists unknown to me, but I had no doubt of their relevant expertise – at least as judged by some committee or other in the Federation embassy in Paris. And such a high-profile jaunt, with a lot of attendant publicity, naturally attracted the famous and the rich. It was rather fun to do some celebrity-spotting as we stood on that windy platform. I thought I recognised our expedition leader: Otto Yulevich Schmidt, well over six feet tall, a scholar and outdoorsman famed for leading expeditions into the Russian Arctic over a decade. I was not surprised to learn that, in addition to Schmidt, there were more heroes of polar exploration among our crew, such as Richard Byrd, first to fly to the North Pole. Our newly crowned King Edward's American wife was aboard too. The union had been seen as a symbol of a new age of transatlantic amity, despite a mild controversy over her previous divorce. But I did not see Queen Wallis. There was even a rumour that the Kaiser Wilhelm III was aboard, taking part in this ambitious flight of the most prestigious of his country's aerial vessels.

'Even more aggressive than his unlamented father,' Eric had murmured to me. 'If we come within biting distance of a real, live Martian we may need to muzzle the man.'

I soon forgot my companions, however, for I was enthralled by our great craft itself.

I first saw the *Vaterland* in bright morning light. Even penned in its hangar it was a tremendous sight, a huge cylinder lying flat on the concrete apron, dwarfing the service vehicles which attended it. Its great belly rested on wheels and rails, and there were stabilising fins on its flanks and at the tail where a vast engine block was fixed.

Then came the call: 'Airship forward!' A kind of netting was fixed over the ship's pale grey surface, and workers like ants dragged the vessel from its shed by hand.

As we passengers walked towards the craft – there was a sickly-sweet smell which I was told was associated with the replenishment of hydrogen – the airship became only more impressive; it was no less than a third of a mile long from bow to stern. But it was the symbolism of the craft that struck me most. A new age of global federations we might be living in, but you wouldn't know it from a glance at the *Vaterland*. Everywhere were the colours of imperial Germany, strong yellow and black, and a mighty eagle, all in black, was emblazoned on the nose – that design alone must have been a hundred feet tall. And Eric pointed out to me the three great compartments which the ship carried slung under its belly. The front was the passenger gondola, the rear was for engines and fuel – but the middle section, Eric said, was essentially a bomb bay.

The passenger gondola, I observed on boarding, was split into two decks, the upper for the kitchens and stores and quarters for the crew, and the lower for our cabins and the lounges and dining rooms – rooms with a view of the ground below. There is always an enormous amount of room on a big airship; even as we boarded, a player at a grand piano treated us to selections from Wagner. It did not take us long to find our rooms and get settled. Later I would explore my cabin's own ingenious features: the padded walls, the fold-away bunk and table, the telephone, the electric lights. For now, though, I could already hear, indeed feel, the throbbing of the great engines transmitted through the ship's frame; I hurried back to the main lounge for the take-off.

I sat with Eric and Hopson – Walter had retired to his room, intent on his note-taking, his endless studies. The lounge was fitted out in the most modern style, all beige colours on the walls and up-lighting on the ceiling, and glass-topped tables and chairs with chrome rails. There was even a small vase with fresh flowers set on our table. It all made the dear old *Lusitania*, fond in my memory, seem shabby.

'Cast off!' came the cry.

And then we rose.

On an airship, you know, the windows are all in the walls and floor, so one can look down at the landscapes that slide silently below, while above your head the sky is shielded by the great bulk of the lift envelope. And the moments after launch offer perhaps the most spectacular views of all. The aerodrome shrank below us, the workers who stood waving by the mooring tower turning into tiny dolls.

The sprawl of Murmansk itself was soon visible to the south, and to the north the Barents Sea opened up, blue water close to the shore but scattered with ice floes not far out. On the horizon the ice merged into a solid mass that, I knew, stretched all the way to the pole. Out to sea I saw a small convoy: a couple of icebreakers and low-slung cargo ships. The Russians' Great Northern Sea Route, a six-thousand-mile passage all along the northern coast of Eurasia, is open for only a few months of the year – mere weeks in a bad season – and it pays to set off early if you don't want to spend a winter trapped in the ice.

Even as we lifted small aircraft jumped into the sky to see us off. Monoplanes, with hulls of glittering aluminium and the sigils of the imperial Russian air force bright on their wings, they ducked and darted around us, making what seemed impossibly tight turns.

Eric Eden was impressed. 'Those must be reaction-engine flyers – following the principle of the Martians' flying-machines, and a product of the German–Russian war, of course. *Our* planes still use screw propellers to drag themselves through the air.'

'Silly asses,' muttered Hopson, puffing on an unlit pipe – smoking was not allowed aboard our hydrogen-lifted craft. 'Flies buzzing an elephant.' But despite this languid dismissal he craned to see the feisty little craft as much as any of us.

7

Across the Arctic

It would be a journey of some two thousand miles to our destination, which was the Taymyr Peninsula. Running at a comfortable speed we would cover this distance in around forty-eight hours. It was on the Tuesday that we set off from Murmansk; we were expected to arrive at the Taymyr some time on the Thursday.

I tended to stick to the company of my companions. It was generally known that I was a friend of Harry Kane, and he had recently made himself notorious by writing a trashy radio drama, produced by his wife Marigold and broadcast on the Edison Broadcasting System, about a sudden arrival of a fresh fleet of Martians in the Midwest. Well, as a new set of close oppositions were approaching, the show had caused a panic – I didn't want to be quizzed about *that* scandal, and I kept my head down. Besides, the company was pleasant. In relaxed circumstances Eric Eden and I properly shared for the first time our reminiscences of the Martian War; it is largely on the basis of those conversations and the notes I made that the relevant sections of the present memoir have been drafted.

We were not allowed to be bored, however.

On the Tuesday afternoon, while a magical landscape of water and ice slid beneath our prow, Otto Schmidt treated us to an off-the-cuff lecture. He was a Russian, despite his name, but he spoke to his international audience in heavily accented German. In his late forties, tall, commanding, and with a beard like Charles Darwin, he looked every inch the Jules Verne hero-explorer to me, and sounded like it too. He described to us something of the history of the Russians' inner colonisation of their own vast empire, which, I was surprised to learn, went back to the days of Ivan the Terrible in the sixteenth century, when explorers and exiles and fur trappers and religious schismatics had wandered east. By the time of Peter the Great the first towns were being established, and in the nineteenth century the construction of the Trans-Siberian Railway was a major triumph. But it was only in the twentieth century – and after the great trauma of war against the Germans and then the Martians – that the development of the region had been accelerated, and conducted in a systematic fashion. Schmidt himself had led the first successful crossing of the Great Northern Sea Route.

Schmidt was a booming braggart, but engaging, and he had a right to be proud of all his country had achieved. And, he claimed, this was the nearest anybody had come to colonising a hostile alien planet. 'So maybe the Russian flag will be the first to be planted on Mars!' We applauded such sentiments politely, and I wondered what the Martians might have to say about that.

But it was thanks to such explorations and surveys, of course, that the presence of the refugee Martians had been confirmed, and as a consequence the Russian science academy had proposed this international mission to the Federation of Federations.

On the Wednesday afternoon we stopped at a town called Noril'sk, which is on the Yenisei river, still some five hundred miles from our final destination. Here a group of companies were mining for nickel ore. We dropped supplies of various kinds; ours was the first significant visit to the town since the winter had relented.

Eric Eden and I took the chance to slip out of the gondola and walk about the town. It was a shabby, functional place, surrounded by a stout wire fence, the buildings mere shacks of cinder blocks and mortar and prefabricated panels, the streets bare, tamped-down dirt where the snow was cleared. There seemed to be cement mixers everywhere. There were elements of mundanity: aside from the factories there was a school, a church, a hospital, all half-built. People lived and worked here, then, and raised children. There was even a small cinema; a handwritten billboard told me it was showing Cherie Gilbert's *A Martian in Hollywood*. But it was a desolate place, and I was chilled to the bone despite my expensive cold-weather gear.

'You know, I spent some time in this part of the world before the Second War,' Eric admitted, for the first time in my hearing.

I grunted. 'Let me guess. You were here to learn how landships fare on the tundra.'

He smoothly ignored that. 'It's not easy out here. Just living,

I mean.' We paused by a half-built shell of concrete and cinder-brick. 'For a start there's the months of darkness, when it gets so cold the mortar will freeze before you can set your brick, and even when the summer comes you get this terrible humidity, and mosquitoes everywhere. The people here are a desolate sort, either drafted in or seduced by false promises of a new life on the frontier – you know the kind of thing.'

'Why the fence? To keep the townsfolk in?'

He grinned. 'Or the wolves out. They call the moonlight the wolves' sunshine, you know.'

A hooter sounded, like a ship's, calling us back to the *Vaterland*. It was time to move on.

And, even as Eric and I turned away from the fence, the snow started to fall – suddenly, without warning, it seemed to me, from a clear sky. We had to cling to each other, and follow other shadowy forms, to make our way back to the airship.

'Even here,' muttered old Arctic hand Eric Eden. 'Even here, at this extreme place, the ends of the earth, the weather is – *odd*.'

Thus, Wednesday. We travelled on overnight.

And on the Thursday morning we woke over our destination, the Taymyr Peninsula.

8

At Cape Chelyuskin

After a hurried, subdued breakfast, we passengers donned our cold-weather gear once more and prepared to descend from the gondola. We were ready for work; many of the scholars had brought cameras, and various other instruments in bags and cases. As we filed down the gondola's ramp I recognised one instrument from the manufacturer's name, stamped on its box; it was a Geiger counter, to measure radiation.

Once outside, standing with Eric and Joe, I discovered that we had come down in the middle of a military camp, over which the flag of the Russian Empire fluttered in a mercifully light breeze. I saw a cluster of buildings, and field guns and heaps of ammunition under tarpaulins, and rows of automobiles, some fitted with skis for travelling on the snow – there was even a landship, a small one, done out in white and grey Arctic camouflage. All of this, along with an airfield large enough to host an airship the size of the *Vaterland*, was enclosed by a fence. And on the northern perimeter of the compound I saw a cluster of watchtowers and gates, and a battery of big Navy guns installed on pivoted mounts.

'*That* way lies the ocean,' came a voice. 'You can smell the salt, I think. And that's the way the guns are set. To the north, beyond the perimeter.' It was Walter Jenkins, bundled in black furs. He wore a heavy-looking Russian fur hat, and what I could see of his face was screened by the lenses of his thick dark sunglasses, and pale skin cream. I wondered if his scarring was made more or less a discomfort by the deep cold.

'Good morning, Walter,' Eric Eden said dryly.

Joe Hopson clapped him on the arm. 'It is good to see you. You mustn't hide yourself away on the return jaunt, you hear? With four of us – well, that's enough for bridge.'

'Bridge?' Walter seemed bemused.

Now Otto Schmidt called us together, the crowd of us passengers with a couple of the crew, and a squad of soldiers. He led us towards the gate on the north side. Towards the sea, then.

Walter walked with me. 'It is not far to our destination. The Russians, having made the discovery by chance – after I had predicted it for years! – have set up shop admirably close to the site. Do you know where you are, Julie?'

'The Taymyr Peninsula. North coast of Russia, a bit of land sticking out into the Arctic Ocean—'

'And separating the Seas of Kara and Laptev, yes.'

We came to the mesh fence, at a heavily guarded gate. A crewman from the *Vaterland* had already taken the passports of the passengers in the party; a junior officer scrutinised these, and called us through. Beyond the fence, oddly, the scent of the ocean seemed much stronger.

'But,' Walter said, 'what is *this* place in particular? Do you know? It is called Cape Chelyuskin. The extreme northern end of the peninsula...'

Now, as I looked around, I could see the ocean. Beyond a swath of dark, hard-frozen beach, the water looked black, but further out sea ice gleamed white as bone. And as we walked slowly forward, I saw a shadow in the ground before us: a circle, a pit, watched over by soldiers with automatic weapons and field wireless sets. A shaft, dug down into the ground: it was just as I had witnessed at Amersham.

'And this Cape,' Walter went on, 'happens to be the northernmost spot on the *whole* of the Eurasian continent. Right here, where we're standing. *The northernmost.* Now do you see?'

I breathed, 'The Martians. They came north. As far as they could.'

'From all across Eurasia, from Berlin, St Petersburg, from Peking, even from Constantinople. As for those who landed in the Americas, it is thought that again they streamed north, and crossed into Asia by the Bering Strait – not much of an obstacle to the Martians, especially in the winter. There were a few sightings in the Canadian territories – Martians on the move! It's odd, by the way, that they made little use of their flying-machines.'

'And Africa? What of the Martians of Durban?'

'That remains a mystery. They left their pits, certainly. There are rumours of sightings in the forests of central Africa: finds of gorillas and chimpanzees, apparently drained of their blood...

435

Some day we may send an expedition into that dark heart and find out. As for South America, no one has yet penetrated the Amazon jungles. That's for the future. Come now. There's something else you must see.'

I walked towards that shadow in the ground, that *pit*, like the one I had explored in the heart of England, now transplanted into the hard Arctic tundra. Its shaft, a little more than thirty yards wide – the width of a Martian space cylinder – was lined, just as in Amersham, with an aluminium sheen. But this pit was not inert, as Amersham had been. This time, as I approached, cautiously like the rest, I could *hear* it, a great *thump-thump-thump*, like a beating heart, deep underground. It was the sound I had heard in England, all the time I was in the Martian Redoubt with Albert Cook, and unwelcome memories crawled.

'They are here,' I said. 'Still here.'

Almost tenderly, Eric Eden took my gloved hand in his. 'Buck up, old girl.'

I saw that a number of the tame experts were drawn away from the pit itself to inspect a broad trench, dug into the ground, perhaps three feet deep and twenty long, and oriented north-south. Those excitable scientists, all spectacles and beards and bald heads – senior academics were still largely men, in those days – were, with caution, using protective gloves, reaching down into the trench and taking samples of what grew there: a plant of some kind, fleshy and crimson and covered in blisters, thick on the earth.

As Walter led us that way I saw that a number of other such trenches had been made across this landscape, running down the narrow beach and into the sea. Walter himself reached down into one of the trenches to grab a handful of the stuff growing there, and gave me a share; it was dry to the touch and rubbery, but otherwise like seaweed. 'No need to be delicate – there's plenty of it around, and more of it every day. Growing in the ground, in a few spots on the surface – oh, and under the sea.'

'How do we know that?'

He pointed to a machine that stood by the shore; it looked like a boiler on fat wheels, but it had a periscope like a submarine, and thick round portholes.

'What's that? Some kind of submersible?'

'Yes, but not a conventional kind. It's a crawler – a design that drives along the sea bed – an old design that never really caught on, but which has its applications. Its brave crew, Russian scientists all, have taken that beast out onto the ocean floor, and far under the ice. And everywhere they went they found—'

'This stuff?' I held up my sample. 'Is it red weed? I remember how quickly it grew, even the first batches the Martians brought to the earth in '07.'

'It seems to be a form of red weed, yes.'

'But what purpose has it?'

For answer, he popped one of the blisters on the frond I was holding. I saw no gas emerge, smelled nothing. 'To collect *this*,' he said.

'The gas in the blister? It is invisible—'

'It is nitrous oxide. A compound of nitrogen and oxygen – the sample is just as reported by the first expeditions, and its purpose is as obvious now as then, to me at least.'

I remembered now Frank's observations of the depletion of the air over fields of red weed in the Abbotsdale Cordon. 'I don't understand. Purpose, you say? What does it mean, Walter? What is the intention?'

'The removal of the world's air,' he said simply.

9

An Unreliable Prophet

That evening, back aboard the *Vaterland*, Walter discussed his ideas further, with myself, Eric, Joe Hopson. We spoke over a dinner of sandwiches and beer and a bowl of fruit. The restaurants were sparsely populated now; those scientists on board – the rest had stayed in the military base – had scattered to cabins become improvised laboratories, and were, no doubt, planning to spend the night in obsessive analysing, experimenting and theorising.

But Walter had already worked it all out.

'Here is the problem,' he said. 'The problem for the Martians, that is. Those stranded here find themselves on a world quite unlike their own in a number of ways. The greater mass, the heavier gravity – there's not much to be done about that. Ah, but what about our atmosphere? From a Martian's point of view there's far too much of it; *their* air is attenuated compared to ours, and a different mix: we have too much oxygen, too little argon, for example.'

Both Joe and Eric seemed to be struggling with these ideas. Eric said at length, 'Are you saying that these Martian Crusoes might wish to *change* the air – to make it more like their own?'

'Precisely. Why would they not? After all, Europeans have spread around this earth, from the Arctic to Australia, and everywhere we have gone we have cleared those lands of native life and made them suitable for our crops and stock animals. It even goes on here – did you know there are potatoes, plants from the Andes, growing above the Arctic Circle?'

'Are there, by golly?' Joe said. He seemed more impressed by that fact than anything else said so far.

'Very well,' I said heavily, thinking it through. 'But how could they do it? To change the air of a world—'

'I have speculated about that,' Walter said calmly. 'I have studied the kinematics of meteorites, for example. We know that the Martians have learned to use the dropping of objects from space as a weapon of war. And, such is the energy released, every such fall blasts away a proportion of the earth's air into space – not much, but some. Once gone it is lost for ever. Well, I wondered, could one use similar impactors – giant cylinders stuffed with rocks, for example – to simply blow all our air away?' He sighed. 'Sadly, I think that's impossible.'

Eric snorted. 'Sadly! The man says sadly!'

'We have studied such impacts since '07, and the natural landings of meteorites even before that. No matter how large a rock you drop, you blast away some air, but only a kind of a skim. I calculate it would take *thousands* of rocks to get all the air away that way. And consider what a mess you'd make of the world if you tried it! No,' he said. 'I think they've been more subtle. I think they've come up with a tool, a biological mechanism—'

'The red weed,' I said.

'Correct. But an adjusted variant, modified perhaps at the level of the germ plasm – we know the Martians are expert at shaping living things for their purposes. No doubt the assembled professors aboard this craft will work it out better than I can, but my guess is—' He glanced at us. 'What's the atmosphere made of?'

'Nitrogen, oxygen, and scraps,' Joe Hopson said promptly. 'That got beaten into us during stinks lessons at school.'

Eric winced. 'Do shut up, Joe!'

'Very well. I *think* it works like this,' Walter said. 'The first goal is to get rid of all that nitrogen and oxygen – yes? Because those are the bulk components. Now, *we* could think of ways to do that – in principle, at least. Nature has provided certain plants which "fix" the nitrogen from the air, that is, draw it down and render it into molecules suitable for take-up by other living things. That's steady, but it's slow if you leave it to the plants. But already we have the Haber process, which fixes nitrogen from the air to use in artificial fertiliser. And a single Haber manufacturing plant can remove as much nitrogen from the air, in a *week*, as all the oceans absorb in the growth of plankton and so on, in a *year*.

'But I believe the Martians have been more subtle yet. I believe the weed encourages chemical reactions among the elements of the air. First, thanks to some catalyst, the nitrogen is made to

439

bond with the oxygen. So the Martians fix the oxide rather than the nitrogen alone, thus removing the oxygen too in a single reaction – the bulk of the air, captured.

'Now, each frond of the weed won't take very much. But what it takes it holds. I have done some tests; *this* version of the weed has a thick, rubbery skin that shows no signs of rotting away and releasing its stolen air any time soon. It just grows, on the ocean floor – and on the ground, and *in* the ground, and then it lies there, just heaping up, a compact, unbreakable store.'

'And the weed grows very fast,' I said. 'It *reproduces* very fast. We saw that even in the First War.'

Walter nodded. 'You start to see it. There is probably more to the system than that. The Martians will need machinery to spread this, to encourage the growth – but they can have that machinery, quickly. In Sheen, I saw myself how one handling-machine could manufacture another in the space of a day . . . It is already fifteen years since the Second War – fifteen years of opportunity for the Martians to develop their system, to spread the operation. And remember, they have *already* rebuilt one world to suit their tastes and their needs – rebuilt Mars itself, over and over as the sun has progressively cooled. They know what they are doing. They know *how* to do this.'

'And already we're seeing the signs,' I guessed wildly, and for some reason I remembered the out-of-nowhere thunderclouds I had seen over Paris, the day I travelled to London. 'The strange weather, the storms—'

'That's it. There's a permanent low-pressure system over this part of the Arctic, as the air is drawn down into the ocean and the ground. As the air thins, you see, it loses its capacity to hold water vapour. In the short term this effect will play merry hell with the normal meteorological processes. We have to expect violent storms of rain, hail, snow . . . Ha! I remember the storms of the June of '07, when the Martians first came to England . . . Coincidental stormbringers!

'But that is merely a phase. As the air thinned further, *if* it did, we would progress beyond meteorological phenomena. Those living at the highest altitudes would suffer mountain sickness. With time such effects must afflict lower and lower heights – there would be refugee flows and so forth. But it won't come to that.'

Eric glowered. 'You know that, do you? Just as every French general *knew* that the Germans' military build-up wouldn't come to an invasion of Paris.'

Walter looked at us as if we were missing the point. 'Did you know that not a single fighting-machine has been seen in these polar wastes? Handling-machines, yes – machines for building, not smashing. Which proves that the Martians are here to stay. This is not destruction. Not war. Not under the eyes of the Jovians! *That's* all over. This is colonisation, not war, and ultimately it will be, it *must* be, of an orderly kind.'

I tried to make him see our obvious concern. 'But, Walter, to strip away our air—'

'Think of it as a negotiation. Of a concrete kind, granted. They are telling us what they want. Well, we must respond by telling them what we will give them – some kind of reserve, perhaps. Even a domed colony. And we are leaving a party of scientists behind to progress that very goal. Perhaps we will find a cosmic Mikaelian!'

Eric said heavily, 'Just hypothetically, Walter – suppose the Martians' sequestration of the air we breathe was not *orderly* after all. Suppose they *don't* abandon it at some polite level. Suppose they just kept on with it. Where would that leave us? How would we survive?'

Walter seemed irritated to have to deal with this – what struck me as a typical hard-headed soldier's question. 'How do you think? As we would on the moon, or indeed Mars itself. In shelters or caves. Shelters with factories that can make, or at least replenish, scraps of breathable air.'

'Scraps of air,' Eric said. 'Scraps of humanity. We will not be able to move around the world – we won't be able to organise – we could not resist.'

'Crikey,' Joe Hopson said softly. 'It would be the massacre of mankind. Just as you wrote in your *Narrative*, Jenkins. *That* would be the very massacre, at last.'

'It won't come to that,' Walter insisted.

'What must we do?' I asked.

Walter seemed surprised by the question. 'As I told you in Berlin, Julie, what, fifteen years ago? Negotiate.'

Eric was still grim-faced. 'Well, we'll know soon enough. The Martian cannons will fire at the end of March, if they mean to come again. If they do *not* fire, then perhaps Walter is right, that all of this business with the air is a mere experiment in colonisation, intended to do us no real harm. But if they *do* launch another invasion fleet—' He looked Walter in the eye, sternly. 'Then we'll know, won't we?'

10

The Epilogue

During our journey westward and back towards Europe and civilisation, I was surprised to learn that Walter Jenkins planned to return to England for his first extended stay in a number of years.

And I was still more surprised when he let slip, quite casually, that he had – evidently on a whim, a nod to the past – bought back the house in Woking where he had lived with his wife Carolyne before the first Martian assault. That was his intended destination now. 'I need to be there,' he told me in that grave way of his, 'on midnight of the twenty-sixth of this month – the date of the next firing, if it comes indeed. When again, history will pivot. I did listen to Eric Eden's objections, you know. I confidently look forward to being proved right.'

Although, to my ears, he sounded anything but confident!

As I have remarked, for months already the approach of the crucial astronomical date had seemed to fuel a world-wide paranoia, and the news of the Arctic Martians, luridly misreported as it was, only magnified that irrational fear (or maybe it was rational, I wondered in the privacy of my own heart). And Walter, bless him, thinking nothing of his own safety – and despite the precedent of the fate of Mikaelian – was all for plunging straight into the maelstrom of public debate, and not only that, returning to Woking, the one address publicly associated with him.

I decided there and then, in the lounge of the *Vaterland*, with Arctic desolation still peeling away beneath us, that I would accompany Walter home. In a way the whole Martian affair had all started in that pleasant house on Maybury Hill – or at least it had for Walter, who had become by default the witness for a generation. It seemed an appropriate place for the story to end – or, more correctly, for a new chapter to begin. And in Woking I could keep him safe. After a quiet word to my old ally Eric Eden I was assured that various irregular elements of the British Army would keep an eye on both of us, 'until the latest Martian flap is over, one way or another.'

But there was more to it than that. We had never been close friends – which in-laws ever are? – and yet he was family. I could hardly bear the thought of him rattling around like a ghost in his old home, alone.

I dashed off a wireless-telegraph message to my sister-in-law in Paris to inform her of my plans, and asked her to tell such colleagues and friends as she felt necessary. All this before I had told Walter of my intention to come with him.

Walter was scarcely gracious when I informed him of my decision. 'Just don't get in the way,' he snapped.

The house on Maybury Hill was almost as I remembered it, as we walked around the place, throwing open windows.

Though it was not far from central Woking, the house had survived the 1907 assaults, and Surrey as a whole had been comparatively spared the damage of the second wave of 1920, which had centred on Buckinghamshire and London. The chimney pots did not match; one had been replaced after the original was destroyed by the brush of the Heat-Ray. Subsequent owners had maintained the character of the place well enough. Here was the dining room with the rather rickety French windows that gave onto the garden and a view towards Ottershaw, where Walter's astronomer friend Ogilvy had lived. Here was the little summer house where, Walter told me, he and Carolyne had enjoyed taking their supper in the good weather. There was furniture in all of the rooms, I noticed, of a more or less appropriate type – a dining table and chairs in the dining room, rather too well-stuffed sofas in the parlour, and so forth. Yet the colours jarred, the sizes and positioning not quite right.

And upstairs was Walter's old study, with its view to the west, towards Horsell Common itself, where the very first cylinder had landed. At some point the study had been done out as a child's bedroom, as I could see from the wallpaper – it had images of Ally Sloper, a favourite from the picture papers, clobbering Martians in their fighting-machines. The only furniture was a solid desk under the window, and a chair, and a light stand, and rows of bookcases, for now unpopulated.

Walter and I stood at the study window and peered out at the ruins of Woking. There were the remains, still distinguishable, of the Oriental College, of the mosque, of the rail station, the electric works. The station had been reopened; the London trains ran. But on the old line, by the stumps of the smashed Maybury arch, the overturned wreck of a train could be seen – a detail that reminded me of Abbotsdale and the Cordon, under the Martians. These ruins, made safe but left otherwise untouched as a monument, were nevertheless being embraced by the green of earth, with grass, rosebay willowherb, even young pine trees growing around the debris.

'Good enough,' Walter said. 'I can work here still.'

'Did you take this place unfurnished, Walter?'

'Indeed. Told the agent to fit it out as best he judged it.'

I tapped the desk; it appeared to have been constructed of old ship's timbers. 'To a budget, I can see.'

'Better things to do than mull over sticks of furniture.' He sat in the heavy office chair behind the desk, and swivelled to and fro. 'This will do.'

I sighed, and patted his shoulder. 'You're not yet a Martian, Walter. You haven't yet discarded all your bodily wants. Will you let me help you spruce the place up a little, while I'm here? A bit of redecoration – some furniture that actually fits the rooms . . . Believe me, if you're comfortable your work will flow more easily.'

He grunted. He opened a briefcase and drew out a calendar, which he set up on the empty desk. And he placed next to it a photograph of Carolyne, a framed portrait – a touch that surprised me. He said, 'Not until after the twenty-sixth.'

It was hard to argue with that.

So we settled into a brief period of domesticity.

I got a cleaner in, to manage the house and do the laundry; I shopped for the pair of us, which was not much of a chore. Walter surprised me by doing much of the cooking. His cuisine, honed by long bachelor years, was quick to prepare, quicker to eat, but nutritionally efficient. Walter had employed a servant, I recalled, before '07. Everybody who could afford it had had one in those days – even a couple making a fairly marginal living from the husband's income as a philosophical writer – but that seems to be a fashion that has passed, probably for the better since most of those 'below stairs' had been women with no other choice of employment.

Walter mostly worked upstairs in his study, putting his notes in order, writing essays perhaps – I was not privy to his drafts. At least, I realised, he was keeping to an orderly schedule, unlike his habits aboard the *Vaterland* where he had treated such things as sleep and food as irrelevant distractions. Whether that was my own relatively orderly influence (relatively! – most of my acquaintances see me as an agent of chaos, I think), or some memory of the calm of his past here with Carolyne, I cannot say. Indeed I wondered if some instinct for lost domestic tranquillity had drawn him back to this house in the first place.

In my own time I worked, and read, and had long telephone conversations with distant friends. I had coffee several times with Marina Ogilvy, widow of the astronomer, who still lived in the house with the observatory at Ottershaw, only a few miles away. And I spoke to Carolyne herself; sometimes she rang me. I urged her to come to visit Walter, or at least speak to him on the phone: 'I know you are divorced, I know it's a burden, but still—'

But still she would not.

So we came to the twenty-fifth.

It was a Thursday. The day itself dawned calm, belying its apocalyptic relevance.

I was up at six, before my alarm clock sounded. I had slept poorly. I knew it would be midnight at the very earliest before either of us slept again.

If the Martians came the launches would begin at midnight that night – and their workings in the Arctic would presumably have to be viewed as a weapon of war – and for all Walter's words the world would be plunged into a new hell. As to the firings themselves, there had been no news yet from the observatories, not even via the channels Walter had the privilege to consult, but I had seen for myself in '20 how partial and tentative those contacts were, and, it seemed, security had only tightened since then.

I washed, dressed, and brought Walter a coffee and a plate of bacon and eggs in his study. He was working at a manuscript, which he put aside; he grunted his thanks. I knew he would not come away to the dining room or the kitchen, not today.

I put in a quiet day of work of my own, reading, writing preliminary drafts of sections of this memoir, writing letters – I paid a few bills on the house.

In the late afternoon I went for a brief walk, down to the

station for the evening papers. I bought the *Telegraph*, the *Daily Mail*, the *Times*, that week's *Punch*, and on a whim *Ally Sloper's Half-Holiday*. I scanned the headlines for news of the opposition; in the serious papers they were variants of 'The World Waits', but there was no solid news.

I walked back home. It had been a fine spring day in southern England; the sun was bright, and the daffodils in the well-kept gardens were brilliant yellow. If the Martians' activities in the Arctic were perturbing the weather, well, there was no strong sign of it that afternoon at least. But it was chill enough that I wondered if there would be a touch of frost that night.

It seemed so safe and tranquil.

I had a quiet dinner. I took Walter sandwiches and soup, but he ate nothing.

About eleven p.m. I made us fresh coffee, and clambered up to the study, where I sat on a small armchair which Walter and I had lugged upstairs from the sitting room. Walter still sat, calmly working. His desk was uncluttered: there was his calendar, a travel clock, a few piles of papers, that photograph of Carolyne in its frame, a battered china mug containing pencils – and a telephone, close by his hand.

The moon was bright that night, I remember, shining through the study window, a brilliant white disc glaring from a clear sky. A full moon! An eerie omen for such a night, as the cold astronomical clock within which both Martians and humans are embedded once again brought our planets to alignment. I wondered idly if the Jovians' great sigil, long vanished to the human eye, had left any mark on that stark surface, to be discovered by spacefaring visitors some day.

I broke the silence. 'I take it there's no news, then, from your astronomical pals.'

'Not *pals*.' He tapped the telephone. 'I wait to hear from the the astronomical exchange, of whom I am privileged to be a priority contact. No news, no. Of course our telescopes see so much better now, but even those early shots, back in '07 – one must remember they were clearly visible even in poor Ogilvy's home device, up in Ottershaw – I saw them myself.'

'An armada – or rather, a colonisation fleet. That's what it would be this time, wouldn't it?'

'That would follow the pattern,' he admitted. 'Ten cylinders in

446

'07, a hundred in 1920, a thousand two years later – could it be *ten* thousand this time? *If* they come, which they won't.'

'There are some who say we should do more than hope for the best.' I flipped through the papers. 'There's a story in here somewhere . . . Ah.' The *Telegraph* had the most complete report. 'Churchill's made another speech. "No more waiting! Did we wait for Napoleon? No! We tackled him before he reached the field of play . . ."'

Churchill, that old warhorse, still in the Cabinet as minister for munitions, had responded to the discovery of the Martians' works in the Arctic by arguing that the 'British space gun', as he called it – that is, the Amersham pit which, in 1922, the Martians had used to launch a cylinder to take them home – could be refurbished and put to use *to send a human missile into space.*

Walter was loftily dismissive of the scheme. 'The world's never been short of murderous idiots. Still plotting a Bacillus Bomb, are they?'

'I believe so. The map shows likely targets . . .'

This was, in a way, an astounding development of the old scratched-together plan to have me carry lethal pathogens into the Martian Redoubt at Amersham. Now Churchill's cylinder would carry a variant of some ghastly archaic plague to infect the whole of Mars itself.

'The most significant known node in the canal network remains Lacus Solis – it says here. And if a bacillus were injected into the global water supply at such a commanding junction, it should spread throughout the planet.'

'At least it is consistent with our own history,' he growled. 'Our European plagues shattered the populations of the Americas and elsewhere, and *that* was what won us empires.'

I said, in a cold tone, trying to provoke him, 'Then Churchill's strategy might work. The precedent shows it.'

'But even so, would it be *right*? Julie, Martian civilisation is immeasurably old, by our standards – counted perhaps in the millions of years. And perhaps it is fragile too. You know that I believe the Martians communicate with a form of telepathy. Whatever the mechanism, what are the greater implications? One oddity that few have remarked upon regarding the Martians is this – *that they have no books.* Or at least, none they brought to the earth. In their cylinders, no scrap of writing or anything like it.

'My own conclusion is this. There *are* no books – or rather, *the Martians are their own books.* If you can talk direct, mind to mind

– memory to memory – what need have you of a book? One could pool thoughts, pool memories, into a communal whole that is greater than the sum of the parts. Nothing need ever be lost, in the vaults of those great capacious memories – as long as they survive. But you see the consequences. Murder the Martians, and you burn their libraries too – gone for all time! We would be like the Huns at the gates of Rome – worse.'

I coughed, rudely. 'But these big-brained librarians of yours came to our earth, and slaughtered us, and drank the blood of our children.'

He ignored that objection. 'Perhaps we need men like Churchill when we must make war, and we must think the unthinkable. But it was you who found a way to make the peace, Julie – not Churchill...'

You must imagine the two of us, arguing in that odd little room with its dim lights and rather ill-judged furniture, and its window looking out over the ruins to Horsell Common, where history had been made – and here was the man who first wrote that history, with some degree of eloquence. I scarce believed a word he said any more. But they were such beautiful words.

'They will not come,' declared the Unreliable Narrator now. 'The Jovians have ensured that. But – and I'm with Haldane on this – I'm not one to argue for an over-reliance on the Jovians to look after us for ever. The Jovians have intervened once in our and the Martians' affairs, like a *deus ex machina* – like the Old Testament God with His floods and plagues. We cannot rely on such help in the future; we *should* not. We cannot bow down before these temporal deities. We ought to stand on our own two feet – perhaps Mikaelian's marvellous Federation is a first hopeful step in that direction.'

'How long, then, Walter? Always assuming the Martians give us the time... How long before we reach some level of social perfection?'

For answer he dug out a manuscript from the pile before him: dog-eared and yellowed, and stained perhaps by spilled coffee, yet he handled this relic with tenderness. 'This is the very paper on which I had been working, in this study, on the afternoon when the first cylinder opened over on Horsell Common. I remember I had a selenite paperweight; I wonder what became of that? It was a paper on the probable development of Moral Ideas with the advancement of the civilising process. When I had to abandon it – I remember I broke off in mid-sentence to get my

448

Chronicle from the newsboy, and he spoke to me of "dead men from Mars" – I was in the midst of a paragraph of prediction. I never went back to the work. I look at it now – how young I was! How ignorant! I was no prophet. And yet, you know, in my dim groping, it seems to me I hit on certain perceptions. Now I have finished that last paragraph. Call it sentimental. Oh, I will never attempt to have the paper published, but . . .'

'Read it to me,' I said quietly.

He picked up the sheet. '"In about two hundred years, we may expect—"'

The telephone rang.

Walter stared at it, as if frozen.

I glanced at the clock on the wall. It was a little after midnight.

Still Walter did not stir.

After three rings, I crossed the room and took the handset. 'Yes? Yes – he is here . . .' And I took the message. 'Walter – *it is Carolyne.*'

He looked at me blankly.

'She says she arranged this with Eric Eden, arranged for your astronomical exchange to call her first, not you. To help you manage the news, you see.'

Walter picked up the photograph of Carolyne, and touched the face behind the glass. 'And the Martians?'

I listened to Carolyne's quiet, calm voice.

'They did not fire, Walter. The cannon did not fire, on Mars.'

'I was right, then.'

'You were right.'

'It's over. The end of the War of the Worlds. Now the Union of the Peoples can begin . . .' He seemed to run down, like an unwound clock. '*Carolyne.*' He touched that photograph once more. 'Once I counted her, as she counted me, among the dead.'

'She's here, Walter.'

He bowed his head. And he took the telephone from my hands.

Afterword and Acknowledgements

For an authoritative and accessible edition of Wells's novel I can recommend the Penguin Classics edition (2005) edited by Patrick Parrinder. Page numbers quoted here refer to this edition, and I have taken spellings and other vocabulary elements from this source. I have also relied on the critical editions by David Y. Hughes and Harry M. Geduld (Indiana University Press, 1993), and Leon Stover (McFarland & Co., Inc., 2001). I have drawn on decades of Wellsian scholarship, beginning with Bernard Bergonzi's seminal *The Early H. G. Wells* (Manchester University Press, 1961), through works like Patrick Parrinder's *Shadows of the Future* (Liverpool University Press, 1995) and Steven McLean's *The Early Fiction of H. G. Wells* (Palgrave, 2009). Biographies of Wells himself include Michael Foot's very accessible *H.G.: The History of Mr Wells* (Counterpoint, 1995). In addition, during the composition of this book I attended three stimulating Wells Society seminars, on Wells and the First World War at Durham University in September 2014, and on Wells and Ford Madox Ford at Kings College, London, in September 2015 and an international conference at Woking in July 2016.

As regards *The War of the Worlds* itself, a recent 'biography of the book' is Peter J. Beck's *The War of the Worlds: From H. G. Wells to Orson Welles, Jeff Wayne, Steven Spielberg and Beyond* (Bloomsbury, 2016), and I am very grateful to Professor Beck for a careful read-through of the text. I. F. Clarke's *The Tale of the Next Great War* (Liverpool University Press, 1995) is a good anthology and analysis of coming-war fictions, an influence on *The War of the Worlds*. On Wells's fascination with London, see '"My Own Particular City": H. G. Wells's Fantastical London' by H. Elber-Aviram, in *The Wellsian* no. 38, 2015, pp. 977–1210. (In our reality the London

450

Roman amphitheatre was not discovered until the 1980s.) Patrick Parrinder's paper 'How Far Can We Trust the Narrator of *The War of the Worlds?*' (*Foundation* no. 77, 1999, pp. 15–24) stimulated my thinking about that troubled character. See also Eric J. Leed's *No Man's Land* (Cambridge University Press, 1979) on shell-shock.

An excellent analysis of Wells's book's internal chronology, military action and strategy was given in three papers by Thomas Gangale and Marilyn Dudley-Rowley in *The Wellsian*, the journal of the H. G. Wells Society (no. 29, 2006, pp. 2–20, no. 30, 2007, pp. 36–56, no. 31, 2008, pp. 4–33). For the purposes of this book I have adopted a date of June 1907 for the Martians' first invasion. Gangale and Dudley-Rowley show that this date is the best fit to the astronomical clues Wells provides – but his text is inconsistent, and indeed the editors of the two critical editions cited above each came to a different conclusion.

On timings: daylight saving time, advancing the clocks by an hour during local summer, was introduced in 1916 in Germany as a fuel-saving measure during World War I, and the practice soon spread, though not universally, to Britain and around the world. In this novel, in which WWI as we know it was never fought, I have assumed that DST has not been adopted, so that British times given are in GMT throughout (as they were, of course, in Wells's novel, which pre-dated DST), and global times are relative to this time zone.

The scientific consensus of the late nineteenth century concerning the evolution of the solar system was a central driver for *The War of the Worlds* – and this sequel is therefore set in a universe in which these theories remain valid, notably the 'nebular hypothesis' of the formation of the solar system to which Wells referred (p. 7), as developed by Kant (1724–1804) and Laplace (1749–1827). In reality Maxwell (1831–1879) raised fatal objections to the theory based on the distribution of angular momentum between sun and planets.

Meanwhile the notion that the sun was cooling was championed by, for example, Lord Kelvin (1824–1907). As for the planets themselves, I have allowed Mars to be as Wells sketched it in his novel and as Lowell and others imagined it, for example in Lowell's *Mars* (Houghton, Mifflin, 1895) and *Mars and Its Canals* (Macmillan, 1906). (In reality the astronomer Giovanni Schiaparelli, on whose misinterpreted observations the theory of canals on Mars was built, died in 1910.) K. Maria D. Lane's *Geographies of Mars* (University of Chicago Press, 2011) was a useful discussion of the cultural background and impact of Lowell's Mars hypotheses. A 'dripping wet' Venus is as, for example, Svante Arrhenius described it in *The Destinies of the Stars* (G. P. Putnam's Sons, 1918). From the 1920s spectroscopic and other evidence would cast doubt on the earthlike models of these worlds, with clinching evidence of the planets' inhospitability provided by the space probes from the 1960s onwards.

For speculation on the Martians themselves I have followed the lead of Wells's own visionary early essay 'The Man of the Year Million' (*Pall Mall Gazette,* November 1893), to which the narrator refers in *The War of the Worlds* itself (p. 151). I have speculated that the Martians' Heat-Ray is an infra-red laser, powered, like other Martian engines, by a compact nuclear fusion energy source. In reality work on 'explosively pumped flux compression generators', ascribed here to Edison, did not begin until the 1950s in the USSR and US, in the course of nuclear fusion research. I'm very grateful to Martyn Fogg of the British Interplanetary Society, the author of *Terraforming: Engineering Planetary Environments* (SAE International, Warrendale, PA, 1995), for a stimulating discussion on the Martian terraforming of the earth.

In a sense Wells's novel (like my sequel) is an alternate history, with a 'jonbar hinge', a branching point, coming in 1894 when a mysterious light on Mars is interpreted as the casting of a huge gun ... I have, however, drawn on a large number of sources for the real-world history of the period, including Malcolm Brown's *The Imperial War Museum Book of the First World War* (Guild, 1991), Charles Emmerson's *1913* (Bodley Head, 2013), Niall Ferguson's *The War of the World* (Allen Lane, 2006), Allan Mallinson's *1914: Fight the Good Fight* (Bantam, 2013), Eugene Rogan's *The Fall of the Ottomans* (Allen Lane, 2013), David Woodward's *Armies of the World 1854–1914* (Sidgwick & Jackson, 1978), and Jerry White's *Zeppelin Nights* (Bodley Head, 2014) on London during the war. On women at war, Kate Adie's *Fighting on the Home Front* (Hodder and Stoughton, 2013); on the aerial war, Kenneth Poolman's *Zeppelins Over England* (Evans, 1960); on the naval war Mark Stille's *British Dreadnought vs German Dreadnought* (Osprey, 2010); on the development of tanks, John Glanfield's *The Devil's Chariots* (Sutton, 2001) and David Fletcher's *British Mk I Tank 1916* (Osprey, 2004) (HMLS *Boadicea* is based on the 'Hetherington Landship' design of 1915). James P. Duffy's *Target: America* (Praeger, 2004) summarises the Kaiser's government's speculative plans to attack the USA. Two speculations on alternate outcomes of World War

I are Niall Ferguson's essay 'The Kaiser's European Union' in his *Virtual History* (Picador, 1997) and Richard Ned Lebow's *Archduke Franz Ferdinand Lives* (Palgrave, 2014). The RMS *Lusitania* was, in our timeline, sunk by a torpedo from a German U-boat on May 7 1915.

I'm very grateful to our good friends Mr and Mrs J. D. Oliver of Whiteleaf, Bucks, for help with local research on the Chilterns; a useful reference is *The Chilterns* by Leslie Hepple and Alison Doggett (Phillimore, 1992). A reference on the Soviet Arctic is John McCannon's *Red Arctic* (Oxford University Press, 1998).

Wells's original 'war of the worlds' was in fact confined to south-east England. But the Martians first came to New York as early as 1897, in the *New York Evening Journal*'s heavily adapted serialisation of Wells's novel – and, in fact the *Journal*, subsequently published the very first sequel to the novel, Garrett P. Serviss's *Edison's Conquest of Mars* (January 12 – February 10 1898). Harry Kane's Edisonade, mentioned in these pages, is an affectionate tribute. *Global Dispatches*, ed. Kevin J. Anderson (Bantam, 1996), is an anthology whose stories contain provocative ideas. Gregory Benford and David Brin suggested that the Heat-Ray could be a laser; Barbara Hambly pointed out how vulnerable the Black Smoke is to water; Dave Wolverton noted how the Martians might prosper in the Artic. My own survey of earlier sequels is in *The Wellsian* no. 32, 2009, pp. 3–16.

In general the interpretation of Wells's great book given here is my own, and any errors or inaccuracies are of course my sole responsibility.

Stephen Baxter
Northumberland
May 2016